the devil

NADIA DALBUONO

SCRIBE

Melbourne • London

Scribe Publications
2 John Street, Clerkenwell, London, WC1N 2ES, United Kingdom
18–20 Edward St, Brunswick, Victoria 3056, Australia

First published by Scribe 2020

Typeset in 12.75/16.5 pt Dante MT

Printed and bound in the UK by CPI Group (UK) Ltd, Croydon CR0 4YY

Scribe Publications is committed to the sustainable use of natural
resources and the use of paper products made responsibly from those
resources.

9781911617945 (UK edition)
9781925713619 (Australian edition)
9781925693607 (e-book)

Catalogue records for this book are available from the National Library
of Australia and the British Library.

scribepublications.co.uk
scribepublications.com.au

For Bruno and Harry

Prologue

'EXORCIZO DEO IMMUNDISSIMUS SPIRITUS.'
I exorcise, O God, this unclean spirit.

The father's voice is soft, yet powerful. In his gnarled hands, he holds the leather-bound book that has been used by the Vatican for over four centuries. Before him, the young woman's body begins to throb and quiver. She lets out a piercing cry, slumps down into her chair, and falls back into a trance. The father places his right hand gently over her heart.

'INFER TIBI LIBERA.'
Set yourself free.

The woman loses consciousness, her long raven hair spilling across her cheek as she lolls back in the chair.

'TIME SATANA INIMICI FIDEM.'
Be afraid of Satan and the enemies of faith.

All of a sudden, the woman begins to thrash violently. The priest and his five male helpers struggle to pin her down. Saliva is foaming on her lips and while everyone else in the room is sweating, her skin is as cold as ice.

'RECEDE IN NOMINI PATRIS!'
Leave, in the name of the Father!

Her features slowly contort and morph into a mask of despair as she continues to convulse and twist. She's trying to rise now; she is trying to attack.

'SANCTISSIMO DOMINE MIGRA.'
Let him go, O God Almighty.

The woman thrusts forward and screams in the father's face, her spittle flecking his lips. 'Never!' she cries. 'Never!'

A low buzzing starts, like the growing swarm of a thousand bees. Everyone in the room is praying: imploring God to keep the devil away; asking him to destroy this evil force. But the woman is beginning to growl and scream again. 'Neverrrrrrrrr!' Her cry fills the room. Then a completely different voice, from somewhere deep inside her, shouts, 'Don't touch her, don't ever touch her!' Her eyes are still closed tight.

'CEDE! CEDE!'
Surrender!

'I am Satan,' the woman screams. The buzzing in the room persists as she becomes increasingly defiant and agitated.

'IN NOMINE DEO QUANDO TU EXIS?'
In the name of God, when are you leaving?

'Never!' she cries. And then, a beat later, 'She is mine! She belongs to me!'

'SHE BELONGS TO JESUS CHRIST!'

2

'We are an army!!' she yells.

'Requie creatue Dei.'
Rest, creature of God.

The father's voice has dropped to a whisper. The woman awakes slowly and sits up. She's dishevelled and seems to have no memory of what has just happened. But then, without warning, she starts to sway from side to side — to writhe and seethe again. One burly priest has to hold her by the neck while another pins down her legs. She thrashes and kicks and bites, but then, finally, her body is still.

Over the course of several minutes, she gradually returns to a normal state. Her long, thick hair, lustrous in the lamplight, frames her angelic features, and to the father she seems almost beatific.

1

SCAMARCIO WATCHED THE GLASSY droplets strike the windscreen like miniature bullets. The world outside remained the same monochrome blur of charcoal and black. It had been over a week since he'd last seen the sun, and, even then, it had risen pallid and hopeless, as if the very act of breaking from the dense cloud mass had robbed it of all strength. He was reminded yet again of how much he hated the Roman winter. It had been different down in Calabria. Of course, they'd had grey days, but with them was always that certainty that March, and the first swim of the year, were just around the corner. In Rome the grey was interminable — a foggy morass that one might never escape, and Scamarcio's low mood felt equally intractable.

He knew that, on paper, there was much to look forward to, but his heart refused to catch up. Sure, there were moments when he felt a surge of excitement at the prospect of becoming a father, but these were greatly outweighed by the nightmares, the sleepless hours spent sweating in the dark, and the waves of anxiety at the sudden appearance of boxes of nappies or baby clothes. None of this was helped by Fiammetta's refusal to learn the sex of the baby. If only he had something concrete to work with — if only he could *plan* — he felt sure that it all would have seemed more manageable. The truth was that he was angry with Fiammetta. He felt she was being selfish, unnecessarily adding to his fear and uncertainty, and he asked himself, yet again, if she truly understood him. Had they been together long enough? Were their foundations solid?

He realised that his attempts to tap out a cigarette against the steering wheel while also navigating a busy roundabout were triggering the ire of an obese guy in a dented white van. Scamarcio quickly stuffed the unlit fag between his teeth so he could flip him the bird.

'Cunt,' he hissed, rooting around in his jacket pocket for a lighter. He'd promised Fiammetta that he'd quit before the birth, but the baby was due in two weeks, and his habit had recently jumped to around twenty-five a day. He had a hunch that all the coming stress would see it hit thirty. It was already bad enough that Fiammetta had banned his trusty dealer, Pinnetta. Scamarcio needed to preserve some kind of outlet.

His mobile started to ring, and he felt the same emotional maelstrom he did every time he heard the brash new ringtone Fiammetta had chosen for him. 'Una Vita in Vacanza' had been the smash hit of last summer, and now it seemed that everywhere you went it was being played on a loop. He hadn't liked it the first time around, and now that it had infected his phone, that dislike had turned to hatred. *Has she gone into labour? Is this the call that will change it all?* He made a mental note to switch the ringtone back to something neutral.

'Scamarcio,' he muttered, his mouth dry.

'Chill out,' laughed Garramone. 'It's only your boss.'

'Which one?'

'You don't sound ready.'

'Who the fuck is? All those guys who go to the classes — join in with the heavy-breathing shit — they're just faking it.'

'You been?'

'Don't be ridiculous.'

Garramone chuckled. 'You want a little something to take your mind off it all?'

'You pushing dope now?'

'I won't dignify that with an answer.' Garramone paused. 'I've just had something peculiar come in. Peculiar but interesting.'

Scamarcio frowned. 'I'm flattered.'

'You heard of Cardinal Piero Amato?'

'That old guy who's always on the talk shows? What is it they call him — "the Vatican's chief exorcist", or something like that?'

'Yeah, that guy.'

'What's happened to him?'

'Nothing, but an eighteen-year-old boy, Andrea Borghese, has just been found strangled in an apartment on Via Po and the cardinal was the last one to see him alive.'

Scamarcio whistled. 'Sex game gone wrong?'

'I won't dignify that with an answer, either.'

'What was the cardinal doing at the flat?'

'What do you *think* he was doing there?'

It took a moment for Scamarcio to make the leap. 'You're kidding me.'

'He was conducting a weekly exorcism along with four of his priests,' said Garramone with aplomb.

'Fuck,' Scamarcio pushed the still unlit fag behind his ear. 'The press will wet their pants.'

'That's why I want you on it.'

Scamarcio rubbed at his stubble. 'My presence will only make things worse. I'm their red meat.'

'No, you'll be a good conduit.'

'What's that supposed to mean?'

'Look, it's a complicated case, and you know your way around the Vatican; you're my choice for this. I'll be waiting for you in my office.'

'My girlfriend's about to …'

But Garramone had already hung up.

2

SEVERAL HOURS LATER, SCAMARCIO set the photograph of Andrea Borghese back down on the coffee table. The boy had the same startling eyes as his mother: a deep amber-brown, framed by soulful dark brows. He could have been a model or an actor. The word 'promise' floated into Scamarcio's thoughts. *A young man with promise.*

'I know you wouldn't think it to look at that picture — he seems so normal, so at ease there,' said the victim's mother, Katia Borghese, slowly picking up the photo and using a manicured nail to gently trace the outline of her son's face, 'but the truth is that Andrea's life has been a living hell. I've lost count of the number of "experts" we've seen.' She put a heavy emphasis on the word, signalling her disdain. 'Psychologists, psychiatrists, neurologists — you name it, we've tried it. Eventually, none of us could take the disappointment anym—' Her voice broke, then shattered. She let out a shuddering sob, then dropped the photo and hid her face behind her hands. Scamarcio returned the photo to the small pile between them, carefully holding it by the edges. He looked up and studied Andrea's father, Gennaro, sitting apart from his wife on the couch. He was staring into the middle distance, face pale and drawn.

'So, that's why you resorted to the Vatican?' Scamarcio asked softly, after Mrs Borghese had stopped crying.

She nodded and wiped the tears away with a ragged tissue that needed replacing. Scamarcio turned to look at her husband again and noticed that his shoulders seemed to have hunched and tightened at the mention of the church. Scamarcio cleared his throat, careful to cover his mouth with a fist. This was Parioli, and he was in polite company.

'Mr Borghese, can you talk me through Andrea's symptoms? I've been given some basic information, but I'd like to hear the details from you.' He pulled out his notebook and patted his jacket pocket for a pen.

The father sniffed and leaned forward in his chair, laying his palms nervously on his smart trousers. Scamarcio took in his reddened eyes and the taut, salty skin beneath. Borghese had already cried many tears for his son.

'Andrea suffered from mood swings, paranoia, tics, seizures, and delusions,' he began stiltingly. 'For the past couple of years, he's been experiencing hallucinations that convinced him he was destined to transform into a monster.' He looked away. Scamarcio watched his eyes film with fresh tears. 'On a certain level, that was true. He could become very aggressive: he would swear, throw things, break things, try to create as much damage as possible.' He paused. 'He'd sometimes take that aggression out on us — he'd punch and slap us both, gave me a black eye once.' Scamarcio watched a tear slide slowly down his cheek.

'When was this — that he became violent?'

'During the hallucinations,' said the mother slowly, as if she was trying to wade through something dense and impenetrable. 'Usually only then. Most of the time he was calm and kind … often thoughtful.' Another low sob escaped her, and she covered her thin mouth with a hand.

'I'm so very sorry,' Scamarcio repeated, feeling, as he always did, that the language was lame and inadequate. 'Can I get you anything? A glass of water perhaps?'

Mrs Borghese threw him a withering look — he was an unwelcome intrusion into her grief. 'A glass of water isn't going to bring back my son.' She rose foggily from the sofa and left the room.

'She's not doing well,' mumbled Mr Borghese.

'Of course,' said Scamarcio, surprised that Borghese felt the need to apologise for her. 'Who would be?'

He considered Andrea's father, sitting there, an entirely broken man in a crumpled designer suit. He must have rushed back from work. He had a worn look about him — furrowed skin, thinning grey hair. Years of stress and struggle were etched across his face. Scamarcio's gaze moved to the man's right hand; his fingers were tapping out some kind of repetitive rhythm against the chair, growing faster and faster, more and more urgent. It reminded Scamarcio of certain kinds of coping techniques he'd heard therapists gave their patients. It made Borghese look unhinged.

God, thought Scamarcio, a disquieting realisation dawning. *This is the lottery of parenthood. You have no way of knowing your child will be OK. You just have to take the hand fate deals you.* He felt a snake of anxiety slither through him. He swallowed and was about to ask if he could smoke, then got a grip on himself.

'Mr Borghese, would you talk me through the routine — how these sessions with the cardinal played out? Was your wife always present?'

Borghese ceased his tapping and nodded. 'Normally, yes. But this afternoon she had to rush away as her father had fallen ill. Cardinal Amato usually brought three other priests with him to help. I imagine it was the same set-up today.'

'And who was it who found your son's body?'

'Me …' Mr Borghese looked into his lap. 'I found him.' His face crumpled.

'I'm so sorry,' Scamarcio whispered, feeling useless again.

'Where is he?' asked Mr Borghese, suddenly looking up as if the thought had just hit him.

'Who?'

'My boy. Where have they taken him?'

'Oh, didn't they explain? They'll have taken the body to the police morgue.' Scamarcio glanced away from Borghese's stricken face. 'The pathologist will conduct an autopsy there,' he added quietly.

Borghese nodded slowly, and peered into his lap once more.

Scamarcio coughed. 'So, when you returned home, sir — could you describe what you saw?'

At that moment, Mrs Borghese walked back in and returned to her place on the sofa opposite, a strangely defiant look in her eyes.

'For years they told us it was epilepsy,' she said, slightly louder than was necessary.

Scamarcio gently laid down his notebook. 'The experts?'

'The experts.' She made two quotation marks with her fingers. 'But their problem was that an epilepsy diagnosis didn't explain certain elements of Andrea's condition.'

'Such as?'

'Before his seizures, Andrea would become paranoid. He was convinced hidden enemies were all around. And then his voice would change, sometimes several times, as if he was taking on different personalities,' she said, more quietly now.

Scamarcio felt his eyebrows rise and tried to return his expression to neutral. 'That must have been difficult to witness.'

Mrs Borghese shook her head at the memory. 'It was unsettling. One minute he'd be loud and booming, forceful, then he'd suddenly become soft and shy like a little boy, then, seconds later, he'd be all wheedling and sly, like some middle-aged salesman. On and on it went, as if he was inhabited by all these different people.'

Scamarcio glanced at her husband.

10

'I'm not making it up,' snapped Mrs Borghese.

'I didn't think you were.'

'Then why are you looking at my husband?'

Mr Borghese sniffed. 'It's true. It was very disturbing to watch — it gave me goose bumps.'

'Could he have been putting on an act, doing it for attention?'

'No, Detective,' said Mrs Borghese, even angrier now. 'He didn't welcome these changes; he hated it. He would have done anything to avoid it. It would happen against his will and would leave him totally drained afterwards.'

Scamarcio felt disorientated. He reopened the notebook, and jotted down the list of symptoms. 'Mrs Borghese, do you work?'

'I used to be an English teacher, but I had to abandon that to look after Andrea when he was still quite young.' There was a jarring bitterness to the words.

'And you, Mr Borghese?'

'I'm in marketing.'

Scamarcio glanced around the large living room and took in the expensive furnishings and the Bang & Olufsen sound system. Marketing must pay well.

'Did Andrea attend school?'

'His education has been sporadic. He was highly intelligent, particularly gifted in maths, but he was disruptive, so he was forced to change schools several times. Then, as he got older, bullying became a problem.' Mrs Borghese's voice was starting to tremble again. 'He was at school again recently, but it wasn't going too well. I suspect they wanted him out.'

'Why was he bullied?'

'Because he was different, of course; because he didn't play the game and always said what he thought. Andrea was incapable of artifice. And then, of course, they liked to get a rise out of him — see a reaction. They'd bait him and try to see how angry they could make him.' She paused and sniffed. 'When he hit puberty, the other kids started calling him the devil.'

Scamarcio swallowed. His heart already felt heavy for this boy. What a tortured life it must have been.

'I assure you, I will do everything in my power to find your son's killer,' he said in a rush, trying to disguise the unexpected emotion that had crept into his voice.

He turned to the husband. 'You were telling me, sir, about what you saw when you came home.'

Borghese sighed. 'Nothing useful. I walked into the living room,' he motioned to the doorway behind him, and then to his left, 'and found Andrea on the carpet, there — exactly as he was when you arrived an hour ago. That was it.' He paused. 'I don't think I'll ever scrub my brain of that image.'

Borghese looked to the spot where his son had lain. There was no blood, no sign of the tragedy that had taken place. Mr Borghese might not have been able to scrub away the memory, but the scene itself looked suspiciously clean to Scamarcio. And sinister. Somehow, the total absence of anything, any sign of struggle, made it worse.

'So, you didn't see anyone leaving the building — nothing out of the ordinary?'

'No. No one coming in or out, no one in the elevator on my way up.' Mr Borghese blinked. Scamarcio caught the blink, but didn't know what to make of it.

'And you returned home earlier than normal? I imagine 4.00 pm isn't the usual time you leave work.'

'My wife called explaining that she had been delayed on her return journey and asking if I could hurry back.'

Scamarcio nodded and made a note. 'And, Mrs Borghese, you came home when?'

'As soon as my husband rang and told me the terrible …' She started sobbing and wiped her nose with the back of her hand.

Judging from her preppy clothes and carefully layered, hennaed hair, Scamarcio imagined that this wasn't something she'd normally do.

'And Cardinal Amato — do you trust him?'

Both Borgheses looked up, startled. Mrs Borghese's thin lips formed a small 'o'. 'You're not suggesting …?'

'It's early days. I have to consider all angles.'

Mrs Borghese shook her head, her voice dropping to a reverent hush. 'No, Detective. There's no way the cardinal could be involved … in … in this.'

'He was the last person to see your son alive. He left an hour before Andrea was found.'

They'd been given that information by Mrs Borghese — he'd need to check it with the cardinal himself, of course, and on the CCTV if there was any.

Mrs Borghese bit down on her thumbnail. Scamarcio watched the red varnish splinter. 'Well, that's crazy. He's a man of the cloth, a *good* man.' She looked away from his gaze, and, for a moment, Scamarcio thought he read flight in her eyes — she wanted to escape. The look had lasted less than a second, but it was enough to convince him that there was something else here, something that needed to be brought into the light.

'I've seen good men do terrible things,' he offered after a few moments.

Both Borgheses just continued to stare at him as if he were a fool.

Scamarcio scratched his forehead. 'So, do you have any thoughts on who else might be behind this?'

The couple shook their heads, almost in sync. Mr Borghese frowned, the lines on his forehead multiplying until they were almost a web. 'I have no idea. At first, I suspected a break in …' his eyes swept the room, 'but then I realised that nothing had been taken.'

'Did your son have any enemies?'

Mr Borghese exhaled softly. The room fell silent, save for the distant hum of a refrigerator. 'Andrea didn't have any *friends*, Detective,' he said eventually. 'He had no *life*. How could someone without a life have enemies?'

3

Scamarcio surveyed Davide Cafaro, the inspector general of the Vatican's Gendarmerie Corps, and decided that the guy was an arsehole. Cafaro might be able to play the king in his little fiefdom of 130 young, impressionable police officers, but Scamarcio wasn't going to allow him to give the Flying Squad the run-around.

'Inspector, you must understand that Cardinal Amato was the last person to see the victim alive. It is crucial to my investigation that I be allowed to interview him, as well as the priests that assisted him during the exorcism.'

Cafaro pushed his thin glasses higher up his long nose. 'I'm not saying you *can't* interview him, I'm just saying that I need to be there.'

'No — that can't happen. That goes against protocol.'

Cafaro pushed his chair away from his desk and rose quickly. 'Then we're done. You've had a wasted journey, and I'm heading home for my dinner.'

Scamarcio threw open his palms. His anger was rising, fizzing and broiling to the surface, and he didn't feel like making an effort to contain it. 'That's obstruction. I must be allowed to investigate.'

Cafaro just shrugged. 'Like I say, nobody's stopping you.'

What a prize cunt. Scamarcio bit his lip — he wanted to smash Cafaro's condescending smile to pulp. But he also wanted to solve this case. That sense of connection to the victim, so crucial to his work, had formed much faster than usual, and he already felt invested.

Reluctantly, he pulled out his mobile and dialled Garramone, Cafaro eyeing him with cold contempt all the while. Scamarcio knew he should probably step outside, but, again, he didn't feel like making the effort.

'I've got a situation with the inspector general of the gendarmerie at the Vatican,' he said, trying to sound calm.

Garramone laughed, and, in his mind's eye, Scamarcio watched his own anger smoulder into a fiery mass of lava. They could all go to hell. Why was Garramone so bloody cheerful of late? It was as if his happiness was inversely proportionate to Scamarcio's own personal misery.

'Of course you do,' said Garramone. 'What did you expect? That they'd just let you waltz in there and do your job?'

'It wasn't such a big deal on the American case.'

'You were looking at a victim not a suspect back then, remember?'

'I was looking at both, actually.'

'Whatever,' said Garramone, bored already. 'What does Cafaro want?'

'To be in on all the interviews.'

Scamarcio heard him exhale slowly as if he was doing yoga. 'How predictable. OK, you have my permission to go ahead and jerk the little prick off.'

'Shit. Why?'

'Because, otherwise, it's going to be a long tedious pissing match, and I have neither the time nor the money.'

'With respect, sir, that's fucking depressing.'

'Welcome to my world,' said Garramone cheerily.

Cafaro knocked three times on the old oak door, and, after a few moments, it swung open, creaking on its hinges like something out of a B movie horror.

Cardinal Amato was slightly smaller and slimmer than Scamarcio had imagined from the TV. He'd read that he was nearing his seventy-fifth birthday, but, in the face, he seemed at least fifteen years younger. There were only a few wrinkles around his bright green eyes, and he sported a full head of thick grey hair. His neck was dense, almost muscular, and, beneath his robes, his shoulders seemed wide and strong.

'Come in. I've been expecting you.' Despite the cardinal's appearance, his voice was light and fragile, as if it barely existed — as if it might be a figment of Scamarcio's imagination. He wondered how such a delicate voice could take on the devil.

'Please have a seat.' The cardinal motioned to a couple of leather armchairs positioned in front of a wide mahogany desk, scattered with papers, photos, and prayer books. Amidst the chaos, Scamarcio spotted a small gold cross, glinting in the light of an overhead lamp. He wondered if this was *the* cross — the one Amato used to expel the devil.

Inspector Cafaro sat down first and opened his hands towards the cardinal in a gesture of apology. Scamarcio wanted to punch him just for that.

'It's OK, Inspector,' said the cardinal. 'The detective is just doing his job.'

Scamarcio didn't appreciate being referred to in the third person and resolved to forgo any pleasantries. 'You were the last person to see Andrea Borghese alive,' he said as he took a seat. 'Is it correct you left the apartment at 1520 this afternoon?'

The cardinal looked momentarily taken aback and scratched below his large nose. 'Yes,' he said quietly. 'It's devastating. He was such a lovely young man with so much to live for.'

There was a sadness in his eyes that seemed genuine, and

Scamarcio's irritation thawed ever so slightly. 'I'd formed more the impression that Andrea had a difficult life and that his parents had been struggling to make things better for him.'

A mobile trilled from somewhere beneath the pile of papers, and the cardinal looked down and started rooting around in the chaos. He eventually located the phone inside a purple file.

'Yes,' he said. 'Yes … Yes … I'm so sorry, but I can't. I have an emergency. My assistant will ring you to arrange another time.'

He cut the call and shrugged as if to say, *What can I do?* Then he leaned back in his leather armchair and folded his arms across his chest. To Scamarcio, the gesture seemed defensive.

'Your initial impression is accurate, Detective, but I had thought that we were making progress with Andrea — that his life *was* going to get better.' Amato rubbed tiredly at the edge of a watery eye. 'I'd actually go so far as to say that my colleagues and I believed he'd turned a corner.'

Scamarcio wondered how that worked — in terms of the mechanics of the exorcism — but decided to save that question for later. 'Could you explain how Andrea came to you? What made you think that you needed to treat him?'

Amato's mobile rang again, and Scamarcio struggled to stifle a sigh.

'Can I ring you back?' said the cardinal, his voice barely a whisper now. 'I'm a bit busy.' There was a pause. 'Sure, I'll call in half an hour.'

He laid the phone on top of the papers, then just stared at it. After a while, he said, 'When I first met Andrea — about a year ago, now — it was very clear that he was suffering from demonic possession, rather than mental illness.'

The cardinal's tone was calm and measured, but Scamarcio couldn't stop himself from frowning at the madness of the statement. Amato seemed to clock his scepticism and just shook his head.

18

'How can you draw a distinction?' Scamarcio asked.

'It's simple,' said the cardinal softly. 'Andrea saw countless medical professionals over the years, but they were unable to help. These doctors might be able to mend brains and fix hearts, but they're not equipped to fight the devil.'

Scamarcio thought it an interesting turn of phrase. What equipment *was* required? But instead he said, 'Maybe they just didn't have a category for what they were dealing with?'

The cardinal shook his head again, and Cafaro coughed to remind Scamarcio of his presence.

'Before conducting exorcisms, I urge people to see a psychologist or psychiatrist, and I ask them to bring me their prognosis. I'm actually in touch with many psychologists who send their patients here. In Andrea's case, his parents had spent years under the care of the medical profession. It seemed reasonable that the church would be their next step.'

Scamarcio looked to his right and noticed a glass cabinet full of small statues of angels blinking eerily in the dim light from Amato's desk lamp. They seemed almost animate; their tiny faces sly and all-knowing. On the wall above them was an official document declaring the cardinal's qualification as devil ridder in chief. Scamarcio figured that descending into a heated philosophical debate about the pros and cons of exorcism was not going to help him find Andrea's killer. 'Can you tell me what happened today? How was the session?'

Amato ran a palm across his forehead. 'It was draining and exhausting, as always. We followed the normal structure, as dictated by the Catholic church's exorcism rites.' He motioned to a tattered leather-bound book on his desk. 'By the end, Andrea did seem to have calmed. I'd say he was more settled than normal, actually.'

'How long do your sessions take?'

'An hour, give or take.'

'And you had colleagues helping you?'

'I normally have three young priests with me, but this time I took a fourth, as Andrea's mother had been called away.'

'Excuse my ignorance, but these other priests — why do you bring them?'

Amato seemed surprised, while Cafaro just looked amused. If he saw that sarcastic smile again, Scamarcio would be liberating the inspector of his teeth.

'You've never witnessed an exorcism, Detective?' asked the cardinal, his tone still reasonable.

'No. I *will* be watching one, as part of my research, but I haven't yet had time. This case has only just been handed to me.'

The cardinal nodded and fixed Scamarcio with a long stare. It felt as if Amato was studying him properly for the first time — as if he'd only just caught his attention.

'The brutal way of putting it, Detective, is that these priests are my muscle. The devil is violent. He has the strength of an army. I'm seventy-five years old with a hip replacement, so I'm no match for that. Maybe I can take him on mentally, but for the physical side of things, I need help.'

'So, the assistants are there to restrain your — erm — your patients? If they become too aggressive?'

'Exactly. If I'm honest, my abiding hope is that one of my young helpers will take over from me one day. The world has never been so awful — these violent acts by people like ISIS are not human. But, so far, I haven't found anyone who is willing to pick up the mantle. Many are just too afraid. Even priests can be scared. It's difficult.'

Scamarcio felt a sudden breeze against his skin. He looked around for a window, but realised there weren't any. Then, all at once, he felt hot and stifled and wanted to leave.

'And you saw nothing untoward when you left Andrea this afternoon, nobody coming in or out of the building?'

The cardinal just shook his head.

'Do you have any ideas about who might have done this?'

Amato raised an eyebrow. 'Certainly.'

He fell silent for a moment and stared at Scamarcio, a cold curiosity behind his gaze. 'It was the devil, of course.'

4

CAFARO HAD ARRANGED FOR the cardinal's young assistants to meet with Scamarcio in an office near Amato's rooms. Scamarcio had made it clear he wanted to interview the priests individually, and when he arrived on the landing, they were sitting waiting in a row outside the door. He tried a smile as he passed, but their expressions remained grave, their eyes hollow. It was late, nearing eleven, now, and Scamarcio hoped that their tiredness might work in his favour.

Cafaro sat down in a chair to the side of the room. Scamarcio took a seat behind an ancient desk and drew out his notebook. 'Come,' he shouted, realising that he was desperate for a cigarette, but that it would be at least an hour until he'd be able to smoke one.

The first to enter was a tall blond boy called Fabio Lania, who Scamarcio soon discovered was from the Veneto.

Once the introductions were out of the way, Scamarcio asked, 'Do you normally accompany Cardinal Amato on his visits?'

'Yes, I've been with him for about a year now.'

'How many exorcisms do you attend with the cardinal?'

'About four a week.'

Scamarcio was shocked at the level of demand, but was careful not to show it.

'What do you think of the work?'

'How do you mean?'

'Are you comfortable with it?'

'Why wouldn't I be?'

'It must be pretty unsettling at times.'

'The more you do it, the more you get used to it. It's God's work, that's all that matters.'

Scamarcio turned a sigh into a small yawn behind his hand. 'How did Andrea Borghese seem when you last saw him? The cardinal told me he believed you were making progress.'

Lania nodded quickly. 'When we first started, it was always difficult to get Andrea to calm; it took a very long time for him to settle. But lately, he's been winding down sooner and he's been in a good place each time we left.'

'And you really believe he was possessed by the devil?'

The young man shrugged. 'Of course — if you believe in God, you must also believe in the devil.'

Out of the corner of his eye, Scamarcio noticed Cafaro shaking his head at his question, as if he were an imbecile. He tried to ignore it.

'When you left him earlier today, how did Andrea seem?'

The priest ran a hand through his long fringe. 'Good. Really good, actually. Probably the best we've seen him. That's what's so strange.' He scratched the back of his neck. Scamarcio knew the gesture might mean he was hiding something; it might also mean nothing.

'And when you left Andrea, he was alone?

'Yes. We talked about it, actually, because it's something we wouldn't normally do. But Mrs Borghese had been called away, and, given Andrea's progress, the cardinal decided it would be all right on this one occasion. He did call Andrea's mother when we were leaving, though, to let her know.'

'And that was at 1520?'

'Yes.'

Scamarcio made a note. 'Did she say she'd come straight back?'

'I believe so, yes.'

Why wasn't mother there when father got home? Scamarcio wrote. He scored a dense box around it along with the word *Traffic??*

'And how would you describe the cardinal's relationship with Andrea? How did Andrea respond to him?'

The young priest crossed his long legs and scratched the back of his neck again. *Twice within a minute?* Scamarcio's instincts took note.

'Well, you know it's not an easy relationship. There's a lot of animosity on the part of the person who is possessed. But, of course, the hatred and the violence aren't coming from them; it's the devil talking,' said the young priest quietly.

Scamarcio closed his eyes and rubbed the bridge of his nose. This was, without doubt, the strangest case he had ever been handed, and that was saying something.

'So, Andrea didn't really welcome the cardinal's visits?'

'With respect, Detective, I don't think you're quite grasping it. When we would arrive, Andrea wasn't Andrea, if you know what I mean. But by the time we had finished the session, it was a different story. Andrea, when he'd calmed, was a very sweet person, and he was gracious with all of us.'

How could Andrea have switched between these two personas so quickly? Scamarcio wondered. *Was it for real or was it an act?* Scamarcio's rational mind was growing skittish at the implausibility of it all.

'These sessions, were they always at the same time?'

'We always visited on a Wednesday afternoon — the times would differ.'

Scamarcio let his biro drop. It hit the mahogany desk, and then rolled off onto the parquet floor with a clatter.

'Sorry, but how does that work? Does the devil just appear on Wednesdays? Does he keep to a schedule?'

24

The priest looked taken aback.

'I don't think much of your interview technique,' said Cafaro drily.

'I didn't ask for your opinion.'

'Andrea had outbursts every day,' said the boy slowly, as if he was trying to explain it to a child. 'But we couldn't go there daily — the cardinal is far too busy. You have no idea to what extent the devil stalks this city. Andrea's mother had decided that Wednesdays would work best, but sometimes she'd phone to say he was becoming agitated and ask if we could come sooner. Or other days, we'd arrive later, depending on the cardinal's diary or how Andrea seemed.'

Scamarcio took a long breath. 'And you always went to the apartment in Parioli? Andrea never came here?'

'At the beginning he and his mother would come to the cardinal's office, but then the cardinal decided it would be better for Andrea if we held the sessions in an environment that was more familiar to him.'

Scamarcio made another note. 'So, nothing in Andrea's demeanour seemed different today?'

'No. Only that he seemed to respond better than usual, like I said.'

'And on your way out, did you see anyone coming in? Did you notice anything out of the ordinary?'

'There were some workmen digging up the road.'

'Were they standing around or actually working?'

'They were using drills and a digger — it was making quite a racket.'

Scamarcio dismissed it. 'So, nothing else?'

The young priest shook his head. 'Nothing that I can think of.'

Scamarcio brought a tired fist to his chin. 'OK, thank you for your time.'

He made a note of the priest's details and how best he could be reached, and then called in the next man.

After just a few minutes, it became clear that this priest's account would match that of the boy from the Veneto. It was the same with the next, the youngest of the three at just twenty-four. He explained that he'd only joined the group that day to provide extra muscle in the absence of Andrea's mother.

When it came to the fourth priest, he, too, delivered a similar account. But it wasn't so much what he was saying as the manner in which he said it that made Scamarcio wonder.

The priest was tall and good looking, with wavy brown hair, dark eyes, and strong cheekbones. He said his name was Meinero. The way he was sitting was the first thing that struck Scamarcio. The young priest was perched on the edge of the high-backed chair as if he was about to be electrocuted. He struggled to maintain eye contact and blinked repeatedly. When Scamarcio asked him about the cardinal's relationship with Andrea, he felt sure he actually observed the priest twitch. 'It was difficult, obviously — because Andrea was always very aggressive when we arrived.'

It was as if they'd all been given a script to memorise.

When Scamarcio had wound up the interview and the priest was heading for the door, Scamarcio decided to give it one final shot. 'One second, please,' he shouted.

The young man turned, and Scamarcio immediately clocked the look of unchecked panic as it spread across his features. It was enough to convince him that there was something here he needed to pursue. But now was not the time, with Cafaro watching — he'd have to make a second approach.

'Oh, nothing,' Scamarcio said flatly. 'You're free to go.'

5

FIAMMETTA WAS FAST ASLEEP when he entered the bedroom. He was relieved, because he didn't feel like talking; he was tired and strung out. But as he climbed into bed, she opened her eyes.

'Where have you been so late?'

'Garramone gave me an inquiry.'

'You could have told me. I'd done dinner.'

'Sorry, it was manic.'

'What's he doing handing you a case at this late stage?'

'He thinks it's complicated and that the press will be all over it. For some reason, that means I'm the only man for the job.'

She propped herself up on an elbow. 'What happened?' Her face was flushed by sleep, and the colour of her cheeks set off the steel blue of her eyes. Scamarcio still couldn't believe his luck sometimes. He kissed her forehead. 'Can I tell you tomorrow, when the dust has settled?'

'You think I'm going to blab to my TV friends?'

'I thought you didn't see them anymore.'

'I don't.'

'I'm not worried about that. I just want to get all my ducks in a row. It almost feels like I could jinx it just by talking about it.'

Fiammetta smiled. 'I get that.'

And there it was, the simplicity from which this relationship seemed to derive its strength. Scamarcio hoped they would be able to preserve it when the baby arrived.

'How's my little lad doing?'

Fiammetta rolled her eyes. 'Leo, I worry you're going to be disappointed …'

He laughed. 'No chance.'

'He *or she* is quiet today. Maybe they're tired, just like their mum.' She yawned. 'I'm sorry, but can we talk in the morning?'

'No worries,' he whispered, kissing her on the lips and turning off the light.

As he lay there in the dark, the anxiety returned. His mind churned on demons and devils and sinister-looking angels, who smiled as if they knew a terrible secret. The gold cross on the cardinal's desk kept breaking through it all, glinting, solid, incorruptible, while all around, shadows danced and writhed and slipped away. Scamarcio felt a tightness in his chest and wanted to switch the light on. But he resisted, until, finally, he drifted into a troubled sleep.

The rain was still beating down the next morning when he arrived at the morgue. He was light-headed with tiredness, and his limbs felt disconnected from his mind. Fiammetta had been tossing and turning all night, and he hadn't once been able to sink into a deep, restorative sleep. When he'd complained, she'd just remarked that he'd better get used to it.

Scamarcio nodded at the bald guy at reception and headed straight for the coffee machine. As he was extracting the tiny plastic cup, he felt a hard grip on his shoulder.

'God, you look like shit. Has the baby arrived and no one's told me?'

Scamarcio looked up into the bronzed face of the chief CSI,

Manetti. They'd missed each other at the crime scene.

'That's quite a tan, Manetti. Do you use a lotion? I thought that was just for girls.'

'Thailand,' said Manetti smugly. 'Four-star hotel, all included — 1200 euros for me and the wife. We had a brilliant time.'

Scamarcio felt a twinge of jealousy. He and Fiammetta hadn't been away for ages — they'd been too worried about the baby putting in an early appearance. 'Glad to hear it,' he said, downing the espresso. 'You here for my exorcee?'

'Is that even a word?'

'No idea.'

'I decided to kill two corpses with one stone. I need to talk to Giangrande, so, as I missed you yesterday, I thought we could catch up.'

'Why did you have to rush off? I had a shitload of questions, and no one was there to help.'

Manetti opened his arms. 'We caught another homicide just twenty minutes after. It doesn't happen often, but it's a clusterfuck when it does.'

'It will start happening more and more. Less resources, spiralling crime — go figure.'

Manetti rolled his eyes. 'You're a little ray of sunshine this morning.'

'Gentlemen,' said Dr Giangrande, as he leaned his head round the doorway to the suite, 'can we get started? I'm on a tight schedule.'

'Who isn't?' muttered Manetti.

Scamarcio tossed his cup in the trash, and they followed the chief pathologist inside.

'Listen,' said Giangrande, as he swept a thick lock of greying hair away from his wide forehead. 'I've already done the autopsy. I needed to get ahead, and I didn't think you'd be that bothered if I just gave you the broad brushstrokes.'

'No worries,' said Scamarcio. 'I'm feeling crap enough as it is.'

'In my opinion, you drink way too much coffee, Scamarcio. It must be playing havoc with your stomach acid.' Giangrande lowered his head to scan the numbers on the outside of the refrigerated storage unit.

'He's about to drink a hell of a lot more,' said Manetti.

'When's the baby due?' asked Giangrande as he consulted a creased piece of paper.

'Any day now.'

'And you're working a case?'

'It's better than staying home and twiddling my thumbs.'

Giangrande looked up. 'Nervous?'

'Why do you ask?' Scamarcio realised that the doctor was now eyeing him closely.

'Because I remember that, when I was about to have my first, I couldn't sleep for weeks. I worried about everything — would she be healthy, would I be a good father, would my wife change, would she still have time for me, etc., etc. …' Giangrande sighed. 'Then, as your kids grow up, the old worries are replaced by new ones. Each phase is a whole new set of problems that you need to adapt to.'

'Thanks for that.'

Giangrande waved the discussion away and placed his hand on the door to one of the units. 'This one has all the makings of a media fuck-fest.' He pulled out the drawer, but didn't remove the sheet that covered the body.

Scamarcio felt a needle of fear prick his gut. 'What have you found that will make it any worse? We've got the Vatican's chief exorcist at the scene, a dead boy — an *extremely good-looking* dead boy — and the son of a mafioso heading up the inquiry; there's meat enough for the vultures without a side dish.' Then a second thought struck him. 'I haven't seen the papers — they're not running it already, are they?'

'It wasn't in *La Repubblica* or *Corriere*,' said Manetti. 'I reckon you've got another twenty-four hours to play with — if you're lucky.'

'Then I'll be lucky,' said Scamarcio, as he watched Giangrande pull back the sheet.

Andrea Borghese's brown hair had fanned out to frame his handsome face. His chiselled features reminded Scamarcio of the bust of a Roman emperor. Scamarcio's eyes tracked down to the neck, and he immediately noticed the purple necklace of bruising.

'As you can see, there're ecchymoses. There's been haemorrhaging in the strap muscles and under the skin. I found abrasions from the movement of the ligature, as well as a few fingernail marks, where I believe the victim tried to remove the rope,' said Giangrande.

'Rope?' echoed Scamarcio.

The doctor nodded. 'He was strangled from behind, taken by surprise. There aren't too many fingernail marks, so there probably wasn't time for much of a struggle. From the marks on the victim's neck, I'd say the murderer used a slipknot. The marks tell me this was a quick and efficient strangulation.' He paused. 'And there's something else. As a rule, in strangling, the killer uses far more force than is necessary, which often results in injuries to the deeper structures. But I've not seen that here. It's as if the murderer knew exactly the right amount of pressure to apply.'

Scamarcio turned to Manetti. 'Doesn't all that suggest a certain level of expertise?'

'Probably,' hedged the chief CSI.

'Professionally trained?' wondered Scamarcio out loud.

'Could be, but I've nothing else to suggest that,' said Giangrande.

'Time of death?'

'Around 4.30 pm yesterday. He'd died very shortly before he was found — but you knew that already.'

31

Scamarcio turned to Manetti once more. 'Any trace yet?'

'Nada. Just the mum and dad and the priests. It's early days, but it's starting to look as if the killer cleaned up after himself.'

Scamarcio's mind flashed on the spotless flat. Then he thought back to his meeting with Cardinal Amato. 'The cardinal believes it's the devil's work.'

'What? Not literally, surely?' asked Manetti, his tanned face screwing tight into a frown. Scamarcio was reminded of a walnut.

'Yes.'

The chief CSI narrowed his eyes. 'What a headfuck. How do you like the cardinal for this?'

Scamarcio sniffed. 'Not a lot, unfortunately.'

'Why unfortunately?' asked Giangrande.

'Because I don't have anyone else — no one seen coming in or out, no motive, no friends, no enemies,' he paused. 'No sodding DNA.' He suddenly wondered about *friends*. He couldn't just take the parents' word for it. Perhaps Andrea *did* have a social life that they'd been unaware of. So much of life was lived out online now.

'Oh, it's only Day Two,' said Manetti breezily. 'You know how these things can shape up.'

'Well, I hope they shape up quick 'cos I need this done and dusted before my life's no longer my own.'

'Christ, Scamarcio, you make it sound like a prison sentence. There are some great things about being a parent.'

'Manetti, you've always complained about your kids.'

'Yes, but the good far outweighs the bad.'

Scamarcio rubbed a tired palm across his stubble. 'Any chance some trace of our suspect will still come to light?'

'I've got a couple of results due in later, carpet fibres and a discarded tissue, but I wouldn't get your knickers in a twist. I've been around long enough to know when a scene's been scrubbed.'

Scamarcio raised an eyebrow. 'That thorough?'

'If I were you, I'd keep my eye on the professional angle.'

Scamarcio nodded towards Giangrande. 'OK, I think we've seen enough.'

Giangrande reached for the sheet, but before he pulled it up, he stopped. 'There's a couple of other things. I found some bruising to the back of the head, recently inflicted, as if he'd fallen and knocked his head against something. I also found signs of malformation in the bowel, areas where it looked like it had been subject to intense inflammation over the years. It might have been a problem from early on in life. I don't know whether that information is of any use to you. If it is, I could ask a gastroenterologist to take a closer look.'

Scamarcio pondered it. He never liked to rule anything out in the early stages of an investigation, but budget was a big issue these days. 'What will it cost?'

'Nothing. I was going to ask a consultant friend of mine to pop by after work and do it as a favour.'

'That would be great, Giangrande.' Obviously, the doctor was still trying to rack up points in the hope that Scamarcio would never speak of a past indiscretion which, if it ever came to light, would kill Giangrande's career in an instant.

'I'll let you know what my friend says. It might be worth asking the parents if he had stomach problems.'

'What was his last meal?' asked Scamarcio, not really knowing why he was interested.

'Looks like a Mars bar — I couldn't find any lunch. Breakfast was a bowl of cocoa pops.'

Scamarcio wondered why the boy hadn't had lunch. Hadn't his mother been home? Maybe she'd fixed it for him, but he'd declined.

Dr Giangrande started replacing the sheet, but a glint caught Scamarcio's eye, and he pushed out a hand to stop him. 'What's that on his finger?'

A simple gold band on Borghese's right index finger was blinking under the halogen lights.

'Sorry, but I couldn't get it off — it seems stuck. And then I forgot about it.'

Scamarcio leaned down to examine the ring. 'Funny, it looks like a wedding band.'

'Yes, I know,' mumbled Giangrande absently.

'Did you take a photo, Manetti?' asked Scamarcio, still examining the ring.

'Of course we took a photo,' Manetti shot back.

Scamarcio let go of Borghese's hand and straightened up stiffly.

'You no longer hitting the gym?' asked Manetti, but Scamarcio ignored him.

Giangrande pulled up the sheet and pushed the body back into its compartment, then shut the door. 'Er, Scamarcio.' He sounded strangely nervous.

Scamarcio was surprised to see that Giangrande was glancing uncomfortably at Manetti, as if he wished he wasn't there. 'Oh, don't worry,' said the doctor. 'It's nothing.'

The full force of Giangrande's 'nothing' hit Scamarcio as he was leaving the mortuary. Aurelia was striding towards him up the path. Her hair was cut short in a new modern style which made her look younger and, if such a thing were possible, more beautiful, and she was talking into her phone and laughing. At the sound of her laughter, Scamarcio's mouth turned dry and his heart skipped a beat. He felt a strange warmth spreading through his lungs, a toxic mixture of joy, excitement, and anxiety. He couldn't tell which was winning. It was as if, after months of stasis, every cell, every fibre in his body, was suddenly coming to life. He willed her to look up.

When she finally did, something dark crossed her features. She muttered a few words into her phone, then pressed a button and pushed it quickly into the back pocket of her skin-tight jeans. She glanced around furtively, as if she was perhaps searching for an exit, but the path through the gardens led in only one direction. Scamarcio stood his ground. She had no choice but to face him.

Once she'd reached the steps, he leaned down to kiss her on both cheeks. He'd been about to say that it was good to see her, but he changed it to a neutral 'How are you?'

'Good,' she said, avoiding eye contact.

'I didn't know you were back.'

'Why would you?'

She finally looked at him and frowned. 'You look tired, Leone.'

'Not sleeping well.'

'You weren't sleeping *last* time I saw you.'

Does she know about the baby? he wondered. He didn't want to be the one to tell her.

'How was Munich?'

'Interesting. I learned a lot.' He'd heard she'd been seeing someone. Maybe they'd split.

'Are you back for good?'

'Until a better opportunity comes along.'

'You didn't feel like staying?'

She turned to him, and he watched her eyes burn with a sudden anger. 'Why? Would that have been more convenient for you?'

His first thought was that she *did* know about the baby, then he wondered if it was all just resentment about what had happened with the Cappadona. And, really, who could blame her? He worried about her being back here now, right under their noses in Rome. Then again, he'd heard that the leadership had changed and priorities had shifted.

His voice fell to a whisper. 'I'm so sorry, Aurelia. About everything. I've missed you, you know. And seeing you …' The words trailed off. He didn't know how to phrase it; he didn't understand his own mind.

She saved him the trouble by holding up a palm and pushing straight past him.

'Aurelia!'

But the doors swung shut behind her, and his voice was lost in a sudden shower of rain.

6

SCAMARCIO WAS STANDING ACROSS the street from the Borghese's apartment building, feeling low and confused, when he spotted Gennaro Borghese getting into a black Porsche Panamera and speeding away. Again, Scamarcio figured that marketing must pay far better than he had first imagined. He made a mental note to ask Mr Borghese more about his work. He also wondered where the man could be heading in such a hurry. Surely his company would have granted him compassionate leave? Perhaps he was dealing with his son's funeral arrangements.

When Mrs Borghese greeted Scamarcio in the doorway to the apartment, she looked destroyed: her eyes were red and swollen, her face pale, and her brown hair lank and unwashed.

'Please excuse my appearance, Detective. I just can't get it together.'

'You don't need to apologise, Mrs Borghese.'

'Please, call me Katia.'

She walked over to the huge TV. 'I found the DVDs of the sessions. I hope they're useful.' She grew pensive for a moment, then said, 'Do you want me to watch them with you?'

'It might be good to get your input, but if it's painful ...'

'No, I *want* to. There could be something there. You never know.'

She slumped down on the sofa. 'Is there any news? From the post-mortem?'

Scamarcio talked her through Giangrande's findings.

'I can't believe it,' she whispered when he'd finished. 'Who would do such a thing to Andrea? And why?' She hung her head, then started to cry softly, and Scamarcio could do nothing but look on and watch.

When her sobs were a little quieter, he said, 'Those are the questions I'm exploring. The pathologist and the chief crime-scene investigator both feel that this murder shows signs of professional involvement. The speed of the attack, the level of pressure exerted — they lead us to believe the killer knew exactly what they were doing, and that he or she had perhaps done this before.'

Katia Borghese looked up. Her face had grown even paler. 'What?'

'You know what a professional hit is?'

'Of course I know what that is.' She shook her head. 'But it makes no sense. Why would Andrea be targeted? I just don't understand ...'

'And when you said yesterday that he had no enemies?'

'Like my husband said, Andrea didn't really have a social life. His schooling had been intermittent, he hadn't formed any real friendships ...'

'What about an online presence? Did he use Facebook, Twitter, social media at all?'

She rubbed her eye tiredly. 'He spent a lot of time on the computer, but it was mainly gaming. I don't think he was big on Facebook and all those things.'

'But you're not sure?'

'No, that was private, really. His private world.' She looked uncomfortable. 'Andrea had so little independence, I always thought that we should grant him what small freedoms we could. I didn't ask him too much about the computer stuff.'

38

Scamarcio was surprised. He felt that, given Andrea's problems with anger, his parents ought to have kept across his online activities. But instead he just smiled understandingly. 'I'm going to need to look at Andrea's computer and other devices — tablet, phone, etc.'

'He just had a laptop and a cell.'

'Did the team take them yesterday?'

'No, they're still here. You want them?'

'Yes, if you could.' Scamarcio was disgusted that the CSI team hadn't bagged them. Leaving the devices would have given either parent ample time to wipe valuable data. He didn't really like either of the Borgheses for suspects, but the case was still very new. He'd have a word with Manetti about the oversight. It couldn't happen again.

While Mrs Borghese was retrieving the devices, Scamarcio took the opportunity to look around. A few tasteful landscapes lined the walls of the living room, and the parquet was strewn with elaborate Moroccan rugs. The sofas were a rich tan leather, on which a few embroidered cushions were carefully placed. Scamarcio struggled to imagine the chaotic madness of Andrea's condition fitting into all this perfection. He wondered about the cushions: what mother, in the throes of grief, would think to plump and neaten her cushions? Or maybe they'd been like that since yesterday. Or perhaps they had a cleaner? Perhaps tidying was a coping mechanism.

'Do you have a cleaning lady?' he asked as Mrs Borghese came back into the room.

She looked surprised. 'No.' She coughed. 'We did for a while, but Andrea was vile to her, so we had to let her go.'

'Why didn't he like her?'

'Oh, it wasn't personal. Andrea didn't like anyone who encroached on his space, his routine.'

A distant bell was ringing for Scamarcio — the memory of a friend's son. 'Did any of the doctors you saw ever mention autism?'

'Oh yes, it often came up. But then they couldn't make some of Andrea's other symptoms fit. It was like he had a bit of autism, a bit of epilepsy, and then a whole load of other stuff. No one seemed to know quite where to place him.'

Scamarcio decided he'd better read up on these conditions when he had a chance. It might give him a clearer picture.

'Here you go,' said Mrs Borghese, handing over a laptop and cable, then an iPhone.

Scamarcio thanked her. 'Are they password protected?'

'I hadn't thought of that. They may be — but if they are, he never told me the codes.'

Scamarcio pulled some plastic CSI gloves from his bag and put them on. Then he perched the laptop on his knees and fired it up. It was locked. Unsurprisingly, it was the same story with the phone. He closed the laptop and laid the devices carefully on the coffee table. He removed the gloves and rolled them into a tiny ball which he popped in his pocket.

'Might your husband know how to get in?'

'We can call him.' She reached for a cordless phone.

'Where is he? I saw him driving off as I arrived.'

'He's gone to see his mother. She's taking all this terribly badly.' She shrugged as if she couldn't understand why.

'It would be hard for any grandmother.'

'Yes, but she never really gave Andrea the time of day. She's a snob, very concerned with appearances. Andrea was a big embarrassment.'

'Ah, I see.'

'Not nice to say, but that's the reality.' She pressed the dial tab on the phone.

The image of Gennaro Borghese speeding away in his black Porsche flashed into Scamarcio's mind once more, and he held his hand out to stop Mrs Borghese. 'Actually, can we hold off on the call a moment?'

Mrs Borghese looked up, surprised. 'OK.'

Scamarcio cleared his throat, trying to buy himself some time while he formulated the thought. 'Mrs Borghese, given this case shows signs of professional involvement, I have to ask: might your husband have links to organised crime?'

Mrs Borghese blinked several times. 'Wow, that was not a question I was expecting.' She paused. 'No, I can assure you that Gennaro has nothing to do with the mafia. In fact, he detests them — never misses an opportunity to complain about them. He thinks the mafia mentality has spread north and corrupted us all. He blames them for everything.'

'I think the same, to be honest.'

They both smiled weakly, and a few seconds of awkward silence followed. Scamarcio wondered if Mrs Borghese had been told about his past. He shifted his weight on the sofa and said, 'Let's make a start on the films. I have a feeling they're going to give me some valuable insight into Andrea and this case.'

'Of course.' She set down the phone and reached for a long remote. She pressed a few buttons, and the huge screen came to life. Scamarcio saw a frozen image of Andrea Borghese flanked by three young men in dark clerical robes.

He threw a quick glance at Mrs Borghese. She was biting her fist and closing her eyes. He couldn't begin to think how hard it must be for her to see her dead son brought back to life like this.

The freeze-frame shuddered, and then began moving smoothly. Andrea was shouting something, but Scamarcio couldn't quite make out the words. The three young priests were pinning his arms back, trying to prevent him from striking at Cardinal Amato, who was standing a few metres away. In comparison to Andrea, who must have been at least six foot, Amato seemed like a tiny wisp of a figure. Scamarcio noticed a battered leather book shaking in his gnarled hands. He felt sure it was the same book he'd seen on the cardinal's desk.

'Neverrrrr,' hissed Andrea, as he thrashed against the grip of the priests. 'Get away! Get away!'

All at once, he managed to break free from their hold. He grabbed a tall wooden chair and, with tremendous force, hurled it towards the cardinal. Amato was able to duck out of the way just before the chair broke against the wall behind him. Andrea reached around him frantically and soon found a glass vase, which also went over Amato's head, crashing and smashing against the wall, and sending small shards scattering across the floor. The cardinal was crouched down and took several moments to assess the situation before rising gingerly to his feet.

'RECEDE IN NOMINE PATRIS!' yelled Amato, in a voice that was entirely new. It was deep and powerful and didn't seem to belong to him. The cardinal was striding towards Andrea, determined now, far less afraid. The dramatic change brought moisture to the back of Scamarcio's neck. It wasn't the bravery that shocked him, but the brute force of the words. This was a different man. It was as if the cardinal were someone else — as if he, too, were possessed.

'SANCTISSIMO DOMINE MIGRA,' Amato boomed as he stepped closer to Andrea, who in turn now seemed cowed and intimidated. He was looking all around him for an escape, but appeared to be rooted to the spot by fear.

'CEDE! CEDE!' screamed Amato as he backed Andrea into a corner. The young priests moved in and grabbed the boy's arms once more. The camera shifted shakily to find a better angle on Cardinal Amato's face. He looked furious — raging, even. His eyes were on fire. The transformation was total, and Scamarcio knew in that moment that he needed to take a step back and reassess: the contours of this case were different from what he'd first imagined. Cardinal Amato was not to be underestimated.

Andrea was quivering now, like a young bird fallen from a nest. The priests were leading him to a chair and trying to coax him to sit. The boy was whispering something over and over.

'What's he saying?' Scamarcio asked Mrs Borghese. He noticed that she had opened her eyes now and was watching the screen.

'"Leave him," probably. That was something he used to say a lot. It was the devil talking — challenging the cardinal.'

'You really believe that?'

Mrs Borghese froze the image and looked Scamarcio hard in the eye. 'It's the only thing that can fully explain Andrea's behaviour over the years. It was our mistake that we didn't recognise it sooner and that we wasted so much time and money. It was only once Andrea started seeing the cardinal that we saw any improvement at all.'

'Does your husband feel the same way? Did he agree with the decision to approach the church?'

Katia Borghese cleared her throat and looked into her lap. 'My husband and I have always had a different opinion when it comes to matters of faith. I have a strong faith; I come from a family with a strong faith. My husband is the son of atheists, and, unfortunately, he has inherited their cynicism.'

'So, it was your decision to approach Amato?'

She glanced up. 'Yes, but what could Gennaro say? Nothing else had worked, so it was worth a try. Even he could see that.'

She returned her gaze to the TV and pressed play. Andrea was still whispering, but he seemed tired. He was resting his head against the wall, and his eyes were starting to close. The cardinal had placed a hand on his leg and was also now speaking in a whisper. The boy's eyes stayed shut. To Scamarcio, there was something disconcerting about the scene, but he couldn't pinpoint why. After a few seconds, the screen turned black.

'Is that it?' he asked.

'I stopped filming because the session ended there. It was a particularly good session because Andrea calmed much earlier than normal. Cardinal Amato hadn't even reached the end of his rites.'

Scamarcio rubbed a palm across his forehead. 'You were able to film this? It must have been hard for you.'

'Actually, I found it easier to watch though a lens than witness with my bare eyes, as strange as that may sound.'

'I guess the camera removes you from the action — there's something between you and reality.' Scamarcio paused. 'How was Andrea after these sessions?'

'After that particular session, he was calm. He slept for a long time. After other sessions, he'd sometimes settle for a bit, only to get fired up again a few hours later.'

'Fired up?'

'He'd become aggressive again: start swearing, throwing things.'

Mrs Borghese went over to the TV and kneeled down to remove the disc. She slipped it into a plastic case.

'Did you film all of them?' asked Scamarcio.

She rose wearily to her feet and sighed. 'Just three or four, I think. I wanted a record of his progress — for when my husband tried to deny it all later.' She smiled sadly. 'And as I say, it was easier to watch through a lens.'

'Can I have the other ones? I'll make copies and return the originals.'

'Of course.' She reached beneath the TV and retrieved a few plastic cases. Scamarcio took them and slipped them into his jacket pocket.

'Shall we call your husband now?'

Mrs Borghese nodded and picked up the phone. She dialled the number, and then she must have put it on speakerphone, because Scamarcio heard it ringing. After a moment, the line crackled, before Mr Borghese said, quite calmly, 'Leave me alone, bitch.'

Mrs Borghese didn't seem in the least bit surprised. She simply ended the call and laid the phone on the table, before folding her manicured hands in her lap and staring off into the middle distance.

'Is that normally how he greets you?' asked Scamarcio quietly.

She laughed bitterly, her eyes empty. 'He blames me. He thinks all this is to do with the church. If we hadn't approached Amato, Andrea wouldn't be dead.'

'Why?' asked Scamarcio. 'Andrea was murdered. He …'

'Don't ask me. Last night we had a huge row. Gennaro is struggling — he is very close to his twin brother, but he's been unable to reach him with the news — Corrado's hiking in Nepal. Because he hasn't been able to talk to him about Andrea's death, he's turned on me. He keeps saying, "This is what happens when you bring the devil into it." He's now convinced that we should have persevered with the science.'

'It sounds like it's your husband who's the true believer.'

She opened her arms. 'It's crazy, I know. But right now, he hates me — deeply. Maybe he'll hate me forever …' Her eyes grew vacant, and she studied her slippered feet. 'I've lost both my son and my husband. It doesn't get much worse than that.'

Scamarcio left the elevator and stepped into the foyer of the Borgheses' apartment block. As he was heading for the front door that led to the gardens, he felt a chill hit the back of his neck and sweep down his spine. It must have been a draught coming from somewhere down the corridor, though when he turned to check, he couldn't spot any doors or windows ajar. He carried on walking, but the chill intensified. He turned again, and, this time, he thought he saw a small shadow disappear around a corner — a fleeting glimpse of black. His mind flitted uneasily to devils and demons, and he relived the strange sensation he'd experienced in Amato's rooms. He swallowed and told himself not to be so stupid. It was probably just a cat.

He stepped outside and immediately felt the cold rain against his skin. To his horror, he realised that several TV news vans were already parked at the kerb. An engineer was rolling out thick black cables through the back doors of one. To the right were a couple of TV reporters Scamarcio recognised. One was adjusting her make-up, while the other was speaking into his mobile phone as he glanced up at the apartment building. Scamarcio was already halfway down the path to the street, which meant there was nowhere left to run. He needed to take a right onto the pavement, but that meant walking straight past them all.

'Fuck,' he whispered.

'Detective Scamarcio,' trilled an uncomfortably familiar voice from somewhere close behind him.

'Go to hell,' he muttered, not wanting to look round.

'Detective Scamarcio, might I have a word?'

He turned to see his least favourite journalist running towards him, a long, lurid red coat billowing out around her. Fabiana Morello snagged a high black patent-leather heel between two paving slabs and swore. Scamarcio smiled.

'Detective,' she said breathlessly, once she'd extracted the shoe. 'Can you give me some details about the Borghese murder? There's been nothing from your press office.'

Scamarcio rubbed a hand across his mouth. Morello had improved since he'd last seen her. She had never been beautiful, but had always worked hard to make the best of herself with expensive clothes and careful make-up. But today, the skin around her eyes seemed tauter and her lips fuller. He guessed she'd visited a top plastic surgeon, and he wondered for a moment where the money had come from. For years, she'd crucified him in her articles, and Scamarcio could never quite shake the suspicion that there was someone in the background pulling her strings.

'The press office will release a statement in due course. There'll probably be a conference. I'm sure they'll let you know,' he said, walking off as quickly as he could without breaking into a run.

'Oh, come *on!*' She was grabbing his arm now. 'You can do better than that. If you would only bother to give me a chance, you might find I have a few interesting things to share.'

He stared at her hard. 'I'm not going to be doing any kind of deal with you, Morello. You're the very last reporter I'd trust, given the shit you've written about me.'

She feigned offence. 'Oh, come on, don't be so sensitive, Leone.'

'It's "Detective" to you. Now fuck off and leave me alone.'

He strode off, knowing that he was exiting the frying pan for the fire. The TV pack was hurrying towards him. In the short time he'd been talking to Morello, they seemed to have swelled in number.

'There'll be a press conference,' he shouted, pushing past them. 'I don't have anything now.'

They were screaming questions, the same ones over and over.
'Was the cardinal a suspect?'
'What was his relationship to the boy?'
'Was it sexual?'

Scamarcio just waved them all away and focussed on the pavement as he hurried for the taxi rank at the end of the Borgheses' street. He hoped they didn't all try to follow. Next time, he'd have to bring the car.

7

'CHIEF MANCINO ISN'T TOO impressed. He thinks you could do with a media-training refresher,' said Garramone as he stopped by Scamarcio's desk.

'For fuck's sake.' Scamarcio looked up from his computer, narked at the interruption. There was so much to do, and he still hadn't been assigned a proper team.

'You come across as hostile in the footage they're running on the news. We mustn't give the impression that they're our enemy.'

'They are.'

'You know that, and I know that, but we're not allowed to say so. Next time, try to crack a smile or something. Don't look so cornered.'

'Crack a smile? A kid was murdered, for God's sake.'

Garramone shrugged. 'We need to show willing, for the good of the department. We all have to play politics now, not just the bosses.'

'I'm a detective. I'm not here to play politics.'

'You have no choice.'

'When's the presser?'

'Gio from media relations is coming up to have a word. She's organising it for 5.00 pm, I believe.'

Scamarcio looked at his watch. 'That's just two hours away.'

'She wants you there.'

He had expected as much, but it didn't make it any easier to digest. He hated press conferences.

'And the Borgheses?'

'Gio called them, and they don't want to do it.'

Scamarcio rubbed his temple. His skull felt tight. 'Why?'

'I dunno. Can you see if you can bring them round?'

Scamarcio reached for the desk phone. 'The mum might be good. The dad, I'm not so sure.'

'The mums are always good,' said Garramone, walking off.

After a long phone call with each of the Borgheses, Scamarcio eventually managed to persuade them that their presence could prove valuable for the investigation. Both had blamed their reluctance on exhaustion and a wish to avoid the public eye, but they'd finally been swayed by examples Scamarcio had recounted from past cases. Unfortunately, when it came to the matter of his son's passwords, Mr Borghese hadn't had any information to share.

Scamarcio decided to use the hour he had left before the press arrived to have one last try at getting into Andrea's devices. But after less than a minute of guessing passwords, it was clear that he was wasting his time. He decided to head over to Tech to ask if they could help.

Negruzzo was the only technician who waved when Scamarcio entered the bunker. All the others studiously ignored him. The air was stale and male and smelled of frustration.

'Have I got the plague or something?' he asked, as he placed Andrea Borghese's laptop and mobile on Negruzzo's desk.

'We've been honing down a child porn inquiry. The guys are focussed,' said Negruzzo, looking troubled.

'Sure,' said Scamarcio, recollecting a terrible case he'd worked on several years back. 'Who are your perps?'

Negruzzo stretched his arms out and rolled his neck, trying to release the tension in his shoulders. 'A ring of Poles living right under our noses here in Rome — but of course they're distributing far and wide.'

Scamarcio sighed. 'I wish we could just hang them all.'

'Yeah.' Negruzzo turned over Andrea's phone, holding it to the light. 'You're not alone in that thought. What curiosities have you got for me here, then?'

'It's the exorcist thing.'

'I just caught a bit of that. You didn't exactly look the picture of happiness, Scamarcio.'

Scamarcio sighed. 'Neither would you if you had that lot up your arse.'

'Did these belong to the vic or the cardinal?' Negruzzo was opening the laptop now.

'The vic. They seem to be locked, and I don't have the passwords.'

Negruzzo shrugged. 'No biggie. As long as they're not encrypted — but they rarely are. What are you hoping for?'

'I want to take a look at the files on the laptop and have a snoop through his life online.'

'Those will be different passwords, but hopefully he stayed logged on to his social-media accounts. What was his full name?'

Scamarcio obliged.

'I'll work on getting into the devices. For the laptop, as long as it's not encrypted, I'll use a live USB. That's a drive that contains a full operating system that can be booted up. That should let me browse all the data on his computer. I could also edit the grub boot-menu options to reset the root password, but ...'

'It's the social media that I'm most interested in.'

Negruzzo pulled up Facebook on a grease smeared tablet, typed in Andrea's name, and scrolled through some photos. 'This him?' he asked after a minute or so.

'Yeah,' said Scamarcio.

'His Facebook account is set to private, unsurprisingly.' Negruzzo paused. 'Just thinking ahead here, but can you provide me with any pets' names, parents' names, favourite football team, favourite rock bands and online games, favourite foods and drinks ...? Might be useful if he has logged himself off. And could help with the devices, too.'

'I don't have all that yet.'

'Can you get it?'

'Don't you have a more sophisticated way of getting in?'

'It'll probably be guesswork. Did the CSIs take a photo of the area around the laptop? That can be valuable. We once got a guy's email password from looking at the number on a scrap of paper he'd pinned to a board, which was actually his dad's prison ID. It was all there on the crime scene pictures — gold dust.'

'The CSIs didn't even bother to lift the devices. I doubt they took pics.'

'That's a bit crap.'

'Yeah, but it was a mad one. They got called away to another homicide almost immediately.'

'It's all falling apart — soon we won't have a police force ...'

'Don't you start.'

'If I can't guess my way in, we'll have to subpoena Facebook. They're obliged to supply us with all his posts, friends, unfriends, etc. Every little bell that has ever been rung.'

'Will that take long?'

'Not usually, if it's a murder investigation. Are we just looking at Facebook for social media?'

'I doubt it. He was probably on Twitter, Instagram. Could you do a search?'

Negruzzo shook his head in faux disbelief. 'Feels to me as if I'm doing more than my fair share these days.' But there wasn't that much animosity in his tone. 'You know a kid that age would probably be on Snapchat or TikTok, too, right?'

Scamarcio made a motion with his hand to indicate that he didn't care what they were called, Negruzzo should just check for them. 'And the iPhone?'

'There are a few vulnerabilities I could exploit — I might be able to get in through the cloud. If he's synced the phone to the laptop, that could also be an option.' He paused to examine the phone once more. 'Hmm,' he murmured. 'It's an 8. The 8 can run iOS 11, which is significant. Apple reconfigured the iOS 11 so you could disable fingerprint recognition by tapping the power button five times. You realise you're about to be nicked — you just reach into your pocket and tap away. The US cops were furious because, whereas before they could force suspects to give up something they *had*, like a fingerprint, they couldn't force them to reveal something they *knew*, like a password.' He fell silent as he touched the screen. 'Let's have a little look-see ...'

'Don't make me wheel over the corpse so you can use the fingerprint ...'

'I'd take the phone to the morgue, Scamarcio,' said Negruzzo, in a *Don't be a twat* tone. 'Ahh,' he murmured, disappointed. 'He's disabled it. It couldn't just be easy for once, could it?'

'I wonder why,' said Scamarcio. 'Surely having fingerprint ID is easier than typing in a password every time?'

'Quite,' said Negruzzo. 'You ought to keep sight of that — it might be a clue for you.'

He set down the phone and began rooting around in a drawer full of USB keys. It was a strange sight — they were all shapes and colours and looked like the haul from a robbery.

'Will you call me or shall I call you?' asked Scamarcio.

'Leave it with me. I'll let you know when I've got somewhere.'

Scamarcio rose to his feet and tried a wave in the direction of the other technicians, but no one looked up.

He was glad to leave the bunker. There was an atmosphere within its walls that brought him down.

52

8

When they arrived for the press conference, the Borgheses
were walking wide apart and didn't appear to be speaking to one
another. Mr Borghese took the door first and almost let it swing
back into his wife's face. Scamarcio managed to catch it just in time.

He led them into a small room next to the hall where the
conference was to be held and fetched them both a coffee from
the machine. He noticed that Katia Borghese had gone to some
effort; she'd put on a smart suit and washed and styled her hair.
Unfortunately, he knew that this didn't always play well with the
public. They'd ask why a grieving mother was composed enough
to worry about her appearance, and they'd wonder if it was a sign
of involvement. At best, her polished image risked eroding any
initial sympathy.

'I really don't want to be here,' she said, as he handed her the
coffee.

Scamarcio wanted to add that neither did he, but instead he
said, 'It's for Andrea. Having the parents at a press conference
always helps.'

At that moment, Giovanna Rinaldi from media relations
strode in. She was a tall brunette with long limbs and a can-do,
easy-going manner. Scamarcio much preferred dealing with her
than the other PR guy, Paolo Gatti, who was a power hungry,
Machiavellian rat.

Rinaldi introduced herself to the Borgheses and gave her condolences. 'We're aiming to start in five minutes. You all set?'

The Borgheses nodded listlessly.

'I know it's hard, but try to remember to speak up, and in complete sentences, if you can. It's easier for them to use your soundbites that way. Detective Scamarcio will be with you, as will I. Any questions you're not happy with, turn to me, and I'll deal with it.'

'Sure,' whispered Katia Borghese. Her husband just studied the floor.

'OK then, I think we can begin making our way inside.'

Rinaldi led them to the conference room. When they entered, scores of cameras flashed and red eyes blinked as the media tracked their arrival. Scamarcio couldn't remember ever having seen the room so full — not even for the case of the missing American girl he'd led a couple of years back.

They took their positions at the desk, and Scamarcio studied the crowd. There were a lot of faces he didn't recognise, and quite a few foreigners among them. He noticed several Asian crews. There was nothing to be done — this story was going global.

Rinaldi introduced them all before handing over to Scamarcio. 'Detective Scamarcio will give you the facts of the case — that is, the ones we have so far.'

Scamarcio coughed and looked down at the bullet points he had prepared. He didn't feel as nervous as he'd expected, just irritated, mainly, at the time he was losing. But he reminded himself that the song and dance might yet be worth it.

He began by talking them through the time and place of death, but he did not mention that they suspected a professional hit or that Andrea had been strangled. He'd agreed with Garramone that they should keep those details quiet for the time being. Scamarcio then gave some general background on Andrea and his sessions with Cardinal Amato. When he finished, the room exploded with a barrage of questions, and it took Rinaldi quite some time to restore order. 'One at a time, please, ladies and gentlemen,' she shouted for the fifth time.

She indicated to a middle-aged man in a smart grey suit near the front. Scamarcio recognised him as a reporter from TG1.

'Go ahead, Paolo.'

'Detective Scamarcio, everyone is wondering — is the cardinal a suspect?'

Scamarcio cleared his throat. 'The murder was yesterday. We're in the very early stages of our inquiry, which means nobody can be ruled in or out.'

'So, he's a suspect?'

Scamarcio wrote tomorrow's headlines in his head. He had enough experience not to fall into the trap that was being set for him. 'As I say, it's very early days.'

'And the other priests who were with him?'

'We're exploring all avenues.'

Rinaldi turned towards another hand held aloft. 'Gina.'

Gina Rizzo was an attractive blonde from Sky News who Scamarcio had made the subject of numerous sexual fantasies.

'How much time elapsed between the end of the exorcism and Andrea's murder, Detective?'

'We believe about an hour.'

She turned her head towards the Borgheses. 'I have a question for Andrea's parents. Could you explain why you'd decided to consult Cardinal Amato? What made you think that your son was possessed?'

Mr Borghese gestured towards his wife and looked at her hard as if to say, *There's no way I'm going to take this one.*

Mrs Borghese wiped her eyes with a tissue. When the words came, they were very quiet. Giovanna Rinaldi placed a gentle hand on Katia Borghese's shoulder and asked her to speak up.

'We'd spent years seeing medical experts. When nothing worked, we decided to try the church.'

'Can you describe your son's symptoms?'

Scamarcio felt there was something mawkish about the question, and Mrs Borghese seemed to feel the same way.

'No,' she said firmly. 'I've given that information to the police, but I don't see why it's of public interest.'

Scamarcio noticed Rizzo purse her lips and look down.

Rinaldi selected another reporter from the throng. Scamarcio didn't recognise him.

'I wanted to ask Mr Borghese if he has any ideas about who might have done this.'

Gennaro Borghese pinched his nose and looked nervously at Scamarcio. Scamarcio just nodded at him to continue.

'Because of his problems, Andrea didn't get out much … he didn't have many friends. My wife and I are at a loss as to how to explain his murder. It makes no sense to us.'

'And how do you feel about the cardinal?'

'How do I *feel* about him?'

'Do you suspect him?'

Mr Borghese's face became pinched. 'No. I don't suspect the cardinal.' He turned to Scamarcio. 'Can we wind this up now?' The words rang out loud and clear over the microphone.

'Just a few more questions,' said Rinaldi softly, as she scanned the crowd.

Scamarcio's heart sank when he saw Fabiana Morello take the microphone.

'Mr and Mrs Borghese, are you comfortable with Detective Scamarcio's involvement in this inquiry?'

Katia Borghese turned to her husband, who looked equally confused. 'Why wouldn't we be comfortable?'

'Because of his background. Detective Scamarcio has a chequered history, he …'

'Can't we move the narrative *on*, Fabiana?' said Rinaldi, exasperated. 'This is about the murder of a young man. Detective Scamarcio's very distant past has nothing to do with it.'

'Not so distant, from what I hear,' muttered Morello into the mike.

Rinaldi rolled her eyes at Scamarcio. Scamarcio frowned back, but, inside, he was wondering what Morello might have in play. Was that comment a first stab at blackmail? Did she have something on him? If anyone did, it would have to be her. Over the years, she'd seemed increasingly obsessed with him, like a dog with a bone. Maybe the dog had been down south, done some digging. The thought made him nauseous. He tried to return his focus to the room.

A Japanese journalist was asking a question about Amato, but Scamarcio hadn't caught the beginning. He turned to look at the parents and noticed that Gennaro Borghese seemed newly agitated. He was struggling to loosen his shirt collar, thick beads of sweat were coursing down his face, and he was blinking rapidly. *Is he unwell?* But before the thought had even coalesced, Borghese had sprung from his chair and was yelling at the crowd. 'You're parasites, the lot of you! You sicken me, you freaks! Fuck off and leave us to grieve.'

Scamarcio rubbed a hand across his eyes and rose from his chair.

'That could have gone better,' he whispered to Rinaldi as she ushered the Borgheses out of the room.

9

SCAMARCIO YAWNED FOR THE fifth time as he made the walk down Via della Giuliana towards the entrance to Cafaro's offices at the Vatican. He felt shaky, and it was an effort to keep his eyelids from closing. He'd been woken at 2.00 am by Fiammetta, who thought she was experiencing contractions. By 3.00 am, she'd changed her mind, but by then he was so on edge that he'd been unable to fall back to sleep and had spent the next few hours trying to banish all thoughts of devils and demons.

He'd sifted through the sparse facts of the case in his head and had tried to form a picture — draw some kind of outline that would tell him which direction to take, but nothing had come to him. He was still mired in 'all avenues' territory, and he needed to get out of the mud, fast. He wanted another meeting with the young priest, Meinero. He had a feeling that exploring his doubts about Meinero — that flicker of fear he'd noticed — would bring him to a turn in the road far sooner than any password on any laptop.

As expected, the chief of the Vatican gendarmerie didn't seem too happy to see him. 'Why didn't you call first?' said Cafaro, tipping back an espresso. He didn't offer Scamarcio one.

'I didn't think I'd find you in so early,' lied Scamarcio.

'Bullshit.'

Uninvited, Scamarcio drew out a seat opposite Cafaro's desk and sat down. 'I just need a word with Priest Meinero. Don't worry about the others.'

'You suspect him?'

'I noticed something in his behaviour that I'd like to explore. It may be nothing.'

'I can't come with you,' said Cafaro as if Scamarcio might be disappointed. 'I have a meeting.'

This was precisely what Scamarcio had hoped for — better to catch the inspector unprepared. 'No problem,' he said quietly.

Cafaro threw him a long stare, it was almost a challenge, but not quite. He sighed then turned to study a document pinned on the wall to the left of his tidy desk. He quickly punched a number into the phone. 'Is Meinero there?' A pause. 'Anyone know where he might be? There's a detective from the Flying Squad who needs to talk to him.' Another pause. 'OK. Shall I send him up?' Silence, then finally, 'Right you are.'

Cafaro cut the call and checked his watch. 'I'm running late. If you head up to the first floor of the Sala Rotonda, you should find him. He's a member of the Congregation for the Doctrine of the Faith, and they're about to meet. I should be free in forty minutes or so. Please report back to me before you leave.'

'Yes, sir,' Scamarcio smiled and rose from the chair.

As he left, he had the distinct feeling that Cafaro was flipping him the bird behind his back.

Scamarcio crossed the Vatican gardens, admiring an array of red and purple primroses that had been sown into the lawn to form the Pope's insignia. He wondered whether he actually liked it. Given his apparent modesty — his refusal to sleep in the Pope's palace and his choice of a simple Fiat to get about — perhaps such an ostentatious display grated with him.

As Scamarcio rounded a corner, he came upon a loud huddle of nuns carrying huge piles of laundry. He'd read in the paper that the sisters had been complaining of late: there was way too much ironing, and they were having to work ever longer shifts to deal with the backlog.

He entered the huge marble lobby of the Sala Rotonda, and the heavy chemical scent of disinfectant on unmoved air hit him immediately. He took the massive wooden staircase, running his palm along the mahogany and wondering at the perfection of the polish. Although he'd lived in Rome for over a decade, he'd never been inside the Rotonda. Scamarcio wasn't one to be easily excited, but the dramatic portraits, the centuries of history within the walls, and the intoxicating brew of power and opulence were stirring something in him. He arrived on the first floor and immediately spotted a group of young priests milling about outside a massive oak door, which appeared to be locked shut with a large gold padlock.

'Is Meinero here?' he asked the small crowd.

They exchanged glances and shook their heads.

'He hasn't turned up yet,' said Lania, the blond priest from the Veneto whom Scamarcio had interviewed the other day.

'Actually, he was supposed to play squash with me last night, but he didn't show,' a small guy with curly dark hair told the group.

'Did anyone see him yesterday?' asked Scamarcio.

They traded quick glances again and shook their heads once more.

'Now I think about it, I don't remember him being at lunch or breakfast either,' said the same curly-haired guy.

What had started as a dull hum of concern was becoming a shrieking alarm in Scamarcio's head.

'Do any of you have an idea where he might be? Perhaps he's had to go away on official business?'

'We'd know about that,' said Lania. 'We're a group. We do things together.'

'Is Meinero a member of any other organisations that might have business in Rome — in the city?'

'He was on the Soup Kitchen Committee, but he left that a few months back,' said the curly-haired guy. 'That would be his only reason for being outside the Vatican, but, even then, they make sure their timetable coincides with other in-house congregation business.'

'Where's Meinero from originally?' Scamarcio asked.

'Piedmont,' answered the curly-haired guy. 'The part near Liguria. I forget the name of his town.'

'Is he still in touch with his folks up there?'

'He's very close to his sister, and she still lives there,' he said.

'Would you have a number for her?'

The young priest shook his head. 'You should try our admin office. We have to give the details of our next of kin. They might have it.'

He gave Scamarcio directions to the office, then said, 'Maybe you should hang around here for a bit, in case he's just running late.' He glanced at his watch. 'We're due to go in any moment.'

As if on cue, an elderly priest arrived and began unlocking the padlock.

'Is Meinero often late?' Scamarcio asked the group.

'Never,' said Lania as he glanced nervously towards the stairs.

It took Scamarcio a long time to find the admin office. It was tucked away behind some steps in a building that appeared to be home to all the Vatican's maintenance workers and their equipment. From one glance, Scamarcio sensed that the elderly lady in charge would be far less amenable than her younger assistant, who had greeted him politely as he walked in.

'What is it you want, exactly?' asked the head secretary as she lowered her half-moon glasses and let them rest on their chain against her thick rollneck sweater. It was stiflingly hot in the office, but the old woman seemed dressed for the outdoors.

Scamarcio pulled out his police ID and passed it to her. She studied it for a few seconds, and then pursed her lips. 'This is all very nice, but you must understand that you have no jurisdiction.'

For a moment, Scamarcio was lost for words. He couldn't believe she was going to give him this level of grief. He'd banked on quickly collecting the information without Cafaro arriving and putting a spoke in his wheels.

'Madam, I'm running a high-profile murder inquiry. You've probably seen it on the news. Priest Meinero attended the Borghese exorcism with Cardinal Amato. None of Meinero's colleagues have seen him for the past twenty-four hours, and I urgently need to speak with him.'

The old woman just shrugged, as if Scamarcio had been complaining about the rain.

'I need to call Inspector Cafaro. He's head of the gendarmerie. This sort of thing needs to go through him.'

'I happen to know that the inspector is in a meeting. I haven't got time to hang around until he gets here.'

'That's your problem.'

'A young man has been murdered. You're impeding my attempts to find his killer.'

She just shrugged again. 'Come back with Inspector Cafaro, and I'll see what I can do.' With that, she replaced the glasses and disappeared into her office, the door banging shut behind her.

'Jesus,' sighed Scamarcio.

The young assistant looked up.

'Sorry,' said Scamarcio. 'I forgot where I was.'

The young woman smiled, and Scamarcio noticed her light hazel eyes.

'Wait,' she whispered.

He frowned, but did as instructed.

She tapped a few keys on her computer, studied the screen, and then began scribbling on a block note. After five seconds or so, she pushed the note onto the counter in front of her and looked away quickly.

When Scamarcio glanced at the piece of paper, he saw two telephone numbers and what appeared to be an address in the province of Alessandria, Piedmont.

He pocketed the note and muttered, 'Thank you.' Then he hurried out, without looking back.

10

BOTH NUMBERS FOR MEINERO'S relatives in Piedmont were ringing out, as was Meinero's cell. Scamarcio replaced the receiver, sank back in his chair, and twiddled a biro across his fingers. His eyes came to rest on the small CCTV camera in the corner of the squad room nearest to his desk. So far, he'd neglected the CCTV element. Sure, he'd done his due diligence on the Borghese's block, which he'd quickly discovered had no CCTV, likewise the street outside. But now he wondered about the cameras near the Vatican: they might prove of use in explaining where Meinero had gone. But experience told him that, at best, they'd just show he'd turned left or right onto Viale Vaticano or Via di Porta Angelica, and then the hunt would start from there. Sure, they could trawl all the cameras along the surrounding roads, but that was a long job, and he wasn't sure they were at that stage yet. There was still too much to do, and he needed to stick with the macro approach for now.

Just as he was lifting his desk phone, Sartori, a detective from Rimini he had worked with in the past, strode over, a finger held aloft. Scamarcio set down the phone.

'You've got me and Lovoti. Then two more, once Garramone has decided who they are.'

Scamarcio frowned. 'You, Sartori, I'm always happy to see, but why the fuck Lovoti? Garramone knows I can't stand him.'

Sartori rolled his shoulders. 'I dunno, you'll have to ask the chief. I think he's just going with who's free. Mancino's probably breathing down his neck because of the media interest.'

Scamarcio sighed. 'They seem to be all over every sodding case of mine.'

'I'd take that as a compliment.'

Scamarcio scratched his head. 'You ready to go? I've got something to start you off with.'

Sartori nodded. 'Knock yourself out.'

'I need you to set up a city-wide alert for a Vatican priest called Alberto Meinero. He was one of the young priests who assisted Cardinal Amato with the Borghese exorcism. When I interviewed him the day of the murder, he was acting strangely, and now it seems that he's gone missing. No one has seen him in the last twenty-four hours.'

Sartori pulled out a chair, and then helped himself to a piece of paper and a pen from the pot on Scamarcio's desk. He wrote down the name, then showed it to Scamarcio. Scamarcio nodded.

'He's from a place called Arquata Scrivia, near Genoa. He's twenty-five, six foot, brown hair, brown eyes, olive skin — good-looking guy. Around seventy-five to seventy-eight kilos, I'd say.' Scamarcio thought of his own weight and the flab that had started to form around his middle. 'Maybe eighty. Thin-framed, anyway. I'll see if we can get hold of a photo.'

Sartori jotted it all down. 'Sexual preference?'

Scamarcio cocked an eyebrow. He didn't have time for jokes. 'No idea.'

'I hear some Vatican priests like to hang around certain Turkish baths and saunas in this city.'

Scamarcio frowned, then realised Sartori wasn't joking. And at that same moment, he understood that Sartori was on the road to becoming a sound detective.

'Yeah, check it out, Sartori. If you have any contacts in those places, use them. On the QT though.'

'Of course.'

'Get the city-wide for ASAP. I dunno, but I've got a bad feeling.'

'And we all know where your bad feelings tend to lead.'

Scamarcio pinched his nose. 'If you see that cunt Lovoti, tell him I don't need him yet. I'll come find him when I want something, not the other way around.'

'Jesus, Scamarcio, he's not that bad.'

'I don't have time to deal with his shit with all this going down.'

'Yeah, but Garramone wants him in.'

'I know, but let me sort it my way.'

'Right.' Sartori got up and pocketed the piece of paper. 'If I don't find you here, I'll try you on the mobile.'

'Thanks,' said Scamarcio. And then, as an afterthought, 'It's good to have you on this.'

But Sartori had already walked off and didn't seem to have heard.

Scamarcio located a photo of Meinero, then tried the numbers in Piedmont a few more times without any joy. He then ran a listless search to see if the police computer network held anything that might connect Gennaro Borghese to organised crime. As expected, there was nothing.

Feeling the need to move, he decided to head down to the Tech pen. He knew Negruzzo would have called had he found anything, but the simple act of leaving the office at least made him feel that he was being proactive.

'Just the man,' said Negruzzo as Scamarcio walked in.

The smell had got worse, and several of the guys looked like they hadn't slept since Scamarcio had last seen them. He spotted Gunbach from the CSI team, who had helped him on the case dubbed 'The Few'. Just the sight of him turned Scamarcio's mouth dry, and he wondered why he'd been brought in.

'You guys making progress?' he asked Negruzzo.

'Almost there. It's been a blinding effort. Those fucks will be left to rot — *if* they're lucky.'

'How many arrests are you looking at?'

'Eight … probably. But, of course, all the contingent pond life — that's a different story. That will be left to local forces, and then, God knows …'

'Sure,' said Scamarcio. He could feel the frustration coming off Negruzzo in waves, and he understood it, perhaps better than most. Whatever they achieved through days, weeks, and months of solid police work would never be enough.

'From your greeting, it almost sounded like you were pleased to see me,' said Scamarcio, wanting to shift the conversation on.

Negruzzo sucked on the end of a silver teaspoon then placed it in a plastic pot. He'd been eating a chocolate Danone. He turned and freed another pot from the pack, ripping off the foil seal and licking it. 'You must be telepathic. I was about to call you,' he said as he tossed the seal into an overflowing bin.

'You got somewhere?'

'I have the cart before the horse. I got into his Facebook, just using one of my brute force programmes, actually. Nothing fancy.' Negruzzo scoffed several spoonfuls, then wiped the chocolate from his chin using the back of his hand.

'Anything interesting?'

The Tech chief rolled his eyes. 'Scamarcio, that's *your* job. I'm just the guy who unlocks the door.'

Scamarcio smiled. 'OK, so do you want to tell me what his password is?'

'"Caligula2000". No spaces, "2000" in numbers.'

'Oh.' Scamarcio wasn't sure what he'd been expecting, but he hadn't been expecting that. 'The year 2000 was the year of Borghese's birth,' was all he could come up with.

'And Caligula was a murderous sociopath who slept with all three of his sisters,' added Negruzzo helpfully.

Scamarcio took a seat on a dirty swivel chair. 'Borghese doesn't have sisters.'

'Thank God for that, then.' Negruzzo polished off the Danone as if his life depended on it and swung back to his screen. 'Forgive me, Scamarcio, but I've got to get on. I'll call you about the others. Have fun.'

Scamarcio smiled, but he wasn't really listening. He was too busy wondering why Borghese had chosen that particular name. Did he identify with the Roman Emperor in some way? Many commentators had declared Caligula insane. Once, when bored at the games, he'd ordered a section of the audience thrown to the lions because he'd run out of prisoners to use. He'd then taken to appearing in public dressed as a god. From what Scamarcio had learned so far, Andrea had been neither tyrannical nor a megalomaniac. Surely, then, it was impossible that he recognised in himself the same degree of insanity. Or was it? The question saddened Scamarcio, yet it also stirred a fire in him. Now, for the first time, he might actually have something to work with.

11

ANDREA BORGHESE'S FACEBOOK FEED was troubling to say the least. It consisted of a melange of blurry pictures of Satanic rituals, posts about the 'artist' Marina Abramović and her practice of 'spirit cooking' (Scamarcio had no idea what that was), and photos of heavy metal groups: Black Sabbath, Judas Priest, and Megadeth. Scamarcio noticed that many of Andrea's posts went un-liked, but, occasionally, the same two or three people left a comment or an emoji of some sort. Scamarcio made a note of their names — one girl and two boys — and printed out their Facebook profile photos. Unfortunately, all three of their feeds were set to private. In all, Andrea had thirty followers, but it seemed that most of them never interacted with him. Scamarcio felt slightly saddened by the paltry number, even though he subscribed to the view that your number of Facebook friends was not a true reflection of the fullness of your life — if anything, the two were inversely proportionate.

He scanned Andrea's private messages. There were just a few from the girl, Graziella, asking how Andrea was doing, and several noncommittal replies back. Scamarcio wondered if she was a girlfriend or had perhaps wanted to be.

He scrolled down the feed and noticed a few more 'spirit cooking' references. He plugged the term into Google.

According to various articles in the press, the performance artist Marina Abramović used pigs' blood as a way of 'connecting with the spiritual world', and it was this she dubbed 'spirit cooking'. Scamarcio came across a video of her using the blood to scrawl various statements on a wall. One read, 'with a sharp knife cut deeply into the middle finger of your left hand eat the pain'. Further parts of the ritual seemed to involve using menstrual blood, breast milk, urine, and sperm to create a painting. The Nutella tart Scamarcio had enjoyed with his last coffee was rapidly making its way back up his gullet, and he had to swallow several times to keep it down.

He closed his eyes and forced himself to read on. Spirit cooking, he discovered, also referred to a sacrament in the religion of Thelema, founded by alleged Satanist Aleister Crowley. Yet, despite this, in interviews, Marina Abramović denied any connection with Satanism and claimed all this was just her own personal take on performance art. She said that spirit cooking was far more about spirituality than anything else.

Scamarcio looked away from the screen and cupped his chin. Why was Andrea interested in this crap? Did he practise it? Could it be that he was simply acting out the role that had been allotted him — namely, that of a boy who was possessed, and who therefore must be interested in all things satanic?

Scamarcio closed his eyes and rubbed his jaw. If that were the case, it was tragic. He thought of Gennaro Borghese and his anger, and for the first time he understood just why the man was so furious with his wife.

Scamarcio didn't want to trudge back to Tech and give them two new Facebook passwords to crack, so he decided to try Andrea's most recent school to see if he could find Andrea's friends in the real world. When he called the school's reception, the secretary was infinitely more obliging than the old woman from the Vatican.

'Yes, all three of those people are students with us,' she announced once she'd run a computer search.

'And they're still attending?' asked Scamarcio.

'They're in their last year and have their exams in June. They'll be home for the afternoon now, of course, but I can give you their phone numbers.'

'That would be great, thanks.'

Scamarcio decided to try to visit the girl, Graziella, first. If there *was* a romantic connection, she might have valuable information.

It turned out that Graziella Feliciano lived just a few streets away from the Borgheses on a road lined with Mediterranean pine and palm trees. Her apartment stood in an elegant pink liberty block with brown shutters. Scamarcio had called ahead and learned that she and her mother would be in and would be waiting for him.

What he hadn't expected was the six-foot-four meathead who opened the door.

'Igor Feliciano,' barked the hulk, locking eyes with Scamarcio. The look said, *Don't even try it, lad.*

'Graziella's father?' said Scamarcio, returning the stare.

'If the police are wanting a word with my daughter, I'd prefer to be around.'

Scamarcio studied the man, taking in his huge shaved grey head, his small rat-brown eyes shrouded by dense brows, and the winter tan on heavy jowls. He looked familiar, but Scamarcio couldn't place him.

'You're thinking you've seen me before,' said Feliciano, as he led Scamarcio into a wide living room. Scamarcio quickly estimated the flat's value at around three million. Sunshine was bouncing off polished parquet and bronze miniatures, forming rich patterns on the pristine walls. There seemed to be a battle of styles in play: a bizarre clash between achingly chic minimalism and nouveau riche vulgarity. A few tasteful paintings hung on the walls, carefully framed and positioned, but the multicoloured sofas and over-stuffed, gold-tasselled cushions covered in cherubim looked as if they'd been lifted straight out of a Bari brothel. Scamarcio wondered if Feliciano and his wife hailed from different backgrounds and didn't quite see eye to eye on certain things.

'*Have* we met before, Mr Feliciano?'

Igor Feliciano motioned Scamarcio to the sofa, and he took a seat. Feliciano inclined his head proudly to the wall on his left. 'Take a look over there.'

Scamarcio did as instructed and immediately spotted a framed photo of Feliciano with his arm around Francesco Totti, ex Roma striker and national treasure. There was another picture hanging beneath of Feliciano with Valentino Rossi, the motor-racing star.

Scamarcio smiled. 'Feliciano, the sports promoter. Forgive me, my mind's a little addled. My girlfriend is about to have a baby, and I'm not sleeping.' Scamarcio thought that it might be helpful to reveal some vulnerability in front of a thug like Feliciano.

Feliciano smiled and lounged back against his strange cushions. 'No worries, been there myself. It's a stressful time. Now, listen,' he leaned forward again, as if suddenly remembering the purpose of Scamarcio's visit, 'what does Graziella have to do with the death of that lad. She barely knew him.'

Scamarcio tried to make himself comfortable. He carefully pulled a bulging cushion out from behind him and placed it to his side. 'Is that what she told you? Where is she, by the way?'

'She'll be in in a minute. I wanted a word, first.' Feliciano was speaking quickly now, and, to Scamarcio, each word felt like a tiny bullet — a quiet threat. 'I don't think that boy had many friends; he was strange, peculiar, prone to outbursts. You're barking up the wrong tree with Graziella. I wouldn't want you to waste your time, Detective.'

'That's considerate of you, but I will need to talk to her. I'm sure you understand that I can't just take your word for it. You must be familiar with police work.' Scamarcio seemed to recall that Feliciano had been caught up in a match-fixing scandal some years back.

The jibe found its target, and Feliciano eyed him for a long moment before moistening his thick lips. 'OK, but don't upset her. She's in an odd mood.'

'Why's that? The death perhaps?'

Feliciano threw open his arms and rolled his eyes skyward. 'There is no "why" with Graziella these days. She's a teenage girl. I'm incapable of understanding her, as hard as I try. And, believe me, I try.' Feliciano looked helpless for a moment, and Scamarcio almost felt sorry for him.

The big man sighed and heaved his bulk reluctantly from the sofa. Then he turned and headed towards some double doors at the back of the room. 'One minute,' he said quietly, as he left.

After ten seconds or so, he reappeared, followed by a glamorous blonde who had to be Graziella's mother, exquisitely dressed in an array of different shades of taupe. From just one look at her, Scamarcio could tell that she was high society, and that Feliciano, the southern boy made good, had married up. Scamarcio was beginning to wonder where Graziella was when an apparition in black materialised in the doorway. It hovered on the threshold for a few moments, as if deciding whether to enter, then slowly started inching forward, a phantom making its approach.

Scamarcio struggled to disguise his surprise. The girl, if, in fact, this creature was female, had deathly pale powdery skin, heavy kohl-darkened eyes, and lips so red they looked like they might be bleeding. Her hair stood up in glassy black peaks, and her ragged black jumper hung to her knees. Her thin legs, in thick black tights, ended in heavy Doc Martens, silver studs lining the huge soles. In the left side of her nose was what looked like a safety pin, and rows of them ran along both ear lobes. Scamarcio stole a quiet breath and glanced at Mr and Mrs Feliciano, smart and respectable. How could *they* have produced *this*?

Mrs Feliciano graciously extended a hand and introduced herself. Graziella hung back.

'Hi, Graziella. I just wanted a word with you about Andrea Borghese,' said Scamarcio, not bothering to attempt to shake her hand as he sensed she'd perceive it as an invasion of space.

The girl just nodded wordlessly.

'If you don't mind,' said Scamarcio, turning to both parents.

Mr Feliciano looked torn. Scamarcio guessed he wanted to throw his weight around, but knew it wouldn't be wise.

'We'll be in the next room,' he muttered, casting Scamarcio an icy stare as he left.

When they were out of earshot, Scamarcio motioned the girl to the sofa. 'Why don't we sit down?'

Graziella complied, but said nothing.

'I wanted to speak with you because you are one of a handful of people Andrea seems to have been in contact with on Facebook.'

'I can't believe he's dead.' Her voice was low and soft and took Scamarcio by surprise.

'How well did you know him?'

There was a long silence before she said, 'He was in and out of school, and I suppose I was one of just a few kids there who actually bothered to give him the time of day.' She paused. 'I liked Andrea, he was interesting to talk to. It turned out that we were into the same sorts of things.'

'How was his behaviour?'

She smiled, seeming to enjoy the memory. 'He totally lost it in a physics lesson once … started screaming and hurling things at the teacher. The school tried to kick him out.'

'But you spent time with him when he was normal, so to speak?'

'He was perfectly reasonable most of the time. Interesting and funny. It's so stupid that nobody in our school bothered to get to know him. They just wrote him off as crazy and that was it. And, if the herd hates you, then it's over. No one is brave enough to go against the herd,' she said bitterly.

'The herd?'

'They're all sheep in my school.'

'What would you and Andrea talk about?'

She rubbed at her eye, and Scamarcio saw some of the black eyeliner smudge. 'This and that. He was into the death metal scene. So am I. He was into the occult, so am I …'

'There's Satanist stuff on his Facebook feed.'

She smiled again, but it was a different kind of smile — evasive, dissembling. 'All that was just for fun. He wasn't really *into* it, if you know what I mean.'

'I thought that was what death metal was all about — the songs talk about murder, torture, the devil.' Scamarcio had done some research before he'd left the office. None of it had been pleasant.

She frowned. 'Just because you like the music doesn't mean you have to practise all that other stuff.'

Scamarcio wasn't convinced. 'Beasts of Satan started with the music, and then look where they ended up.'

She scratched at the corner of her mouth. 'Those kids murdered their friends. Andrea would never do anything like that.' Her voice started to rise, indignation taking over. 'No one understood Andrea when he was alive, and it seems that nobody understands him now.'

'Where are we going wrong?'

Another long silence. 'Andrea was highly intelligent, but he had problems controlling his emotions. His mother should never have got the church involved — it was all bullshit. Bullshit Andrea didn't need, stress he didn't need. *She* was the crazy one in that family, if you ask me.'

'Did Andrea ever speak about her?'

'He couldn't stand her.'

'What?' Scamarcio looked up from his notes.

'He said she was a controlling bitch who made his father's life hell. She's an alcoholic, you know. Andrea said that from 5.00 pm she'd be out of it. By 7.00 pm she'd be aggressive.'

Scamarcio took a long breath. 'What kind of aggressive?'

'Verbal, I think — Andrea was too big to beat up. But I got the feeling she'd tried when he was little.'

'He said that?'

'No, but reading between the lines ...'

'It sounds like you two were pretty close for you to know all this about his mother.'

'We were ...' The words trailed off, and she looked away.

'Were you a couple, Graziella?'

She sighed. It was a long, laboured sigh, as if she was trying to drag something heavy to the surface. 'I don't think Andrea was interested in sex. He never seemed to want to take things to the next level ...' She looked away, embarrassed.

Scamarcio drew a large question mark on his page and boxed it. Then boxed it again.

'You never saw him with anyone else?'

She shook her head. 'Like I say, most people didn't want to give him the time of day.'

A small question had been troubling Scamarcio, niggling away at the fringes of his consciousness. Finally, it broke through. 'Why didn't Andrea dress like you, if he was into the same things?

When we found his body, he was in normal clothes — preppy cords, a striped shirt. He seemed a long way from being a goth.'

She shook her head sadly. 'He didn't want his parents to find out about that aspect of his life because he knew they'd make hell for him. He chose to keep it a secret, and just live it out online.'

'His parents kept him on a tight leash?'

'He felt totally suffocated by them; he blamed them for all his problems.'

'But from what I've been told, he had serious mental health issues from a young age.'

'Who's to say they didn't cause them?'

Scamarcio wanted to frown, but looked down at his pad instead. He'd never been able to understand how kids from good families ended up hating their parents. *He* had a valid reason; they just seemed spoiled and naïve.

'His other friends on Facebook, Castelnuovo and Pombeni — do you know them?'

'They're both good guys. They're the only other people who talked to Andrea at school. I hang out with them sometimes.'

She looked away quickly, and Scamarcio had the feeling that she was trying to make the relationship sound more casual than it really was. The question was, why?

'Graziella, do you have any idea who might have done this? Did Andrea have any enemies?'

She closed her eyes for a minute, and when she opened them, Scamarcio saw that they were brimming with tears. Her make-up was quickly becoming a mess. 'Andrea was such a nice guy, such a sensitive soul … I just can't, I *can't* … understand.'

Scamarcio drew in his bottom lip. This was a weird one: her sadness was real, but he felt sure her confusion wasn't. She had an idea of who might have done it — he could feel it. He could *see* it in the way she held her shoulders, in the quick movements of her fingers against the hem of her jumper, in the set of her jaw. But experience told him he couldn't push too early or too hard. He'd talk to the others, and then come back around to her.

'Thanks, Graziella. I appreciate you talking to me.'

She looked up, surprised. 'Is that it?'

'For now, yes.' Scamarcio rose from the sofa. 'I'll see myself out.'

She just stared at him, worry etched across her forehead, her eyes wide, and he knew he had her exactly where he needed her.

12

It was getting late, and the scarlet light had long since faded from the sky, but it was just two streets' walk to Alessandro Castelnuovo's house, so Scamarcio decided to make one last push before heading home to Fiammetta.

The address from the school secretary brought him to a stop outside an impressive glass and chrome block, palms lining the walkway to the entrance. He scoured the list beside the intercom for the surname, and then tried the buzzer. A nervous female voice with a foreign accent told him to come up to the fifth floor.

Scamarcio was greeted by a maid with South American features, who led him into a vast living and dining area, divided in two by a wide arch resting on two pillars. Spotlights lined the ceiling. The furniture was contemporary and expensive, and the pine floors were covered with bright rugs in modernist designs. Tall windows ran from floor to ceiling, offering a glimpse of an illuminated balcony crowded with potted palms and ferns.

The maid asked Scamarcio to wait a moment, and then hurried back down the corridor, knocking on several doors until she found somebody in. The young Castelnuovo eventually emerged from a cloud of smoke and slammed the door loudly behind him. From the looks of him, he modelled himself on Robert Smith from The Cure. *What is it with these privileged kids that they all have to dress up like the living dead?* wondered

Scamarcio. Castelnuovo was whistling a gentle tune, as if he hadn't a care, and was walking slowly, ever so slowly, as if he'd never had to rush for anything in his life. If he was in any way cut up about Andrea's death, he was doing a great job of disguising it.

'Alessandro Castelnuovo?' Scamarcio asked as he stepped into his path.

'You're the police?' The boy looked him up and down, but seemed untroubled.

Scamarcio produced his card and handed it over. 'I'm investigating the death of Andrea Borghese.'

'Of course you are, of course you are,' said Castelnuovo in a tone that let Scamarcio understand that he considered himself rich and untouchable.

'Where are your parents?'

'Still down at the parliament, I expect. Probably drinking with friends by now.'

Scamarcio frowned, while Castelnuovo smiled. 'You must know who my father is? You will have done your research ...'

That settled it. Castelnuovo was an arrogant little shit, and Scamarcio was going to make him sweat, crackle, and burn like a pig on a spit, whether or not he actually had anything to do with Andrea Borghese's death.

'Oh, sure, now the penny drops. Your father's the leader of that pitiful crew of politically correct fuckwits who have no idea how most people live.' Scamarcio cast a long look around the living room and shook his head. He knew he shouldn't be allowing himself to get so angry, but domestic politics had been enraging him of late.

Castelnuovo took him by surprise and laughed warmly. 'That's a solid analysis, Detective. Right on — fuckwits they are.'

He threw himself down onto the sofa and pulled a pack of Camel Lights from the top pocket of his black shirt. He tore off the plastic and waved the pack at Scamarcio, who nodded reluctantly.

When Castelnuovo had lit up for the pair of them, Scamarcio said, 'You've heard about the death of Borghese?'

'I saw it on the news. I hope you don't mind me saying, but you didn't look too pleased to be involved.'

'I just hate the press, that's all.'

'We have that in common.'

Castelnuovo spoke like someone older than his years. Scamarcio wondered if growing up hearing his father's cumbersome speeches had taken its toll.

'How well did you know Andrea?'

'Let's be quite clear, Detective, we weren't great friends. But I felt sorry for him. I could see that he was deeply troubled, and that he was lonely.'

Scamarcio studied the boy sitting across from him: floppy dyed-black hair, wide brown eyes, and pouting lips. If it hadn't been for all the goth crap, he'd probably be considered attractive.

'Did you speak to him much?'

'I'd usually sit with him at lunchtime because I could see he was on his own. My father always taught me to be kind to the weak and the vulnerable.' There was no pomposity or bravado to the words, but Scamarcio's initial assessment of Castelnuovo remained unchanged.

'Once I got talking to Andrea, it became clear that he was very intelligent. He'd read all sorts of books, and he was really interested in physics and the universe. He quoted that man in the wheelchair — what's his name ... Stephen something — all the time. He'd read all his work.'

'And the goth stuff?'

'Well Andrea had a penchant for death metal, but I don't think he'd totally embraced the goth scene. He dressed pretty normally, you know.'

'I listened to some death metal earlier. Cannibal Corpse, I think they were called. I don't know how you can stand it. It's the musical equivalent of a car crash.'

Castelnuovo just shrugged, unimpressed. 'What do you old guys listen to?'

'Old guys?'

Castelnuovo's expression remained neutral.

Scamarcio frowned. 'Depeche Mode, Modest Mouse, a bit of LCD Sound System on occasion.'

'Never heard of any of them,' said Castelnuovo.

'You've never heard of Depeche?'

Castelnuovo sniffed. 'So, what's the score with Andrea? Who do you people think did it?'

'You don't seem that upset …'

'Like I say, I didn't really know him.'

'Still, a school friend murdered is a big deal.'

'Bad things happen in Parioli. It wouldn't be the first time.'

'It's hardly the Bronx.'

'Those mums pimping out their daughters a few years back — that was quite a shocker. Then the Circeo slayings …'

'The Circeo case was decades ago.' Scamarcio paused. 'You take an interest in crime?'

'I like to read the odd novel. I'm an admirer of James Lee Burke — you know him? *Dixie City Jam* is a masterpiece.'

Scamarcio muttered a 'no' and tried to drag the interview back into focus. 'So, you can't think of anyone who might have been angry with Andrea?'

'Angry enough to kill him?'

Scamarcio didn't answer.

'Andrea didn't hang out with many people. When he wasn't doing the crazy act, he kind of faded into the background — you wouldn't even notice him. I can't really think of who he would have aggravated to that level. But, you know, maybe he had a whole other life I wasn't aware of.'

'What about Graziella? She seemed quite close to him.'

Scamarcio watched a cloud cross Castelnuovo's features, it drew in his brows and darkened his eyes. His hand rubbed behind his neck, and he blinked several times. 'I think Andrea wanted them to be close, but she wasn't interested.'

'Funny, she gave me the opposite impression.'

'How do you mean?' Castelnuovo sucked down hard on his Camel Light.

'It was Andrea that didn't seem interested in taking things to the next level.'

'She told you that?'

Scamarcio nodded wordlessly and observed the boy. He couldn't take his eyes off him, now. He watched as his Adam's apple bobbed up and down, watched as the Camel shrunk to the filter and Castelnuovo continued to chug away, as if it was providing oxygen, watched as his right foot began to jiggle while he rubbed his wet palm slowly along the thigh of his drainpipe jeans.

'Yes, Graziella told me that,' continued Scamarcio. 'I got the impression that she was very keen on Andrea and extremely cut up about his death.'

Castelnuovo rooted around in his shirt pocket for the fags and lighter, tossed the spent butt into a chunky marble ashtray, and lit up again. He bit down on his lip, scratched below the corner of his left eye, and blinked. If he didn't say another word, that would be fine.

13

THERE WAS A SPRING in his step and a song in his heart as Scamarcio rounded the corner to Via Boncompagni. It was an intoxicating moment when that sense of floundering around in the dark was finally replaced with the firm knowledge that you had a direction: a motive. Its presence alone was enough to throw everything else into some kind of relief.

It was par for the course that your initial suspect would have to be the son of a powerful politician, and that your balls would be broken by every one of your superiors on your journey to the truth, but Scamarcio's years in Rome had taught him that nearly everyone was entangled and compromised, and, whoever your suspect, eventually you'd come up against a connection that would prove tricky to navigate. Scamarcio wouldn't go so far as to claim that he relished the challenge, but it no longer disheartened him like it used to. The way he saw it, it was like a computer game. You had to deftly manoeuvre your way to the next level, and there was always a certain satisfaction in the simple act of trying.

'Honey, I'm home,' he shouted sarcastically as he tossed his jacket onto a chair full of old newspapers and took in the severe chaos that was now his flat. Scores of Fiammetta's shoes lined the corridor, and a couple of large plastic bags of dirty shirts and jackets blocked his path to the living room. Fiammetta had said she'd take the shirts to the drycleaners, but she must have forgotten. She often forgot.

He rounded the corner and saw his girlfriend lying on the sofa, a generous bowl of chocolate ice cream on her lap. She was watching the evening news.

'Hi, darling,' she said without looking up.

Her blonde hair was scraped up into an untidy bun, and she wasn't wearing a scrap of make-up, but she still looked beautiful.

'This new vaccine law is a shitstorm.'

'What?' he murmured, coming up behind her and planting a kiss on her cheek.

'Cinque Stelle are saying they'll abolish it. Looks like they're going to pick up a shedload of votes for that.'

'Are there that many people against?'

'Many more than they say on the news, I reckon.'

'But who could possibly be against protecting their kids?'

She turned to look at him, her expression grave. 'It's not that simple, Leo. Sure, vaccines are important, but this law ignores the fact that not every child is born identical. MMR may be perfectly fine for most, but there are always going to be a few who have an adverse reaction — whose bodies can't take it. And if that's the case, you simply cannot make it compulsory. You're forcing parents to give something to their child that might not be right for them. Sure, the rich will find private day care or alternative arrangements if their unvaccinated kids get kicked out of a nursery, but what about the single mum from Taranto who has no spare cash and has to work? Maybe she had some doubts, maybe she wanted to space out her vaccines, do singles, or none at all. With this new law, she's forced to do it all in one go. It's a disgrace, Leo. It's blackmail. The parent must be allowed to choose what's right for their kid. It can't be forced on them by the state.'

Scamarcio sighed. 'Maybe the state felt it had no choice. Maybe they were just trying to prevent an epidemic.'

'An epidemic of what, Leo? Measles? They tell us measles is so deadly, but I had measles and I was fine, my sister had measles and was fine. Did you have measles?'

'I don't remember …'

'I'm sure you did, and you lived to tell the tale. And, anyway if they are so bloody worried about measles and its complications, then offer it as a single jab. At least give parents a choice! This is the first step on the road to fascism. Our government is for sale, and the sooner people wake up to the fact, the better.' Her cheeks were flushed, and her eyes were burning with an anger Scamarcio had rarely seen.

'Jesus, what's got into you?'

She put the bowl down on the floor, and the spoon fell out, leaving a creamy trail on the parquet.

'If the Italian military takes eighteen years to conduct an investigation into illnesses afflicting their soldiers stationed abroad and comes to the conclusion that no soldier should have more than five vaccines at a time, then why the fuck are we giving our kids eight in one go? Eight, Leo!!' She paused to draw breath. 'I'm about to have a child — *we're* about to have a child. I'm not going to let some corrupt fuck tell me how to manage my baby's health. I'm not stupid: I went to liceo scientifico, I graduated cum laude. I will not let myself be dictated to by people who are at best ignorant, at worst compromised.'

There was even more colour in her cheeks, now, and he watched a vein throb in her slender neck. He wasn't sure it was a good idea for her to get worked up like this, but just watching her now reminded him of why he'd fallen in love. What had first attracted him to her was not what had ultimately won his heart. Her fierce intelligence and strength had only come to the fore later on. But, unhelpfully, right at that moment, his mind, ever disobedient, flashed on the chance meeting with Aurelia the day before, and he struggled to push the memory away, eradicate it.

He stroked Fiammetta's huge stomach and closed his eyes for a moment. 'Do you think it'll be soon?'

'He or she are still quiet.'

'I don't like this waiting.'

'Leo, you've just caught a case — the case of the moment, if the news is anything to go by.' She turned to look at him. 'Sorry, but you looked like shit on the TV. I thought you were about to punch those reporters.'

'I nearly did.'

'Yeah, but shouldn't you try to hide all that?'

'Why? They know how I feel about them. What's the point in lying?'

She smiled and shook her head in mock despair. 'You solve your case as quick as you can, and then I'm sure our child will put in an appearance. Maybe they're just waiting for you to make a breakthrough.'

'I can really sense it today — it's going to be a boy,' said Scamarcio, looking away so she couldn't see his face.

'Hmmm,' murmured Fiammetta, noncommittal.

The more Scamarcio thought about it, the more it had to be a boy. The threat seemed bigger with a girl, the vulnerability greater. At a certain point, a boy could fight back, defend himself from attack. But a girl? Could she really? He knew that Fiammetta would be furious with that analysis — she'd deem it sexist — but Scamarcio was from the south, and he knew how it worked. A boy, *his* boy might be able to wrestle his way out of this mess, eventually drag himself free. But a girl? With a girl, the dangers were many, and they were more acute.

It was going to be a boy. It *had* to be.

When Scamarcio woke the next morning, a thin patch of blue was visible above the curtains, and the birdsong was louder and more spirited than the half-hearted chorus of days past. He felt hopeful. A few hours of sunshine would give him the psychological boost he needed to hone down his theory. Namely, that the politician's son Alessandro Castelnuovo was in love with Graziella Feliciano and deeply jealous of Andrea. Whether that jealousy had led to murder was a different question, but at least Scamarcio had a place to start. At some point today, he'd fix up a meeting with Pombeni, the third Facebook friend. Perhaps Pombeni would be able to fill in some missing detail.

As he entered the squad room, Sartori waved him over, a telephone clamped to his right ear. He switched the receiver to the other ear so he could scrawl something down.

'OK,' Sartori was saying. 'Yep, got it. We'll be there ASAP. Don't let the CSIs leave before they've spoken to us. Who's lead?' A pause. 'Don't know him.'

'What the fuck is going on?' asked Scamarcio, not caring that Sartori was on the line to someone else.

'One second,' said Sartori to the voice on the other end. He clamped a hand across the mouthpiece. 'An adult male has been discovered dead in a room at the Hotel Ducale on Via Caselli in Testaccio. Hanged himself. Your missing priest's ID has been found on the corpse.'

'Priest Meinero?'

Sartori nodded.

'Fuck,' said Scamarcio, scrambling to get his brain into gear. 'Tell them I'm on my way.'

'I just did.'

'Can you call Manetti. Get him to come?'

'It's a different CSI.'

'I know, but I want Manetti to see the corpse. Make the call.'

'OK.'

Scamarcio hurried back down the stairs, his mind racing in a thousand different directions at once. What had seemed, a few minutes ago, like the beginnings of clarity, now felt like a morass.

When he arrived at the hotel, a CSI was already loading up the van with gear, and the mortuary truck was parking up outside. Scamarcio grabbed the nearest uniform and asked for the floor number.

'Don't move the body yet,' he shouted as he ran into the room. 'This may tie into a case I'm working. I need to take a look.' He turned to the CSIs present. 'Who's in charge here?'

A young guy stepped forward who Scamarcio hadn't seen before. 'Gianluca Pizzotto.' He extended a damp hand that smelled of soap and plastic.

'Where's the body?'

The CSI motioned over Scamarcio's shoulder. 'In the bathroom.'

Scamarcio turned. He saw part of the corpse before he crossed the threshold. A leg, seemingly suspended from above, was hanging over the side of the bath. As Scamarcio entered, the naked body came into view, muscular, but now lolling limp and white from the shower fitting, a noose around its neck. The face was pale and drained, but Scamarcio immediately recognised the young priest. Meinero. The faintest hints of decomposition were already peppering the air.

'Fuck,' he whispered. Then, 'Definitely a suicide?' He sensed that the CSI had come up behind him.

'No, he choked on a peanut.' It was Manetti's voice this time. He must have just arrived.

Scamarcio took a step closer to the corpse. The priest's eyes had rolled back in his head, and his tongue was hanging out as they always did with hangings. Scamarcio averted his eyes back to the body. The young man was in good shape. There was a dense band of muscle running across his stomach, and his thighs were honed and solid. Scamarcio studied the arms: the biceps, the thick wrists missing a watch. He exited the bathroom. The young CSI was scratching his chin and looking at Manetti, a worried expression on his face.

'Before you say anything, it's not that we think you can't do your job. It's just that Scamarcio can't go anywhere without me,' said Manetti, opening his case and searching for something among the tweezers and scalpels and thin rolls of plastic. 'Call it puppy love or whatever, but he needs me to hold his hand.'

Scamarcio wondered if Manetti had been dragged away from somewhere he really wanted to be. Probably a Thai massage parlour, if the rumours were anything to go by. 'I'm just aiming for continuity in the case, that's all.'

'No worries,' said the young CSI, looking embarrassed. 'I'm easy.'

'You're about the only thing on this case that is,' sighed Scamarcio.

Manetti took his kit into the bathroom and started whistling. It sounded like the theme tune from one of the Bond films.

'He could just have asked me for my notes,' murmured the young CSI.

'I guess he prefers to do it his way.'

Scamarcio turned to the two attending officers. What with the mortuary team, the CSIs, him, and Manetti, the hotel room was getting pretty crowded, and the smell was intensifying. 'What time were you guys called?'

'Eight-fifteen. The vic had asked for a 7.00 am wake-up call, and when he didn't respond, reception sent someone up. They told us he'd been quite insistent about the call — said he had an important meeting — so they thought they should double check.'

'Right,' said Scamarcio, pulling out his notebook and flicking to a blank page. 'When did he check in?'

'Last night,' answered the officer, scrolling down his notes with his finger, '10.00 pm.'

'They notice anything odd about him at reception?'

The officer scratched behind an ear. 'Not that they mentioned. Maybe you should have a word.'

'Don't worry, I will. Any visitors to his room?'

'None that they noticed.'

'CCTV on all the floors?'

The young officer glanced up, anxious, his cheeks red, then he looked back down at his notes. His finger had stopped moving.

'Don't worry, I'll ask them,' said Scamarcio. 'Anything else of note?'

'The name on his ID ...'

'Where is the ID?'

'It's already bagged,' said the chief CSI, pointing to the bed. 'With the others, over there.'

Scamarcio saw a stack of plastic forensic zip-locks in a large case. He walked over and spotted the ID near the top. When he examined it, the name and photo confirmed it was Meinero. He rifled through the bags underneath. He saw bubble gum, metro tickets, some coins, and some jewellery — it looked like a gold cross on a chain, a watch, and a ring.

Scamarcio turned back to the officer, the ID still in his hand. 'Why did you mention the ID? It seems hunky dory to me.'

'But that's not the name he checked in with.'

'Oh? What name did he give?'

The officer glanced back at his notebook. 'Amato. Piero Amato.'

'Who was on shift last night?' Scamarcio asked the manager at reception, a clean-shaven guy in his forties without a hair on his head. 'Would they still be at work?'

'No. Your officers have already spoken to them by telephone, but we can ask them to come in if you want. We had two staff manning reception when Mr Amato arrived.'

'Get them here straight away,' said Scamarcio, struggling to believe that the officers hadn't already requested this. 'Did Mr Amato have to show ID?'

'Of course, all our guests are required to do so.'

'Do you have a photocopy of the ID?'

'Yes, I showed it to your officers. One second, please.'

Scamarcio took a moment to glance around the lobby. It was a three-star hotel and didn't seem to deserve a higher ranking. The beige faux-leather sofas looked worn and dirty, and the carpet was a couple of decades out of fashion.

The manager came back with the photocopy and handed it to Scamarcio. The photo was of the young priest, no doubt about it. But the name did indeed read 'Piero Amato'. The date of birth matched that of Priest Meinero. Why was Meinero using this fake ID with the surname of his superior, and where was that fake ID now?

'Do you have CCTV?' Scamarcio asked.

'Sure.'

'On all the floors?'

'Just the lobby.'

Scamarcio found himself wishing that the priest had chosen the Marriott.

'Can I have a look at your footage for last night, around the time Mr Amato checked in?'

The manager led him into a back room and tapped the keyboard of a desktop computer. The footage was already up on screen, and Scamarcio guessed he'd been scrolling through it, knowing he'd be asked. 'This should be it. That's him, isn't it?' said the manager, looking pleased with himself.

Scamarcio leaned in closer. 'That's him,' he whispered as he took in the scene. The priest was facing the desk. His brown hair looked tousled by the wind, and his robes were obscured by a thick patterned scarf and heavy black overcoat. He was rubbing the small of his back and placing something on the ground to his right — a large suitcase. Where was this young priest of the Vatican heading with such a heavy bag, and what was he doing checking into a nondescript hotel on the wrong side of town?

The check-in process passed quickly, and, after a couple of minutes, the priest left the desk and headed for the elevator. After that, all trace of him disappeared. They fast-forwarded through the footage, slowing it down if anyone entered the lobby. Scamarcio observed a couple of drunken tourists (English, according to the manager) staggering their way to the lifts, a Japanese family stopping to examine some leaflets from a table near the sofa, and an elderly gentleman (Polish, according to the manager) approaching reception. They watched the Polish gentleman for several minutes, but it seemed he just wanted to make chit-chat with the pretty girl on shift. After that, the lobby was empty for half an hour — from 11.30 pm till 12.00 am according to the time stamp — until the pretty receptionist and her male colleague disappeared into the back room for a moment. They'd only been gone for a few seconds when a figure, medium height, wearing a baseball cap, sunglasses, and a long winter coat quickly crossed the lobby and headed straight to the lift. Within seconds, the two receptionists were back at their posts, none the wiser. Scamarcio spooled through the footage, waiting for the figure to reappear. But the hours passed, and there was no sign of him/her. 'Is there any other way to leave the hotel?' he asked.

The manager looked up from the screen, his eyes slightly glazed over. 'You could go down to the basement, that leads onto a parking garage. But the garage is locked at midnight. I don't see how anyone could have got out from there. And it was a fourth-floor room, so they could hardly have jumped out the window.'

'Any CCTV down in the garage?'

'Yes, but it wasn't working last night. I've called in a repair-man, but they can't get here till tomorrow.'

'What time did it go down?'

'Around 8.00 pm, I think.'

Why couldn't it be simple for once? thought Scamarcio as he lit his fifth fag of the morning.

Scamarcio felt quite nervous as he approached the mortuary. The chances of running into Aurelia were high, and the chances that she now knew about the baby, even higher.

He stubbed out his Marlboro on a broken paving slab and breathed out slowly. The two hotel receptionists from the night before had proven less than useless; he'd have got more from the shabby pot plant on their desk. The missing CCTV in the garage was still eating away at him. When did he ever get what he needed? The odds always seemed to work in the other direction. He stopped halfway up the steps. *Shit. That's it.*

What if it wasn't just bad luck? He'd had a case last year where the CCTV had been deliberately tampered with. It had been a professional hit, and professionals always planned ahead. Was it the same deal here? But who knew the priest would be staying at that hotel, and how could they know? Was it perhaps a place he used frequently? The staff hadn't mentioned it, but Scamarcio hadn't asked — an oversight. He pulled his mobile from his pocket and scrolled through his recent calls for the number of the hotel.

'We'd never seen him before,' said the manager, sounding disappointed not to be able to help. 'I was pretty sure we hadn't, but I also consulted our records, and there was nothing there.'

'But which names were you checking?'

'I searched for both names you gave me: the name he checked in with, Piero Amato, and the other name, Alberto Meinero.'

'And nothing for either of them?'

'Nothing.'

Scamarcio struggled to sound polite. He thanked the manager, then hung up. He was about to make another call when a male voice shouted his name.

Dr Giangrande was standing in the hallway, holding open the swing doors, his white overalls flapping in the breeze.

'I've got something, come see.' Giangrande rarely looked excited, and Scamarcio felt his unease stir again. He followed the chief pathologist through to the suite, trying unsuccessfully not to inhale the heady clash of bleach and body fluids. Despite the hours Scamarcio had spent here, the smell still shocked him every time.

Meinero's corpse was lying on the autopsy table with his torso cut open, his intestines pushed to one side to reveal the abdominal cavity. The stench was overpowering. Scamarcio swallowed and closed his eyes. When he reopened them, Giangrande was looking at him impatiently. 'We haven't got all day.'

'I had *polpette* …'

'The first thing you need to know is that this was no suicide.'

'He was hanging from the shower fitting. There was a noose.'

'He was put there after.'

'After what?'

'After he'd had a massive heart attack.'

Scamarcio was shaking his head, although he knew Giangrande was never wrong. 'What was he — twenty-four, twenty-five? Was he sick?'

'No. He'd ingested a large quantity of a drug that can cause cardiac arrest if taken in too high a dose.'

Scamarcio frowned. 'But why would he do that? Did he make a mistake — get the dose wrong?'

'I suspect that he didn't even know he'd taken it. I found the drug mixed up with a brioche in his stomach. It had been ground down, and I'm inclined to think that it had been hidden. The victim probably had no idea he'd ingested it.'

Scamarcio threw his arms open. 'What the fuck? Why would anyone do that?'

'You've been a policeman long enough to know why someone might want to do that.'

'For God's sake, there are easier ways to kill a man.'

'If you know what you're doing, it's not that difficult.'

'Yeah, but you have to get it into the brioche, and then make sure he eats it. And then where does the hanging fit into it?'

Giangrande looked at him as if he were simple. 'Well … I'd hazard a guess that perhaps they wanted to make it look like a suicide …'

Scamarcio let the sarcasm pass. 'Yeah, but they must have known we'd do an autopsy?'

Giangrande scratched his head. 'Yes. And we were meant to conclude that the drug had nothing to do with his death. And maybe that's what I would have written, had I not taken the trouble to send it for analysis.' Giangrande looked momentarily sheepish. 'On the fast track.'

'The fast track? Garramone has practically banned that.'

'Yeah, but I've been around long enough to know when something might crack a case open.'

'Did he sign off on it?'

'I … may have faked his signature.'

'You *what?*'

Giangrande dismissed the worry with a wave. 'The lab just called me to say that the separate chemical components I found only appear together in one product.'

'And what product would that be?'

'It's called Tamazol, and it was banned from sale five years ago because it was shown to cause cardiac arrest, as I said, if taken in too high a dose.'

'What was it used for?'

'Erectile dysfunction.'

'What??'

'You heard me.' Garramone paused. 'You know, certain elements of organised crime in this city have been known to use contraband drugs to kill.'

It was all too much. Scamarcio felt disorientated. 'I'm not sure how they'd figure in this.' He paused. 'This is getting crazy.'

'Yeah,' sighed Garramone. 'It's a weird one, I'll grant you that.'

Back at his desk, Scamarcio turned off his computer screen and rested his head in his hands. He had a headache that was moving up from the troublesome joint in his neck. The squad room was quiet, but the low hum of the coffee machine, the slow tick of the wall clock, and the distant clackety-clack of reports being typed still felt too loud. He pulled out a notepad from his desk drawer and closed his eyes.

As a child, he'd had difficulty with maths. His teacher, Mrs Guzzi, had always maintained that it wasn't a problem of competence, but confidence. He'd fly into a panic if he felt like he might not know the answer, and then the numbers would blur on the page, until he could no longer see his way to the solution. Mrs Guzzi had taught him to stay calm, take a breath, and work it through: step by step, digit by digit. It had taken him a while to adopt the strategy, but once he had, the numbers no longer danced, and he eventually found himself at the top of the class. She'd been a lovely woman, Mrs Guzzi. But then her son was murdered in the wars of the eighties, and no one ever saw her again. She never left the house. He remembered someone saying that she'd died that day along with her boy, and only an empty shell remained.

He opened his eyes and started writing down what he knew so far about the case. Then he made a list of the questions that needed answers, including the angles and suspects each question related to.

When he'd finished, he had three A4 sheets full of writing, but he felt better.

Distilled down to its essence, at the heart of his inquiry were two possible suspects: the politician's son, Castelnuovo, and Cardinal Amato or someone with links to Amato. As improbable as it seemed, Amato had to remain a suspect because he'd been one of the last people to see Andrea Borghese alive, one of the cardinal's assistants was dead, and the cardinal's name had been used on the fake ID found with Meinero's body. Until these questions were clarified, Scamarcio could not eliminate the old man from his enquiries. Besides, on a non-factual, purely instinctual level, the dramatic change in Amato's behaviour on the DVD still troubled Scamarcio. It had demonstrated that the cardinal was capable of more than Scamarcio had first assumed.

Top of Scamarcio's to-do list was a return to the Vatican. He needed to find out as much as he could about Meinero and his life or secret life. He wondered how far Sartori had come with his own enquiries. There was no sign of him in the office, and when Scamarcio dialled his mobile, it rang out. Frustrated, he called Negruzzo in Tech, hoping that he'd got somewhere with the other passwords.

'It's a ballbreaker,' murmured Negruzzo through a mouthful of food. 'I've drawn a blank with brute-force attempts, so I'm going to have to try something else.'

'Is that significant, that you're having to work so hard?'

'Hmm, yes and no, yes and no.'

'Well, which is it?'

'It's tricky. It could just be that your vic came up with a highly unorthodox password … or he's popped something in the system to defeat us.'

'Wouldn't you be able to spot that?'

'Not necessarily.'

'Christ, I thought computers were supposed to be straight-forward.'

Negruzzo sighed. 'Scamarcio, it's not really about computers. It's coding, encryption, algorithms and maths we're dealing with. In some ways, it's a dark art.'

Scamarcio wanted to hurl his phone across the room. 'Well, when you finally see the light, let me know.' He hung up, immediately feeling guilty. Negruzzo was trying his best, and Scamarcio knew it. It was just that everything felt so bloody slow. He needed to see movement.

For some reason Chief Inspector Cafaro seemed in a good mood. The fact that he was happy worried Scamarcio. He suspected that it might signal some kind of problem coming his way.

'You're very cheerful, given the circumstances.'

'What circumstances?'

'The murder of Father Meinero. I thought it might be weighing heavily on your mind.'

Cafaro set down his cup of coffee and blinked. 'Meinero is dead?'

Scamarcio filled him in on the details he was prepared to share.

'Why did nobody think to inform us?' said Cafaro once he had finished. Scamarcio had been about to say, 'No idea,' when he realised it was probably his responsibility to have made that call.

'I'm sorry, Cafaro. What with everything going on, it slipped my mind. I apologise, I should have let you know.'

Cafaro surprised Scamarcio by brushing the apology away and saying, 'OK. I'm going to need to inform a load of people. Are there any suspects? Does it link back to Borghese?'

'I'm working on the assumption that it does, but I have no factual evidence to back that up yet.' Scamarcio told him about the scarce CCTV. 'I'll need to talk to those priests again, and I'll need to speak with Cardinal Amato once more.'

Cafaro moved a palm across his eyelids and sighed. 'What a mess.'

'It gets worse. Meinero used a fake ID in Amato's name to check into the hotel.'

Cafaro frowned. 'Why would he do that?'

'I've no idea, but it points to another connection between the two of them.'

Cafaro fell silent for a moment. 'You're not saying ...'

Scamarcio scratched his temple, 'No, I wasn't ... I mean, I hadn't arrived at that conclusion.' He wondered why Cafaro had got there so quickly.

Cafaro smoothed his sharp chin. 'You know, some of these priests ... Well, let's just say that on occasion I've had to deal with the odd situation that, if made public, would be pretty uncomfortable for the church.'

'Hmm.' Scamarcio rooted around in his jacket pocket for his fags. He knew that the less he said, the higher the chances that Cafaro would continue.

'There are certain places in this city a few of our priests like to frequent. Well, once or twice there have been incidents — incidents that were best kept quiet.'

'Criminal?'

Cafaro turned his hand in the air, indicating 'half and half'.

'You're not saying Cardinal Amato was part of the sauna scene?'

Cafaro looked shocked. 'Oh no, I wasn't saying that at all. Not the cardinal, but ...'

'Our dead priest?'

Cafaro steepled his fingers in front of his long nose. 'Perhaps.'

'You had to handle the fallout?'

Cafaro sniffed and neatened the edges on a pile of papers. 'We need to crack on. Let me round up Amato's assistants. It'll take me a few minutes.' He gestured to the door behind Scamarcio. 'If you want to grab a coffee from the machine, I'll come get you when it's sorted.'

Scamarcio thanked him and rose. As he was leaving, he noticed a photo of Cafaro on the wall in his official dress uniform. Standing next to him was a small dark-haired woman, who Scamarcio presumed was his wife. Two little boys were on Cafaro's right, one of them in a wheelchair. His head was lolling back on a headrest, and Scamarcio could see that he was severely disabled.

'Is this your family?' Scamarcio asked, immediately regretting it, because he knew it would seem like an invasion of privacy.

But Cafaro surprised him again by saying, 'Yes, those are my boys. We had some great news yesterday — my eldest, the one in the wheelchair, has just got the all clear from a major health scare. We thought we were in for a very rough ride, but it's all now looking much better.' Cafaro was smiling again.

Scamarcio felt a hard lump forming in his throat. Christ, what the hell was wrong with him?

'I'm really pleased to hear that, Cafaro. You have a lovely family.' He turned and hurried out of the office.

Lania, the tall blond priest from the Veneto, appeared to be in quite a state when Scamarcio entered the room in the gendarmerie quarters that Cafaro had set up for the interviews. In keeping with his shift in temperament, Cafaro had seemed content to leave Scamarcio alone with his interviewees this time. Lania was sniffing and rubbing his eyes repeatedly. 'I can't believe it,' he whispered when Scamarcio took a seat across from him. 'You didn't know him, but he was a good man, Alberto. He had a good heart.'

'Of course, he was a priest,' said Scamarcio. And then kicked himself for the inanity of the remark.

'Not all priests are good men,' said Lania.

'What makes you say that?'

'I'm just stating a fact. We all know by now that there has been evil in the church. The Pope has admitted it.'

'Mr Lania, do you have any idea who could have done this? Were you aware of any problems in Alberto's life? Any difficulties of late?'

'Chief Inspector Cafaro said Alberto was found hanging. They wanted you to think it was suicide?'

Scamarcio nodded, and the priest fell silent. After a few moments, Lania said, 'The only real difficulty for any of us was the Borghese thing — it had us all shaken up. We'd come to care about Andrea. We wanted to see him get well.'

'And there's nothing else you can think of? No worries Alberto shared with you?'

The boy shook his head. 'Alberto and I were friends, but he wouldn't necessarily have confided in me. I think you should speak with Michele — he's the one with curly hair you met outside the Sala Rotonda. Michele and Alberto were at the seminary together; they've known each other a long time. I think if anyone would know what was going on in Alberto's life, it would be him.'

'What's Michele's surname?'

'Cogo.'

'Would you have a number for him?'

The priest pulled out an old Nokia and began scrolling through his contacts. He showed the screen to Scamarcio, and Scamarcio took a note.

'And what about Alberto's relationship with Cardinal Amato? Did they get on? Were there any issues there?'

Lania pushed up his bottom lip and shook his head. 'No. Like me, Alberto had been with the cardinal for about a year. I know he had great respect for the cardinal and his work. I'd never see them argue or anything like that.'

'And how did Alberto seem during the sessions?'

Lania shrugged. 'Just like the rest of us: focussed, concerned. We all wanted to do the best job we could.'

'Do you think he believed in the work — that he really thought it had a purpose?'

Lania frowned and opened a hand. 'Of course. Why wouldn't he have? He wouldn't have been helping the cardinal if he didn't.'

'How exactly did you guys get chosen for this work?'

'Recommendation, mainly. A lot of places for young priests in the Vatican are through recommendation.'

Scamarcio nodded. 'And what do you think of Cardinal Amato and how he goes about his job?'

'Like I say, we all have the utmost respect for him. I've never seen him do anything out of line. He cares deeply about the souls he treats.'

Scamarcio knew when he was on the road to nowhere. 'Thank you, Father Lania. I'll be back in touch shortly.'

Lania rose from the chair. 'I appreciate you're busy, but please let us know if you find out who did this. Alberto meant a lot to us.'

'Of course,' said Scamarcio.

Michele Cogo didn't seem able to speak properly. The grief was tearing him apart. Scamarcio had seen many people in the early stages of grief, and, in his experience, it fell into two camps: a numb denial, which saw you slip into a kind of ghostlike autopilot, or a searing pain, which ripped you asunder. It seemed that Cogo fell into the latter category.

'You were close?' Scamarcio tried, when Cogo finally found some breath between sobs.

'I'd known Alberto since I was seventeen.'

'That's unusual — that you both found a place at the Vatican.'

'We were both mentored by the same priest. He got us in here,' said Cogo absently, his mind elsewhere.

'Michele, I know this isn't pleasant to think about, but do you know why anyone might want Alberto dead?'

Cogo sighed and rubbed his palms across his eyes. 'I wish I could help, but I can't. I just can't get my head around it. I can't think of anyone. Everyone loved Alberto, and I'm not just saying that. He was widely liked.'

'And had you noticed any change in him recently?'

Cogo fell silent and studied his palms in his lap. 'You mean a negative change?'

'Not necessarily,' said Scamarcio quickly. 'It could be a positive change. Just a change in the way he was, his behaviour.'

Cogo rubbed his jawline. 'You know, we weren't as close as we used to be. Alberto didn't confide in me like he did when we were younger, but I have to say that he did seem really happy lately — happier than usual. As if some— ... something really good had come into his life.'

Scamarcio had the distinct feeling that Cogo had been about to say 'someone'.

14

Frustratingly, after his interviews with the priests, Scamarcio was informed that Cardinal Amato was away on a two-day retreat in Umbria and could not be disturbed. If he'd had any proper hold on his prime suspect, Amato would not have been allowed to leave town. Scamarcio felt like calling Garramone to complain, then figured it would get him nowhere and he had better things to do with his limited time. He was heading over to Andrea's third Facebook friend Tommaso Pombeni's house in Parioli for an evening visit, when his mobile rang. 'Scamarcio,' he grunted, not recognising the number.

'Detective Scamarcio, I've just picked up your messages. I'm sorry, I've been abroad on holiday and had my mobile switched off.' It was a woman's voice, but Scamarcio had no idea who she was.

'Who's speaking, please?'

'Oh, sorry, I should have introduced myself. I'm Anita, Alberto Meinero's sister.'

Fuck, she was way too cheerful.

'Has anyone called you from the Vatican, Anita?' Scamarcio asked quietly.

'No, er … has something happened? … To Alberto?'

Scamarcio turned into a side street to escape the noise from the traffic.

'Anita, I'm sorry, but I have some very bad news.'

There was a sharp intake of breath. Then a long exhale. 'Oh God, what is it? You're scaring me …' She laughed nervously.

'Alberto was found dead this morning. We believe he was murdered.'

The crying started as a loud shuddering, before it turned into something soft, wet, and broken. Scamarcio closed his eyes. He hated it. It never ever got any easier.

'I'm so sorry.'

'But, why…why? My parents … oh my God, how will I tell them? They're very old … they won't be able to take it. It will destroy them.'

'Do you have someone you can call? Are you alone in the house?'

'My husband's at work,' she stuttered.

'Is there a neighbour who could come over until he gets back?'

'Yes, yes, I … but … who would do this? To Alberto?'

'That is what I'm investigating, Anita. I'd like to come and talk to you as soon as possible. Would that be OK?'

Her crying grew loud again, and she was struggling to speak.

'Yes … I'll need to go to my parents … I'll need to …' Her voice faded, lost in tears.

'I'll look at the trains and call you straight back. I'm so very sorry, Anita.'

He cut the call and stamped out the spent fag he'd been smoking. *God, what a mess.* The correct procedure would have been to phone the local police and ask them to inform her, but there'd been too much going on. He'd have to make it right now, though. She couldn't be left alone with that news. He dialled Sartori.

'I'll put a call in, get them to send a car,' he said between loud slurps of something. Scamarcio guessed it was his usual king-size

Coke. Sartori might have the makings of a good detective, but there was a risk his body would give in before he got there.

'I'm glad you called, Scamarcio, because I did a bit of asking around. Well, to be precise, I showed your dead priest's picture to a few contacts, and somebody recognised him.'

'*Who* recognised him?'

'One of my friends at the Turkish baths on Viale Angelico. Your guy had been in a few times. That may or may not be significant, but, as my friend says, "Anyone coming here knows the kind of clientele they'll meet." So, your priest might have been visiting the baths with a purpose, if you get my drift.'

'I get it, I get it,' muttered Scamarcio, wishing he didn't. He needed to head north to Meinero's sister first thing tomorrow.

'If you had a brother, would you tell him everything?' he asked Fiammetta while they were slumped on the sofa watching an irritating documentary about a serial killer. Scamarcio gladly would have chosen anything else, even *Wheel of Fortune* or that bland show on La7 with Lilli Gruber (the least curious journalist he had ever known), but Fiammetta was engrossed and refused to switch over.

'Depends on the relationship, I guess. A sister, maybe. But brother and sister is slightly different.'

'Hmm, I know,' said Scamarcio, already worrying that Anita Meinero might not have the answers he needed.

'Why do you ask?'

'Oh, nothing really.'

'Is it to do with your case?'

'Yes.'

'You don't want to tell me the details?'

'No, not really.' He squeezed her hand, and she squeezed back. 'It's not easy having a cop for a partner,' she said cheerily.

'You don't seem too cut up.'

'You know me, I take things in my stride. And I knew what to expect.' She fell quiet so she could listen to the breathless narrator. When he'd finished delivering what Scamarcio thought was a particularly crass line of commentary, she said, 'I guess we should count ourselves lucky that you're not investigating a serial killer like this bastard. Jesus, that would really screw you up.'

Scamarcio gazed out the window to the night sky beyond. He felt an unfamiliar anxiety move through him, like a beast that had long lain dormant, but was now finally beginning to stir.

15

SCAMARCIO HAD DECIDED TO take the 6.00 am train
to Genoa because the connections to Arquata Scrivia were
good, and a quick glance at the map had told him that Anita
Meinero lived just a few minutes' walk from the station. At
least the journey would give him the chance to study his notes,
and perhaps make a few calls. In light of the late conversation
with Meinero's sister, he'd delegated the visit to Borghese's last
Facebook friend to Sartori, filling him in on the possible love
triangle. He'd have preferred to have conducted the interview
himself, but he knew he had to start using Sartori, and not just
for his own selfish ends. If the man was going to develop into a
good detective, he had to be given the chance to grow.

Amidst his notes, Scamarcio returned to the question marks
he'd scored boxes around. Again, he wondered why, if Amato
had called to advise her that the session was over at 3.20 pm, Mrs
Borghese had arrived home so much later. Perhaps her father had
simply been too ill to leave, but hadn't one of the priests said she'd
been heading back when they called? Had she hit traffic? Scamarcio
needed to speak with her again, lay these small doubts to rest.

He glanced up from his papers. They'd finally left the outskirts
of Genoa and were passing what looked like a refinery on their left.
Winking in the sun were large circular containers with metal tubes
running in every direction. A few brightly coloured villas stood

lonely on the brows of small hills, empty rolling green all around. He noted that it was a different green here, up north. It was denser and deeper — like the Kodachrome green of a Super 8 film. As he rested his head against the window, the backdrop morphed into rugged cliffs, black and unforgiving. Scamarcio noticed pile after colourful pile of storage containers, many bearing the names 'Maersk', 'Hanjin', or 'MSC'. After a few minutes, they passed a car park full of truck cabs, and he guessed that Arquata Scrivia served as a transportation hub between Genoa and the north.

The train slowly rolled into the station, and Scamarcio took in the drab apartment blocks and ragged pylons. The place could not be described as beautiful.

He pulled out the map he'd printed from his computer and started the walk from the station. There was a small fountain and a few benches across the road from where the cars pulled up, and he noticed three or four black men sitting around, apparently idle and bored. They were smartly dressed in clean denim and fashionable trainers, but a few locals were standing some distance away, eyeing them with concern.

This is it, a nutshell tableau of Italy's immigrant issue, reflected Scamarcio. Boatloads of migrants made the harrowing crossing from Libya, saw their friends, family, babies drown — only to end up somewhere like Arquata Scrivia, where the local population had never seen a black man, and where the chances of finding a job were non-existent. For the life of him, Scamarcio couldn't understand how the Italian government expected to create a living, a future for these people, if they had nothing to offer them. It was hard enough for the average Italian to find work; there was no slack in the system. Scamarcio had sympathy and compassion for these migrants — everyone deserved the right to a decent life — but he also knew that Italy was the very last place these poor souls would find it. The EU seemed happy to dump the problem firmly in Italy's backyard. It was just Italy's hard luck that the peninsula lay thirty miles from Africa and was perceived as the gateway to paradise.

As he walked further up a main road lined with tiled apartment blocks and bars with blacked-out windows, Scamarcio spied another trio of Africans in neon-yellow safety jackets. They were pushing a cleaning cart and seemed to be sweeping the street. At least the local council had found something for these men to do. Maybe he was wrong: maybe the guys on the benches *would* find work; maybe it would be better than what they'd left behind. But, somehow, he doubted it. Somehow, he'd sensed their disappointment as he'd passed.

He swung a left and then a right and took a road that led to the foot of a steep hill covered in pine trees. On the right were a series of attractive villas, small palms in their gardens. He stopped outside the first of these, checked the address on his piece of paper, and rang the bell. A muffled voice crackled over the intercom.

Scamarcio introduced himself and pushed open the gate at the sound of the buzzer. Anita Meinero was standing in the doorway to her home, a little girl clutching her knee.

Scamarcio extended a hand, and Meinero took it. She was good looking, with strong cheek bones like her brother, but unlike him, she had blonde hair and blue eyes.

'Do you have any news?' she asked, her heartbroken eyes searching his.

'Not yet, but we're pursuing several theories.'

She seemed to remember her manners. 'I'm sorry, please come in. It's cold.'

She led Scamarcio into a long hallway with a light wood floor. The hallway opened onto a modest-sized living room with a large window that looked onto the front garden. The furniture was dark and solid and didn't match the pale floor.

'Please sit down, Detective. You must be tired after the journey.'

The little girl was eyeing Scamarcio with a mixture of fear and curiosity. Anita Meinero turned on the TV and said, 'Oh look, it's *Masha and the Bear*.'

The child tottered over to the TV and sat down on the carpet, quickly engrossed.

'I don't like to let her watch too much TV, but it's the only way we'll be able to talk,' she said. 'Can I offer you a coffee?'

Her eyes were red-rimmed and her hands were shaking slightly. Scamarcio didn't want to cause her any extra stress.

'No thanks, I'm fine. I've just had one. At the station.'

He took a seat on a wide-patterned sofa, then stood up again immediately and removed a large piece of Lego that had been lying beneath him.

'Sorry,' said Anita Meinero, her voice fragile. 'However much I try to keep things tidy, I can never keep up.'

'I'm about to have a child myself,' said Scamarcio, not quite sure why he'd brought it up.

'Your first?' She also seemed a bit surprised.

'Yes, I'm quite nervous, actually.'

'I think that's normal.'

'I'm sorry,' said Scamarcio, 'I didn't come here to talk about me. Would you like me to tell you the circumstances in which we found Alberto, or would you prefer I didn't? It's up to you.'

Anita Meinero nodded wordlessly, thinking. Eventually, she said, 'Tell me.'

As Scamarcio started to speak, she closed her eyes. He talked her through the details of the scene in the hotel room, and then explained Giangrande's findings and theory.

'What is the drug they found in his body normally used for?' Anita Meinero asked, looking up. Scamarcio had hoped he wouldn't have to mention it.

'Erectile dysfunction.'

She closed her eyes again.

Scamarcio sighed. 'Anita, it would really help if you could tell me a bit about your brother. I've spoken to his colleagues at the Vatican, but none of them knew him like you did. If he had a secret or a problem, I figure it would have been you he confided in. Am I right to think that?'

She nodded and wiped a tear from her eye.

'So, what I want to know, Anita — what I *need* to know — is whether something had changed in his life of late, or whether *he* had changed.' She kept nodding, and Scamarcio felt a small spark of hope.

'He called me,' she said, her voice starting to break. She glanced at her daughter and swallowed, trying not to cry. 'It was before I went on holiday, so that would be about ten days ago now.'

'Was it a routine call?'

'No, he was worried about something.'

'What did he say?'

She sniffed and brought a hand to her mouth. 'He was concerned about his boss, the cardinal.'

'Cardinal Amato?'

'Yes, the one who does the exorcisms.'

'What was the problem with Amato?'

'They were treating this young lad, in Parioli, I think, or a nice suburb like that, and they'd been treating him for quite some time ...'

Scamarcio's heart was starting to race. 'Anita, have you seen the news since you've been back?'

'No, I haven't really had a chance. I got your message, and then, well, my world came crashing down. Why?'

'Never mind for now. So, this lad in Parioli?'

'Well, Alberto told me he thought that the cardinal was obsessed with him. He said the situation wasn't healthy — it was making my brother uncomfortable.'

'Obsessed in what way?'

113

'I'm not sure it was sexual — it might have been, but Alberto didn't spell that out, as such. He just said that the cardinal gave this boy far more time than the others ... that he was always calling him on his mobile, that he seemed to care about him more than the rest, that he was always asking about him.'

Scamarcio said nothing. His felt a buzzing between his shoulder blades.

'I told my brother to talk to someone — one of his superiors in the church — let them know that he was worried.'

'And what did Alberto say?'

'He said, no way, he couldn't do that, it would be career suicide.' She fell silent for a moment and appeared to be thinking something through. 'I was worried about him after that call. He'd seemed so preoccupied and worked up. I actually tried to ring him back the next day, before I went away, but I couldn't get hold of him.'

Scamarcio sat back slightly on the couch. The sister's testimony dragged Amato back into the frame and threw him right down in the middle of the picture. But there was also something subtler here, something that had repercussions on a different level, and Scamarcio made himself focus. The deeper question was, why had Alberto been so troubled by the cardinal's 'obsession' — troubled enough to mention it to his sister? As his friend had said, Alberto had a good heart. Maybe his morality meant that he was struggling to accept the cardinal's behaviour. But then, why had none of the other priests raised this supposed obsession with Scamarcio? Were they *all* just trying to avoid career suicide? Was it really just a case of uniform self-interest? As much as he tried, Scamarcio couldn't simply write it off as that. Sure, it had seemed as if they were all keeping to a script, but they had also seemed genuine in their ways. There had to be something significant to the fact that Alberto was worried about this so called 'obsession' and that the others were not. Now, Scamarcio just needed to work out what that was.

16

ANITA MEINERO CAME BACK into the living room with glasses of water for herself and Scamarcio. While she'd been gone, her daughter had sat staring at him intently. He'd found it unsettling, and he realised that he didn't have a clue what you were supposed to do with a child of that age: what games they liked, how you played with them, or even how you spoke to them. He was totally unprepared for fatherhood. He'd need to read a book or two. He probably should have started months ago.

He took a sip of the water and tried to concentrate on the task in hand.

'Anita, I'm sorry to have to ask you this, but I feel it's pertinent. Did you have any sense that your brother might have been gay?'

Maybe he'd expected a look of outrage, an angry word or two, but instead, Anita Meinero just nodded sadly. 'Yes ... I mean, it's not like he ever spelled it out or anything, but I could tell. I actually picked up on it quite early on — from when he was fourteen or so. It was the way he'd talk about certain boys. Girls just didn't seem to hold his interest in the same way.' She paused for a moment. 'But, please, you won't be asking my parents about this, will you? They don't know. I don't think they'd be able to understand — they're from a different generation.'

'Don't worry — I don't need to discuss this with them.'

She breathed out slowly and studied the floor.

'Had he mentioned anyone of late? Did you get the feeling that he had someone in his life?'

She looked up slowly. 'Well, he was a priest, so obviously that would be strictly forbidden.'

'I know, but ...'

She blinked. 'But, now you mention it, he did sound happy, upbeat, whenever we spoke over the last few months. It was only when he called worried about the cardinal that he seemed low. That was the first time I'd heard him down in a while.'

Scamarcio nodded. He was trying to connect the dots ... and was failing.

Meinero was still thinking. 'Actually, I did wonder at one point if there might be someone — and whether that person could be from a different walk of life.'

'What made you suspect that?'

'Alberto's vocabulary changed. He was using words I hadn't heard from him before, and, a few times, he said that he was bored of his fellow seminarians — the ones who'd graduated with him ... that he wanted to spend time around different kinds of people.'

'Did you ever meet any of his colleagues at the Vatican?'

'No, just Michele. They were at college together; they'd known each other a long time. He's a lovely man, Michele.'

'Yes, I spoke with him.'

'He must be devastated by this.'

Scamarcio said nothing. He didn't want to make things worse.

'I should probably call him.'

'I wouldn't be putting any extra pressure on yourself right now, Anita.'

She smiled tightly and looked at her daughter, who was now playing with a wooden train.

'This is hard,' said Anita Meinero, her voice breaking.

'I know,' said Scamarcio softly.

On the train journey home, staring out the window, he wondered about Cardinal Amato's 'obsession' with Andrea Borghese. Could it really have been sexual? That seemed the most obvious conclusion from Meinero's statement. And Borghese had been a strikingly good-looking young man. Maybe his beauty had stirred something in the cardinal — something he couldn't control. Scamarcio pulled a sceptic's face in the glass and was reminded of a gargoyle. He'd have to pursue this line of enquiry, but he wasn't convinced. He couldn't square it with what he knew of Amato. Then again, the DVD had been a surprise. With Amato, what you saw wasn't necessarily what you got.

He turned away from the window and surveyed the empty carriage. Whichever way you cut it, it was a hornet's nest in the middle of a shitstorm. The media frenzy would reach frightening new heights if the gay angle came out.

He dialled Garramone.

'What you got?' barked the chief, sounding considerably less cheerful than of late.

'A possible homosexual obsession on the part of Cardinal Amato towards Andrea Borghese.'

'Say it ain't so, Scamarcio. Say it ain't so!'

'I wish it wasn't.'

'For fuck's sake, we can't field the fallout from that. Can't you just ignore it? Focus on other things?'

Scamarcio said nothing, knowing that the chief had taken temporary leave of his senses. He'd give him a few seconds to compose himself.

'Why don't they just let them marry? That's what I don't understand. All these scandals, all this secret suffering could be so

117

easily avoided if the Vatican just accepted that their priests have basic animal urges like everyone else. We're in the twenty-first century, for fuck's sake. It's absurd. Totally absurd.'

Scamarcio had heard it all before. He rubbed a hand across his eyes. 'What do you want me to do? Shall I up the ante and go into the Vatican all guns blazing with a warrant, or shall I stick to the softly-softly?'

'What do you make of the cardinal? Is he the type to get ruffled and make a mistake?'

'He spends his days fighting the devil. I wouldn't say he's someone who spooks easily.'

'Stick with the softly-softly. That gives us some time to play with before the shit hits the fan and the Vatican seals itself tight shut.'

'The shit might *not* hit that particular fan. It's just Meinero's word for it at this stage — in a private conversation with his sister. I suspect Meinero might also have been gay. He liked to frequent certain saunas at any rate.'

'What does the sister think?'

'She's thought so for a long time.'

'So Meinero's dead — *and* gay,' muttered Garramone as if the whole thing had been deliberately contrived to create problems for him personally. 'It's a huge bloody gay priest boomerang that's going to come back and smack us in the face one way or another. We need to get prepared. Work out how we're going to handle it. I'm thinking I'll give media relations a heads-up.'

'No, don't do that,' snapped Scamarcio. 'Just let me do a bit more digging first, so we have a clearer idea.'

Scamarcio could hear the boss sucking air in through his teeth. 'OK, but don't leave it too long. Why aren't you using Lovoti, anyway? It seems to me that you need all the help you can get.'

'I don't want him on this.'

'Why the fuck not?'

'I don't trust him.'

'He's solid.'

'A solid detective who's got it in for me.'

'You sound unhinged.'

'Whatever. I don't like him, and this thing is way too sensitive for a leaky ship.'

'Lovoti's not a leaker.'

'I don't want to take the risk.'

'Scamarcio …'

'Sorry, sir. I've got another call coming in.'

Scamarcio cut him off. He knew it was a mistake, but really, he didn't have time to be dealing with arseholes like Lovoti.

Cardinal Amato answered his door in a thick red-and-blue checked dressing-gown. He was dabbing at his nose with a paper tissue, and his eyes, red and rheumy, blinked out from behind his spectacles like two sickly crustaceans unaccustomed to the light.

'What —?' The words were lost on a hacking cough.

'Are you unwell?' asked Scamarcio.

The cardinal was still coughing. Eventually he said, 'I caught a cold. It went to my chest. I have a weakness in my lungs, unfortunately.'

'I'm sorry to disturb you, Cardinal,' said Scamarcio, feeling more frustrated than sorry.

'Could you perhaps come by another time?' said Amato, tightening the cord on his dressing-gown. 'It's past nine.'

'It's just that we're working against the clock on this case. It's …'

Scamarcio felt a firm grip on his bicep, and turned to see Cafaro glaring at him. 'What do you think you're doing? You have no right to be up here unaccompanied.'

'I couldn't find you.'

'Bullshit. We watched you on the CCTV. You sauntered in here, plain as day. You made no effort to drop by my office.'

Scamarcio gritted his teeth. 'If I have to run every tiny detail past you, Cafaro, I will never solve this case.'

'I'd hardly describe the cardinal as a tiny detail.'

Cardinal Amato hacked and spluttered. It sounded as if he was bringing up his insides. Scamarcio wondered for a moment if he was seriously ill — whether he should be in hospital.

'Please, gentlemen, can we deal with this later. I just need to be in bed.' With that, the cardinal shut the door in their faces.

'I'll come back tomorrow,' said Scamarcio, half pushing Cafaro out of the way.

'I doubt he'll be better by then.'

'Well, I'll be coming. There's a heads-up for you, Cafaro.'

'And here's a heads-up for you, Scamarcio: bring a warrant.'

Scamarcio turned back slowly. 'You really want to go down that road, Cafaro?'

'You heard me.'

'I just want a quick chat.'

'You're wanting way too many chats with the cardinal for my liking. It's starting to seem as if he's a person of interest.'

Scamarcio tried not to let his simmering rage boil over. 'Why are you doing this, Cafaro? Why can't we just cut each other some slack? We both know how this game works.'

Cafaro brushed something off his sleeve. 'Yeah, and that's why you'll be needing a warrant. If I were you, I'd hurry back to my desk and start sounding out some judges. Good luck finding one with balls.'

Scamarcio stormed off, his pulse pounding. *If Cafaro wants a war, that's precisely what he'll get.*

17

SCAMARCIO DROPPED HIS SPENT fag onto the dirty plate. The ash soaked into the greasy trail of tomato sauce and made him think of blood and gore.

'You still have a face like thunder,' said Sartori. 'You need to take it easy or you'll be heading for a coronary.'

Scamarcio watched Sartori stuff another forkful of French fries into his mouth. 'I hardly think you're in a position to comment.' He tapped out a second fag from a new pack and lit up. 'So, now your terrible hunger has been seen to, maybe you can tell me what you made of our young friend in Parioli?'

Sartori knocked back the rest of his pint glass of Coke and belched behind his fist. 'I don't get it, all this goth crap. The guy was wearing a Beasts of Satan t-shirt with the pictures of the killers across the front.'

'He what?'

'I kid you not. Honestly, this shit should be banned. How can you be allowed to sell t-shirts depicting killers?'

'When are those bastards out?'

Sartori picked up another cluster of chips and used them to sponge up the sauce from his braised beef. 'I think they have just a few years left inside. God knows what the parents are going to say when they come face to face with their children's murderers in the street.'

Scamarcio shook his head, troubled by the thought. The Beasts of Satan were a group of young heavy metal fans who'd carried out a series of satanic ritual killings in a town north of Milan during the late '90s and early 2000s. The group had been convicted of three murders, although to this day it was suspected that their victims may have numbered as many as eighteen. The killings were considered to be among the most shocking crimes to hit Italy since the war.

'Did Tommaso Pombeni shed any light on my love-triangle theory?' asked Scamarcio, trying not to think any more about the Beasts of Satan and how they had buried one of their victims alive.

Sartori swallowed down the last of the chips. 'Yeah. You have it about right. Pombeni said that the politico's son, Ale Castelnuovo, did indeed have the hots for the girl, Graziella, but that her interest appeared to lie elsewhere.'

'But he didn't specify Andrea Borghese?'

'I pushed him, and he said he'd suspected it might have been Andrea, but that she'd never spelt it out.'

'And did he offer anything interesting on Andrea?'

'Just the same as you got from the others, really. That he was OK when you got talking to him, but that he could throw the most terrible fits, and that's why a lot of the other kids gave him a wide berth.'

'And he didn't have any ideas on who might have wanted Andrea dead?'

'Not really.' Sartori scratched at his huge stomach. 'But he said something I think you'll like.'

'Spit it out then.'

'Apparently the politico's son has a bit of a temper. Pombeni has seen Ale Castelnuovo lose it big-time on several occasions, and one time, the guy on the receiving end ended up in hospital with a broken jaw. Apparently, Ale's father paid the boy's family a shitload of hush money not to go to the press.'

'Hmm,' said Scamarcio, drawing the nicotine down deep. It felt medicinal.

'And it gets better.'

Scamarcio just rolled his eyes.

'Ale is obsessed with true crime and forensics apparently. He gets all those weird magazines that describe the murders of serial killers, that pore over every last little detail. He told Pombeni that he wants to be a pathologist when he's older.'

'Funny,' said Scamarcio. 'He neglected to mention his career ambitions to me.'

Sartori finally laid down his fork and wiped his mouth with a paper napkin. 'It might explain what Giangrande said about the strangling — the professional element.'

Scamarcio nodded slowly. 'You were right. I do like it, Sartori.' He tried not to sound half-hearted.

While Sartori had provided two great leads, neither of them brought Scamarcio any closer to understanding why Meinero had been murdered.

'Be a glass-half-full guy, for once,' said Sartori, easing his bulk out of the chair. 'Sure, you don't have the whole picture, but I've just given you a big chunk of it. A thank you wouldn't hurt.'

Scamarcio looked up, surprised. 'You've done great work, Sartori. I guess I'm just in a hurry to close this.'

'Don't be in a hurry — enjoy it. In a few weeks, you'll wish you'd taken your time, believe me.'

'What's that supposed to mean?'

'When you're up to your eyeballs in shitty nappies, and you and Fiammetta are screaming at each other because neither of you have slept in a week, a leisurely lunch discussing a case will seem like a taste of paradise.'

'Christ.'

Sartori surveyed him, his expression grave. 'God, Scamarcio, I worry. I really do. I don't think you know what's coming.'

'Maybe it's better that way.'

'Hmmm.'

Scamarcio just looked at him and said nothing.

Sartori winked. 'Here's something to buoy you up — lunch is on you.'

'What?'

But Sartori was already halfway out the door. Scamarcio just stared into space, his mind stalling from stress and tiredness. Eventually, he decided the best thing to do would be to light another cigarette.

'Cocksucker wants a search warrant,' said Scamarcio to Garramone, across a sea of papers, and empty cups from the machine. Garramone looked addled and pale, the colour in his cheeks from a few days past had all but disappeared. Scamarcio wondered what was amiss.

The boss yawned and cupped a hand across his mouth then rubbed it up and down. 'It's just the usual chest-beating. I saw a wildlife documentary once where they showed these apes fighting about who was in charge. Eventually, the weaker ones would submit by showing the stronger one their backsides.'

'What exactly are you suggesting?'

'I'm not suggesting anything. I'm just trying to get you to understand that it's all a farce. Life is a farce.'

'Are you OK, Chief?'

Garramone sighed and scratched the crown of his head with a biro. 'I've been around a long time, Scamarcio — seen a lot of shit. On the one hand, it's depressing, because you never see a break in the cycle or an improvement, but on the other hand, it teaches you to pick your battles — to recognise when it's not worth the fight.'

'You reckon we'll find a judge who'll play ball, then?'

'I've got a couple we could try. I'll call them — it might be better coming from me.'

Scamarcio tutted. 'If only we could just haul the cardinal in for questioning.'

'It'll be easier to get the warrant, believe me. Besides, you wouldn't want the press to get a whiff of him arriving here. It wouldn't look good, and it would generate a whole load of fresh shit for you to deal with.'

''Tis true,' murmured Scamarcio.

'Look at it this way: once you've got a warrant, you've got a warrant. Even if you weren't ready to go full guns, now you have the right.'

'If I get it.'

'If you get it.'

'What if all this *isn't* just Cafaro swinging his dick? What if he knows something or suspects something? What if he's been told to cover it up by the powers that be?'

Garramone sniffed. 'Could be, I suppose. But Inspector Cafaro has a solid reputation — I checked him out. He's a stickler for the rules, and my assessment is he's just marking his territory.'

'And blocking my inquiry.'

'I'll let you know how I get on with the warrant. Don't sweat it.'

Back at his desk, Scamarcio ran a comprehensive web search on Cardinal Amato. He read every article he could find and made a note of every friend and acquaintance mentioned. The cardinal was born in Bologna in 1943 and had spent more than fifty years as a Roman Catholic priest. He became the Vatican's official exorcist in June 1988, under the tutelage of Father Carlo Quattrocchi. Amato, it seemed, was a member of the Society of St Paul, the congregation founded by Giacomo Alberione in 1914. In 1992, Amato created the International Association of

Exorcists, and remained president to this day. Scamarcio was surprised to learn that the cardinal claimed to have performed over thirty thousand exorcisms in the course of his life and referred to himself, modestly, as the most important and most successful exorcist in the history of the Catholic church. The high number started to make a little more sense when Scamarcio read that Amato believed that a person could be possessed by more than one demon at a time, and that some victims were overrun with hundreds. As he tracked the press coverage over the years, Scamarcio noticed a growing pessimism in Amato. The cardinal began to lament that, 'People have lost the faith.' The rise in popularity of superstitions and magic was giving the devil a foothold, he said, and the problem was only going to get worse.

Scamarcio's concentration was starting to wane when he came across an article in the online archives of *La Repubblica* that made him sit up. The headline read, 'Vatican's chief exorcist claims to know truth about Cherubini kidnapping.'

Scamarcio wet his lips and tried to focus. 'Cardinal Amato, the Vatican's chief exorcist, has revealed in his new book that he fears that Martina Cherubini may have fallen victim to a sex ring involving an ambassador to the Vatican, other foreign diplomats, and members of the Vatican gendarmerie.'

'What the fuck?' whispered Scamarcio. Why the hell hadn't this been on his radar or why hadn't someone put it there? The disappearance of fifteen-year-old Martina Cherubini from outside a basilica in Vatican City over twenty years ago had gripped the nation. Her body had never been found, and various conspiracy theories abounded, some involving elements of the Roman mafia, others international intelligence agencies, and some both. But Scamarcio had never been aware that Amato had commented on the case, and he had also been unaware of the gendarmerie link.

He read on:

Cardinal Amato says that rumours had circulated for a long time about sex parties with underage girls for diplomats belonging to a foreign embassy inside the Vatican. The girls were allegedly procured by a member of the gendarmerie and a parson of the Vatican church of St Mary. The cardinal's testimony seems to line up with an anonymous letter sent to Cherubini's mother that claimed her daughter had been procured for a sex party and had been murdered shortly after. When contacted for comment, Cherubini's brother, Massimo, said the theory could hold weight. According to Massimo, the family had never been able to explain his sister's disappearance from outside a busy church at 7.00 pm as she'd never have accepted a ride from a stranger. But Martina knew the priest at St Mary's, and if she'd been asked to get in a car with him, she may well have agreed.

Scamarcio looked away from the screen and pinched his nose. It could be nothing or it could be everything. He needed to ask the cardinal about the case. More importantly, he needed to find out what Chief Inspector Cafaro was doing in 1995. Was it possible that Amato had some kind of hold over him, and, if so, would the inspector be prepared to cover for Amato — protect him from his own troubles twenty years later?

Scamarcio closed his eyes, and an image from the opening sequence of the film *La Grande Bellezza* swam into his mind. The writhing tango line of those first frames revealed a world where everyone was entangled — priest, politician, sinner, saint. The film director, Sorrentino, had it right: it was impossible to escape the spider's web in Rome. You were constantly having to ask yourself, *Cui bono?*

18

It was 8.00 pm, and as Fiammetta had said she was going to bed, and as he hadn't been able to find out anything useful about Cafaro's career history, Scamarcio thought he'd head to the gendarmerie barracks and do some casual asking around. He hoped that the chief inspector might have gone home, and that the visit might give him a chance to speak to the young priests once more.

The golden dome of St Peter's was looming into view when his phone rang.

'Could you come right away?' said Mrs Borghese. There was a tremor in her voice, and Scamarcio couldn't decide if she'd been hitting the bottle or crying. Perhaps both, he reasoned.

'Has something happened, Katia?'

'No. Yes. Well … kind of. I don't know, it's hard to explain. It would be much better if we could talk in person.'

Scamarcio stifled a sigh. 'OK. I can be there in half an hour.'

'Thank you.'

He turned back the way he'd come, searching for a taxi. Friday at 8.00 pm was not a good time to try. The traffic was backed up for miles, and the usual pointless cacophony of horns was starting up. What did she want? He hoped it would be worth the effort.

An hour later, when he finally arrived at the Borghese's apartment, Mrs Borghese welcomed him with what looked like a tumbler of whisky in one hand and a burned-out cigarette in the other. She was wearing a silk dressing-gown that was sagging open.

Great, he thought, *a tired attempt at seduction in the middle of a nightmare inquiry. Could it get any better?*

Katia Borghese led him into the living room and flopped herself down on the sofa and yawned. The dressing-gown gaped wider.

'I'm worried about my husband,' she said quietly.

'Your husband?'

'He keeps disappearing for long periods, and when he does eventually show up, he barely speaks to me.'

Scamarcio tried to push back against a wave of frustration. He'd changed his plans for *this*?

'He's grieving, Katia. Grief affects people in many different ways.'

'Yeah,' she said, unconvinced. 'But I think he's trying to pull something off.'

'What do you mean?'

'My husband's a mover and shaker. He doesn't just sit back and deal with what comes — that's not his way. He's got to be in the driver's seat, calling the shots.'

'So, how does that relate to your son's death?'

'I think Gennaro is up to something. I think he may have found out who's done this and is out for revenge.'

'What?'

She shrugged and opened her palms. 'Like I say, he's proactive.'

'But surely he knows that's *our* job?'

'Maybe he doesn't trust you to find the killer? I don't know, I just have a strong feeling he has a plan in motion.'

Scamarcio sat down on the sofa and pulled out his mobile. But before he placed the call, he asked, 'And do you have any idea who your husband might be targeting? Who he suspects?'

She shook her head quickly. 'None. That's the frustrating thing. Right now, I'm the last person he'd talk to about it.'

Scamarcio patted his jacket pocket for his fags. There were only three left. 'Mind if I smoke?'

'As long as you offer me one,' said Mrs Borghese, readjusting the dressing-gown.

Although it was nearly 9.30 pm by the time he'd dealt with Mrs Borghese, Scamarcio decided to head back to the Vatican as the chances were now high that Cafaro had left. As Scamarcio approached the Ponte Sant'Angelo, the milky pale faces of the statues stared back at him, sombre and pensive in the moonlight. He thought of the body he'd found hanging here the year before last and the way in which that one murder had changed his world view, had perhaps changed him. His mobile rang, and he looked away from the river and checked the screen. Sartori was finally returning his call.

'See if you can locate Gennaro Borghese, and once you do, put a tail on him,' barked Scamarcio.

'What's cooking?'

'No idea, but his wife thinks Gennaro doesn't trust us to do our jobs and that he might want to strike out on his own.'

'Who does he have in his sights?'

'I don't know.'

'Jesus,' hissed Sartori down the line.

St Peter's rose up out of the darkness, and Scamarcio upped his pace. 'Jesus, indeed. Let me know if you get anywhere.'

He finished the short walk to the main entrance of the Vatican and produced his badge for the Swiss Guard.

'What are you doing here?' one of them asked, his expression cold.

'I just need to ask someone a question in relation to my current inquiry.'

'We've heard all about your current inquiry.'

Scamarcio said nothing.

'Who do you want to see?'

Scamarcio did not feel like sharing his plans, and the reception at the gate was putting him off a trip to the barracks. 'Priest Lania. He's from the Veneto,' he heard himself say.

The guard frowned, but handed back his ID and motioned him through. 'You have half an hour, then we will be coming to check.'

'Right you are, then.'

Scamarcio walked away as quickly as he could, then pulled out his mobile and dialled Lania. 'Any chance you, Michele, and your colleagues from the exorcism could meet me in the next fifteen minutes? Somewhere near the main entrance.'

'I'm not sure I can round up everyone so quickly,' said Lania hesitantly.

'Please try. It's important.'

The boy said he'd do his best, so Scamarcio slumped down on a cold stone bench in the gardens and spent the next few minutes scrolling through emails. He hoped that the Swiss guards hadn't alerted the gendarmerie, but he knew there was rivalry there and collaboration wasn't always a given. There was, of course, the possibility that one of Cafaro's cronies would be scanning CCTV, but, hell, sometimes you just had to try.

Scamarcio had replied to most of his emails, most of them pointless, when he felt a hand on his shoulder. He looked up to see Lania with one of the other, younger, priests, whose name he couldn't remember. The third one was nowhere to be seen.

'I couldn't get hold of Riccioni,' said Lania. 'He's not answering his mobile.' Scamarcio remembered Riccioni as the priest who had only joined the group on the day of Andrea's murder, so his absence seemed less of a loss. 'And Michele has the flu — he sounds awful, says he's got a fever of thirty-nine.'

'It might be the shock,' said Scamarcio, wondering quietly if Michele Cogo was trying to avoid him. 'No worries,' he added, rising wearily. 'Thanks for coming at such short notice.'

'You said it was important.'

'Is there somewhere we can talk?'

'The library's just around the corner. It's closed, but I can get the key.'

'Sure.'

The boy led the way inside, stopping at a small office, where he muttered a few words to a plump grey-haired man behind a counter and was promptly handed a large key chain.

The library was less than a minute's walk down a wide wood-panelled corridor, which smelled of sandalwood and expensive polish. When they entered, Scamarcio was struck by the hollow ring of their footsteps across the enormous marble floor. As the overhead lights spluttered to life, he glanced up to see a magnificent corniced ceiling adorned with pastel frescoes depicting the Ascension. Row upon row of massive books stretched to the end of the hall, and when he examined the cover of one, the beaten leather and Latin inscriptions made him wonder if it was penned around the time of the Magna Carta.

The priests were pulling out a couple of heavy chairs from a wide oak table. Scamarcio joined them and took a seat.

'I'm sorry to have disturbed you so late, but, after speaking to Meinero's sister, I have some new questions.'

Lania pushed his long fringe away from his eyes and blinked. 'How's she holding up?'

'As well as can be expected. It's a huge shock for his family, obviously.'

The other priest frowned. 'It seems that the deaths around this case are mounting. It makes you wonder if you might be next.'

Scamarcio hadn't considered it from their perspective. 'I don't believe either of you are at risk, but if you feel uncomfortable or notice something out of the ordinary, please call me immediately. You both still have my card?'

They nodded solemnly.

'So, what is it his sister said?' asked Lania.

'She told me that Meinero had called her shortly before his death, and said he was concerned about the cardinal's behaviour. Apparently, he believed Amato was obsessed with Andrea Borghese.' Scamarcio wasn't sure what reaction he'd been expecting, but no response came other than a stony silence and a brief exchange of glances.

'So, neither of you have anything to say on this?'

The young man from the Veneto sighed and looked at his colleague who just nodded slowly, as if giving permission.

Lania took a long breath. 'We'd all noticed it. Meinero was not alone in his worries.'

'Ah.' Scamarcio sat up straighter in his chair.

'He treated Borghese differently from all the rest: gave him more time, seemed to be totally obsessed with curing him. He'd always be getting us to move other appointments around to accommodate Andrea and his family.'

'Did you have any sense about why?'

The other priest rubbed a hand along his jaw and shook his head. He said nothing.

'No. None of us could understand it,' said Lania.

Scamarcio had been hoping he wouldn't have to spell it out for them. 'Might the cardinal have been in love with Andrea?'

The younger priest screwed his face tight into a frown and raised his eyes heavenward. 'Cardinal Amato is a seventy-five-year-old priest. Are you crazy?'

Scamarcio sighed. 'Well, what else would it be?'

'It's *anything* other than that,' said Lania, looking around him at the vast library. 'Strange rumours do fly about this place, but the one thing I know is that I've never heard anything like that in connection with Amato — he's totally focussed on his work, to the exclusion of everything else.'

Scamarcio couldn't come up with anything other than, 'Hmmm.'

'This obsession thing did trouble us, as we felt it wasn't fair on the other cases, but to my mind it was always an *intellectual* obsession. As a subject, Andrea intrigued the cardinal. He told us he was one of the most complicated cases he'd seen, and I think he was absolutely determined to succeed where all the doctors had failed.' He glanced at his colleague. 'Wouldn't you agree, Bruno?'

The priest nodded. 'That's always how I saw it, too. I did think it was unhealthy, though — the constant phone calls to the mother, the constant rescheduling, the interrogations after.' He looked to his friend. 'After every session with Andrea — and *only* Andrea, because he didn't do it with the others — the cardinal would ask us how we thought it had gone: was Andrea improving? Did we think he'd make it through? It was almost ...' The priest stopped as if he didn't want to use the word.

'Embarrassing?' offered Scamarcio.

'Kind of,' said the priest, looking away.

Scamarcio rubbed at an eyebrow. 'You know, I've been in this game a long time, but I confess I don't know what to make of this.'

'Because it's new to you,' said Lania. 'It's a world you don't know.'

'Perhaps,' said Scamarcio softly. He paused for a moment, trying to find a comfortable way to phrase his next question. 'I've reason to believe that Alberto Meinero was gay — that he may recently have started a new relationship. Is that something either of you were aware of?'

Lania actually blushed. He cleared his throat. 'Alberto was a lovely person, but he was a very private man. This was never something he would have discussed with any of us.'

His colleague confirmed it with a sad nod. Scamarcio found it interesting that neither of them had tried to deny it. 'So, what links these two deaths? *That's* my problem right now.'

The priest pulled at the corner of his lip. 'I don't envy you. It's odd, I can see that. None of it makes any sense. I wish we had more information to give you.'

Unfortunately, Scamarcio believed him.

19

'JUDGE GARIBALDI HAS COME good,' said Garramone over the phone as Scamarcio tried to finish an apricot brioche at an up-scale bar he sometimes liked to visit for breakfast. 'I called in a favour.'

'What favour was that?'

'None of your business.'

Scamarcio wondered for an idle moment if Judge Garibaldi was 'The Judge' — the subject of a hot rumour last year that had entertained the squad room. A team from Vice had raided an orgy at a Thai massage parlour, but almost immediately a call had come in from on high leading to the instant release of one of the 'clients' arrested at the scene. All the other customers had gone on to face charges. The Vice team had been sworn to secrecy or risk losing their jobs, so, unsurprisingly, no one had been willing to give up a name. All anyone in the squad knew was that the guy had been a high-powered judge.

'Thank God for Thai massage parlours,' said Scamarcio under his breath.

'What did you say?'

'Nothing. So, it's all signed, sealed, and delivered?'

'Swing by my desk, and I'll hand it to you in person.'

'How's it going to play out with the whole jurisdiction thing? Can Cafaro still put a spoke in my wheels?'

'He's the one who requested the warrant, but in theory, yes. I'm sending one of our lawyers with you. He will outline to Cafaro the consequences of not complying. Having spoken to our man, I think it's likely that Cafaro will choose pragmatism. Well, if he's wise, he will. It's not worth the legal firestorm if he doesn't.'

'Right,' said Scamarcio, feeling suddenly on edge. The brioche sat heavy in his stomach.

'I'll give you three officers and Sartori. Between the lot of you, you should manage to organise a decent sweep through Amato's stuff.'

'The cardinal's under the weather with a chest infection.'

'This probably won't make him feel any better.'

Scamarcio raised a hand to his chin. 'What I really need is something that links him to Borghese in a way that it shouldn't.'

'How do you mean?'

Scamarcio filled him in on the obsession angle. When he'd finished, Garramone asked, 'And you buy the young priests' version that it was a purely professional interest?'

Scamarcio fell silent for a moment. 'Yes. I was awake most of last night, and I spent a long time thinking about the nature of obsession. I came to the conclusion that perhaps it doesn't have to be sexual to be dangerous.'

'Go on.'

'Well, you know that guy — that psychiatrist — who did that controversial research where people were persuaded to inflict pain on one another with a fake machine, ramping up the severity with a dial each time? And everyone said, "Oh God, this proves that, as a species, we humans are basically evil."'

'Hmm, yes, I think I know the man you mean, but what does this —'

'Let me finish. For a long time, the world took that research seriously. It was discussed, cited, referred to time and again. Only

137

now, it's come out that he faked a lot of the data to reach the conclusion he wanted. His research subjects were lied to and manipulated. Then they discovered that this psychiatrist had had a terrible childhood: he'd witnessed unbelievable cruelty and suffering during a massacre. His distortion of the research was basically an attempt to come to terms with what had happened to him as a kid.'

'I still don't see why this is relevant, Scamarcio.'

'That psychiatrist was obsessed with evil, he went to enormous lengths to pin it down, identify it, explain it. In a way, Amato is doing the same thing, except he's not just saying, "Here it is," he's trying to rid the world of it. And he's been on a mission for the last thirty years. Perhaps, near the end of his life, he feels like he's failing, he's desperate to see real results. Perhaps he returned to Andrea after the session, perhaps he tried to get him to do something, behave in a certain way, perhaps it went wrong ...'

'Andrea was strangled. The cardinal ...'

'Before you say it, the Vatican clean-up machine is efficient, and you know it. If there'd been a mistake, the cardinal could have summoned help to sort it — make it seem like something else.'

'So quickly?'

'It's possible.'

'Scamarcio, you've impressed me many times, but I'm not buying this. It's Occam's razor. We know that murder victims are often killed by someone they know and that romantic entanglements are high on the list when it comes to motive. Ignore those young priests — go for the likeliest explanation: sex. As much as I wish it wasn't. It might be something sexual involving those Facebook friends, or it might be something sexual involving Amato.'

'Amato is seventy-five.'

'So? Ever read *Death in Venice*? Maybe it was love, rather than sex?'

Scamarcio clicked his tongue. 'No, there's professional obsession, and then, behind it, there's something else that I need to identify. Something that pushed it all to the next level.'

'You think the cardinal killed Andrea or had him killed? *And* Meinero? But why? It remains a fucking big *why*, Scamarcio.'

'Because Meinero knew something he shouldn't, or he'd discovered something that others preferred to keep hidden.'

'Perhaps Meinero walked in on Andrea and the cardinal ...'

Scamarcio drummed the counter top. 'Too simple, too Occam's knife or whatever it is.'

'In my experience, simple is often right.'

'Not in mine.'

'Jesus, Scamarcio, just think it through, step by step. You'll catch a break, I'm sure.' Scamarcio exhaled sharply and turned to see a few customers at the bar observing him over their newspapers. He'd forgotten he was in a public place. Garramone sighed. 'Let's talk more when you come by my office. I've got an early meeting in five.'

'Sure,' said Scamarcio, now keen to leave the café.

The rain was beating down hard against the windscreen of the Panther as they made the turn into Via di Porta Angelica, which led to the Vatican.

'Bells and whistles?' asked the police driver seated beside him.

'Nah,' said Scamarcio. 'No need for a fuss. We're just here for a friendly chat.'

'You think it will be friendly?' asked the Flying Squad's top lawyer, from the back seat. Lucio Baldini was a good-looking, lanky forty-three-year-old, who had graduated magna cum laude from Bocconi University in Milan, and had then made it to the prosecutor's office in record time. How he had been persuaded to join the police was a mystery to Scamarcio, although it was probable that his bureaucrat's salary was considerably higher than those of the detectives he assisted.

Scamarcio frowned. 'It's rarely friendly at the Vatican.'

'I blame it on the nuns,' muttered Baldini. 'There's a malevolence there. Makes for a bad atmosphere.'

'You were a convent kid?'

'Good guess.'

'I hear they're terrible places.'

'They *were*. They've improved, I believe.'

Baldini fell silent and Scamarcio wondered if he'd hit a raw nerve. He rested his head against the seat and spooled through his conversation with Garramone. Was simple always right? Was it possible that the two priests had done a good job of obscuring the truth in steering Scamarcio away from the sexual angle? Would he be foolish not to keep that element alive, however off it felt?

They approached the main vehicular entrance to Vatican City at Porta Sant'Anna, and the police driver buzzed down the window. The gendarme studied their documents, and then got on his walkie-talkie. Scamarcio guessed that Cafaro would soon be making an appearance, and, indeed, as they rounded the turning circle, the chief of the gendarmerie was waiting for them, legs apart, arms crossed, and flanked by five of his armed officers. *What was he expecting*? Scamarcio wondered. *A shoot-out*?

Scamarcio stepped out of the car and handed him the warrant. 'I'd like to point out that it was you who brought things to this point,' he said quietly.

Cafaro smiled tightly and shook his head. 'I'm not so sure.' He waved the paper in the air, holding a corner of it by his fingertips as if it was a piece of litter about to be lifted by the breeze. 'I'm not even convinced this actually means anything.'

'I'm here to assure you it does,' said Baldini, stepping out from behind Scamarcio and extending a hand, which was ignored.

'And who the hell are you?' asked Cafaro.

Baldini apprised him of his credentials.

Cafaro stared at him hard, then said, 'Well, this is all very nice, but the cardinal is unwell.'

'We'll make sure he's comfortable. We don't need his help to search his rooms,' said Scamarcio, checking his watch.

'I just hope he doesn't have a heart attack with the stress of it all,' said Cafaro, leading them inside, his officers falling into step. To Scamarcio, it sounded like a thinly veiled threat, and a quick glance at Baldini told him that the lawyer felt the same.

When Cardinal Amato came to the door, Scamarcio was shocked by the change in his appearance. He was very pale, and his shoulders now seemed hard and bony beneath his dressing-gown. There were dark rings beneath his eyes, and his voice was raw and shaky. Scamarcio seriously wondered if they should get him to a hospital.

'The cardinal looks bad,' whispered Baldini. 'If he's unwell, his lawyers could challenge the validity of any interview.'

'I'm aware of that,' said Scamarcio. 'But I'm not really here for an interrogation. I'm just looking to confirm or deny a hunch.'

Baldini shrugged and shuffled inside behind the police team.

The cardinal watched aghast as the team started to examine papers on his desk and pull out books from his shelves. They were doing it with care, as instructed, but Scamarcio knew it would prove an alarming sight nevertheless.

'Is all this really necessary?' asked Amato, struggling to lift his voice above a gravelly whisper.

'I believe it is,' said Scamarcio, examining a crystal paper weight bearing a gold plaque that read 'Honorary visit of Cardinal Amato, Archdiocese of Boston, Massachusetts, 24th of July, 1989'.

He signalled to Sartori that he was leaving, and then asked, 'Is there somewhere we can go where you can sit comfortably, Cardinal?'

Amato tutted in frustration and whispered, 'Follow me.'

Scamarcio was dismayed, but not surprised, to see Cafaro hurry out behind the cardinal.

Amato led them out into the corridor and knocked on a door opposite his rooms. An elderly priest answered, wide-eyed.

'The police are using my rooms, could I borrow your study for a while?' said Amato, not looking the least bit embarrassed.

The old priest seemed taken aback for a moment, but then waved them all in, saying, 'I'm just on my way out, so go ahead.'

He turned to Scamarcio as he passed and gripped his arm. 'Please go easy on him. He's having a terrible time.' The man's eyes were as hard as steel, and Scamarcio found his dark stare unsettling. 'Leave the key under the mat when you've finished.'

Scamarcio just nodded.

When Amato had been made comfortable on a wide sofa and a blanket draped across his knees, Scamarcio asked, 'Have you seen a doctor?'

'I've always had a weakness in my chest — it's just an infection. I prefer to avoid antibiotics if I can.'

'Even so, it might be good to get yourself checked out.'

'So, all this fuss is because you're concerned for my health?'

Scamarcio sighed. 'No.'

'Of course not.'

'I spoke with Meinero's sister. She told me that he'd called her, worried about what he perceived to be an unhealthy obsession on your part towards Andrea Borghese.'

The cardinal said nothing, just steepled his bony fingers in front of his mouth. The silence in the room was a dark void. Scamarcio couldn't even hear breathing or the tick of a distant clock. *How can a room in the very centre of Rome be so quiet?* he wondered.

When it seemed that the cardinal wasn't going to speak, Scamarcio turned to Cafaro and said, 'You understand my problem?'

Cafaro just blinked.

'Cardinal Amato, from my perspective, this is just a chat. I haven't called you to the station, you haven't phoned your lawyer. I'm not looking to bring charges, I'm just hoping for some clarity, so I can steer this investigation in the right direction.'

Amato coughed. It was a thick phlegmy cough that came from deep in his lungs, and Scamarcio felt even more convinced that the man needed medical attention.

'Meinero was right, in a way,' said the cardinal slowly, the words barely audible. 'Andrea Borghese was the most interesting and challenging case I had ever come across, and I was determined to succeed. Andrea had so much promise — so much talent. I so desperately wanted to see him lead a normal life.'

The cardinal's voice broke into a cough once more, and he reached beneath the blanket and pulled out a crumpled cotton handkerchief. He dabbed at his cracked lips and sighed.

'But what was so interesting about Borghese in particular?' Scamarcio pushed.

'His intelligence, his perspicacity, his cunning. Often, it felt as if the devil was trying to manipulate Andrea's talents for himself. I had to fight hard to win them back.'

Scamarcio hesitated. 'And your interest went no deeper than the professional?'

The cardinal looked up from his handkerchief, his mouth agape. 'What on earth?'

It was Scamarcio's turn to fall silent.

'That's disgusting,' muttered Amato.

Cafaro just grimaced and glanced away. He looked like he'd rather be anywhere else.

'It's a question I have to ask,' said Scamarcio quietly.

'And I have to tell you that it's a revolting insinuation. I'm nearly seventy-five, I'm a man of the cloth, I'm dedicated to my job ...' Amato had raised a small fist in the air. It was starting to shake.

'Police work is often uncomfortable,' sighed Scamarcio. 'One is forced to ask terrible questions of good people.'

The cardinal lowered the fist and stared into his lap.

'So, you were not in any way in love with Andrea Borghese?'

The cardinal looked up again, his eyes wide. 'No,' he almost shouted, the word shaking and quivering before breaking into a terrible wheezing whistle that turned into a coughing fit. When Amato's voice finally returned, it was weak and fragile: the voice of a child. Scamarcio had to lean forward to hear him.

'I was just fascinated by him. I was keeping a diary of his progress so that I could perhaps draw on it for a future book — if I ever got around to writing another.'

Scamarcio considered the old man sitting before him: his thin wrists bunched in his lap, the old dressing-gown sagging around his wheezing chest, the echo from the force of his 'no' still heavy on the stale air. If there was ever a moment to realise that you had to cut a particular theory adrift — let it go — this was it. The 'sexual obsession' angle would do nothing but drag Scamarcio down a blind alley. It was time to call it quits.

On his way to the squad car, the brief interview over, Scamarcio considered the rest of his conversation with Amato and his claims that he hadn't known Father Meinero well. The cardinal had insisted that he had no idea why Meinero would be using a false ID in his name. If Amato had been lying, and Scamarcio's instincts told him otherwise, it was a performance deserving of an Oscar. Instead, Scamarcio was left with the impression that the cardinal lived almost entirely in the world of his exorcisms, and that he had no time for those the devil chose to leave in peace.

Scamarcio knew full well that Garramone and his Occam's razor wouldn't like it that the man at the very centre of the investigation, the man to whom all roads led, appeared to have nothing to do with both murders. But Scamarcio was comfortable: the confirmation that he was dealing with an intellectual rather than sexual obsession was liberating and freed him to consider other angles. There was much he now needed to do: first and foremost, he wanted to take a closer look at the politician's son, Castelnuovo. After that, he'd turn his attention to the Borgheses, their life, and their apparent wealth. He needed to find out if Mr Borghese, still AWOL, was planning an act of revenge, as his wife suspected.

Just as the police driver was opening the car door, Scamarcio heard Sartori shouting from some distance away. 'Scamarcio, wait up.' Sartori was running towards him, something white flapping in his clenched fist. Scamarcio felt his heart skip a beat.

'I thought you'd want to see these,' Sartori panted, thrusting what appeared to be photographs into his hand. Scamarcio turned them towards the pale sunlight. The pictures were black and white and were portraits of Andrea Borghese: Borghese looking out a window; Borghese leaning on a balcony, azure sea in the background; Borghese at a restaurant. But it was the last photo, the smallest, that really took Scamarcio's breath away. It was a shot of a boy of eight or nine riding a bicycle. It took him a moment to realise he was looking at Andrea Borghese as a child.

'Where did you find these?' he asked Sartori.

'They were at the end of a row of books on one of the cardinal's shelves.'

'What's Amato doing with a picture of Borghese as a kid?'

Sartori shrugged. 'Fuck knows.' He paused for a beat. 'I've saved the best for last.'

'Show me.'

Sartori handed over another small photo, printed on thicker paper than the rest. A toddler of two or three was pushing a small wooden cart. The carefree grin was unfamiliar, but the wide eyes were unmistakable — the same soulful brown.

'What the hell?' whispered Scamarcio.

'Quite,' muttered Sartori, pulling up his collar against the wind.

20

SCAMARCIO TOOK HIS FIRST swig of espresso for the day and studied the photos fanned out in front of him. He drained the cup, then dialled Mrs Borghese.

'Perhaps you could solve a mystery for me,' he said quietly. 'Why would Cardinal Amato be keeping childhood photos of your son in his private rooms?'

There was a sharp intake of breath, then silence. 'What?' she asked eventually.

'We found a stash of pictures of Andrea, some showing him as a toddler, some as a teenager. I'm perplexed.'

There was no sound at the end of the line. She was either blindsided by shock or she was thinking, hard. Finally, she said, 'The cardinal claimed he was writing a book. He asked me for some photos, a few weeks ago now. He promised to return them.'

Scamarcio realised that he shouldn't have phoned through a question like this: he needed to see her face, read her expression. But he'd been impatient, wanted a quick answer. 'I see,' he murmured, unconvinced.

'Nothing sinister there, I'm afraid,' added Mrs Borghese in what seemed a poor attempt at a lighter tone.

'Any sign of your husband?' he asked, drawing the nicotine from a fresh fag down deep. 'We issued a police alert, but we've got nowhere. He didn't come home last night, did he?'

She fell silent again. After a few seconds she answered, 'No.'

'Any idea where he might have gone? His mother's?' asked Scamarcio, knowing full well that Borghese hadn't pitched up there.

'No. Not his mother's. And his brother is still away hiking in Nepal …' Scamarcio had delegated chasing the brother to Sartori, but, despite numerous attempts, he'd been unable to reach him. Katia Borghese let out a tired sigh. 'Gennaro's at his mistress's probably.'

'Ah.' Scamarcio took another long drag and closed his eyes, trying to calm his frustration. 'That been going on long?'

'I found out about it around six months ago. How long it had been going on prior to that, I have no idea.'

'I should have been told.'

'It's not an easy thing for a wife to admit to.'

'It might have a bearing on the case.'

'You've watched *Fatal Attraction* too many times, perhaps.'

'Mistresses can sometimes behave irrationally.'

'Only if they feel they're on the losing side. Anyway, she's not that kind of woman.'

Scamarcio heard something glug in a bottle.

'Are you sure?'

'She was one of my best friends.'

'Jesus.'

'Women are vipers. You can't trust them — any of them.'

'That's bleak.'

'It's the truth.'

He took another long smoke, refusing to give up on the fag, though it was down to the filter. 'Don't take it personally.'

'What?'

'I don't think women understand men. Well, as much as men don't understand women. Men, given half a chance, will cheat. We have too many hormones we don't know what to do with. It can get us into trouble if the wrong woman comes along and leads us by the leash. We don't want to stray, but, given the opportunity, we will. You were just unlucky that your so-called friend decided to try her luck when she did. If she hadn't intervened, your husband probably wouldn't have betrayed you.'

'You southerners, my God ... I think my husband bears some share of the responsibility, don't you? He's not a robot. You can't pin it all on the woman.'

Scamarcio said nothing.

'My marriage was in a mess for a long time,' she added.

'Why was that?'

'Do you have any idea what a problem child can do to a relationship?'

Scamarcio swallowed. 'No.'

'The pressure is enormous, unbearable. You're constantly pitted against one another, there is no time to breathe, you're desperate for peace, even just five minutes of it. You have no time for yourself, no time for your partner: nothing left to give. The relationship withers, then dies.'

'God,' muttered Scamarcio, feeling the old unease stir again. He noticed that the second fag he'd only just lit was already halfway through.

'Let me know if you find my husband,' sighed Mrs Borghese, sounding as if she didn't really care anymore.

Scamarcio replaced the receiver. As he was shuffling the photos back into a tidy pile, he reflected that he didn't yet have the measure of Katia Borghese. He still hadn't checked why her return home had been delayed. His earlier sense that there was something going on behind the scenes was deepening.

He noticed the stack of DVDs of the Borghese exorcisms and reached for them. He wanted to watch them all, in case there was anything — any tiny detail that might provide some clarity. He loaded the first of the discs and pressed play. The scene appeared to mirror the one on the DVD he'd watched with Mrs Borghese. The only difference was that Andrea's hair was shorter.

Amato was running through the usual rites, his voice building in intensity as Andrea's angry cries threatened to drown him out.

'I hate you!' screamed the boy for a third time, before he finally ceased shouting and slumped into a chair, his hair caked to his forehead with sweat. The priests massed around him like a black swarm, holding him down, and then Amato approached and stood over him.

'Requie, creature dei,' he said, firmly but quietly. Scamarcio knew he was instructing Andrea to rest.

Andrea's head lolled against his chest, and the screen turned black. Scamarcio wondered why Mrs Borghese had stopped filming.

The next DVD offered nothing new, and the third was shaping up to be no more enlightening. Scamarcio continued watching until the exorcism arrived at a point where the aggression on the part of both Amato and Andrea was so overwhelming that he feared they might strike each other. They were screaming in each other's faces, spittle flecking their cheeks and sharp fists raised. Scamarcio found it almost unwatchable. Andrea's face was red with fury, his eyes dark with intent, but then, as in the previous films, a sudden change swept over him, and he closed his eyes and collapsed into a chair. It was like watching the power being drained, as if a switch had been flicked.

Yet again, Scamarcio asked himself if this was for real or just theatre. He was about to fast-forward through the rest of the film, when he noticed something and paused. On the screen, the cardinal had struggled painfully into a crouching position and was reaching out to place a calming hand on Andrea's upper arm. There was nothing particularly unusual about the gesture, but it was the reaction of Meinero, standing to Amato's left, that stole

Scamarcio's breath. Meinero's forehead contorted into a frown, and his eyes narrowed. His right hand bunched into a clenched fist, which hung at his side like a club. He seemed outraged, livid even. Almost instinctively, Meinero inclined his shoulder towards the cardinal, and Scamarcio wondered if he was about to hit him. Scamarcio studied the other faces in the room. None of the other priests seemed to have a problem with what Amato had done, so why was Meinero so very troubled?

Scamarcio closed his eyes and massaged his aching forehead.

Really, there was only one obvious answer to this question, and it also explained why Meinero had complained to his sister about the cardinal's so called 'obsession'.

Meinero was jealous.

21

'I'VE GOT A DEAD priest possibly in love with the victim, the vic's father gone AWOL, and a hothead schoolkid with a serious axe to grind. Not to mention a weirdly obsessed cardinal. There's something off about the vic's mother, too, but I haven't figured that one out yet.'

Scamarcio didn't want to tell Sartori that the cardinal had commented on the Cherubini disappearance. The cold case had been playing on his mind, and the background to the young girl's disappearance was a potential crime huge enough to have triggered serious fallout inside the Vatican, but discussing it now felt like a step too far: Scamarcio didn't want to complicate things for Sartori at this delicate stage.

'If you ask me, the only weird thing about the mum is the booze. Drink can make people seem stranger than they really are,' said Sartori, ripping the wrapper off a Snickers bar.

'She hasn't seemed that pissed when I've seen her.'

'Maybe she knows how to handle it by now.'

Sartori took a bite that encompassed three quarters of the bar. Scamarcio grimaced. 'How can a drunk be a good mother?'

'How can a drunk be a good wife?' Sartori popped the last piece delicately in his mouth.

'Are we 100 per cent sure she's a drunk?'

'Hmm.'

'We just have that schoolgirl Graziella's word for it. I've seen the odd thing, but I wouldn't necessarily conclude she's an alcoholic.'

'Maybe we need to look for some signs.'

Scamarcio rubbed his eyes with the heel of his hand. 'Do you know anyone in marketing?'

Sartori stopped chewing. 'What the hell has that got to do with anything?'

'Do you or not?'

'A friend of my wife's, I think.'

'Does she earn well?'

'As far as I know, nothing spectacular. Again, why are you asking?'

'But maybe a marketing director would? If he's in a lucrative sector?'

'Lucrative like what?'

'What kind of salary would you need to afford the kind of apartment the Borgheses live in? What would you have to earn to afford a Porsche Panamera and a Bang and Olufsen sound system?'

Sartori scratched his chin. 'No idea. My wife's friend lives in San Basilio. It's hardly Manhattan.'

'Is she senior?'

'I don't know.'

'Mr Borghese works in the pharmaceutical sector. All I can think is that it might pay highly compared to other industries.'

Sartori stared at him. 'It may do, and I can get that kind of info in a flash, but if you have any kind of hunch, Scamarcio, we should probably be running it down. Now.'

Scamarcio pulled his last Marlboro from the pack and waved it at Sartori. 'Get the spit and cough on who Borghese works for. And take a stroll through his bank accounts. Let's just check it's all above board, so I can cross it off my list and worry about something else.'

'Sure,' said Sartori, rising from his seat.

'And while you're at it, find out who he's screwing.'

'What?'

'You heard.'

Sartori shook his head. 'Why is it that on every sodding case, there's some loser cheating on his wife?'

'It's life.'

'Life down here in the pit. Up in Rimini, the family is sacrosanct.'

'You're just the exception that proves the rule, Sartori.'

Scamarcio felt torn: the centre of gravity of this case did seem to be shifting towards the Vatican and the Borgheses, but he knew from experience that he couldn't just write off Andrea's other life and the entanglements that came with being a teenager. Even if it didn't immediately feel like it, any knowledge gained here might have a bearing on other things. With this in mind, he resolved to pay a visit to Andrea's Facebook friend Tommaso Pombeni. He needed to hear his testimony about Castelnuovo and his violent tendencies first-hand.

He was making the turn into Pombeni's street when his phone rang.

'You're an arsehole,' said Aurelia softly. Scamarcio didn't know whether to be more surprised by the phone call or the words.

'What?'

'Why didn't you tell me you were about to become a father?'

He clenched his jaw — this was the last thing he needed.

'It didn't really feel like the right time. I hadn't seen you in over a year. What was I supposed to say, "Hi, welcome back and, by the way, my girlfriend's about to have a baby"?

'Oh, fuck right off.'

'*You* called *me*, Aurelia.' But he was glad she'd called. Worryingly glad.

'I deserve an explanation.'

Scamarcio fell silent for a moment, then said, 'Yes, that's the very least you deserve.' He stalled, hesitated, but he heard himself ask the question anyway. 'Can you meet me — in an hour and a half? Trastevere? So we can talk.'

'It's Saturday night.'

'Would you prefer another time?'

'No, it's OK. Where?'

'Bar Solari?'

'You remember what happened last time we met there?'

'I promise it won't get violent.'

Aurelia tried to stifle a laugh. 'OK, see you then.'

'See you.'

Scamarcio looked at his phone and sighed. If he wasn't very careful, he'd soon be on the road to disaster.

Tommaso Pombeni was a strange looking kid. Very skinny, with big, almost bulbous, eyes, a wide flat nose, and a huge brow. Altogether, the effect was of a sorrowful frog. And the voice didn't help. It was unusually deep and raw: exactly the kind of voice a frog might have could it speak.

'I saw it a few times. Castelnuovo is a spoilt little shit. If he doesn't get what he wants, all hell breaks loose. He's not used to anyone saying no to him.'

'But I thought you two were friends?'

'We hang about in the same group. That's it.'

Scamarcio frowned. He couldn't make sense of these adolescent relationships.

'And you told my colleague you'd seen him beat up a guy?'

Pombeni tucked his legs beneath him on the settee, as if he was getting comfy before telling a tall tale. 'Yeah, it was fucked up. This guy had said something snide about an expensive jacket

Ale was wearing, Ale saw red and smashed the guy's head into a wall, hard. And I mean fucking hard. The guy passed out.'

'What happened next?'

'The paramedics were called, and they brought him around — I don't know how. The guy was taken to hospital, though.'

'Was he OK?'

'As far as I know, yes. They didn't keep him in long, anyway.'

'And how was Castelnuovo after this happened?'

'Well, it was creepy, actually. He looked like he really couldn't give a shit. Like it had been nothing. He wasn't smiling or anything, but he just shrugged and carried on as normal.'

'He wasn't afraid of being arrested?'

'If he was scared, he certainly didn't show it. I reckon he thinks he's immune — what with such powerful parents and everything.'

'And that's exactly what happened, isn't it?'

'How do you mean?' The boy stuck a thumb in his mouth like a baby.

'Well, you told my colleague that the boy's parents wanted to kick up a fuss, but that Castelnuovo's family had it all hushed up.'

'Oh yeah. The kid's folks were furious, understandably — furious with the school, too — then it all just disappeared, as if it had never happened. The principal told us not to talk about it to anyone.'

'The school principal?'

'Yeah.'

'And you're sure it was the Castelnuovos who've had it all swept under the rug?'

'Not *sure*, exactly, but that's the logical conclusion, isn't it? And I remember Castelnuovo saying that it would all get covered up like it always did.'

'That's what he said? "Like it always did"?'

'Yeah, I definitely got the feeling it had happened before.'

156

Scamarcio took a breath. 'And getting back to Andrea Borghese and the girl, Graziella Feliciano ...'

'Graziella had the hots for Andrea, and Castelnuovo had the hots for Graziella. Big time — he wasn't going to let anyone get in the way.'

Scamarcio paused before he posed the question. 'Do you think he could have killed Andrea?'

The boy nodded eagerly. 'To be honest, that was my first thought when I heard the news.'

Scamarcio rubbed a hand across his mouth. This was the tricky bit. 'Who is Castelnuovo really good friends with?'

'Him and Jacobini are tight.'

'Jacobini?'

'Samuele Jacobini.'

'Do you think if he did something terrible, like kill a man, he'd confide in Jacobini?'

The frog-boy paled slightly, as if the seriousness of the situation was finally dawning on him. He took a long breath. 'I don't know. Castelnuovo's the type to keep his own counsel, but I guess, if he did want to unburden, Samuele would be the one.'

Scamarcio nodded and thought to himself for a minute. Then he looked at the boy. 'Tell me, have you ever considered a career in the police?'

Pombeni looked surprised. 'Me? Oh, uh, no. Not really.'

'You'd make a good detective, you know,' said Scamarcio. 'You've paid close attention to the dynamics between all your peers. You know how to read them. You've got good instincts. And being a detective is all about instinct.'

The boy blushed and looked pleased.

'So listen,' said Scamarcio, 'I need you to do something for me.'

Frog-boy paled again. 'Oh God, really?'

'Right now, all we have is supposition, and that counts for shit in the courts. We need to take it to the next level.' Scamarcio paused and looked into his lap — he couldn't just ride roughshod through the rules, much as he wanted to. He had to check. 'How old are you?'

'I just turned eighteen last week.'

'Good.'

'What?'

'Never mind. I need you to have a little chat with Jacobini, find out if Castelnuovo told him anything.'

'You've got to be joking. Jacobini thinks I'm pond slime.' It was an unfortunate analogy.

'Just try — see where you can get. If you ever want a career in the police, assisting with an investigation will help.'

'I don't know …'

'It might be fun,' said Scamarcio.

'What — the police or this gig?'

'This gig. But police work has its moments.'

'I'm not sure. I'll need to tell my parents.'

'Why? Do you tell them everything? Like when you screw a girl? Or fart?'

The boy looked uncomfortable. *He's probably still a virgin*, thought Scamarcio.

'OK, you're right. No need to get them involved.' He opened his spindly arms. 'I'll be glad to help in any way I can.'

'Excellent,' said Scamarcio, extending a hand.

Aurelia was waiting for him when he entered the bar. A couple of men at a table to her right were giving her the once-over, but she seemed oblivious. She already had a large glass of red in front of her, and it was half full.

'I'd mention that you're late, but what's the point,' she said, getting up to kiss him on both cheeks. That she'd even deigned to do that surprised Scamarcio.

'Sorry,' he said. 'I'm working that exorcist case, and it's pretty much round the clock.'

'Nothing's changed, then.'

'Nope.'

'Except that you're about to become a father.'

Scamarcio took off his jacket and draped it across the back of a chair. He sat down and waved the waiter over. 'I hope you don't mind if I get a drink first.' His heart was hammering in his chest.

'Of course.'

Once he'd ordered a large glass of Nero D'Avola, he folded his hands on the table and looked at her. There was no denying she was beautiful. But in a different way from Fiammetta. Aurelia's beauty was of the solid kind. From whichever angle, the beauty remained indisputable, perfect, unchallenged.

'I'm sorry I didn't tell you,' Scamarcio said, meaning it. 'But I wasn't even sure you wanted to hear from me.'

'I didn't.'

He shrugged. 'Well, there you go.'

Aurelia sighed and took a long slug of wine. 'I appreciate what you did for me — in Munich, I mean. I know you had me kept an eye on, so to speak.'

'It was the least I could do.'

'It wasn't your fault, Scamarcio.'

'Yes, it was.'

'You couldn't know they'd come for me.'

'I might have guessed.'

'No. It was a high-stakes game, and it was new to you. Nobody in your position could have foreseen what happened.'

Scamarcio sniffed and looked away. Then he looked up at her and said softly, 'It's decent of you to say that. But I worry about you being back here. I'm still not sure it's safe.'

'I heard that the Cappadona had changed leadership and dropped the hunt. I wouldn't be back here otherwise.'

159

'You can't ever be certain,' said Scamarcio.

She smiled sadly. 'I can't stay hidden forever. My life is here, Scamarcio. My family is here.'

'I'm so sorry,' he said into the table.

'I want to lay the past to rest.'

He looked up. There was a cold finality to the words. He felt both relieved and disappointed.

'I don't want to be carrying around hate and resentment and all that negative shit.'

He said nothing.

She pushed her short hair behind her ear, but it refused to stay and fell back against her cheekbone. Scamarcio had to look away again.

His wine finally arrived, and he drained it in one.

'I hear you were awarded the medal of honour.'

He smiled. 'Last year. It was a bit of a headfuck.'

'Giangrande told me all about it. Why is it you always find yourself in the middle of this shit?'

'That's a question I'm still trying to answer.'

'It will have to change with a kid.'

'I know.'

'Are you worried?'

'Just a little.'

There was a silence. But Scamarcio didn't feel uncomfortable.

'Your girlfriend — how did you meet her?'

'It was on a case last year involving some people who work in TV. She worked in TV at the time. She —'

'It's OK, I know who she is.'

'Why are you asking, then?'

'I dunno, I …'

Scamarcio leaned forward across the table. The wine had emboldened him. 'Aurelia, this is very difficult having you back here. I'd be lying if I said I didn't still think about you. It was easier when you were abroad. But now …'

'But now you're about to have a child, so you need to move on. As do I.'

Scamarcio let out a long sigh. 'Things could have been different, I think.'

'Everything could be different. There are multiple potential outcomes for any situation. Our outcome was what it was.'

He rubbed his cheek. 'Right.'

'I wish it was me who was having your child, but it's not to be.'

He looked up from his glass. 'You do?'

'Of course.'

'Your guy in Munich?'

'That didn't work out. We were too different — call it culture clash.'

'I'm sorry.'

'No, you're not.'

'No, I'm not. I want to sleep with you.'

'But you can't.'

He grabbed his jacket and threw some money down on the table. 'I can't. What kind of man would I be?'

'And what kind of woman would I be, going to bed with a man whose girlfriend was nine months pregnant?'

'We'd both be total shits.'

'And we're not.'

They headed outside. The air was damp and cold, and there was a strong smell of old rubbish and wet stone. She gave him a perfunctory kiss on both cheeks.

'Look at the moon,' she said. He followed her gaze. It was full — fat and bright.

'Good luck, Scamarcio. I love you.'

And with that, she was gone. He wanted to smash his head against the wall.

161

22

It was 8.00 am on Sunday, and Fiammetta was sleeping soundly for once, but Scamarcio knew a lie-in was not an option. He was wired — both Aurelia and the case had spun his mind into overdrive.

He dialled Sartori. 'Any trace of Gennaro Borghese?'

'He pitched up home late last night, apparently.' Sartori sounded like he was struggling to shake off sleep.

'Any idea where he'd been?'

'The mistress's. Katia gave us an address in Parioli, which Lovoti was staking out. No joy, so he did a trawl of the local neighbourhood. Found them in a restaurant a few streets away. She's quite a piece, by the way.'

'Lovoti …'

'For fuck's sake, Scamarcio, we need all the help we can get. I'll deal with Lovoti so you don't have to.'

'He tried to fuck me over on a case last year. He's only out for himself.'

The line fell silent.

'Anyone spoken to the mistress?' asked Scamarcio, trying to rein himself back in.

'I thought you'd want first dibs.'

'I'll head over there this morning. You got a number?'

Sartori scrambled around for something, then reeled off the

details. 'I can't do much on the whole financial angle, today being Sunday.'

'Do what you can, leave the rest until tomorrow.'

'And there was me thinking you'd say, "Don't sweat it, you enjoy Sunday with your kids."'

Scamarcio felt like an arsehole. 'Don't sweat it, you enjoy Sunday with your kids.'

Melissa Melandri lived in small but immaculately kept apartment in a smart modern block just behind Via Ruggero Fauro in Parioli. She was tall with long brown-blonde hair, wide blue eyes, and dense brows, and reminded Scamarcio of the actress Brooke Shields. He could see why Gennaro had slipped up.

'Can I offer you anything, Detective — coffee? Juice, perhaps?'

'I'm fine, thank you.'

She led him into a neat living room painted in calming shades of grey. The sofas were a crisp white.

'You have a very nice place.'

'I've just had it redecorated. This is supposed to be "New England" style, according to the brochure.'

'I lived in the States awhile. West Coast, though.'

She motioned him to the sofa. 'I've never been. It's on my bucket list.'

Scamarcio smiled and sat down.

'I'm so sorry about Andrea.' She stretched out her long legs in front of her. He noticed the bottom of her calves, where her designer jeans stopped, were very tanned. Maybe she and Gennaro had been away. Maybe she had other lovers.

'Did you know him well?'

'We'd been family friends — I saw him grow up.'

'It must have been very difficult for his parents.'

'Katia didn't make it any easier.'

163

'What do you mean?'

'Well, you'll know that she took to drink — when the stress became too much?'

'I'd heard something along those lines, but I wasn't sure how seriously to take it.'

'It's quite true. She took to drink, and she never quit. The problem for Gennaro and Andrea was that she was a bad drunk. Became aggressive. In the end, she was aggressive most of the time.'

'And she's still drinking now?'

'Yes.'

'I can't say I've seen much sign of it.'

'I believe she kicks off in the evening. In the daytime, she can just about keep it together. I mean, she'll drink, but you won't notice.'

'And Andrea, how did he cope with this?'

'By shutting himself away in his room. I suspect her drinking exacerbated his condition. I know that's what Gennaro thinks, anyway. The stress of the arguments she'd start certainly did not help Andrea.'

Scamarcio sighed. 'What a mess.'

'Indeed.'

'But then, you didn't exactly improve things, did you?'

'My relationship with Gennaro has nothing to do with it.'

'How can you say that?'

'I was there for him when he needed me.'

'But that wouldn't have helped Mrs Borghese's drinking any.'

Her back stiffened, and she took a quick sip of water from a cut-glass tumbler. 'She'd be drinking anyway. She's too far gone.'

Scamarcio rubbed his mouth and studied the woman before him. She was the picture of composure, she had it all together.

'So, as Andrea's mother — I mean, how did it work? Was she able to be a responsible parent for him?'

Melandri sighed and looked away for a moment. 'In the beginning, I have to say, she did her utmost — gave it all she had. Then, I think there came a point when she just couldn't handle it anymore. It all became too much. Maybe a lot of us would have broken under the pressure — maybe I would have, too. Who knows?'

Scamarcio looked at her and doubted it. 'So, in recent times, how were things between her and Andrea?'

'Gennaro told me that often she didn't bother to prepare meals — didn't even show up.'

Scamarcio thought of the solitary Mars bar found in Andrea's stomach. He returned again to the question of why Mrs Borghese hadn't been home on the afternoon of the murder. Perhaps she couldn't face it. Took some time out. He thought of Andrea — the lack of friends, cheating father, absent, alcoholic mother. Poor kid.

'And Gennaro and Andrea, how did they get on?'

'It was a strong bond — a good relationship, as far as it could be. Andrea looked up to his father; he knew he'd always be there for him.'

'Did you see them together much?'

'Gennaro and Andrea?'

'Yes.'

She frowned, then tried to soften it at the edges, but couldn't quite muster a smile. 'We sometimes went for walks together. I could tell there was a lot of love there.'

'Did Andrea know?'

'About Gennaro and I?'

Scamarcio nodded.

She shook her head firmly. 'No, I'm sure he didn't.'

Scamarcio wasn't convinced. He paused to change tack. 'A friend of Andrea's told me he'd claimed his parents had ruined his life.'

'Isn't that just something all teenagers say?'

'Perhaps.'

'Do you think Gennaro hates his wife?'

She stared at him, her eyes narrowing. 'Hate is a very strong word.'

Scamarcio just shrugged, he wasn't going to give ground.

'I don't think he hated her before the death. He was exasperated, frustrated, angry, but I don't think he hated her.'

'But now?'

'He holds her responsible. If she hadn't brought the church into it …'

'I don't follow the logic.'

'Gennaro believes it's all connected. I don't think he's clear on how, exactly, but he feels that there's a link to the exorcisms.'

'He's not planning anything, is he?'

'How do you mean?'

'Revenge of some kind? Perhaps he has someone in his sights?'

She shook her head slowly. 'He's certainly not said anything to me.'

He believed her. Melandri was no fool and didn't seem the type to withhold information. She'd want to keep things tidy with the police.

'Will you tell me if you hear anything?' He handed over his card, and she took it quickly.

'Of course, Detective.' She paused. 'Do you have a theory yet? On who did this?'

'Unfortunately, I have several. The task, now, is to whittle them down to one.'

'It must be a fascinating job.'

He blinked. It was a strangely detached comment from someone whose lover's son had just been murdered. 'What will happen now?' he asked, locking eyes with her.

'I don't quite follow ...'

'Between you and Gennaro?'

'Oh,' she placed a smooth manicured hand across her heart, as if trying to steady it. 'I hadn't really thought. We'll probably just keep going the way we are. I don't think Gennaro has the energy for a divorce.'

'It would cost him too much?'

'Oh, it's not that; I don't think he's bothered about the money. It's just the emotional turmoil of dealing with Katia.'

'And you don't care?'

'I've never been big into marriage.'

'Is Gennaro from a rich family?'

'No, quite the opposite.'

He was about to push her further, but then figured it would be unwise to tip off Borghese that he was interested in the financial element.

'Thanks for your time, Miss Melandri.'

'No, thank *you*. I do hope you find who did this.'

He held her gaze. 'Oh, don't worry, we will.'

23

'"TAKE A STROLL THROUGH his bank accounts," you said. You made it all sound so easy.'

Scamarcio lit another fag and blew the smoke just clear of Sartori's reddened face. 'What's the hold up?'

'The bank is being arsey — wants us to go the official route.'

'Did you tell them about the case?'

'They seemed to know all about it already.'

'Borghese?'

'Could be. Or they saw it on the TV.' Sartori pulled the tab on a can of Coke and slumped down into a dented plastic chair. 'You'd better watch that,' he wiggled a fat finger at Scamarcio's cigarette.

'Fuck off. You know what happened to Moia? They just lopped off his left leg due to diabetes.'

'Don't screw with me.'

'I'm not. I got a text from him a few days back. He won't be running down the criminal underworld for a while.'

'He'll be like the big guy in a wheelchair on that American show.'

'There's no way Moia will accept being in a chair. He'll just limp about with a stick.'

'They'll hear him coming for miles.'

Scamarcio sucked down hard on the fag, then, as if finally heeding his conscience, stubbed it out half-smoked and tossed it in the bin — which he realised too late was full of crumpled-up papers. He bent over and tried to fish it out.

'We digress. I'll get that perv judge onto it, the one Garramone keeps in his pocket.' He had to pause. The effort to retrieve the fag had left him out of breath.

'Yeah,' Sartori tried to stifle a belch, but failed. 'That's probably the quickest route. I get the feeling we need to move fast.'

'Why?'

'If Borghese's up to something, he may have transferred the money out.'

'We'll see it if he has.'

'Sure.'

'It's all evidence — of what, I still don't know.'

Sartori handed Scamarcio a sheet of A4. 'Borghese's work history. I've listed the companies, their details, and the dates Borghese was there, along with the positions he held.'

Scamarcio took the paper. 'Did you get salary details?'

'Oh no, I didn't think it was important,' said Sartori, sarcasm rammed to maximum. Scamarcio ignored him. Sartori conceded: 'For the first two, but I'm struggling with the current one.'

'Why?'

'They're bleating about data protection.'

'I'll give them sodding data protection. We're the police.'

Sartori shrugged. 'Maybe Garramone's perv judge will grease the wheels?'

'Yeah, don't sweat it — once he waves his dick, they'll start singing.'

'I hope he's got a big one.' Sartori pulled his notepad from his pocket and flipped through a few pages. 'I've honed down some family background on Borghese. He doesn't come from money. His father was a low-level accountant, and his mother a housewife. Sure, they were comfortable, but nothing spectacular.'

'The mother's still alive, I think. Mrs Borghese mentioned her.'

'Yeah, living in Garbatella.'

'Decent area, but not exactly luxury.'

'It's not Parioli.'

'And Mrs Borghese's parents?'

'Even less spectacular. Her father was a farmer, her mother did odd jobs cleaning. God-fearing folk.'

'It seems to have rubbed off on their daughter.' Scamarcio scratched his palm, and studied the sheet of information Sartori had handed him. 'The highest salary on here is 40K. And looks like it's his current company that won't spill?'

Sartori nodded.

Scamarcio sighed. 'I want to see those bank records, and I want to see that salary. I want to see this giant leap of social mobility explained. I could understand it if Borghese was an entrepreneur, had his own company, but ...' he pushed a hand under his armpit, he needed to take a shower, '... all that for an employee. I don't know — it may be nothing, but my instincts are trying to tell me something.'

'You want me to ask Garramone to get his puppet dancing?'

'No, I'll do it. I need to see him about something else.'

'Fucking banks,' said Garramone, when Scamarcio was seated across from him. 'When I was young, they treated you with respect, wanted your business. Now it's like they're doing you some fucking huge favour holding your cash. And all that "too big to fail" shit — what bollocks — nobody's too big to fail.'

Garramone still looked haggard. His skin was grey and saggy, and his hair unwashed.

'Everything OK, boss?'

'Not exactly. But if I told you, I'd have to kill you, so let's just leave things as they are. I'm short on detectives as it is.'

Scamarcio smiled.

'So, you want me to get on to my buddy,' said Garramone as

he tapped at his keyboard and frowned.

'I didn't know you two were friends.'

'We're not, but that prick thinks we are. A couple of rounds of golf do not a friendship make.'

Scamarcio rubbed at an eyelid. He was bone-tired. 'I need it as comprehensive as possible. We may need to dive back in later for something else — you know the score.'

'I'll ask him to give you the works. It should allow you access to Borghese's entire banking history.' Garramone looked at him for a moment. 'You just want his?'

'Let's get the wife's, too.'

'Good lad. Are we just talking about bank records — I don't want to have to go cap-in-hand a second time.'

'Employer salaries, too. One of them's holding out on us.'

'Right.'

Scamarcio thought for a moment. His last major case came to his mind. It had ended with a trip to the stock exchange.

'Can we see if he holds other assets — shares maybe?'

'Shares is a longer job, but certain assets are doable. I'll add it to the request, and then we'll take it from there.'

'For the wife, too.'

'For the wife, too.'

'Hmm.'

'What's bothering you, Scamarcio?'

'Borghese has a mistress.'

'Ah.'

'If he's clever and he's hiding something, he may have used her.'

'Good thought. Give me her details, and we'll add her to the mix. But we'll have to stop there. It'll start to feel like a fishing expedition otherwise, and my guy will get antsy.'

'I thought you had his balls in your pocket.'

'I do, but they could still slip out at any time.'

Scamarcio grimaced.

24

TOMMASO POMBENI HAD CALLED just after lunch.

'Can you meet me? Not at my place though — there's a café on Via Civinini. Caffè Giò. I'll see you there in half an hour?'

'Has something happened, Tommaso?' Scamarcio fingered the plastic on a fresh pack of Marlboros and tried to stop thinking about Aurelia. She'd been playing on his mind all morning, and he felt guilty, but the more he tried to push any thoughts of her away, the more they persisted. Maybe it was something about being in the office — sitting at a desk allowed his mind to wander.

'Not on an open line,' said Pombeni dramatically. He sounded slightly breathless.

Not on an open line. Scamarcio mouthed the words silently and rolled his eyes. The boy thought he was in *Miami Vice*.

'I hear you,' said Scamarcio, gravely, deciding to embrace it. 'I'll see you in thirty. You'd better not be packing.'

'Packing?'

'Thirty minutes, Pombeni.' Scamarcio rolled his eyes again and cut the call. Still playing with the unopened cigarette packet, he turned his attention to the document Sartori had drawn up of Borghese's employment history. For the past twenty-five years, Borghese had worked for one pharmaceutical company after the next. He'd left Sapienza with a degree in marketing and communications, and had been taken on by an American firm called Delaware Pharmaceuticals as an intern. After six months, they'd offered him a permanent position, and he'd gone on to stay with them five years. Scamarcio made a note of the company's name — he'd run a search on them later. He noticed that Borghese's final salary was 65 million lire — around 35,000 euros in today's money. Good, but not spectacular. After Delaware, Borghese had been hired by a firm called Genesis Pharmaceuticals, but had only stayed for two years. Final salary, 74 million lire — around 40K. Most of Borghese's career had been spent with his current company, Arrow Communications, who specialised in providing marketing and media consultancy for various healthcare and pharmaceutical firms. He'd joined Arrow just before his son was born. Among the companies Arrow counted as clients were several European and US pharmaceutical businesses. Scamarcio typed the names of each of the companies into Google and had a look around.

The US firms seemed to have a presence in several European countries, including France, Italy, and Spain. They specialised in vaccines for influenza and cervical cancer, as well as drugs for epilepsy, prostate problems, and migraines. Their annual turnovers were around the 100-million mark. None of them were in the mega-league with the likes of Sanofi or GSK, but they all sat comfortably in the middle. Scamarcio searched some of the firms' drugs, but it seemed none had featured in the news — only a few trade periodicals. He noticed that the Italian Ministry of Health had chosen one of the firms, DC Pharmaceuticals, as their key supplier for epilepsy medicines and influenza vaccines — a huge contract which had seen the DC share price soar.

Scamarcio looked away from the screen and scored a dense box around the word 'epilepsy'. He wasn't sure why — he just knew it had figured in the early discussions of Andrea's condition. It probably wasn't significant, but he found himself drawing a second frame around the word, nevertheless.

He studied the wrapped box of fags — the perfect envelope corners, the smooth glittery lettering, the sheen of his desk light playing on the plastic. He picked up the pack and slipped it back into his shirt pocket. But two seconds later, he pulled it out again and tore it open.

He looked up and realised that Sartori was watching him. 'What number are you on?'

'I haven't been counting.'

'Start. You can't smoke around a baby.'

'Then I'll smoke outside.'

'Then you'll always be on the balcony, and your girlfriend will be inside doing all the work.'

Scamarcio inhaled, drew it deep into his lungs, waited for his synapses to sing back their response. 'You joined women's lib?'

Sartori gave him a pitying look, then slapped another sheet down in front of Scamarcio. 'Ninety grand.'

'You won the lotto?'

'Borghese's current salary.'

Scamarcio fell silent and cupped his nose in his hands. 'Again, good, but not spectacular.'

'I don't think it can explain a 200-square-metre apartment in Parioli.' Sartori chewed down on a nail.

'Or a Porsche.'

'That rat you smelled is starting to stink, Scamarcio.'

Scamarcio leaned back in his chair and swung around so he could see the window. He observed his own reflection in the glass. His face was tired and drawn, his eyes sunken. Beyond his distorted form, Via San Vitale was bleak and empty — the rain must have been keeping everyone inside.

'How come Arrow coughed up the info?'

'Our pervy judge has just been onto them, urging cooperation.'

'That's what I call good service.'

Sartori shrugged and followed Scamarcio's gaze to the street. As if from nowhere, a hard flurry of rain hit the glass, turning the world outside into a grey blur. 'It's bad when you can smell the corpse, but wherever you look, you still can't find it.'

'That's a recurring nightmare of mine,' muttered Scamarcio.

Sartori eyed him with concern. 'So, what now?'

'Our judgeship seems on the ball. Get back onto the bank, see if he's already ruffled *their* feathers. You might point out that it will look a hell of a lot better for them if they cough up the data before we slap them with an official order.'

Frog-boy was pale — well, paler than normal. There were dark rings beneath his eyes and a sprinkling of acne had broken out across his forehead. Scamarcio wondered if it was stress-related.

'So, Tommaso, how's it hanging?'

Pombeni took a hurried swig of Sprite and coughed when it went down the wrong way. He glanced around nervously. 'Did you come alone?'

'What?'

'I asked if you came alone.'

Scamarcio leaned forward. 'Pombeni, this is not *Law and Order*. Yes, I came alone.' He sat back in his chair and pulled a Marlboro from the pack. His lighter was refusing to respond, but Frog-boy leaned forward and helpfully produced one from his pocket. Scamarcio noticed a sketch of a topless woman on the front.

When Scamarcio was good to go, the boy said quietly, 'They threatened me.'

'Who?'

'Castelnuovo and that cunt friend of his, Jacobini.'

'Threatened you how?'

'I did as you said, tried to get Jacobini to talk a bit. After less than five minutes he calls Castelnuovo over — I hadn't realised he was around — and goes, "This guy's trying to make me grass on you." That's when all hell broke loose.' The boy lifted up his AC/DC t-shirt — his abdomen was a mess of bruises: purple, yellow, and brown.

Scamarcio breathed in quickly, but forgot to breathe out. 'Jesus,' he said after a moment. Then, 'I'm sorry.'

'I'm just a kid. There's some serious shit going down, and I don't want to find myself slap-bang in the middle of it.'

Scamarcio nodded. He was right, he needed to lift him out of this before there was blowback. But instead he said, '"Trying to get me to grass on you," is an interesting choice of phrase.'

The boy shrugged. 'I dunno if they'd be that stupid. But there's something else.' He was playing with a sachet of sugar, squeezing it, and the paper suddenly broke. The granules left a glittery trail on the table top.

Scamarcio frowned. 'Go on.'

'Just as I was about to approach Jacobini, I heard him on the phone to someone. He was trying to keep his voice down, but he was talking about Castelnuovo. He was bragging that he had him by the short and curlies — that Castelnuovo had fucked up big time, and that *he* had to help him out of it. Jacobini said he owned Castelnuovo. He said he'd own him for the rest of his life, and that he'd own his bastard politico parents, too. I waited for Jacobini to finish the call, hung about a few minutes and then I made my approach. But, like I say, he didn't want to talk to me.'

'After that call, I'm not sure he really needed to.'

Frog-boy's lower lip drooped. For a moment, Scamarcio imagined him on a lily pad, trapping flies with his tongue. 'Did I make a mistake?'

'No. You did right. You have any idea who he might have been talking to?'

'It could have been his girlfriend, Maura Valentini. He has another good friend Stefano — Stefano what-is-it?' He looked at

176

the ceiling, as if he hoped to find the name scrawled up there. 'Rosati! Could have been him.'

Scamarcio's mind whirred over the possibility of tracking them down, getting them to spill what they'd heard.

'And when Ale Castelnuovo came over, how did he seem?'

The boy's eyes clouded for a moment at the memory. 'Angry, obviously.' He fell silent for a beat. 'But what was different was that he wasn't his normal self. At least, he didn't give off the usual relaxed rich-boy air that nothing or nobody could touch him. If anything, he seemed a bit worried — stirred up.' He fell silent again, then added, 'Perhaps even scared.'

25

FIAMMETTA WAS LYING ON the sofa, her eyes closed, when Scamarcio walked in. Her long blonde hair had spilled across her cheek, and she was breathing in and out slowly, drawing long controlled breaths. Scamarcio's stomach flipped.

'Has it started?'

'It may have.'

'What does that mean?'

'It means I'm not sure.'

'How can you not be sure?'

'It hasn't been going on for long enough for me to know, but they feel like labour pains.'

'What should we do?'

'I don't think it's time to go to hospital. Let's just see how it pans out.'

Scamarcio hovered by her side. He didn't know whether to sit or stand. He had never been a big fan of waiting to see how things panned out. 'But it might all kick off — and we're not prepared.'

'It doesn't just *kick off* with first babies. It's a long process. If you'd come to the classes, you'd know that.'

Scamarcio let it ride. Those classes were more than he could have managed: work always got in the way.

'Don't bother to blame it on work,' said Fiammetta, breathing more quickly now, her eyes still closed.

'Can I get you anything? A drink?'

'No.'

'Something to eat?'

'I'm not sure that would be a good idea.'

'Shit,' said Scamarcio running a hand through his hair and starting to pace.

'What's the matter?'

'I just feel a bit useless. Do you want me to hold your hand?'

'No, not right now.'

He scratched his forehead. 'I think I might try to get some work done, then — get it out of the way while I still can.'

'OK.'

'You want me to stay in the flat or is it OK if I go out?'

She opened her eyes. 'Leo, I think it might be best if you stay.'

'Right. I'll just be in the kitchen making calls, then. Let me know if you need anything.'

She nodded and closed her eyes again.

He padded into the kitchen and took a bottle of Nero D'Avola from the rack. He tore off the foil, but was having trouble getting the screw into the cork: he couldn't make it grip. Then, when he'd finally pushed it deep enough, he couldn't pull the cork up. He swore softly and started again, trying to get his hands to stop shaking. When the cork was finally clear, he poured himself a large glass and sat at the kitchen table, which, as if for the first time, he noticed was greasy and pocked with stains of different colours.

He took a long drink. The lights of a thousand apartment blocks blinked back at him in the darkness, a thousand little lives in the eternal city, a thousand souls who had never asked to be born, but who were trying to make the best of it. Would his child be happy? Would it be grateful for the life it had been given? Scamarcio felt as if he was setting sail across an unknown sea without a compass; he didn't know if he could bring them all safely to the other side.

He picked up his mobile and dialled Sartori. He wanted to ask if the bank had finally given him access to the Borgheses' accounts. But the question was also an excuse. Sartori knew the ropes; he had four kids. It might be comforting to talk to someone who had been through this.

'Scamarcio,' Sartori was gruffer than normal, as if he wasn't too happy to have been disturbed. 'I'm still at the bloody bank. We're going through it all now.'

'Anything?'

Sartori exhaled, and it made a loud rattle down the line. 'It's looking pretty normal so far — for both husband and wife. Gennaro has around 30k in his account, and she has fifteen. The mistress is with another bank, Intesa, and she's sitting on around 70K — seems legit.'

'And none of them have other accounts?'

'Not with this bank, but I'm running a trawl on the others.'

'And the money in and out of Mr Borghese's is regular?'

'Yep, just his salary payments from Arrow, around the same time every month.'

'And the wife doesn't have anything coming in?'

'Nope, nada. The mistress does freelance work — translation. You see a thousand arriving every month or so.'

'She seems to have a good lifestyle. And 70K is a healthy little nest egg.'

'Inherited money — dad was rich. She put most of it in that property apparently.'

'You didn't spot any sign of shares, trading, anything like that?'

'Negative.'

'Maybe I'm barking up the wrong tree.'

'No, let's stay with it, Scamarcio. The Borgheses' apartment must be worth going on two million. It doesn't add up.'

'Thanks, Sartori. I'm glad you see it that way, too.'

Sartori fell silent for a moment. 'Everything OK? You don't sound like your usual self.'

'Oh.'

'What's the matter?'

'Fiammetta's in labour.'

'*What?!*' It was almost a shriek. 'And you're calling *me?*'

'I didn't know what else to do.'

'You should be with her, making sure she's OK, for fuck's sake.'

'But these first babies take a long time; it'll be hours until anything happens.'

'Not necessarily. First babies can take you by surprise, believe me.'

'Oh.'

'Scamarcio, don't take this wrong, but you need to forget about work tonight. Your family needs you. I'll hold the fort and let you know if anything breaks.'

'Right, then.'

'Keep it together, mate. It'll be OK.'

Scamarcio hoped he was right.

By 2.00 am, Fiammetta had decided that it probably wasn't contractions she was experiencing. By 4.00 am, she was quite certain it was indigestion. By 6.00 am, Scamarcio gave up on sleep and stood under the shower like a corpse trying to rise from the dead.

He was at his desk by 7.30, a fact not unnoticed by Garramone, who said he'd come in early for a meeting with the chief of police.

'To what do I owe this honour, Scamarcio?'

'Insomnia.'

'Try a glass of red before bed.'

'I tried several.'

'They do this magnesium stuff — mag-something — I found it helpful.'

Scamarcio nodded listlessly.

'You look like shit.'

'Fiammetta thought she was having contractions, then it turned out she wasn't.'

'God.'

'I just want it to come now. I can't take any more false alarms.'

'I bet.' Garramone tried to make himself comfortable on the corner of Scamarcio's desk, but looked awkward. 'Other news?'

Scamarcio filled him in on the bank accounts.

'And you're looking into other banks?'

'Sartori is on it.'

'Good.' Garramone paused. 'Trust your instincts, Scamarcio. They're sound — usually.'

With that, he rose with difficulty from his perched position and headed for his office.

'What if I've got two murderers?'

Garramone stopped and turned. 'What?'

'I've come across some intelligence that the politician's son, Castelnuovo, may have been involved in Andrea Borghese's death. But there is no link between Castelnuovo and Meinero — well, no link I'm yet aware of. It's possible I'm looking at two crimes.'

'But you can't think they're unrelated?'

'They might be.'

'No, Scamarcio. That's impossible — they have to be connected. They occurred just twenty-four hours apart.'

'That might not mean anything.'

Garramone scratched beneath a baggy eye. 'But Meinero was at the exorcism. And he had concerns about Andrea and the cardinal. You sure you're right about Castelnuovo?'

'No, I'm not.'

'Then work it hard, and then ditch it as soon as you can. There's no time left for you to take another false path.'

What did he mean 'another false path'? Scamarcio's jaw clenched. He'd been running this right.

As Garramone shuffled off, Scamarcio's desk phone trilled. He prayed that it wasn't another contraction — for real, this time. He realised that, for all his talk of being sick of false alarms, he still wasn't ready, and could do with a few more days to get his head together.

'Scamarcio.' It was an effort just uttering his own name.

'Detective.' It was a man's voice, middle-aged, educated, smoothed out by privilege.

'Who's calling?'

'That's of no importance. I just wanted to tell you to look at Zenox Pharmaceuticals.'

'What?'

'Maryland, USA.'

There was a click on the line, and Scamarcio realised that the guy had already hung up. He quickly punched the button for the switchboard. 'That call you just put through to me, can you trace it?'

'One second.'

Scamarcio waited. The one second was starting to feel like one hour.

Eventually the controller came back on. 'Dead end.'

'*No.*' He'd almost shouted it.

'Untraceable. Probably a burner. Was it a nark?'

'Of sorts.'

'Sorry, Scamarcio.'

'Don't sweat it.'

Scamarcio sank back in his chair. As far as he could remember,

183

the name Zenox had not come up in his previous searches. He googled 'Zenox Pharmaceuticals, Maryland'. The company's website was at the top of the results list. Scamarcio checked their Italian site and discovered that they were a medium-to-large-sized US multinational, who had been doing business in Italy for over twenty years. They specialised in drugs for prostate disorders, heart conditions, epilepsy, and cancer. They also made an influenza vaccine.

Scamarcio checked out some of their top brand names in Italy, but could find no smoke around them, no court cases or negative press.

He looked away from the screen and ran his hands across his eyes. Was there a link to Arrow Communications? Did Zenox use their services in Italy? Maybe he'd overlooked the name on his first search.

He repeated his previous steps, but there was indeed no mention of Zenox on the Arrow website.

He called Sartori. 'Can you get down to Arrow Communications and see if they've ever had any dealings with a US company called Zenox Pharmaceuticals?'

'Why?'

'I just got an anonymous tip-off.'

'Hmm.'

'When you've done that, can you see if any of Borghese's previous employers had any links or dealings with Zenox?'

'Affirmative. When do you need it by?'

'Yesterday.'

26

Scamarcio headed over to Parioli, feeling discouraged by the online brick wall he'd hit trying to find a link between Borghese's previous companies and Zenox Pharmaceuticals. He wondered whether the person who'd made the tip-off was really trying to throw him off track. He hoped Sartori might make more progress in his house-to-house visits to the companies themselves. Not everything appeared online, and if the relationship was old, it might have been consigned to the paper files. Wishful thinking, but he needed hope.

Pombeni had named two people Jacobini could have been talking to on the phone when he'd boasted that he 'owned' Castelnuovo — Maura Valentini or Stefano Rosati. A quick scan through Jacobini's phone records around the time Frog-boy had overheard the incriminating call revealed that he'd been talking to Rosati. Rosati lived on Via Carlo Allioni in western Parioli: a street lined with elegant baroque buildings. To Scamarcio, it still felt as if he was being distracted by a high-school melodrama when more serious clouds were gathering at the fringes of his investigation, but he knew he had to 'work it hard', as Garramone had advised.

When Scamarcio reached Rosati's house, his mother explained that her son could be found at the skate-park five minutes away on Via Dorando Pietri.

The first thing Scamarcio noticed was a group of youths in ridiculously wide shorts with flat black piercings through their ears hanging about by the skate ramp. They didn't look like goths — they seemed one branch up on the evolutionary tree.

'Stefano Rosati?'

A boy with a mop of blond hair hanging across one eye looked up. The other side of his head was completely shaved. 'Who's asking?'

Scamarcio flipped open his badge, and a murmur rippled through the group.

The boy took a long drag on his fag, squinting at Scamarcio through the smoke, then said, 'Follow me,' in a manner which seemed to impress his friends.

They walked twenty metres away to a bench pocked by dried bird dung. The boy took a seat and pulled out a dented pack of Camels from an enormous pocket. He offered one to Scamarcio, who took it. Anything to make his own pack of Marlboros last longer.

'So, you're here about Castelnuovo,' said the boy, drawing the smoke down deep and blinking into the sunlight. The first promise of spring was finally in the air, and Scamarcio removed his jacket.

'I just wondered what Jacobini had told you on the phone. I believe he was bragging that he had some kind of hold over Castelnuovo.'

'This is deep shit,' said the boy, letting the smoke escape through the gap in his yellow teeth. 'Deep, deep shit.'

'I'm aware of that.'

'No, I don't think you are.'

'Enlighten me, then.'

'Castelnuovo killed Andrea Borghese.' Just like that, no preamble, no notes of hesitancy.

'You sure?'

'He told Jacobini, and I'm not going to get myself in trouble with you guys by holding anything back.' He took another long drag and stared into the middle distance while he seemed to organise the facts, as he knew them, in his head. 'Castelnuovo had been to Andrea's flat to talk to him about Graziella. Castelnuovo knew that she had a thing for Andrea, and he wanted Andrea to call it off. Castelnuovo was used to getting what he wanted. When Andrea told him to forget it, he saw red and killed him. Castelnuovo has a fierce temper, always has done.'

'Killed him how?'

The boy waved a hand through the smoke as if the question were irrelevant. 'I don't know the details.'

'And this is what he told Jacobini?'

'Yes, he'd been drinking and confessed the whole thing. Jacobini now thinks he owns Castelnuovo and his famous family. Says he's going to use it.'

'What a nice friend.'

Rosati shrugged.

'Is Castelnuovo scared?'

Rosati took a long suck on the fag while he followed the progress of a female jogger in skin-tight lycra. 'Shit-scared. That's a first.' He smirked, as if the thought gave him pleasure.

Scamarcio wondered at the lack of remorse. Did these rich city kids not have souls? He'd encountered more morality down south.

'Did you know Andrea?' he asked, trying to make the Camel last a few drags longer.

'I made small talk with him once or twice, but no, we didn't hang out. He was too weird. You never knew if he was going to lose it.'

'What, lose it like Castelnuovo?' Scamarcio felt his anger rising.

187

The boy frowned through his smoke. 'I guess.' He stubbed out his cigarette on the ground, grinding it in hard with his pristine Converse boot. 'What now, then?'

'Well, if what you say is true, it looks like Castelnuovo will be heading up the road to Rebibbia.'

The boy shook his head sadly, as if some great injustice was about to be done. 'Fuck,' he whispered.

Scamarcio fixed him with a steely stare. 'In the meantime, I don't want you breathing a word of this conversation. I won't have you fucking up my timing. If I find out you've spoken to anyone about our meeting, I will charge you with obstruction, that clear?'

The boy frowned again, then nodded lamely.

'Give me that.' Scamarcio pointed to his mobile phone.

'What?'

'Your phone, give it to me.'

The boy held it to his chest as if it were part of him — a limb he couldn't lose. 'No way.'

Scamarcio reached across and ripped it away. 'I will be keeping this for twenty-four hours so you can't set the grapevine alight. Show up at the station on Via San Vitale tomorrow, and you can have it back.'

'I don't know where that is.'

'Buy a bloody map.'

Scamarcio rose quickly and stormed off. A cauldron of fury was seething in him. He wanted to punch the boy, teach him some respect for the dead.

27

JACOBINI WAS STRUGGLING FOR breath, his head hanging over the fence at the edge of the rugby field. He didn't look in shape for sport: there was a tyre of fat visible beneath his white t-shirt, and his pale legs were large and flabby. The coach was eyeing him with dismay.

'It's the smokes,' panted Jacobini as he removed his mouth guard. Scamarcio noticed a thin dribble of saliva running down his chin.

'What are you on?'

'About twenty a day.'

'I didn't mean the fags. What drugs?'

The boy said nothing.

'Sad to see a lad of your age reduced to this,' muttered Scamarcio.

Jacobini narrowed his eyes and turned so his back was now resting against the fence. He rubbed his sweaty forehead and looked at Scamarcio. It was a look that said, *You've caught me unawares, and now I have no cards left to play*. 'This Castelnuovo business is giving me sleepless nights,' he murmured.

Scamarcio was not surprised by the sudden candour. A visit from the police spelt trouble; events had quickly turned serious for fat boy.

'Why is that, then?'

'It's not a great feeling when you realise your best friend could be a murderer. It's disorientating. And then I keep thinking about

Andrea. That poor guy, his life cut short — and such a difficult life at that.'

Scamarcio exhaled and watched his own warm breath hit cold air. Finally, someone with a soul — or a very good actor. He erred towards the second hypothesis, given the way he'd shopped Frog-boy to Castelnuovo.

'You knew Andrea?'

'Not well, but I always felt sorry for him. He was constantly isolating himself from the world with his out-of-control behaviour, then trying to get back in.'

'The world didn't seem to make much of an effort to embrace him, as far as I can tell.'

Jacobini shrugged. 'Some people did; Graziella did.'

'And that was Castelnuovo's problem.'

Jacobini nodded. 'It was.'

Scamarcio wanted to smoke, but knew he'd have to offer Jacobini one, and that wouldn't look good in front of the coach. He bit down on a dirty stub of nail instead.

'So, what happened? How did Castelnuovo tell it?'

Jacobini turned to look at him, an earnest sadness in his small brown eyes that actually took Scamarcio aback. 'Castelnuovo arrives at the apartment, asks Andrea nicely to leave off Graziella. Andrea tells him to go fuck himself.'

'You think it was nice? The way Castelnuovo asked it?'

Jacobini raised a knowing eyebrow. 'I doubt it.'

'Go on.'

'They get into a struggle. Castelnuovo rams Andrea's head against the wall, and he passes out. Castelnuovo bends down to check Andrea's wrist, but he can't find a pulse.'

'He rams his head into the wall?'

'Yes.'

'And then what?'

'Castelnuovo freaks — knows he has to get out of there,

knows he has to run. Besides, he hears someone in the corridor.'

'Does he pass them on the way out?'

'I don't know, you'd have to ask him. Why, is that important?'

Scamarcio waved the question away. 'So, he just leaves?'

'He leaves.'

'And he doesn't call an ambulance?'

'No.'

Scamarcio fell silent.

In a small voice, Jacobini asked, 'It's murder, isn't it?'

Scamarcio sighed. 'Well, it would have been if he'd strangled him.'

'What?'

'Borghese was strangled. That's how he died.'

'Oh.'

'Would Castelnuovo lie about the way he'd killed him?'

'Well, no ... I mean, I don't know. Why would he, though? What would be the point?'

'Indeed,' repeated Scamarcio, his brain stalling, refusing to turn over.

'So, Castelnuovo was mistaken? He didn't actually kill him?'

Scamarcio reached for his pack of Marlboros and lit up. He couldn't give a shit about the coach anymore. He took a long desperate drag, and tracked the thin trail of smoke as it spiralled up into the evening mist. 'No, he didn't.'

Scamarcio had worked it hard, and it hadn't held. Garramone would be delighted, whereas he just wanted to roar at the darkening sky.

28

ALE CASTELNUOVO WAS NOT the same boy Scamarcio had met in the apartment. All the swaggering bravado was gone: the confidence, the jokes, the smirk. He had been reduced to a hunched shadow, small and thin and barely communicative.

'I want to know exactly what happened in that apartment, and I want to know now,' said Scamarcio leaning back in the rickety chair. He knew the chairs in the police interview suite were kept deliberately uncomfortable, but he didn't understand why that rule had to extend to those of the detectives, too. He took a sip from his small plastic cup of espresso and scowled.

'Why is Jacobini outside?' asked Castelnuovo in a tiny voice.

'Because I decided to keep him where I could see him until I'd spoken to you.'

'The fucker,' muttered Castelnuovo under his breath.

'It wasn't Jacobini who got you into this mess.'

Castelnuovo frowned and angled his rigid body even further away from Scamarcio.

'We can stay here all night if that's what it takes. I don't care, Ale. I really don't.'

Castelnuovo picked at his bloodied nails and blinked. He was thinking about it. Scamarcio heard the plastic tick of the wall clock marking out the seconds, then the minutes. He looked down at his gaping shirt, his scruffy cords, the scuffs on his shoes.

He remembered that he'd got dressed in the dark.

Finally, Castelnuovo said, 'I was jealous of Andrea, I admit it. I just couldn't understand what Graziella saw in him. And the worst part was that he seemed totally unfussed, which I guess just made her like him more.'

'So, you went around to his flat to talk to him?'

Castelnuovo nodded. 'That's all I wanted to do — talk. Believe me. I had no intention of getting into a fight. I had no idea he'd even be home alone. I guess I just wanted to say to him that, if he wasn't interested, could he at least clear the pitch so someone else could have a try. But his reaction was so out of proportion. He just got so angry, so quickly. Started screaming at me, saying how dare I come to his place, intimidate him like this. He seemed furious that I thought he wasn't interested in Graziella. He kept saying, "Why do you think that? Why do you think I'm not interested? Why do you say that?" His anger was so wild and disturbed, it was more like he was in a panic, like it was out of his control.'

Castelnuovo paused to take a long shaky breath. 'To be honest, I was getting quite scared. He did really seem crazy. Then, at some point, he got right in my face and put his hands on my neck, and I freaked. I thought he was going to kill me. So I pushed him hard against the wall, and he passed out.' Castelnuovo hung his head. 'But I really didn't mean to kill him. Believe me.' The last words were almost inaudible.

Scamarcio let out a long breath. 'You didn't.'

'I didn't what?'

'You didn't kill him. Someone else did.'

Castelnuovo's head jerked up, his mouth open.

'Did you hear anyone outside when you were in the apartment?'

'I heard voices, yes — that's why I was in such a rush to leave. I was freaking out, not thinking clearly. But —'

'Male or female?' Scamarcio interrupted.

'What?'

'The voices.'

'Male, I think.'

'Did you notice anyone on your way out the flat?'

Castelnuovo shook his head slowly, still dumbfounded. Then he stopped and looked at Scamarcio. 'Yes, I ...' he stuttered. 'There were two men hanging about by the elevator. They were wearing baseball caps and sunglasses. I thought they might be foreigners, staying in an Airbnb, that kind of thing.'

'Why?'

'They were dressed like tourists, and I think one of them was holding a map, but I can't really remember — it might have been something else. I didn't stop to take a good look.'

'Did they get in the lift with you?'

'I didn't wait for the lift, I took the stairs. I wanted to get out of there.'

Scamarcio sighed. It was less than useless as there was no CCTV inside the building or on the street that might help match these descriptions to someone.

'What will I be charged with?' asked Castelnuovo, his voice shrinking to nothing once more.

Scamarcio narrowed his eyes and raised his chin, defiant. 'Unfortunately, nothing, because Andrea is in no position to sue you for assault.'

Castelnuovo bowed his head in an attempt at humility.

'But I swear, Ale, as far as the police are concerned, your card is marked. If you ever try anything like this again, there is no way your arsehole parents are going to be able to pay your way out of it. We'll be watching, and we'll have you behind bars way before your dad has time to open his Gucci wallet. Got it?'

'Got it.'

'Now fuck off. I never want to set eyes on you again.'

29

SCAMARCIO KNOCKED BACK HIS second cappuccino of the morning and tried to convince himself that he wasn't exhausted. How would it feel to wake refreshed, for once, ready to tackle the day, rather than to live permanently with the feeling that you were dragging a huge weight around and constantly counting the hours until you could sleep. He knew the answer to his troubles lay in cutting out caffeine, but the thought terrified him — he didn't think he'd be able to put one foot in front of the other.

He left the bar and made the short walk down the street to the Italian offices of Zenox Pharmaceuticals. He'd told Sartori to leave this one to him. When Sartori had found no link at the Arrow offices between them and Zenox, Scamarcio had deemed it worth his while to visit unannounced.

The beautiful blonde at reception managed to muster an icy smile when he produced his badge. 'One moment, please.'

He took a seat on an expensive-looking leather sofa and admired the grey-and-chrome lobby. It created an impression of cool efficiency, rather like the woman behind the desk. After a few minutes, a good-looking guy in his early thirties strode over and extended a hand. 'Morning, Detective. I'm Giuseppe Conti from public relations.'

Scamarcio rose reluctantly from the sofa. 'That's all very nice, but it was the managing director I was wanting.'

Conti nodded as if he'd been expecting this. 'Sure, but can you fill me in a bit first? Our MD is a busy man, and if I walk in there unprepared, he'll eat me for breakfast.'

Scamarcio smiled. 'If you put it like that …'

'Let's go to my office. Can I offer you a coffee?'

Scamarcio's mind yelled, *No*, but he heard himself say, 'Thanks, that would be good.'

When he was seated across from Conti, opposite a vast window that offered a spectacular view of Parco di Villa Torlonia, Scamarcio said, 'I'm investigating the exorcist killing.'

'The thing that's been all over the news?' Conti sat up straighter in his chair, more excited than worried.

'Yeah, that one.'

The guy seemed to suddenly remember his job. 'But what's that got to do with Zenox?'

'Your company's name came up in the course of my investigation.'

'Came up how?'

Scamarcio pinched his nose and pulled his notebook slowly from his pocket. 'Maybe it's best if we start at the beginning — take things one step at a time.'

Conti opened his palms, as if to say, *Go ahead.*

'The father of the victim, Gennaro Borghese, works in marketing for drug companies — his firm is called Arrow Communications. You heard of them?'

Conti scratched his cheek. 'Yeah, I know Arrow. We don't use them, though — we have our own in-house marketing team.'

Scamarcio nodded and made a note. 'Is the name Gennaro Borghese familiar to you? Has he ever been employed by you?'

Conti shook his head. 'No. I've never heard of him, at least.'

'Hmm,' murmured Scamarcio. He tipped back the espresso

he'd been given. It was excellent.

'How long has your MD been in the job?'

'Twenty years.'

'Ah, finally my luck is changing.'

'Why?'

'He's the institutional memory I need.'

'Never heard of him,' said Ennio Burrone, his ski tan glowing in the morning light from his massive window.

'You quite sure?'

'One hundred per cent. I have an excellent memory for names.'

'Do you have a database of past employees?'

'Yes, but I'm telling you, he hasn't worked for us.' Burrone had the look of a predator — his nose was thin and hawk-like, his eyes glassy and dark, and his brows strong and arched. Scamarcio was glad he didn't have to do business with him.

'So why is your company's name coming up in my investigation?'

'Coming up how?'

Scamarcio said nothing and studied the to-and-fro of joggers and tourists in the park below: the silent interplay of lives, the absurd dance.

'I want your payroll data.'

'What?' Burrone arched a brow so high it looked like it would meet his hairline.

'Your payroll data.'

'But that's pointless — we've already told you we don't know him.'

'Yep,' sighed Scamarcio. 'But I wouldn't be doing my job if I didn't check. Don't make this harder than it needs to be, Mr Burrone. We both know that I can be back here with a warrant if I have to.'

'Oh, for God's sake.' Burrone ran a deeply tanned hand through his flop of silvery hair and picked up the desk phone. 'Get me the finance manager,' he said, the words taut with suppressed anger. Scamarcio couldn't be sure whether Burrone was riled by having his authority undermined in front of the young Conti or whether there was something more interesting at play.

After a few seconds, Scamarcio heard a low crackle on the other end of the line. 'Marco, can you prepare our payroll data? There's a detective from the Flying Squad here who needs to see it.' A pause. 'It's a long story — I'll escort him down myself.'

For a busy man, as Conti had claimed, Burrone seemed to be giving Scamarcio a lot of his time.

The finance manager was waiting in the doorway to his office when they arrived, his all-female team trying to look busy as Burrone passed. Scamarcio got the feeling they'd been told he was the fuzz. The man introduced himself as Marco Quercini. He was a tall dark-haired guy in his late forties. After he'd shaken Scamarcio's hand, he gestured to a computer with two large screens. 'Over there, Detective. It's all yours.'

Scamarcio walked over to the desk and pulled out his notebook.

'It's alphabetical,' Quercini added helpfully, as if Scamarcio couldn't work that out for himself. Scamarcio had expected he'd be there for the long haul, checking names that might have a connection to the Borgheses, so he had to look twice when he came across 'Borghese, Andrea' after just twenty seconds.

'Andrea Borghese?' he turned and looked at both men. Burrone seemed more mystified than worried. His finance manager looked like he was trying to trap a fleeting memory.

'Let me see,' he said, stepping behind Scamarcio and peering over his shoulder. 'That's a red entry, which means it was stipulated by our head office in the States. One moment — I'll need to ask one of my people.' He stepped out of the office, and Scamarcio heard him say, 'Debora, can you come in here, please?'

A short dark-haired woman with glasses hurried in clutching an A4-jotter and pen. She nodded nervously at Burrone before Quercini motioned her to the computer. 'Do you know anything about payments to an Andrea Borghese? They seem to have been stipulated by HQ.'

The woman squinted at the screen, and then brought a finger to her mouth. 'That comes out every month, I think — seven thousand each time. It's a payment Maryland requested.'

'Do we know what it's for?'

'I've never asked, to be honest.'

Scamarcio couldn't believe it worked like this. 'How long's it been going on?' he asked.

She looked up at the ceiling for a moment. 'Quite a while. I can check my records for you, but I think it's been at least eight years or so — the whole time I've been working here, anyway.'

Scamarcio leaned in closer to the screen. 'That number, next to the name — is it his bank account details?'

The woman tapped the screen with a long burgundy nail. 'Bank account number and IBAN.'

'But that employee code is wrong,' said Quercini, leaning over Scamarcio's other shoulder. 'It's only four digits; it should be seven.'

'It's always been like that,' said the woman.

'Can I have the computer a moment?'

Scamarcio moved out of the way for Quercini. He started pecking and scrolling through various screens. 'This guy is not an employee. So why is he on our payroll? Why haven't I noticed him before?'

The woman named Debora just shook her head vacantly. Burrone was starting to look irritated as well as mystified. The three of them were either extremely confused or they were all heading straight for Broadway.

'Who is this person, anyway?' asked Burrone. 'Detective, you mentioned a Gennaro Borghese, not an Andrea.'

Scamarcio thought he picked up a strange undertone in the way Burrone posed the question — it was as if he already knew the answer, but needed Scamarcio to say it.

'Andrea was the son, the victim. He was strangled,' he said, suddenly feeling as if he was delivering a line in a play.

A hush swept through the small office, and Scamarcio thought he saw Burrone blink. 'Impossible,' he whispered. But his tan lost none of its colour under the halogen lights, and Scamarcio failed to detect any chink in his managerial composure. For someone caught up in the middle of a major murder inquiry, Burrone was displaying remarkable sangfroid. Scamarcio wasn't sure if it was just art-of-the-deal training — a necessary trait for the job. What he did know, though, was that it bothered him. It had raised a red flag.

30

'IT'S A MATCH,' SAID Sartori, studying Scamarcio's computer screen. Burrone had requested some time to investigate their records and interview staff, but Scamarcio was due back there in an hour. Sartori tapped the screen triumphantly. 'We're definitely talking about the same Andrea Borghese. That's his bank account number. He was with the same bank as his dad.'

'Fuck,' muttered Scamarcio. 'Have they told you how much is in there?'

'No, I'll need Garramone to fast-track us another warrant, then I'll head straight down there.'

'Why the hell were Zenox Pharmaceuticals paying Andrea Borghese? What was the money for?' Scamarcio pulled the last Marlboro from its box. The cigarette was dented, with a tear in the filter paper. He'd sat on the pack by mistake. He tried to straighten out the tip so it was smokable, but then he just gave up and lit it. He closed his eyes.

'The answer to that is probably the answer to the entire investigation,' said Sartori, turning from the computer.

Scamarcio exhaled and watched the smoke wind its way to the office ceiling, scarred brown and yellow from years of similar abuse. 'I could kick myself.'

'Why?'

'Because I should have checked the boy's bank account to begin with. I did the parents, but not him.'

'Well, it's not the first thing that springs to mind. He wasn't exactly leading an independent life.'

'Yeah, I just wrote him off as a minor — but he was eighteen, an adult.'

'It doesn't matter. He was receiving payments for the past eight years, at least.'

'Yeah, but I should have thought it through.'

Sartori frowned and started pulling on his jacket. 'Don't sweat it. We're here now, and this smells like progress.'

'As soon as the warrant's in, call and tell me how much he's holding.'

Sartori made a silent salute then headed for the boss's office.

Scamarcio took another long drag and let the smoke escape through his nostrils. 'Assets,' he said out loud, causing a colleague at the next desk to turn and stare. Scamarcio scrolled through the contacts on his mobile and dialled the number for Dino De Blasi, an old university friend who had helped him on a case the previous year.

Once the pleasantries were out of the way, Scamarcio said, 'Dino, if I want to find out if someone's holding shares in a particular company, what's the quickest way to do it?'

'Maybe just ring around the big brokers — there are only a handful. If you don't get lucky with that you could try the asset services firms, they're the guys who administer the shares on behalf of the companies themselves. Again, there are only a few.'

'How much time would I be looking at?'

'A few hours, probably. Unless your guy's right under the radar.'

'Could you give me the names and numbers of these firms?'

'No worries — hang on a minute.'

As Scamarcio was waiting for Dino to return, he spotted Lovoti making his way to the coffee machine. 'Lovoti, come here,' he hollered. Lovoti did not look pleased to be summoned.

'What's the matter? I was on a break.'

'Not anymore.'

Lovoti just rolled his eyes at no one in particular.

'Stand by. I'm about to give you something important to do.'

Lovoti threw him a look which said, 'Don't patronise me.'

Dino De Blasi came back on the line, and Scamarcio jotted down the information. He thanked him and said goodbye.

'It's your lucky day, Lovoti. If you crack this, I'll stick a big gold star on your report card.'

'I'm not your performing monkey, Scamarcio.'

'Whatever. I need to find out if the boy, Andrea Borghese, held shares in any companies. According to a contact of mine at the exchange, if you call these brokerage firms, they'll tell you if he did. If you don't get anywhere with them, try these asset services firms below. You should have it done and dusted by tea time. Then you can go get yourself a nice coffee.'

'Warrant?' Lovoti cocked an eyebrow.

'See where you get without it. If they get shirty, Garramone will have one ready.'

'Is Judge Garibaldi still giving him a lap dance?'

'How do you know about that?'

'Everyone knows about Garibaldi.'

It was the first time Scamarcio had heard someone other than Garramone mention the name, and it riled him deeply that it had come from Lovoti. The prick always had to be one up on everyone else.

'Good luck, Lovoti. I'm counting on you.'

Scamarcio saw a look of confusion cross his brow.

The MD of Zenox Italia poured himself a large measure of Scotch, then placed it next to his blotter and stared at it.

'I'm not going to drink it,' he said, almost as if he was trying to convince himself.

'You're not?' Scamarcio shifted uncomfortably in his seat. He pulled a fresh pack of Marlboros from his pocket. 'But I *am* going to smoke these — that's if it's all right with you.'

Burrone waved the courtesy away. 'I used to be an alcoholic. I've been on the wagon for ten years. I stopped when it started to interfere with my work.'

Scamarcio felt wrong-footed by the candour, but tried not to show it.

'But you still pour yourself a Scotch?'

'I pour it at the same time every day. It's an act that I could not give up, a part of the routine I've allowed myself to keep.'

'But then what do you do with it? It looks like an expensive make.'

'It is — it costs sixty euros a bottle. I study the colour of it, the texture, the trace on the glass, and, most importantly …' Burrone picked up the tumbler and brought it to his nose, '… the aroma. The smell is everything.'

'I thought alcoholics did all they could to avoid the smell of alcohol.'

'Not this one.' Burrone set down the glass, then rose and took it into the bathroom next to his office. Scamarcio heard a tap running, then the quick suck of air as it closed. Burrone returned with the empty glass. Was it just a show? Had he drunk it? Scamarcio wondered.

Burrone sat back behind his desk, folded his arms across the blotter, and looked at Scamarcio expectantly. Scamarcio rested his cigarette in a chunky glass ashtray and coughed. 'Sir, why are you confiding in me?'

Burrone stared at him hard. 'Because I'm an honest person. Because I believe in telling the truth …' He let the words hang heavy on the air, as if they bore some secondary meaning —

some hidden message. Scamarcio just held his gaze. It was starting to feel like the OK Corral of stare-outs. Scamarcio wondered whether they'd make it to thirty seconds.

Burrone finally broke the silence. '… And I want you to know that neither myself nor my finance manager have any idea why our company was paying that boy.' He steepled his hands in front of his chest and began rotating his long fingers.

'I would have thought the finance guy would have been on top of all that stuff.'

'Marco has an enormous quantity of names and data to deal with — not just employees, but consultants, vendors, etc. It runs into the thousands. He can't be expected to know every entry in the system.'

Scamarcio tried not to frown. 'This payment that was stipulated by the States, didn't you notice the money was missing every month — if it came out of your budget?'

Burrone raised a finger. 'That's a good question, Detective, and that was the question that was bothering me. I asked Marco to explain it, and he's just found that the US had set aside a contingency — a kind of permanent fund for the boy's payments that we were holding. Debora knew about its existence, but doesn't recall who told her or who set it up in the first place.'

'And you believe her?'

'Of course. Why would she lie?'

'But you've been here all these years …'

Burrone shook his head slowly. 'Like I just told you, I had no idea. The fund could have been set up remotely. It's not impossible that the IT team in the States created it without us being initially aware.'

'But surely when they moved the money in …?'

'Marco has a vague memory of questioning HQ about a large sum that had appeared some years ago from America and being told not to worry about it. He was instructed to leave it where it was until asked — it wasn't to be touched or entered onto any balance sheet. Phantom cash, as it were. He says he had too much else going on to ever chase it up again.'

'So he took no further action?'

'He was just obeying orders.' Burrone shrugged.

'How curious.'

'I must admit that I also find it curious.'

Again, the emphasis he put on the word 'curious' made Scamarcio glance up from his notepad, as if he was supposed to pick up on some secret sign. But Burrone's expression remained inscrutable, the tan glowing. Scamarcio wondered if he visited a salon. 'Have you spoken to anyone in America about this?' he asked.

'I've tried to call Mike McCain — my counterpart over there — but I've been told he's on the golf course entertaining clients. I'm expecting him to ring back in the next few hours.'

'You know what?' said Scamarcio, extinguishing the spent cigarette and patting his pocket to check the pack was still there. 'I think I'll talk to him myself. If he doesn't call you back, don't chase him.'

'With respect, Detective, I'll do what the bloody hell I like. I run this company in Italy, and I need to understand what's going on.'

Scamarcio smiled and rose tiredly to his feet. 'Right you are, Mr Burrone — as you wish.'

'Fuckers.' Scamarcio slammed his mobile onto the plastic tabletop and took a long swig of chilled Ichnusa. He hadn't wanted to go back to the office and figured he could call the States just as well from the bar at the end of his road. He studied the frosty sheen on the neck of the bottle and thought of

Burrone and his strange addiction story — thought of the weird, unidentifiable something that niggled at him about the MD. He pressed redial for the fifth time.

'Detective, as I just told you, there's no one here to deal with your enquiry at this time,' said the whiny, nasal East Coast voice, slightly shriller and higher than last time.

'I find that difficult to believe. It's 11.00 am there — the office must be full.'

'But the people you need are out with clients. And, as I've now informed you many times, I will make sure they give you a call as soon as they're back.'

'Don't they have mobiles?'

'I can't disturb them at this time.'

'Not even for important enquiries?'

'I believe their mobiles are switched off.'

'You believe? Why don't you try to call them while I'm on the line? I have no problem holding.'

'I can't do that, sir.'

'Why on earth not? This relates to a murder inquiry, for God's sake.'

He heard a sharp intake of breath. 'I've been given strict instructions not to disturb them.'

'I think they'd want to know about this.'

Another dramatically laboured breath. 'I've sent an email message; they will call you back promptly, I'm sure.'

'Listen ...' But she'd hung up on him. Would she have hung up on the US cops, he wondered?

He laid his cell phone gently on the table and studied the passers-by. A beautiful woman with short brown hair hurried past, and he thought of Aurelia. The thought started in his head, but inevitably ended up in his groin. He took another long drink of beer and was about to leave and head home to Fiammetta, when Lovoti's name flashed up on his mobile.

'I should be so lucky, lucky, lucky, lucky,' sang Lovoti down the line, loud and cocksure. Scamarcio wouldn't have taken him for a Kylie fan. He looked up at the violet sky and decided to let him enjoy his moment.

'One million euros,' whispered Lovoti smugly.

'Is that what the hookers on Via Ostiense charge you for a hand job these days? Is there a penalty for syphilis?'

'Very funny. One million euros is the value of the shares held by your vic, Andrea Borghese.'

Scamarcio fell silent.

'Various companies, quite a few pharmaceuticals — including several US firms, which he traded on the exchanges over there.'

'He traded them himself?'

'According to the brokers, the dad did it for him.'

'Gennaro. Was this all money invested or did they turn a big profit?'

'Steady accumulation, according to the brokers — there were no fantastic investments with miracle returns, but the money was being invested regularly, and then allowed to grow.'

'Really good work,' said Scamarcio before he'd even realised he was about to say it.

'Gee, thanks, Scamarcio — a thank you from you is high praise indeed.'

'Credit where credit's due.'

'Sartori wants a word.'

He heard the phone being handed across and then someone mutter, 'Fuck off.'

'There's half a million in the bank account. Can't find any other accounts,' said Sartori as he took a loud slurp of something. Scamarcio guessed it wasn't an organic smoothie.

'Our victim seems to have been pretty rich for an eighteen-year-old,' said Scamarcio.

'Pretty rich for a forty-year-old …'

'Any other money coming into Andrea's account other than the Zenox payments?'

'Nope — just Zenox.'

'To have all that wealth in shares, those payments from Zenox must have been going on for years.'

'Yeah. You can ask Lovoti, but he told me that some of the shares were bought when Andrea was just a young kid — probably six or seven years old.'

'Six or seven years old,' Scamarcio echoed, his mind sticking on something, but he wasn't sure what. There was something about the age. How old was Andrea when his parents first noticed a change in his behaviour? He'd need to ask Mrs Borghese again. Maybe it wasn't even important, but, on the other hand, perhaps there was a connection here, a symmetry he didn't yet understand. He'd need a word with both Borgheses first thing tomorrow.

31

FIAMMETTA WAS DOING BREATHING exercises when he walked in, the enormous bulk of his child resting on her thighs. There was something almost obscene about it; it didn't even look natural anymore.

'How are you feeling?' he asked, wondering for the thousandth time how women could put up with this.

She stopped the strange breathing and shifted around on the parquet to face him. 'It's getting a bit much. It's starting to feel too heavy, now. My ribs are killing me.'

He bent down and kissed her forehead. 'I'm sorry, Fiammetta. I wish there was something I could do to help.'

'You could get me some fries and a burger.'

'Do we have any?'

'Would you mind popping out?'

'I've only just got in.'

'You just said you'd do anything to help.'

Scamarcio supressed a sigh. He just wanted to flop down on the sofa and relax. 'What kind of burger?'

'Double cheese with extra-large fries and ketchup.'

'Isn't that a bit greasy?'

'I'm the one carrying our child, so I'm the one who decides what I eat.'

Scamarcio put his jacket back on and cast his eyes to the

ceiling so he didn't have to look at her. Sometimes he noticed a new imperiousness to Fiammetta, a hardness he didn't recognise. He hoped it would pass once the baby was born.

The air was bitingly cold as he stepped back out onto the street. He felt a wetness against his cheek and realised too late that it was raining, but he couldn't be bothered going back inside for an umbrella. The nearest burger joint was fifteen minutes' walk, but on the plus side, at least it would give him the chance to smoke. The traffic on Via Venti Settembre sounded like it was tuning up for a fight. The rain was making people impatient. He watched as a rusty white truck rearended a black people-carrier. The drivers poured out onto the pavement and an 'in your face' argument ensued. He looked the other way.

He felt his mobile vibrate, and, through the raindrops, he saw Katia Borghese's name appear on the screen.

'Detective, you've got to help.' She sounded choked, as if she was fighting back tears.

'Has something happened?' He stepped into a small alleyway, where several pigeons were rooting around in an overturned dustbin. The arrival of two stray cats quickly saw them off.

'It's Gennaro — he came home briefly last night, but then he disappeared again.'

'You haven't seen him since?'

'He said he was going to work — he said he wanted to go to the office because he needed the distraction. But I called him there as I couldn't reach him on his mobile, and they said he hadn't been in all day.'

Scamarcio cleared his throat then swallowed. 'Katia, I don't know how to put this, but …'

'Oh, save yourself the trouble. I already called her, and she hasn't seen him either.'

'Was she expecting to?'

211

'She claims that he hasn't been answering her calls and that she hasn't heard from him in hours.' She paused for a beat. 'Unusual, apparently,' she added bitterly.

'And his mother?'

'She phoned me about an hour ago, wondering where he was — he'd promised to pop in on his way back from work.'

Scamarcio let out a quiet sigh. He noticed that one of the cats was making good progress with a chicken carcass. For a moment, Scamarcio felt like the one being mercilessly picked over.

'Where do you think he might be, Katia?'

'I've no idea, but I've got an awful feeling that it could be connected with this secret plan of his. I think he might be in trouble.'

Scamarcio held the phone away from his ear for a moment and tried to ease out a sudden crick in his neck. 'Listen, Katia, try to stay calm. One of my detectives is going to call you — you're going to need to give him Gennaro's mobile phone number and the service provider he uses.'

'Don't you have his number?'

'We do, but we need to double-check it with you, and we need the provider — do you know it off the top of your head?'

'I think it's TIM, same as me, but I'll find a bill so I'm sure.'

'Good. Once we have that information, we'll triangulate his phone — that means we'll try to identify the phone masts his cell most recently checked in with.'

'OK.'

Scamarcio thought for a moment, then said, 'I'm going to stop by your place. It might be best not to buzz anyone in until I arrive.'

'You think I'm at risk?'

'No, but it costs nothing to take a few precautions. There's something I need to do first — I should be with you in about an hour.'

'All right, I'll be waiting.'

Scamarcio hung up and exited the fetid alleyway. He was sorely tempted to ditch the trip to the burger bar, but he knew there'd be hell to pay if he did. He hurried up Via Venti Settembre, pushing past groups of confused-looking tourists, then swung a right onto Via Goito towards Termini, where he knew there was a McDonald's.

His heart sank when he saw the queue inside. Desperate times: he pulled out his badge and pushed his way to the front.

'What's going on?' asked an acne-ridden boy on the till.

'We think an armed criminal might have come in here — you seen anyone acting strangely?'

The boy looked terrified and started scanning the faces in the queue. 'No, I mean, I don't think so, but you know …'

'Listen, stay calm — we don't want to worry the customers. Just let me stand here a moment so I can survey the scene. To make things less conspicuous, could you fetch me a double cheeseburger and extra-large fries — I don't want to be noticed.'

'Sure, got you.' The boy hurried off, and Scamarcio saw him whisper something to a tall guy with a headset. He was wearing a shirt and tie and looked like the manager. After a moment, they both glanced furtively in Scamarcio's direction. Scamarcio turned away and cast his gaze around the restaurant, pulling out his mobile as he did so.

The boy was soon back with the food, the manager beside him. Scamarcio produced his wallet, half-expecting trouble.

'No, officer — it's on the house. Thank you for your service. We greatly appreciate it,' said the manager, handing him the big brown bag.

'That's kind.' Scamarcio waved the bag in the air. 'I'll remember this. The place is secure — he must have headed somewhere else. Sorry for the inconvenience.'

'No, we're just glad you checked.'

Scamarcio threw them a wave and hurried out, ignoring the angry stares from the other customers.

The strange thing was that, as he headed home, he thought he spotted a figure, or the shadow of a figure, darting down a side street: a ghost gone as quickly as it had appeared. Once again, he felt a chill hit his spine — it was almost as if his armed criminal had become real and was on his tail.

32

'GENNARO'S ALWAYS BEEN A hothead,' said Katia Borghese as she took a sip of something clear from a grubby tumbler. 'To be honest, that's what attracted me to him in the first place. Another guy tried to chat me up on one of our early dates, and Gennaro practically obliterated him.'

'You *liked* that?'

'What's not to like — a woman needs to know a man will defend her.' She shrugged a beat too late, and Scamarcio realised that she was drunk.

'How long will it take your colleagues to find him?'

'The phone companies are usually efficient when it comes to helping the police. I'm sure we'll get an idea in the next half-hour or so. Of course, if he's turned his phone off, it's another story.'

'No way to trace him?'

'We'd only be able to see roughly where he was when he turned it off.'

'God.'

'Try not to worry.'

They fell into a semi-comfortable silence, and Scamarcio decided to chance it. 'Katia, there's something I've been meaning to ask you for a while: why weren't you home that afternoon? Cardinal Amato said he called you to let you know they were leaving and you said you were on your way back. Did you get stuck in traffic?'

'My father, he …'

'Yes … I know he'd been taken ill.'

'Yes, he … Oh, to hell with it.' She took a long drink and then set the glass on the coffee table, precariously near the edge. 'My dad was fine to leave. He was comfortable by then, and his carer had already arrived — a lovely Filipina girl, two kids back home. You have no idea of the hardships those …'

'Katia, please.'

'Oh yeah, sorry.' She waved a hand through the air. 'You don't need to know all that.' She rubbed at the corner of her eye, her movements slow and uncoordinated. 'The truth is, there's no good reason why I wasn't home when my boy was murdered.' She was pale-faced with grief. She paused, lowered her head, and seemed to be trying not to cry. 'I'd had a very stressful morning, and I felt on edge: the business with my father just made it worse.' She stopped, took another drink, but held onto the glass and cradled it. 'I couldn't face going home. Andrea was often very calm, much better than usual, after the exorcisms, so I thought he could be by himself for an hour or so, until Gennaro got back. So I went to the park near my dad's and just sat on a bench for a while. I just wanted a few moments of peace. Some time for myself.' She hung her head, miserable.

Scamarcio leaned forward on the sofa. 'I think that's perfectly reasonable. Anyone would understand you need a break sometimes.' But what he was really wondering was what in particular had upset her that morning. He wanted to ask, but at the same time he didn't want to scare her into silence.

'Yeah, but if I'd been home like I was supposed to, Andrea wouldn't have been killed, would he?' Her voice fractured into a thousand pieces, and she broke into long powerful sobs.

Scamarcio waited, then said, 'Katia, you can't think like that. It's destructive — how were you to guess what would happen?'

'I know, but I feel like I always let him down — from start to finish.' The last words were lost to tears.

Scamarcio let out a long sigh. 'If you ask me, guilt is the ruin of us all.'

She looked up slowly, still sniffling. 'Catholic guilt?'

He shrugged. 'I didn't want to give it a name.'

She wiped her eyes and face with her sleeve, then picked up a piece of plain paper from the coffee table and started folding and refolding it. Scamarcio wondered what it would become.

'I think my faith is starting to shake. Something like this, well —'

Scamarcio's phone rang, and he glanced at her apologetically. He fished the mobile from his pocket, taking the opportunity to pull out his depleted pack of fags at the same time. He answered the call as he walked out into the hallway.

'We've placed him somewhere near Frascati, then the picture becomes a little blurry,' said Sartori, a low hum of excitement in his voice.

'What do you mean "blurry"?'

'His cell checks in with a few masts, then drops off the grid, then pings back in again three hours later.'

'Pings back in again where?'

'Frascati still.'

'What the fuck is he doing?'

'If you're with the wife, you should ask her if he has friends there, or family maybe.'

'Should I, Sartori? Thanks for the steer.'

'No need to get shirty, we're all tired.'

'I'm tireder than most.'

'No, you're not.' Sartori fell silent for a beat. 'Seems to me that while I'm with the phone people and can get my hands on Gennaro's call history, we should take a look.'

'Yeah,' said Scamarcio quietly, trying to sound reasonable

217

now. 'Do that. Run reverse searches on any numbers that stand out for frequency.'

'Sure.'

'Call me as soon as you've got anything.'

'Shall we alert Frascati?'

'Yeah, get his picture over to them. I'll stay with Katia and see if I can learn more.'

'*Katia* now, is it?'

'Fuck off, Sartori.'

33

SCAMARCIO WAS ON HIS way to the squad room, morning birdsong in the trees, when a little voice in his head told him to take a detour via the Vatican. Borghese, it seemed, was in Frascati, but if his wife was right, and her husband was planning some kind of revenge, it seemed sensible to alert Cafaro to the possibility. Scamarcio very much doubted that Borghese would try to harm an aged cardinal, but the threat provided a useful pretext for asking Cafaro about his work history. Scamarcio still needed to know whether his time at the Vatican had ever overlapped with the case of the missing girl Martina Cherubini.

When Scamarcio arrived at the gendarmerie barracks, the young policeman on desk duty threw him a look of disdain. Scamarcio ignored it and asked if the boss was around. The youth examined his badge for a few seconds longer than seemed necessary, then rose and muttered, 'Wait a minute.'

Scamarcio studied the walls and noticed a line of pictures of the gendarmerie corps with different popes throughout the years. He thought he spotted a young Cafaro with Pope John Paul II, which would mean he must have been in the corps at the time of the Cherubini disappearance. Scamarcio was about to scan through the list of names beneath the picture when a booming voice behind him made him jump.

'Scamarcio!'

He turned and saw Cafaro standing in the doorway to his office. It was as good an opportunity as any. Scamarcio pointed to the picture. 'This you?'

Cafaro frowned then walked over to the wall.

'Well spotted. I must have been about twenty-four at the time.'

'Did you like him?'

'Who?'

'Pope John Paul.'

Cafaro's frown deepened. 'Er, yes. He was a good man — decent, kind.'

'And Ratzinger?'

Cafaro turned to Scamarcio. 'I'm finding your behaviour a little odd this morning. For once, you don't try to slope in unannounced, and now you're asking for gossip about the popes.'

Scamarcio smiled. 'Can we step into your office for a moment?'

Cafaro nodded, his face marked with distrust. Scamarcio noticed that the desk officer was observing them both closely.

When they were seated either side of Cafaro's immaculate desk, Scamarcio said, 'This is a courtesy visit, really.'

'A what?'

Scamarcio cleared his throat and crossed his legs. He spotted a red-wine stain on his beige cords that he hadn't noticed when he was getting dressed. Cafaro, as usual, was pristine in his perfectly pressed uniform.

'Gennaro Borghese has gone AWOL, and his wife thinks he might have hatched some kind of plan to take revenge on his son's killer.'

'Why are you telling me this?'

'Gennaro blames the church, blames Amato. I don't quite follow the logic myself, but if the man is unhinged by grief, who knows where it might lead him.'

Cafaro pouted and scratched beneath his starched collar. 'Really, you think so?'

'I don't know. In my heart of hearts, I doubt it, but I thought you should know. Plan for the worst and all that.'

Cafaro picked up a round glass paperweight and weighed it in his palm. 'This is a fucking weird one.'

Scamarcio snorted. 'That's the first time I've heard you swear, Cafaro.'

Cafaro ignored him and shook his head, thinking. 'I mean, there's no way Amato did it: he's in his seventies ... he's a good man. None of it makes any sense.'

'I dunno, either, Cafaro. I'd be lying if I said I wasn't struggling.'

Given the surprising first hints of camaraderie, Scamarcio took the plunge: 'Talking about weird cases, were you here when the Cherubini disappearance happened?'

Cafaro carefully laid down the paperweight and stared at his empty blotter. Scamarcio wondered if he was trying to recompose his expression. If he was, he'd failed, because when he finally looked up, there was a new darkness in his eyes. Sorrow or fear — Scamarcio couldn't tell.

'That was a terrible thing. I can't imagine how her family have lived all these years with no answers. No closure.'

Scamarcio was taken aback by the humanity, by Cafaro's empathy. He knew Cafaro probably wasn't as much of a dick as he pretended, but this was more than he'd expected.

'Yes, it must have been dreadful for them.' What Scamarcio really wanted to say was 'You haven't answered my question', but he knew he just had to sit back and wait now.

A few moments of silence followed, before Cafaro said, 'I'd only been with the gendarmerie a year, and I was as low down the pecking order as you can get, but there were rumours ...' He broke off and looked up, and Scamarcio cocked an eyebrow. 'This off the record?'

221

Scamarcio nodded vigorously.

Cafaro sighed. 'Our boss back then — Filippo Battaglia — word was that he was into some nasty stuff. They said he organised parties for the diplomatic corps and that Cherubini may have been taken for one of those.'

'He'd taken her?'

'Oh, that wasn't really clear. He may have ordered someone else to take her, or he may have helped in the cover-up after.'

'Cardinal Amato commented on it, you know — to the media. I came across it when I was going through his press.'

Cafaro sighed again. 'I did know that. People here weren't happy. The thinking was that Amato should have kept his mouth shut — Vatican laundry should not be aired in public.'

'God, a child disappeared. There was a duty to speak out, surely?'

Cafaro frowned, seemingly perplexed. 'I'm just telling you what was said — I don't necessarily agree with it.'

'So, Filippo Battaglia …' Scamarcio stopped. He hadn't heard a knock at the door, but now realised that a massively tall, extremely broad man in uniform had entered the room.

'Ah, Battaglia,' boomed the hulk. 'Cafaro here was his protégé. Quite the golden child.'

Cafaro remained quite still, but Scamarcio could feel the air leave the room. A look of consternation crossed the stranger's face. He extended a hand to Scamarcio, more hesitant now. 'Sorry to interrupt. Alessandro Giuliani — Cafaro's deputy.' He turned to Cafaro. 'I heard you had the detective in here, but I needed to tell you that a security meeting has been summoned for 10.00 am.'

'Why?' There was colour in Cafaro's cheeks.

'Call from Interpol apparently — some new intel just in. It's the terror threat. Again.'

'If we respond to every terror threat that comes in, we'll spend our lives in security meetings.'

'Don't we already?'

'It's probably worth listening to. I was caught up in the siege last summer, and it was no joke, I can tell you,' offered Scamarcio, trying to ease the tension in the room.

'Yes,' said the stranger decisively, as if a puzzle had just been solved. 'I remember. Didn't they give you the medal of honour?'

'They did,' confirmed Scamarcio, ashamed.

'Blimey,' said the hulk. 'That must have been intense.'

Scamarcio tried not to remember. It still gave him nightmares. 'Not something I ever want to repeat.' He rose from the chair. 'You're busy, Cafaro, so I won't take up any more of your time. I just wanted to give you that heads-up.'

Cafaro finally looked at him, his cheeks still flushed, then rose to shake his hand. He stared at Scamarcio, as if he was unfinished business — inconvenient business. He seemed about to say something, then stopped. Instead, he murmured, 'I appreciate it, Detective. I'll put a guard on Amato's room — as you say, no harm in being prepared.'

His deputy's face formed a question, but Cafaro ignored it. 'Stay in touch, Scamarcio. Seems to me that you and I could work together better if we tried.'

Scamarcio smiled. 'I thought you might say that.'

Back at his desk, Scamarcio studied the highlighted telephone numbers on the sheets Sartori had given him. It would have been helpful if Sartori could have coded them for frequency: a sea of fluorescent yellow didn't mean much after a while. Scamarcio wondered if they could get the phone records in digital form and then ask Negruzzo to run them through a pattern-finding programme, but all that took time. It was probably simplest to just go the old-fashioned route for now.

Sartori had managed to supply a list of the numbers of frequently dialled friends and family — mother, wife, son, work, mistress, Gennaro's twin brother, who, despite daily attempts, they still hadn't been able to reach. Eliminating all these was painstaking work, and Scamarcio cursed himself for letting Sartori and Lovoti head out to Frascati. *He* could have been there, enjoying the views, while they sifted through the minutiae.

After thirty minutes of scoring through digits with a pen and ruler, Scamarcio glanced out at the windswept vista beyond his window. The trees were bare and scarred, the pavements black and cold. Summer felt like an ever-fading figment of his imagination.

'Battaglia's golden boy.' The words had been chasing each other around his head ever since his meeting with Cafaro. Did it mean that Cafaro could have been involved in the Cherubini case? Did it mean Cardinal Amato knew that? Or did it mean nothing at all? Cafaro might have been a favourite of the boss, but it didn't necessarily follow that he would have taken part in Battaglia's extracurricular activities. Scamarcio almost wished he hadn't found out about the link. It didn't feel helpful.

He rolled his head and tried to click out the stubborn knot in his neck. When he glanced back down at the papers, the figures had finally stopped swimming. Once relatives, mistresses, and the rest had been eliminated, he was just left with four highlighted numbers. The simplest option seemed to be to call them. He tried the first.

'Desert Orchid,' answered a sing-song foreign voice. She sounded Asian — Thai, maybe, or Filipina.

'Are you a restaurant?'

'No, darling, not a restaurant.'

'A shop?'

'Depends on your definition of shop.'

'I don't follow.'

'I think you are having wrong number, darling.'

'No, wait, don't hang up.'

'You just embarrassed maybe?'

'Ah, yes, that's it. I'm embarrassed. A bit shy.'

'Don't worry, darling, many are. You want to make appointment?'

'An appointment, yes.'

'What for, darling?'

'What are the options?'

'There's whole night, three hours, an hour, thirty minutes. All depends on what you're looking for?'

'Blow job,' Scamarcio chanced.

'Oh, OK — for that you can just walk right in.'

Scamarcio sighed and cut the call.

The next number appeared to be a telephone banking service. The bank was the same as the one they had for Borghese, so no surprises there. Scamarcio tried the third number. 'Giovanni De Luca's office,' answered a woman with a Milanese accent.

'Oh, excuse me, I'm not sure I have the right number. Could you tell me where I've come through to?'

'This is the office of Dr Giovanni De Luca, director-general of the National Pharmaceutical Service,' said the woman impatiently.

Scamarcio frowned. 'The pharmaceutical service of the Ministry of Health?'

'Yes.'

'Here in Rome?'

'Yes. Who is this?' Her irritation was plain.

'I'm sorry, I do have the wrong number. Apologies for wasting your time.'

He hung up and stared at the wall. Why had Borghese been calling the National Pharmaceutical Service so often? Was it for work?

He looked back at the sheets of paper. Sartori had obtained records going back six months. Scamarcio studied the dates of the calls to the pharmaceutical service. They all seemed to fall around the beginning and the middle of each month. He went further and further back, checking whether the pattern held. It did.

He dialled Sartori. 'I need you to get Borghese's call history for the last five years.'

'Five years?'

'I've seen something. Get onto the phone people ASAP — ask them if they can send the stuff digitally. Soon as, Sartori.'

Scamarcio hung up. There was one number left to try — a mobile. He dialled. The office was quiet, and his pulse hammered in his ears as he waited for whoever it was to pick up.

'Benedetti,' snapped a gruff voice.

'Sorry, is this Lorenzo Benedetti?' Scamarcio tried.

'Eugenio Benedetti. You've got the wrong number.' He hung up.

Scamarcio opened Google and typed in the name, but he already knew who he'd just spoken to — his instincts were telling him it was so. The first result was a Wikipedia entry. Scamarcio clicked on the link.

'Eugenio Benedetti, Italian Secretary of State for Health. DOB: 24 July 1967. Member of the Partito Democratico.'

Scamarcio returned to the list, his fingers running down the numbers. He checked the times against the calls to the director-general of the pharmaceutical service. The calls to Benedetti were made on exactly the same day, and were also twice monthly. They didn't last long — no more than five or ten minutes. The ones to the pharmaceutical service ran to fifteen, twenty minutes sometimes.

Scamarcio rested his head against the back of his chair and ran his biro-stained fingers through his hair. Why would someone doing drug-marketing have a direct line to the health secretary?

That they might call the pharmaceutical service seemed slightly more probable, although the fact that Borghese seemed to be speaking to the director-general himself gave him pause for thought.

Scamarcio brought a fist to his mouth. A picture was starting to form that he didn't much like. It was the spider's web again: fine and intricate; taut and deadly. It would only spell trouble for him and the department.

34

SCAMARCIO WAS DIALLING NEGRUZZO in Tech, when, over his shoulder, someone said, 'Isn't telepathy wonderful?'

Negruzzo was standing there in a wash-faded Comic-Con t-shirt with a flaky picture of Chewbacca on the front. He seemed pleased with himself.

'Have you guys mastered teleportation as well now?' said Scamarcio, slightly unsettled.

'Nearly there, give or take a few months.'

'I was just about to ring you.'

'Yes, I saw you dial. Hence my comment about telepathy.'

'I'm about to get five years of mobile records. I'll need to run a search through them, looking for two numbers. But I need to be fast.'

'Piece of piss,' muttered Negruzzo, shifting his weight from one foot to the other. He seemed to want to move onto something more interesting. 'You could do it yourself from here.'

'What brings you out of the cave, then?'

'I cracked your vic's iPhone.'

Scamarcio had almost forgotten about the phone. 'Oh, good work.'

'Not really, it took me longer than anticipated.'

'Don't sweat it. I'm not even sure it's crucial.'

'You may want to rethink that.'

'Don't tease me, Negruzzo.'

'I'm not.' He handed over Andrea Borghese's phone and said, 'The password was "Sexypriest".'

'Was what?' Scamarcio swivelled round in his chair to face him.

'"Sexypriest". Seems to me that if you've got a cardinal and a dead priest involved in this inquiry, that particular choice of wording may yet prove significant.'

'Jesus.'

'"Caligula", "Sexypriest" ... there's a story there.'

'The only priests Andrea saw were men.'

'The only priests in the Catholic church are men.' Negruzzo scratched at a temple. 'I don't want to tell you how to do your job, but I think you may need to consider the possibility that your victim was gay.'

Scamarcio closed his eyes. 'Of course. *He never wanted to take things to the next level.*'

'What?'

Scamarcio's mind flashed on Meinero's anger during the exorcism. He'd already picked it for jealousy, it just hadn't occurred to him that Andrea might reciprocate Meinero's feelings. It had been there all along, but he'd missed it. He wanted to punch the wall.

Negruzzo was observing him, rather like a scientist might observe a rat during an experiment. 'Scamarcio, you can't be expected to know everything from the get-go. That's why you have a team. That's why it's called *detective work*. Cut yourself some slack.'

Scamarcio pulled his Marlboros from his pocket and waved them at Negruzzo, who glared at the pack as if it were radioactive.

'Don't touch the stuff.'

'Good for you.'

'When you get those numbers, send them my way and I'll sort it.'

'Thanks. And thanks for this.' Scamarcio hefted the iPhone in his hand.

'You don't actually look grateful, Scamarcio.'

'It's just another new layer of complication, isn't it?'

'Nature of the game.'

'Nature of the game,' Scamarcio conceded.

His journey through the contents of Andrea Borghese's phone had given him a full-blown headache. Scamarcio reflected that it was not the kind of sharp headache you got from the exhaustion of a successful search, but the persistent, dull, throbbing kind that came from over an hour's worth of frustration.

Despite the promise of the password, the phone itself seemed to hold little of interest. Andrea's emails were mainly of the circulars kind — he hadn't seemed to communicate with anyone who was actually a human being. Another insight into Andrea's life that saddened Scamarcio. Andrea's Instagram and Twitter accounts were largely inactive and his documents dull and schoolwork-related, although Scamarcio did come across an interesting essay on Caligula. The boy's photos were mainly of the family cat, an obese mud-brown creature that seemed to smirk sarcastically, with a couple of the girl Graziella holding it. Scamarcio wondered if she came to the house often, and if she'd visit when the parents were out. He checked the Google Drive for further photos and documents, but as expected, Andrea had left nothing there — he was either worried about privacy or didn't have anything to store. He laid down the phone and was about to step out to the pharmacy to buy something for his headache when his mobile rang.

'Some woman thinks she spotted Gennaro Borghese in a bar on the outskirts of town.' Sartori's heavy breathing on the line made Scamarcio worry. 'That was almost twenty-four hours ago now.'

'What's he playing at?'

'Maybe he's done something awful and is hiding out.'

'We've not heard about something awful.'

'The connection might not be obvious yet.'

'Anything awful happened in Frascati, Sartori?'

'No'.

'Or there's another possibility,' said Scamarcio.

'What's that?'

'Maybe he's scared. Maybe he's worried the same people who killed his boy will come for him.' Scamarcio started drumming the edge of his desk with a cracked biro. 'You guys need to find him — we can't have another death.'

'We're trying, Scamarcio, believe me.'

Scamarcio's email pinged. 'The phone records are in.'

'They're quick, I'll grant them that.'

Scamarcio opened the email from the phone company and started downloading the attachment. When it had loaded, he said, 'If my pattern holds, we're looking at trouble.'

'Care to fill me in?'

'Just let me talk to Garramone first.'

Sartori tutted like an old Rimini fishwife. 'Jesus, Scamarcio, I don't get the need for the cloak-and-dagger all the time. We're on the same side.'

'I don't trust Lovoti.'

'Then I won't tell him.'

'I can't take that risk, Sartori.'

Scamarcio hung up — he didn't have time to be pussy-footing around people's feelings.

'I can see you now,' shouted Garramone from his office doorway. Scamarcio patted down his jacket, which he'd tossed across the back of his chair, and extracted his fags and the pack of ibuprofen he'd just bought at vast expense. The price of drugs never ceased to appal him. In the US, it would have cost him 70 per cent less, but, then again, they had this thing called 'competition' over there. Years ago, Italian pharmacists had neatly formed themselves into a hermetic little lobby, which allowed them to charge the earth for the most basic of medicines. Scamarcio popped out another tablet from the blister pack and washed it down with cold coffee.

'Coming.'

He shut the boss's door gently and threw the huge bundle of phone records onto his desk. Normally, this point in a case would have marked a moment of triumph, but Scamarcio just felt debilitated and anxious.

Garramone seemed to pick up on his mood and said quietly, 'Take a seat.' He steepled his hands in front of his mouth and studied Scamarcio carefully. He didn't look impressed by the wine-stained cords. 'Why do I have the feeling you're not bringing me good news?'

'Experience.'

Garramone sighed and drained the last of the water from the plastic cup on his desk. He tossed it expertly into the bin, and then leaned back in his chair. 'OK, hit me with it.'

'I've got five years of phone records that show Gennaro Borghese was calling first the director-general of the pharmaceutical service and then the secretary of state for health twice a month. I've got a stack of bank records that demonstrate that, despite an annual salary of less than 100k for his entire career, Borghese has managed to squirrel away over one and a half million euros in cash savings and shares — all in his son's name.'

Garramone pulled out his top lip and stared at Scamarcio hard.

'I've got monthly payments of seven thousand euros passing to our victim, Andrea Borghese, from Zenox Pharmaceuticals, going back at least eight years, but I suspect longer.'

'Any connection between Borghese's marketing company and Zenox?'

'None that I can find. And I've checked thoroughly.'

Garramone stroked his chin. 'So, what exactly are we looking at?'

'Perhaps you know what we're looking at; perhaps you've seen it before.'

When Garramone said nothing, Scamarcio continued: 'Gennaro Borghese was doing some kind of clandestine work for Zenox; they were paying him on the side for something that had to do with the health secretary and the pharmaceutical service.'

'He was moonlighting?'

'Yes.'

'And Zenox might have had a hand in Andrea's death?'

'It's a possibility we need to consider.'

'But why?'

'Maybe they needed Gennaro to keep a secret. Maybe they wanted to send him a warning of some kind.'

'What drugs do they make?' asked Garramone, unmoved.

Scamarcio consulted one of his print-outs. 'In Italy, they sell medicines for epilepsy, prostate problems, heart conditions, and cancer. They also make a flu vaccine, I believe.'

'Have you found any negative press around any of these drugs?'

'None to date, but my search hasn't exactly been extensive.'

Garramone flopped his head against the back of his chair and studied the ceiling. 'I'd like to tell you that you're clutching at straws …' He fell silent. 'But the money and the calls — undoubtedly there's something there, the question is what.' He frowned. 'As much as I want to, I don't think we can walk away from it.'

'Neither do I.'

Garramone let out a long sigh and placed a hand on his desk phone. 'I'll need to inform Chief Mancino, and then I'll probably have to alert the financial police.'

'How will they want to proceed?'

'They may want to do a wire tap first, they may not. If a judge is convinced, and if they can find one that isn't bent, I imagine they'll be raiding the homes and offices of the health secretary and his pal at the pharmaceutical service. It's probably wise for you to give Borghese's place the once-over first to see if there's any extra evidence there. That might help matters with the judge.'

'Aren't you going to use your usual guy?'

Garramone shook his head firmly. 'No, it's time to cut him loose. I wouldn't trust him as far as I could throw him on this. Besides, the finance police probably have their own judge on call.' He paused for a moment to scrawl something on the notepad in front of him. But the biro wasn't working and he had to root around in his desk drawer for a new one.

'What you and your team need to do now is compile a comprehensive list of which Zenox drugs are licensed in Italy and *when* they were licensed. Does the timing match up in any way with the calls placed by Borghese? We also need to look at whether the licenses are proportionate to Zenox's usual market share in other countries — are they somehow getting a bigger slice of the pie in Italy? These will all be elements we need if we're to build a convincing case.'

'Sure,' said Scamarcio, feeling overwhelmed by the scale of it all.

'This needs to be a tight ship, Leo. Not a word to anyone for the time being.'

'Of course.'

Garramone bowed his head sadly. 'When will it ever end?'

Scamarcio wanted to say 'It won't', but really, what was the point? Garramone knew. The tumours would just keep multiplying; corruption was not a disease you could cure overnight, or in one generation, or even two. They could all

234

dance around the subject as much as they liked, but the bottom line was, they were fucked. Unless the people bothered to get off their backsides and take to the streets, Italy was fucked. Anyhow, the way Scamarcio saw it they all deserved to be screwed. Apathy was the greater sin here.

'Regarding our other victim — Father Meinero,' he said, attempting to tune his mind to more productive thoughts, 'I'm working on the theory that he perhaps saw something he shouldn't have — maybe he'd left something at the flat, had gone back to retrieve it, and had walked in on the killers? That would explain his fear and hesitancy when I met him.'

'Would it explain why he was murdered?'

'Yes, if they wanted to keep him quiet.'

'But that strange hanging?'

'Don't forget the banned drug in his system. The Zenox people would have ready access to substances like that.'

'Hmm. Good point, but doesn't organised crime sometimes use dodgy meds? They sell contraband.'

Scamarcio remembered that Giangrande had mentioned the same thing. 'On occasion.' He paused. 'There's one other discovery I've made, and it doesn't exactly slot nicely into all this.'

'Tell me.'

'I think Meinero had the hots for Andrea Borghese, and it may have been reciprocated.'

He watched Garramone's thick eyebrows merge in surprise.

'Tech cracked Andrea's iPhone password — it was "Sexypriest".'

'And from that you deduce that he was in love with Meinero?'

'No, not just from that. But I've got a girl who was keen on Andrea saying that he never showed any interest in her. I've also got Meinero caught on camera during the exorcism session looking extremely jealous.'

'You need more than that.'

'I've …' Scamarcio stopped. His mind skipped over the useless iPhone, then, for some reason, settled on Father Meinero's body hanging in the hotel bathroom: the muscular torso, the arm, the hand. There was something about the hand — what was it? It was bare, no jewellery. Why? Why hadn't Meinero been wearing the watch and the ring that were in the CSI pouch? Surely, the CSIs would have known *not* to remove the jewellery, that they should leave it in place. But Scamarcio now realised that he had to double-check this, and probably should have done so earlier. He thought back to the ring in the bag — a simple gold band … *a bit like a wedding ring*.

'Oh …'

'What's the matter?'

'I think I might have something else. I'll need to make some calls and let you know.'

'OK, whatever,' said Garramone, raising a tired hand to his temple, 'but we need to clarify our angle. Does the fact that Andrea and Meinero might have been in a relationship have any bearing on your theory that the drug company may have killed them?'

'No, not really — only in the sense that it could explain why Meinero might have gone back after the session to see Andrea.'

'Do we know for sure that Meinero went back?'

'No, it's still just a theory at this stage.'

'Did you check CCTV on the street?'

'Yes, the camera was down that afternoon.'

'Another faulty camera? Wasn't the one at Meinero's hotel down, too?'

'Yes. The chances of this being a professional job seem high.'

'I'm inclined to agree, Scamarcio.'

'But I've still got two orphan elements: one is the stack of childhood photos of Andrea that Cardinal Amato had in his rooms.'

'He could have been preparing to write a book, like the mother claimed.'

'Yeah, but aren't photos the last stage of the process, rather than the beginning?'

'Maybe he was using them for inspiration.'

Scamarcio shrugged. 'The second is Chief Inspector Cafaro of the Vatican gendarmerie.'

'What the fuck does Cafaro have to do with anything?'

'When I was looking into Cardinal Amato, I found out that he had spoken to the press about the Cherubini case. He expressed his belief that she may have been seized by someone from the gendarmerie who was organising sex parties for the Vatican diplomatic corps.'

Garramone whistled softly. 'Amato said that?'

'He did.'

'But what does that have to do with Cafaro?'

'Cafaro was in the corps at the time, twenty-four years old and a favourite of the boss, Battaglia. It's Battaglia who Amato implicated in his comments.'

'But just because Cafaro knew Battaglia doesn't have to mean he was involved.'

'I know.'

'And why is this relevant anyway?'

'If Cardinal Amato has dirt on Cafaro — has some kind of hold over him — then Cafaro might have felt the need to help him cover up a crime all these years later.'

'Bullshit. Anyway, there is no crime. You've just told me your theory lies with Zenox Pharmaceuticals.'

'It does, *for now*. But in my experience, it pays to keep conflicting theories alive until the final stages.'

'Your experience is still relatively short, Leo. I didn't want to say this before, but I think there's been way too much fuzziness. You need to start working one specific angle, otherwise we won't cross the finish line. Forget Cafaro and Cherubini. It's a minefield.'

Scamarcio's felt his heart begin to pound and a small pulse fire in his head. 'Forget it because it's a minefield or forget it because it doesn't hold?'

'Both!' shouted Garramone, exasperated. 'You've finally come up with a working hypothesis, so run with it. It's one fucking huge headache of a hypothesis, anyway, and we really haven't got time to be wetting our pants about anything else.'

Scamarcio tried to keep his voice from trembling with anger. 'Oh, so sorry to have brought you such an inconvenient discovery.'

Garramone sighed. 'No, you're not. You love rooting out this country's moral decay.' He sounded properly on edge now.

'Actually, I don't. I'm fucking sick of it.' Scamarcio rose, stuffing his crumpled stack of papers under his arm. His heart was hammering now, and his fist was about to take on a dangerous life of its own. He headed for the door.

'Leo!' shouted Garramone, but Scamarcio didn't turn. He was fed up with the rough and tumble, the politics. What was the fucking point of the job? What was the fucking point of him?

He'd never change a thing.

Aurelia had agreed to meet at her flat. She still had the old place with the pink stucco walls and flower boxes. Scamarcio felt sad memories stir as he took the stairs. How many times had he come here after the Cappadona attack, trying to reach her, trying to get her to talk? How many times had he failed?

He knew that he was probably about to make the biggest mistake of his life, but he didn't care. There was a mad anarchy running amok inside him; he felt like an arsonist about to set his world ablaze. He wanted to cast everything to the wind and just live. The rest of it was farce, a stilted comedy of manners, and he couldn't be bothered playing his role anymore. It bored him. Deeply.

Aurelia was standing in the doorway when he reached her floor. She read his expression and looked startled. 'Everything OK, Leo?'

He didn't answer. He just strode towards her and kissed her like he'd been wanting to kiss her ever since he'd seen her that first day. He didn't know what he'd been expecting, he hadn't even thought about it, and when she kissed him back and drew him into the flat, he felt no surprise. It was primordial, this thing between them. It had to *be*.

A long time later, when it was finally over and she was standing by the window, looking out at the pale wintry dusk, he said, 'I love you.'

'No, you don't.'

'Don't tell me how I feel.'

She stood quite still, her eyes fixed on the darkening rooftops, as if she was determined to catch the very moment it all turned to night. Eventually she said, 'Why do I already know that you loving me will count for fuck-all?'

'You can't know that.'

She sighed. 'Scamarcio, even you don't sound convinced.'

'Aurelia, I want to work this out.'

'You won't work it out. Or not in any way that benefits me. I know you, Scamarcio. Perhaps even better than you know yourself.'

He couldn't think of a reply.

She turned from the window, her eyes blank and cold. 'I'd like you to leave now, and then I never want to hear from you again.'

35

To Scamarcio, it felt as if someone had kicked him in the stomach then ripped his heart out from between his ribs. He was winded by grief and a searing longing that he thought would never leave him. He reflected bitterly that none of this left much room for remorse about the terrible betrayal he had just committed towards his pregnant girlfriend. Truth be told, he could no longer like himself — he was a selfish arsehole, a philanderer, a liar. What he really deserved was to be left by both of them. But just the thought of splitting from Fiammetta made him nauseous. He couldn't lose his kid, he had to have his kid. He wondered for a moment if he should confess, tell Fiammetta what had happened. But that crazy idea filled him with a different kind of panic — a panic that the stress of it all would harm her and hurt their unborn child.

No, he'd fucked up, and now he needed to swallow the misery he'd created all on his own. It would be a lonely meal for one.

The wind was starting up, and he thought he felt the first spots of rain against his skin. Or were they tears? He tried to hail a passing cab, but the driver ignored him, even though he wasn't carrying any passengers. Scamarcio rooted around inside his jacket for his smokes, but when he pulled out the pack, it was empty. Why hadn't he just thrown it away? What was wrong with him?

He spotted a newspaper kiosk up ahead, but when he reached it, the guy was already winding down the shutter. Scamarcio peered through the gap into a thin chink of light, but couldn't see the man's face in the darkness. 'You got any Marlboros back there?'

'Till's closed.'

'Come on, give a guy a break. I'll pay you double.'

The man hesitated for a minute, then threw a pack through the hole. 'On the house. Anyone that desperate deserves my sympathy.'

Scamarcio laughed. It felt strange hearing his own laughter echoing out across the cobblestones, and he realised it was something he hadn't heard in a long time. But the sound didn't reach his heart; that had become a very distant place.

'Something funny, Scamarcio?'

He swung around. The Calabrian accent was as familiar as the howl of an ambulance or the blast from a gun. Scamarcio's hand froze in midair, the cigarette unlit.

'Can I help you with that?'

A gold lighter materialised in the darkness and glistened under the glow of the streetlamps. A small flame hissed up into the blackness, a serpent's kiss.

'It's been a while,' said Scamarcio, drawing the nicotine down as deep as he could, willing it to reach his gut and restore calm there.

'Congratulations on your medal.'

'It was a surprise.'

'I'll bet. For a while there, I thought they wanted to *kill* you,' said Dante Greco quietly.

Scamarcio didn't much like the emphasis he placed on the word. 'So, I'm thinking this isn't just coincidence, Catanzaro being some six hundred kilometres away and all.'

'I like to come to Rome from time to time — it's helpful to have a reminder of one's limitations.'

'You talking about your politician friends?'

'I'm talking about the monuments, Scamarcio. The history.' Greco swept an open palm around him and seized it to his chest, as if he wanted to scoop up the entire ancient city and keep it for himself. 'What are we, in all this magnificence? Pitiful nothings, that's what we are.'

Scamarcio took another long drag and closed his eyes. 'Funny, I'd been thinking much the same lately.'

'Perhaps we're both having a midlife crisis.'

'I've had them throughout my life.'

Greco snorted. 'You know, Scamarcio, there's a part of me that has always liked you.'

'Good to hear.'

'That's why I wanted to warn you.'

'Warn me of what, Greco?'

'You're about to tread on a few people's toes. Don't. You're at an important juncture in your life and have way too much to lose.'

'Ah.'

'Now is not the time to be ruffling feathers. You have the chance to lead a happy life, Scamarcio. Take it.'

With that, Greco melted into the darkness, like the flame from his gold lighter.

The rain started falling in earnest now, but Scamarcio didn't move. He let the water cascade down his face and soak his collar. It didn't seem important.

Fiammetta was already in bed when he got in. 'It was the only place I could get comfortable,' she said, trying to rearrange the pillows behind her shoulders.

'Let me help you with that.' He kissed her cheek. She looked radiant; he'd never seen her eyes so bright. He sorted the cushions, then carefully removed his jacket and placed it on the chair, worried that something incriminating — he didn't know what — might fall out. He wondered if the gesture might seem strange; normally, he just tossed his clothes wherever, and if they landed somewhere other than the floor, it was a bonus. He needed to take a shower, but that was also something he never normally did when he came home.

'I've got a funny feeling,' she said, resting her head back down and running her hands along her stomach.

'That the baby's about to come?'

'No, that something bad is about to happen.'

'Don't say that.'

'I can't help it. I've had it all afternoon. It's been eating away at me.'

Scamarcio swallowed and started unbuttoning his shirt. 'We all have feelings of anxiety. It doesn't mean you should take them seriously.'

'I've had this before in my life — my instincts were always right. Something bad *did* happen.'

'Like what?'

'I had the same feeling in my early twenties before I ended up in hospital with a severe kidney infection. They had to remove the kidney, as you know.'

'Yeah, but that bad feeling was probably just you feeling unwell.'

'No, I felt fine at the time. It's like a sixth sense.' She paused. 'You know, I watched a documentary about 9/11 and many of the relatives of the people who died that day claimed that their loved ones had an awful inkling something was going to happen. Some even said they knew they were about to die.'

'That's bullshit.'

'It was in the documentary.'

Scamarcio sighed and sat down on the bed. 'Fiammetta, you're about to have your first child. That would cause anxiety in anyone. I've been away a lot, which I'm sure hasn't helped. You and I haven't known each other that long, which is another question mark to add to the mix.'

'What do you mean by that?'

'Nothing, I'm just saying that perhaps it causes some degree of insecurity.'

Her eyes flashed with indignation. 'It certainly doesn't in me. I know how *I* feel.'

He closed his eyes for a moment. 'That's not what I meant.'

'Are you happy in this relationship?'

He opened his eyes and saw her staring at him. She was biting her bottom lip; the skin was turning white there.

He opened his hands. 'Why are you asking?'

'Don't deflect the question.'

'I'm not deflecting anything.'

She was still staring; there was no way out. 'Of course, I am.' He leaned over and kissed her on the lips this time. He took her hand. It felt hot and clammy.

Fiammetta took a long breath and turned away. After a while she said, 'Maybe you're right. Maybe it's just a load of different anxieties mounting.'

He stroked her arm. 'Everything's going to be OK, Fiammetta. Don't worry.'

She turned back to him, and he read a question in her eyes. It was like she already knew. But how could she? It was impossible.

He kissed her again, then left the bedroom and walked to the kitchen. The fact that there was half a bottle of Nero D'Avola on the counter felt like nothing short of a miracle.

He pulled out a glass from the cupboard and filled it to the brim. The threat from Greco was rattling around his head like a crazed phantom. It was being chased by memories of sex with Aurelia, which left his mouth dry and his legs weak. Aurelia was a problem he had to walk away from, however hard that was.

But Greco? Walking away from the head of 'Ndrangheta wasn't exactly an option.

Scamarcio thought of his unborn child and the world they would be entering. The dangers were everywhere, and they were mounting. But what kind of country would he be leaving his kid if he was cowed into inaction by the likes of Greco? He took a long drink and closed his eyes. He couldn't just throw in the towel. He had to try to make a difference, however tiny. Even if it often felt futile, he owed it to the next generation to at least try.

He finished the glass, then poured another.

36

'You look like shit again,' said Garramone, tipping back an espresso from the machine. For some reason, the smell of it turned Scamarcio's stomach.

'Nice to see you, too.'

'What the fuck got into you yesterday?'

'I don't like being told what to think.'

'I'm your boss.'

Scamarcio shrugged, as if this were an irrelevance. 'Am I still entitled to my own opinions or are we all supposed to become automatons? Is it part of another new efficiency drive?'

'Is this about Cherubini?'

Scamarcio shook his head. 'I just don't get why you want to dismiss it out of hand. It might have a bearing on the case.'

'Like I said, I've already got one political shitstorm brewing. Why the hell would I want another?'

'That shouldn't be my problem.'

'Well, unfortunately for you, it is.' Garramone paused. 'You'll never make management with your attitude.'

'Why the fuck would I want to?'

Garramone rolled his eyes, then cracked the plastic cup in his palm.

Scamarcio ripped a piece of paper from the pad on his blotter, then couldn't remember why he'd done it. 'Look, let's just leave

246

it. There's enough going down without any extra hassle.'

Garramone held his hands aloft, the crumpled cup squeezed inside a tight fist now. 'Honestly, Leo, the way you talk to me takes my breath away.'

'"No respect for authority." That's what they wrote on my school reports. My dad was pleased; he thought it was healthy.'

'I hardly think your dad was in a position to judge.'

Scamarcio shrugged. 'Depends.'

'If you want to make it in the real world, you need to acknowledge there's a hierarchy. No doubt your dad thought you *wouldn't* need to get on. He imagined you'd jump straight into control, the prince anointed ...' Garramone seemed lost in thought for a moment and studied the scuffed floor. When he looked up, he asked, 'Do you ever regret it — your choice?'

'Not for one second,' Scamarcio lied, rising quickly to his feet and gathering his notes. 'Is this meeting about to start? Or did I haul my arse out of bed at 6.00 am for nothing?'

The boss pointed to his office. 'They're a bit "A-Team". Just take it in your stride.'

'A-Team?'

But Garramone was already walking off.

Garramone had it about right. The guys from the financial police certainly were not what Scamarcio had expected. Rather than a bunch of pale-faced accountants, they looked like they'd been hand-picked from the marines — all three were tall, broad, and ski-tanned, with impressive biceps straining beneath their smart-casual attire. Scamarcio wondered why they'd dispensed with uniform. Perhaps they wanted to stay under the radar.

After introductions had been made, Garramone asked, 'You've all had a chance to look at the documents I sent?'

The three of them nodded. The oldest-looking of the group,

who had introduced himself as Chief Inspector Puglisi, smiled thinly. 'It's not watertight by any means, but there's enough to stir one's interest. Our legal team didn't have much trouble getting the judge on board, at any rate.'

'I figured they might want more, some telephone intercepts first, before you went in all-guns?'

'No,' said Puglisi, offering nothing else.

'So how do you want to play it?' asked Garramone, folding his arms and looking slightly worried.

'We'll coordinate three raids in the next twenty-four hours — one at the director-general's office at the pharmaceutical service, one at his home, and the other at the house of the health secretary,' said Puglisi, looking to his colleagues for confirmation.

'You won't search his offices?' asked Garramone.

'It's a bit of a logistical and legal hornet's nest, that one. We think it best avoided.'

'Right you are,' said Garramone, looking absently at something on his desk and scratching his hairline.

'How will they work these raids?' asked Scamarcio. 'In practical terms, I mean.'

'We're going to send a helicopter over the director-general's residence, as it's pretty extensive and there's a risk he could leave by car or foot and take any evidence with him. For his office and the home of the health secretary, we'll go in by car. We'll probably be deploying three separate units.'

'That's six men a unit?' asked Garramone.

Puglisi nodded. 'Affirmative.'

Scamarcio rubbed at a cheekbone. 'Is there any chance they could have got wise to this — been tipped off?'

The trio exchanged glances. 'Not by us,' said Puglisi defensively. 'Have you heard anything along those lines?'

Scamarcio thought of Greco and felt a wave of nausea move up from his gut. 'No, nothing. I was just wondering, that's all.'

Puglisi nodded his head sharply, keen to push on. 'When will you search Borghese's place?'

Scamarcio looked at Garramone. 'We were planning on doing it before you guys went in.'

'What do you think, Chief Puglisi?' asked Garramone politely.

Puglisi scowled. 'I don't really see a need. Especially if the guy has gone AWOL. It would probably make most sense for you to start at the same time we're doing our raids.'

'Understood,' said Garramone.

Scamarcio felt a twinge of disappointment. He would have liked to have seen the A-Team in action. 'Scamarcio, let's exchange numbers so we can communicate from the scenes. What we find might have a bearing on what you need to look for, and vice versa,' said Puglisi, pulling out a smartphone.

'Sure,' said Scamarcio, reaching for his mobile.

When contacts had been shared, Puglisi said, 'We don't want to leave it too long. We're going to head back to base, and then we'll kick off the raids within the next two hours.'

'That quick?' asked Garramone.

'They've been in the planning all night. Your detective was right to ask the question — the longer we wait, the greater the risk of a leak and evidence being scrubbed.'

'Very efficient,' said Garramone quietly.

Puglisi rose to his feet, and his colleagues followed. 'You've got to stay one step ahead or they'll eat you for breakfast.'

'That they will,' murmured Garramone.

'You want one?' asked Katia Borghese, waving a pristine pack of Gitanes right under Scamarcio's nose.

'I didn't know you smoked.'

'I didn't, until last night.'

'Gitanes is quite a heavy brand to start off with.'

Mrs Borghese swatted the comment away as if it was an irritating bug. Scamarcio wondered if she'd been at the bottle already.

'Do I care? No. What have I got to lose? Nothing.'

The cigarette was leaving a long trail of ash all over the parquet, so Scamarcio relieved her of it and placed it carefully in an ashtray. She seemed to have a problem with the sudden physical proximity and a slight shiver rolled across her.

'Why are you here, Detective?' she asked. 'Have you found him?'

Scamarcio moved over to the sofa to put a more comfortable distance between them. 'No, not yet. I need to look through Gennaro's stuff.'

'What are you hoping to find?'

'You know anything about a company called Zenox Pharmaceuticals?'

Her face was a blank. A believable blank.

'What about Mr Borghese, did he ever mention them?'

'No.'

'Quite sure?'

'I've never heard my husband mention them.'

She didn't blink, didn't flinch. He wondered for a moment if drink made you a better or a worse liar. Maybe it depended on your personality.

'Does your husband keep a computer here?'

'He has a laptop in his study for when he needs to work at the weekends.'

'Anything else?'

'A tablet, but he may have taken that with him.'

'Can you show me?'

He followed her down the long beige corridor, past a bedroom, then past the kitchen. He glanced quickly through the doorway and noticed a bottle of Smirnoff on the counter. The top was off.

She came to a stop outside the study. 'I hate this room,' she said, with what seemed like unnecessary passion. 'Gennaro never lets me clean it. It's a pigsty.'

Scamarcio cast his eyes around the small office. There were lots of piles of papers on the desk, and some of the books on the shelves were spines out, others spines in, but he would never have called it messy. He spotted the black laptop in the centre of the desk, but instead of getting his hopes up, he reasoned to himself that if it held anything important, Gennaro would have taken it with him.

'OK, thanks, you can leave me to it.'

'I hope that whatever it is you're looking for helps you find him.'

Scamarcio turned. 'You still care?'

'Of course. He's my husband. He's …' She stopped. 'He *was* the father of my child.' Her voice started to crack. Scamarcio willed her not to cry. It was shit of him, but he simply didn't have the energy and needed to press on.

'If he left his mistress and tried to improve things between you, would you still hang around? You wouldn't want to divorce?' he heard himself ask.

She stared at him as if he'd said something in another language. 'That, Detective, is exactly what I'm praying for: that he dumps that manipulative bitch and comes back to me. It's the only way I can handle the grief. I'll fold, otherwise. I'll crumble. I can't do this alone.'

Scamarcio frowned. Unfortunately, it seemed more that Gennaro Borghese's overwhelming grief, not to mention his conviction that his wife was somehow responsible, was just driving him further away.

'You need to quit the drinking, Katia. And I'm not saying that in any sanctimonious or judgemental way — I come from a rough family and have seen terrible things, so I'm the last one to get on my high horse. But I'm a man, and I know that no man wants a drunk for a wife. I also know that alcohol only intensifies whatever feelings you already have, it doesn't help you handle the pain. Quit, and you'll see that things will improve for you. Believe me.'

Suddenly he realised, with a pang, that this was the conversation that he'd always tried to have with his own mother. Tried and failed. For much of his teenage years, he hadn't had the guts. Then, when he was old enough to finally face it, she was too far gone to listen.

'It's in the blood,' she said quietly. 'My father was a boozer.'

'My father was a mafioso, but it doesn't mean I've decided to go around killing people.'

'Your analogy doesn't hold. I'm talking about a genetic predisposition, you're talking about a life choice.'

'They say violence *is* a genetic predisposition. Babies who hear violence in the womb, feel it, will grow up to be violent. And believe me, I have the impulse.'

'That's nurture not nature.'

Scamarcio sighed. 'Whatever. Just listen to me on this — I know what I'm talking about.' He headed over to the desk. 'It's going to be a bit dull for you to watch me looking through your husband's things, so I don't mind if you want to go and rest.'

'Rest? That's the very last thing I want to do. I must keep busy, stay occupied, or the grief breaks the dam.' There was a quiet but terrified urgency in her voice.

Scamarcio just needed space and some time to think.

'Excuse my rudeness, Katia, but if you want to stay occupied … I haven't had breakfast and I'm starving. I was going to pop out to a café, but, by the looks of your husband's desk, I may be here a while.'

'No, don't go out,' she said quickly. 'It will be nice to have somebody to cook for.' She hurried out the door, and Scamarcio thought again of the solitary Mars bar in Andrea's stomach.

He turned and started pulling out the desk drawers. There was a lot of stuff inside: papers, files, expired driver's licenses and ID cards, USB drives, even some old floppy disks. He pushed the stacks of papers to one side and tipped it all out onto the desk, then repeated the process with the next drawer. He started flipping through the papers from the drawers, but couldn't find anything of note. It all seemed to be related to household admin: utility bills, insurance, wage slips — which, at a quick glance, seemed to match up with the figures Scamarcio already knew. The thin piles of papers on the desk told a similar story. The documents in the next drawer seemed to concern health matters regarding Gennaro Borghese himself. A diagnosis from a private hospital detailed a protruding disc on the spine, another listed the results of a heart check, which appeared to be in order. And there was a smaller piece of notepaper bearing a prescription for a new pair of glasses. It was all just dull, everyday life.

Scamarcio pushed the floppy disks and USB sticks out of the way, and then pulled out the third drawer.

'I've made scrambled eggs,' said Mrs Borghese, coming back in with a tray.

'That's very kind of you.'

She left the tray on a side table, then, to Scamarcio's relief, said, 'I'll be in the sitting room if you need me.'

Scamarcio walked over to inspect the tray. The eggs looked a bit runny, but they would do. He ate quickly, then returned to his task. The third drawer seemed to hold a collection of memorabilia from various periods of Borghese's life: a small leather rugby ball; an old school picture in which Scamarcio struggled to identify Gennaro; a plastic entry pass; a polaroid of a young Gennaro with a girl Scamarcio didn't recognise; a few packs of photos of the old kind you sent away to develop; two expired passports; and three old pairs of spectacles, one broken.

He pulled the laptop towards him and pressed the *on* button, but nothing happened. He looked around for a power cable, but couldn't find one. He'd ask Mrs Borghese in a moment.

He sat down in Borghese's desk chair and tried to think. There was something wrong about this scene. Where were the photos of Andrea and Katia? Where were the documents relating to *their* lives? It was as if Gennaro Borghese had no family. Sure, Scamarcio could understand that Mrs Borghese might take care of her own affairs, but he'd at least expect Gennaro to keep some paperwork relating to his son's health or schooling. Scamarcio cast a glance at the shelves, but there were no files there, just novels. And the occasional nonfiction book — it looked like history mainly — stuff on the Roman empire, a few books on the Second World War. Interestingly, there didn't seem to be anything relating to medicine, which Scamarcio found odd.

There were a few pictures on the wall — all Tuscan landscapes — and Scamarcio took a quick peek behind them, running his fingers across the backs. There were no surprises: no hidden keys or safes.

He was about to trouble Mrs Borghese for the power cable, when his phone rang.

'Scamarcio.' He tried to sound as put out as possible, so whoever it was would quickly leave him in peace.

'Detective, this is Chief Inspector Puglisi.'

'Puglisi. How's it going down there?'

'Our time at the director-general's home has proved productive. More so than his office.'

Scamarcio's pulse quickened. 'What did you find?'

'So far, we've got half a million euros in five hundreds, five twenty-four-carat gold bars, weight 12.4 kilograms — which would net you around 2.5 million dollars on today's market — and diamond jewellery, which I'd say, at a rough estimate, would probably fetch about three hundred grand.'

Scamarcio wanted to ask if he was joking, but he could already tell Puglisi wasn't one for humour. 'God,' was all he could come up with.

'I have to admit, I'm surprised. If there was anything, I didn't think it would be hidden in plain sight, so to speak.'

'And the health secretary?'

'Well, we did find something, but it won't help a court case.'

'What do you mean?'

'He was hanging from the ceiling when we went in. Offed himself.

'You sure?'

'Well, that's for you guys to establish, but it certainly looked like it to me.'

'And no money there? No evidence?'

'Nothing. He's taken his secrets to the grave.'

'Jesus,' sighed Scamarcio.

'The devil is certainly on the march in Rome,' muttered Puglisi.

37

Scamarcio made a small pile of the laptop, USB sticks, and floppy disks.

'It's weird there's no cable,' said Mrs Borghese. 'He usually keeps it attached.'

'No worries,' said Scamarcio, almost glad that he'd be able to examine the contents of the computer in peace. As much as she'd tried to stay away, Mrs Borghese had spent the last ten minutes hovering in the doorway on one pretext or another, and Scamarcio knew it was time to leave.

'Do you think Gennaro might have killed himself?' she said out of nowhere, quite matter of fact. 'I mean, grief can do that to people. Maybe he can't handle it?' Her voice was unusually steady.

Scamarcio took a breath. 'We're doing all we can to find him, believe me. I don't know your husband well, but he didn't strike me as a quitter. It's more like you were saying: he was looking for some kind of solution.'

'This Zenox Pharmaceuticals thing …?'

Scamarcio frowned. 'You've remembered something?'

'No. As I said, I've never heard of them. But what if they want to hurt Gennaro for some reason?'

'What reason would that be?' he asked, unable to keep the suspicion from his voice.

'I don't know!' she shouted, frustrated. She opened her arms, her hands shaky. 'I know *nothing about them*. I just have this *bad* feeling.'

Scamarcio sighed. 'I get it, Katia.'

'You'd tell me if Gennaro was at risk … or in trouble?'

Scamarcio's mind flashed on the health secretary, hanging. 'Yes, I would.'

She smiled tiredly. 'OK, thanks. Sorry.' She paused. 'I can't think for the life of me what he's doing in Frascati. He has no family there. No friends. His brother's in Calcata.'

'I thought he was still in Nepal.'

'He just got back this morning.'

'He hasn't returned my calls.'

'I'm sure he means to, but he's just learned about Andrea and he's heartbroken. And now he's busy trying to track down his crazy brother.'

Scamarcio thought for a moment. 'Are he and Gennaro similar, being twins and all?'

'They're close, but completely different. Corrado is a homeopath and has no truck with modern medicine. He thinks Gennaro sold his soul to the devil.'

'What's he doing up in Calcata? That's a strange place to live.'

She smiled. 'All those artist types love homeopathic remedies — he's kind of established himself as the village witchdoctor.'

'Can you give me his address?' said Scamarcio, his mind moving onto next steps.

While she was looking for her address book, he wondered if it might be better to turn up in Calcata unannounced. Gennaro's brother hadn't exactly gone out of his way to make contact.

She returned and handed Scamarcio a small sheet of pink notepaper, which he glanced at and then pocketed. He tried to negotiate his way out the door, his arms full with the haul he had to take to Negruzzo. A memory drifted into his head, and he turned. 'Mrs Borghese, there's something I should have asked you a while back, but it escaped my mind.'

He noticed her spine stiffen. 'Go on.'

Scamarcio coughed, hoping that he wouldn't lose his grip. 'The autopsy on your son — it revealed a problem with his bowel. It seemed inflamed, and the pathologist believed it was a chronic condition — something Andrea would have had for a long time.'

She nodded quickly. 'Yes, he was right. It came on about the same time as Andrea's behaviour started to worsen. It has plagued him his whole life.'

'How old was he when you first noticed it?'

'The change happened at around six years old — that's when his behaviour became very erratic and he started to show a lot of aggression towards us, as well as himself.'

'Do you think the two things could be connected?'

She shrugged. 'It's hard to know — like I say, they appeared about the same time. That's as much as I can tell you, really.'

There was the same evasive quality again, a hesitancy behind her eyes that made Scamarcio wonder. It didn't feel as if she was lying to him, exactly. More like she might be lying to herself. But why?

He tried a smile. 'Thanks for your time, Katia. I'll call you as soon as I hear anything.'

'Please do,' she said, turning away quickly.

But he'd already seen the tears.

It felt odd to be heading up to Calcata again so soon after the last time. Scamarcio relived for a moment the events of last summer, and a small shiver ran through him. The stress of those thirty-six hours was something he hoped never to experience again. He thought of Alessandro Romanelli in his new position as head of the country's foreign intelligence service and smiled. Who would have thought that threadbare hippy harboured such an interesting secret?

Soon, the jumbled red and brown rooftops of the village came into view, tiny windows winking in the sun like glass beads. From a distance, it seemed as if the houses grew out of the wall itself — as if the entire village was a living, breathing organism, a rejection of that other world that began in the valley below.

Scamarcio parked the car and made the steep climb to the square. He thought of the laptop and USB sticks he'd deposited on Negruzzo's desk before leaving. He hoped Negruzzo would get to them quickly. Scamarcio could sense that he'd reached that point in the case when he needed to maintain momentum; if he slowed, or hesitated, he might lose that fleeting first glimpse of an answer before it coalesced. With his mind working that theme, he dialled Manetti for the third time that day. He still hadn't managed to speak to the chief CSI in person.

'Ah, finally,' sighed Scamarcio when he picked up.

'I'm not your personal consultant, Scamarcio. I also work for other people. *Many* other people.'

Scamarcio closed his eyes and let the comment pass. 'OK, but I have an important question — and only you will do.'

'Knock yourself out,' sighed Manetti. 'And you better not be badgering me again about the DNA comp. I'm doing the best I can in difficult circumstances — they're as slow as fuck down there this week.'

Scamarcio muttered 'Shit' under his breath. The DNA comparison between Meinero and Andrea's corpses should have been in days ago.

He struggled to push his frustration aside. 'You know that young guy — the CSI on the scene when we got to the hotel room for the dead priest?'

'Yeah, bright spark.'

'You know how the ring and watch were already bagged when we arrived? Would he have taken them off the body?'

'God, no. He'd know better than to do that. It's the first page of the textbook.'

'You sure?'

'Absolutely. Anyway, I remember his report — the ring and watch were on a bedside table, along with the wallet and other stuff. I've also seen the crime-scene photos that show them lying there.'

'Right,' said Scamarcio breathing out slowly. 'I need you to do me a favour.'

'Another one?'

Scamarcio couldn't think of what the first favour had been. 'Can you go take a look at that ring? Can you see if there's a watermark or an engraving of any kind? If so, can you send me a photo?'

'Is that all?' Manetti asked, the sarcasm plain.

'Yes, that's all. I need it as soon as possible.'

Manetti just tutted and hung up.

Scamarcio slipped his phone into his pocket and studied the piece of paper Katia Borghese had given him. She'd written that her brother-in-law lived on a tiny street behind the church in a house with a bright-red door. Scamarcio soon spotted the door beneath a dense wall of ivy. Running to its right was a steep stone staircase leading to an upper floor. The house, like so many of the others in Calcata, looked as if it might topple over at any moment.

Scamarcio knocked loudly three times before a gravelly voice said, 'Come in.'

Scamarcio pushed the heavy door and entered what appeared to be a small consulting room. In one corner was a desk with an Anglepoise lamp, two chairs either side. Against the other wall of the narrow room stood a bed covered with a disposable paper sheet. The exposed stone walls were lined with books and jars and boxes of various shapes and colours. A variety of intricate Indian rugs covered the terracotta floors, and the air smelled faintly of incense and oranges. Scamarcio noticed a tall man crouching awkwardly before one of the book shelves. He was running his finger along the spines, looking for something.

'Corrado Borghese?' Scamarcio asked, pulling out his badge.

The man turned, and his eyebrows formed a small arc of surprise as he took in the police ID. He rose to his feet, and Scamarcio noticed that he seemed slightly taller than his twin. But if you took away the beard, this would have been the only difference: they might have been the same man. Scamarcio wondered for a moment if he was being played. Then he told himself that Gennaro couldn't have grown a full beard in such a short space of time.

'You seem surprised. I take it Katia didn't ring ahead.' Scamarcio extended a hand, and the man shook it politely, confusion troubling his brow. He smoothed his beard with long tanned fingers.

'Oh, I did speak with her this morning. But she didn't mention you. I just got back from trekking in Nepal.' He paused and looked at the terracotta beneath his feet, downcast. 'Then the world caved in. You're here about my nephew, I take it?'

'Yes,' said Scamarcio, glancing towards the desk. 'Would you mind if we had a chat?'

The man followed his gaze and said, 'Of course.' He shuffled to the front door and removed a sign from the back. 'I'll just shut up shop for a second. I didn't really feel like opening anyway — heart's not in it.'

Once he had placed the sign, he said, 'Let's talk on the patio. It's a bit more convivial, and I could do with some air.'

'Could I see your identity card first? It's police procedure,' Scamarcio lied.

The man walked over to an empty-looking backpack propped against the far wall. A few items were scattered around it in stages of unpacking — Scamarcio spotted a compass, a silver thermos, and several brightly coloured ropes. Borghese pulled out a plastic wallet from the front of the pack and showed Scamarcio the ID. He scanned it: *Corrado Borghese. Same date of birth as his brother. Same place of birth, too.* Scamarcio had noted Gennaro Borghese's date of birth when he'd first learned it as it was the same day as Scamarcio's father's — albeit some twenty years later.

'OK,' he said, satisfied.

Corrado Borghese smiled tiredly and led him through a narrow kitchen, which opened onto a patio with a small wooden table and two iron chairs. It was covered by a gazebo. The patio ended abruptly at a crumbling wall, beneath which Scamarcio glimpsed a sheer drop to the Treja Valley below.

'Spectacular view,' he said.

'Spectacularly scary. I worry the wall might give in at any moment.'

Scamarcio had been thinking the same thing. Corrado Borghese motioned him to a chair. 'Can I get you anything, Detective?'

Scamarcio waved the offer away. 'That's kind, but I've just had my fifth coffee of the day.'

Corrado Borghese grimaced as he took a seat. 'You know it's poison? The only coffee I drink is made from orzo and chicory.'

'Mr Borghese, I fear if I relayed my daily diet to you, you'd be appalled.'

'Better to ditch the junk now than go through chemo in your sixties.'

'That's bleak.'

'Why is there so much cancer around? Because we're all eating shit. Cut out plain flour, sugar, dairy, and meat, and I guarantee you, you'll live a long life. Simple.'

'That doesn't leave much I can eat.'

'It leaves a lot.' Corrado Borghese sighed. 'But that's not why you're here.'

'That's not why I'm here,' Scamarcio echoed.

'I'm very worried about Gennaro.'

'Have you heard from him?'

'He called me when I was in Nepal, but I only picked up his messages the day before yesterday — just before I was due to fly.' He paused. 'I feel so guilty not to have been there for him.'

'Are you close?'

Corrado Borghese nodded. 'We usually talk every day.'

'In the messages, how did he seem?'

'Well, devastated obviously.' Borghese slowly scratched at his temple, as if he still couldn't believe what had happened. 'But you know, Gennaro, he ... well, Gennaro ...' He stopped. The words wouldn't come.

'It's OK, Mr Borghese. We have plenty of time,' said Scamarcio, not at all sure that they did.

Corrado Borghese took a deep breath. 'He sounded a bit off, a bit crazed, if I'm honest. Not his usual rational self. But I guess, shit, his son had just died ...'

'What made him sound crazed to you?'

Borghese's gaze moved off to the side as he thought it through. 'He was talking about retribution, you see. He kept saying he'd get his revenge. But, you know, he didn't specify any details — who, why, where, etc. He just spoke in generalities.'

'So, you have no idea who your brother might hold responsible for his son's death?'

Corrado Borghese shook his head sadly. 'I don't, no. That's the problem.' He paused. 'I was going to head straight to his apartment from the airport — I was concerned. But I couldn't reach him, and then Katia told me he's in Frascati, but no one can track him down. It's not like him to fall off the radar, especially with me. I figure he doesn't want me involved in whatever it is he's up to; he doesn't want me around.'

Scamarcio rubbed his stubble. 'Yeah, Katia also suspects he might try to put some kind of plan into motion, but she doesn't know what, either.'

'And you still have no idea where he is exactly?' asked Borghese as if the fault somehow lay with the police. *It probably does*, reflected Scamarcio.

'Once he arrived in Frascati, the trail went cold. Do you have relatives there? Or does he have friends there?'

Corrado's face was expressionless. 'I can't think of anyone.' He sighed. 'God, why does he have to be so impulsive? He's been like that since we were kids. I'd think things through; he'd just act then deal with the consequences later.'

'And you chose such different careers too …?'

Borghese shrugged. 'I started out in general medicine, actually, then turned to homeopathy a bit later.'

'Did you and Gennaro ever argue about it? The whole homeopathy versus chemical medicines thing?'

'No, not really.' Borghese shrugged again. 'Gennaro is in marketing. I never got the feeling he was that invested in the medical science behind it — it's just a job for him.'

'You two surprise me a bit,' said Scamarcio. 'For twins, you aren't much alike …'

'Then I take it you've not met many — sure, there's the physical similarity, but it often ends there.'

Scamarcio pulled out his notebook and flicked through several pages — not because he was looking for something, but because he needed a few seconds to plot an approach. 'Did you know your nephew well?' he asked. 'Were you close?'

Corrado nodded slowly. The sadness was like a mist descending: it had started soft and subtle, but now seemed to grow thick and dense around him. Scamarcio feared it might become impenetrable.

'I've never married and don't have children of my own. Andrea filled that vacuum — we'd spend weekends together, go camping when his parents needed a break, that sort of thing.'

'And his mood swings didn't bother you?'

Borghese waved the comment away as if it were inconsequential. 'He didn't have many with me and ...' — he took a long breath — '... when he did, I just gave him space. I didn't really react. To me, it seemed as if Andrea felt caged — we just needed to unlock the door, let him vent as much as he needed.' He opened his palms, as if it was all very simple.

Scamarcio had been about to ask what Corrado thought of the decision to approach the church, but his mind had snagged on something else. 'You have medical experience, Mr Borghese. Do you have any thoughts on what might have caused Andrea's illness?'

Corrado Borghese looked up quickly from the fog of sadness and stared at Scamarcio. 'Haven't they told you?'

'Told me?'

Borghese swung his head from side to side, disbelieving. 'No fucking way — all these years ...'

'Sorry ...'

Borghese leaned forward on the creaky iron chair, which made a precarious scraping sound against the stone. 'Andrea was given medication for ADHD as a small child. Some idiot my brother worked for at the pharmaceutical company recommended it. Andrea had been a very difficult kid, agitated, moody, aggressive, distracted. Katia was at her wits' end. So, they gave him a stimulant, methylphenidate. He was six years old, and after that,' Borghese clicked his fingers, 'Andrea changed. He became much worse. Tics, mania, delusions. The tragedy was that they kept him on those meds for over two years. The quack of a doctor, again recommended by the same arsehole at the pharmaceutical company, told them they needed to stick

265

with it, but any idiot could tell that the drug was the problem. It was new, I believe. They did go on to try other stimulants, but the damage had already been done, and they just seemed to exacerbate his condition. I firmly believe that first drug, followed by all the others, caused Andrea long-term damage.'

'Was he still taking any of those stimulants when he died?'

'I think they stopped a few years ago, but, if you ask me, it was way too late by then. There was no going back for Andrea.'

'The side-effects from these drugs — do you think they might be misconstrued as demonic possession?'

Borghese opened his palms. 'But, of course. It was idiocy to approach the church. Aggression, agitation, psychosis, delusions, mania, motor or vocal tics — these are all very well-known collateral effects of methylphenidate. And they're also all on the list for your average possession syndrome. Gennaro knew that — he's no fool. But I guess he and Katia had grown desperate; they'd tried everything and none of it had worked.'

'I've watched some videos of Andrea's exorcism sessions, and I have to say that they seemed to have a calming effect on him. I don't know how to explain it.'

'There's no hidden mystery there, Detective. He was just exhausted. These episodes are draining: highly physically demanding. In the end the "possessed"' — he made two quotation marks with his fingers — 'can't go on. The body has to rest.'

Scamarcio fell silent for a moment as he took it all in. 'Why didn't your brother tell me Andrea had been given these drugs?' he asked eventually.

Borghese passed a hand across his mouth then down his beard, as if he wanted to rub the whole thought away. 'Because he doesn't want to admit it. He knows he made a mistake, and he just can't face it.' He paused. 'But, if you ask me, some fault lies with Katia, too. She didn't want to be stuck at home with a difficult kid, and she put pressure on Gennaro to fix the problem.'

'Understandable, I guess,' said Scamarcio. 'I mean, what would you have done in their position? Could Andrea really just have been left untreated?'

Corrado didn't hesitate. 'I think the outcome would have been far better for him. With the right environment and the right stimuli, he could have lived a much more satisfying life. And who's to say he wouldn't have grown out of those symptoms eventually — they may not have been permanent.'

Scamarcio thought about all the years Andrea had been medicated. All the damage done. 'Couldn't Gennaro have sought compensation from the manufacturers?' he asked.

'That whole thing is like trying to enter Kafka's Schloss. It's very hard, if not impossible, to prove liability.'

Scamarcio wondered for a moment if Corrado's personal beliefs were clouding his judgement, then he thought back to the strange sensation he'd had earlier that Katia had been lying to herself about something.

'Did you ever talk to your brother about this?' he asked.

'I tried to — once. He became extremely angry and said he never wanted to see me again. After that, I didn't dare broach the subject.'

Scamarcio nodded and made a pointless note on his pad. A shape was starting to form, but it remained shadowy and oblique. 'You ever heard of a company called Zenox Pharmaceuticals?'

Corrado considered it. 'I don't think so ...'

'We believe your brother may have been involved in trying to bribe officials at the Ministry of Health to license and buy certain drugs made by Zenox.'

Corrado Borghese's face seemed to fold in on itself. But a few seconds later, the shock was followed by something else: a kind of dawning realisation. He covered his eyes with his hands and said nothing for a long time. Scamarcio heard someone on the street shout, 'See you later.'

'No,' Corrado finally whispered.

Scamarcio shifted in the uncomfortable chair. 'What's going on, Mr Borghese?'

All at once, Corrado Borghese was on his feet and heading back into the house. 'I need to make a call.' He shuffled inside, and Scamarcio followed, worried that Borghese might be about to make a run for it. But instead, he stopped at his desk and quickly began flicking through a Rolodex, which seemed to hold various business cards. He stopped at one and recited the number out loud as he picked up his desk phone and dialled.

'Mrs Pavesi?' he asked after a few moments. Another pause. 'I'm sorry to disturb you. You probably won't remember, but I'm Corrado Borghese, we met at that homeopathy conference in Florence some years back — you'd mistaken me for someone else.' A long silence. 'Ah, I'm sorry to hear that.' Borghese looked up and motioned Scamarcio to leave the room.

Scamarcio felt as if he had no choice — he didn't want to rile a witness at such a potentially important juncture. He hovered in the kitchen for a moment, but sensed Borghese knew he was still there, so he retreated back onto the patio, feeling like an idiot. But witnesses were delicate — they needed to be nurtured, you couldn't ignore their sensibilities and hope to get somewhere. What would Garramone have done? Scamarcio sat down tentatively, then rose again and was about to re-enter, when he heard footsteps hurrying towards him across the stone floor.

Borghese was flushed. He pulled a cotton handkerchief from his shirt pocket.

'You triggered something for me, Detective,' he said, wiping his brow.

Scamarcio said nothing, just studied the man carefully.

'A few years ago, I was at a homeopathy conference in Florence, and, after I'd been on a panel about alternative cancer treatments, this woman came up to me ranting and raving and saying how dare I call myself a homeopath. I was a disgrace to the profession, not to mention the human race. It was all quite embarrassing, but when she'd finally calmed down a bit, I bought her a coffee and tried to get to the bottom of what was eating her so badly. For some reason, she was convinced that I'd been round her house offering her a wad of cash to keep quiet about a very adverse reaction to a prostate drug her husband had taken. It had left him with serious heart trouble. They'd been desperate for money to pay the medical bills, so they took the hush money and signed something, but she claimed she bitterly regretted it, because her husband had died just six months later.'

Scamarcio felt the rhythm of his blood change. 'Do you remember the name of the company that made the drug?'

'I'd always kept that woman's card, as our encounter had been so strange. It was her I just called, and she confirmed to me that it was Zenox Pharmaceuticals. I know we're twins, but it never occurred to me that it could have been Gennaro she'd met. He was in marketing, he was my brother. It just never could have crossed my mind — I mean, what was he doing being the bagman for a pharmaceutical company?'

'That's precisely the question I'm trying to answer,' said Scamarcio.

38

As he was driving back to Rome, the pale winter sun already low over the darkening hills of the valley, the outlines of the case finally seemed to arrange themselves into a sequence, a pattern he could work with: Gennaro Borghese had tried to buy off the woman from Florence and her poor husband after an adverse drug reaction. Borghese's son may have also suffered an adverse reaction to a drug. Was Borghese himself being bought off? Was he being paid huge amounts of cash in return for acting as a bagman and errand boy between Zenox and the Ministry of Health? But surely, if Borghese really believed the stimulant was to blame for his son's condition, he would never have accepted that kind of deal? He'd want to pursue Zenox through the courts, seek justice. But, as Corrado had said, those cases were tough. Perhaps Gennaro Borghese knew he'd never win or perhaps he simply couldn't admit the drug had played a role ...

Scamarcio's thoughts were interrupted by his mobile ringing on the seat beside him. He was approaching a bend, and didn't have time to check the caller display before responding. His mind jumped to Fiammetta, prone, alone in the flat, in pain. He swallowed.

'Scamarcio,' he answered, his voice a question.

'I've just sent you a photo. There *is* an engraving on that priest's ring. It reads *Andrea forever.*'

'God.'

'And because, for some reason even I don't understand, I always end up going that extra mile for you, I called Giangrande.'

'Why?'

'To see if the ring was still on Andrea's body, of course.'

'And?'

'Giangrande had it in his tray — he'd had to take it off with pliers in the end because of the swelling post-mortem.'

'Was there anything on it?'

'We managed to piece it together. Same dedication as the other ring, but this time it read *Alberto forever.*'

Scamarcio punched the steering wheel. 'Fucking fantastic, Manetti. You're a diamond.'

'I do what I can.' The line went dead.

Scamarcio's brain hadn't had time to process all the implications when the phone rang again.

'Oh, thank God.' Katia Borghese was breathing fast.

'What is it, Katia?'

'I've just found a letter from Gennaro — in the mailbox. It reads like a suicide note. I think he went to Frascati to kill himself.'

'Now, Katia, try to stay calm.'

Scamarcio was struggling to negotiate the tight bends of the valley without dropping his phone.

'Don't tell me to fucking stay calm. You've been looking for hours and you still haven't found him. I refuse to lose my husband, too. What the fuck are you all doing anyway? Why aren't you *getting* anywhere?' Her voice was thick with drink now.

'Listen, Katia. You need to tell me what's in the letter. There might be something that could help us locate him. People contemplating suicide often want to be found.'

There were a few seconds of silence before she said, 'Of course, yes.' He heard paper being uncrumpled, smoothed out.

'OK, right,' she said, trying to steady herself. 'Oh … my glasses?'

Scamarcio raised his eyes to the darkening sky.

'Ah, got them. They were on my head.' She sounded as if she was running a sprint. 'Here you go. He says,

Dear Katia,

I know I have been very angry at you for bringing the church into all this, for letting the devil into our lives. But, the truth is, it's me who first allowed him in — me who set this whole nightmare in motion. Many years ago, I made a pact that has now come back to haunt me. It was a mistake, something I should never have contemplated, but I was young, naïve, and worried about our boy.

Finally, after all that has happened, after our unspeakable loss, I must break that pact if others aren't to suffer like Andrea. I've hesitated for too long. Our son's death was a warning: a threat to keep quiet and not go public with what I know.

Strange strategy, thought Scamarcio. *Why not just kill the father, rather than the son?*

As if reading his thoughts, the letter continued:

But they should have killed me first. Now, I must finish what they started.

Katia Borghese's voice was lost to one long sob, before the line crackled and died in the curves of the valley. Scamarcio swore and pulled into a potholed layby.

'Listen,' he said, after he'd called her back. 'That might not be a suicide note. He may mean something else. I'm going to send someone round to stay with you while I organise my colleagues in Frascati. We'll find him, don't worry.'

There was no time to wait for her reply. He dialled Sartori. 'You still in Frascati?'

'Yeah, nothing's cooking,' he said casually, as if he were looking for a stolen bike.

'Well, you need to get a grip on this. He left a note — sounds like he might have suicide in mind.'

'Fuck,' Sartori sounded more weary than worried.

'You got anywhere left to look?'

'Frascati's full of people — we don't have the resources for a house-to-house.'

'Hotels, B&Bs …'

'You don't think we've been trying those?'

'Well, fucking find him, Sartori. I need him alive. Do your job.'

Scamarcio cut the call and slammed the dashboard. He thought of the letter. *If others aren't to suffer like Andrea.*

He needed to find out which Zenox drugs had recently been licensed. They'd been looking at licences that corresponded to Borghese's calls to the pharmaceutical service, as Garramone had instructed, but they hadn't yet brought it all up to date — they hadn't been thinking much about the present. But now it seemed that Borghese was hinting at something imminent, some new medicine, as yet unknown. Scamarcio opened the browser on his phone. The Zenox website had a list of medicines in Italy, but it was long and alphabetical, and offered no further information other than the trademark and generic name, which told him nothing. There was no news about upcoming products. He wasn't going to find the information this way.

He called the offices of Zenox Pharmaceuticals in Rome and asked for the MD, praying to the God he still didn't believe in that Burrone hadn't left for the day. Scamarcio cursed himself that he didn't have his mobile number with him.

The woman on the switchboard was predictably officious, prompting Scamarcio to say, 'I met Mr Burrone yesterday. If you don't put me through immediately, I'll be forced to send round a police team with a warrant, which might make its way to the news, given the high-profile nature of this inquiry. Believe me, it will be your head on the block for not putting me through in the first place, as I so politely requested.'

'One moment, please.'

'Burrone,' barked the MD.

'It's Detective Scamarcio.'

'Ah, Scamarcio, what a pleasant surprise. I'm actually in the middle of my daily routine.'

'The one with the sixty-euro Scotch?'

'No, the one with the hooker.'

Scamarcio said nothing. Burrone laughed tightly. 'My superiors in the US have instructed me not to speak to you,' he said, not sounding particularly apologetic or worried.

'Then I'll have no choice but to issue you with a warrant *and* a subpoena. Believe me, it makes far more sense for you to piss off some arseholes across the pond than face the might of the Italian justice system.'

'Does it have any might?' asked Burrone tiredly.

'You'd be surprised.'

'I would.'

Scamarcio sneered at his own reflection in the glass. 'I need to know which of your new drugs have been licensed in Italy recently.'

'Can't you just go and find that out some other way?'

'I could, but it'll take too long. If you help me now, we'll look on you kindly when the shit hits the fan.'

'Oh, I'm not concerned. My hands are clean.'

'Others may try to shift the blame onto you.'

'They might, but I'm sure a good detective like yourself would see straight through it.'

'Come on, Burrone, I haven't got all day.'

Burrone yawned down the line. 'Do I need to call my lawyers?'

Scamarcio had never known anyone caught up in an inquiry of this scale to sound so relaxed. Maybe the MD simply had no idea of what had been going on under his nose. But somehow, Scamarcio doubted it. That sharp mind, those hawkish eyes — Burrone was too smart. Maybe he just felt supremely confident that the police wouldn't be able to build a case.

'In the last few months, we've brought a vaccine for influenza and a new drug to treat childhood depression onto the Italian market.'

Just like that, no further protest. Without revealing his surprise, Scamarcio asked, 'The names?'

'They trade as EffeVax and Sequilex.'

Scamarcio pulled out his notebook and jotted down the information. He asked Burrone for the generic names, too, which Burrone helpfully supplied.

'You may want to call the Centre for Disease Control in the US about one of those, Detective.'

'Why would I want to do that?'

'You just might.'

Scamarcio paused. 'Burrone — why the sudden change in tune?'

'Well, I suppose I felt contractually obliged to put up a fight, but at the end of the day, really, what would be the point?'

'Sorry?'

'I'm riddled with cancer, you see. I'm what they term "inoperable".'

Scamarcio breathed out slowly and watched as a small mist formed on the windscreen. The rain was starting to fall again, and he observed his own reflection twist and distort.

'I'm very sorry to hear that, Mr Burrone.' He paused, tried to refocus. 'But may I respectfully ask why you're still at your desk? Why aren't you sailing around the world, checking off your bucket list?'

'I had a little job to do before I left.' Burrone sighed. 'You're my resignation letter, Detective. My swansong. Check the CDC.'

With that, he hung up, and Scamarcio suddenly felt sure that the anonymous call to Police HQ had come from Burrone — the MD had been the one to lead him to Zenox in the first place.

Scamarcio guessed that the drug of interest would be the one for childhood depression — why else would Borghese mention others suffering like his son otherwise? But what was the question he needed to ask the CDC? Burrone had neglected to mention that.

Scamarcio stared at the rivulets of rain running down the glass and watched as they thickened and spread. If the drug had been licensed in Italy illegally, through bribes, was it possible it would have been licensed in the US, too? Or would it be a different story there? Was that in fact the point?

He dialled the number for the CDC he had found online and explained that he was calling about Sequilex. His heart sank when the girl on the switchboard put him through to what she termed the 'legal department' — he feared that, at best, they wouldn't have the answers he needed and, at worst, they'd be obstructive.

He carefully explained the nature of his inquiry, as loosely as he could for now, and asked about the drug for childhood depression, supplying both trade and generic names. 'Do you happen to know if it's licensed in the US?' he asked the mildly friendly guy who had picked up his call.

'One moment, please.'

After half a minute or so, Scamarcio heard the receiver being lifted again. 'According to our computer records, that drug was not given a licence. A licence was applied for in May of last year, but it was rejected.'

Scamarcio felt a heat in his chest. 'Do you know why?'

The guy coughed, as if he was perhaps revealing something he shouldn't. 'Studies indicated that it was causing dramatic mood swings, aggression, delusions, and even epilepsy in several cases. In some subjects, the depression worsened. We decided that deeper research needed to be done before the drug could be brought to market.'

Scamarcio scribbled it all down, cursing the fading light in the car.

'Thank you. That's all very helpful.'

'The drug's been licensed in Italy, you say?'

'Yes, it has.'

There was a pause on the line before the guy said quietly, 'If you ask me, that's criminal, given these studies.'

'Yes, *criminal* is the word I'd choose, too.'

39

SCAMARCIO ARRIVED BACK IN Rome as darkness fell. He was heading for his flat and feeling newly guilty about Fiammetta when Sartori called.

'We've got him,' was his opener.

'Is he alive?'

'Yes.'

'Where was he?'

'In a B&B in the hills above Frascati — it was new and hadn't been on our original list,' Sartori added cagily.

'How does he seem?'

'Like he wants to talk.' Sartori sniffed. 'Listen, I don't think we should bring him to the station. I reckon you'll get more out of him if you speak to him here, first.'

Scamarcio knew what Sartori meant — drag a fragile witness into an intimidating legal environment, and, more often than not, they clammed up.

'OK, I'll head over now. It'll take me about forty minutes — you think you can keep him sweet until then?'

'I'll do my best.'

The B&B stood atop a hill surrounded by dense olive groves that seemed charred and deformed in the grey winter half-light.

Scamarcio spotted a woman in her late fifties or early sixties hovering anxiously on the patio. She didn't look too pleased about the uniformed officer Sartori had placed on her front-door.

'You the owner?' Scamarcio asked, extending a hand while pulling out his ID. She studied his ID, but ignored the hand.

'I must say, all this creates a very bad impression. I have six other guests staying.'

'I know it's not ideal, but we're in the middle of a major inquiry — we'll be out of your hair shortly.'

She nodded, clearly unconvinced. Scamarcio stepped inside and took a steep flight of stone steps to the first floor, which had been converted into a breakfast room. It was all achingly tasteful — exposed wooden beams, white paint and white furniture, a few bronze sculptures dotted here and there. Scamarcio often had a problem with such contrived aesthetics — he felt as if he was being forced to take someone else's acid trip. Sartori's voice boomed down a flight of steps. 'I needed it done yesterday.'

Scamarcio followed the shouting to the next floor.

'You think all that is good for the mood of our star witness?' Scamarcio asked as Sartori came out onto the landing.

'I wasn't talking to him,' said Sartori angrily, shoving his phone back in his pocket. 'Anyway, he's taking a nap.'

'I doubt he is now.'

Sartori shook his head, irritated, and pushed the door open. Gennaro Borghese was sitting up in bed, smoking a cigarette.

'This is a no-smoking establishment,' Sartori observed helpfully.

'Like I give a fuck,' murmured Borghese.

'We've been pretty worried about you,' said Scamarcio, trying to perch on a corner of the bed. Sartori stood behind him.

'Oh, spare me the crap, Detective.' Borghese took a long desperate drag.

'What are you up to, Gennaro?'

Borghese finished the fag and stubbed it out in an empty yoghurt pot. The bedside table was strewn with greasy sandwich cartons and crisp packets. Scamarcio spotted a pizza box on a desk. Borghese had been lying low.

'I'm not up to anything. I'm just trying to get over the death of my only child. It ain't fucking easy, believe me.'

Scamarcio sighed. 'You got another one of those?'

'Another one of what?'

'Fags.'

'It's no-smoking, like the policeman said.'

'I'm the police, I can do what I like,' said Scamarcio softly.

Borghese reached for a packet on the bedside table and waved it at him reluctantly. Scamarcio took two and tucked one behind his ear — he was all out of Marlboros, and there'd been no time to restock. 'You got a light?'

'Next you'll be wanting the shirt off my back.'

'No, you can keep that — it looks well worn.'

'I've had no access to a washing machine.'

Borghese flicked his lighter, and Scamarcio closed his eyes for a moment as the nicotine hit. 'I haven't had Davidoff in a while,' he said. 'I may give them a second chance.'

Sartori huffed and headed to the window, where he made a big show of opening it as wide as possible.

'What is this? Nice cop, nasty cop?' asked Borghese.

'No, we're both nice,' said Scamarcio. Sartori rolled his eyes. 'I'm sorry about him,' Scamarcio added.

'You've been onto Zenox,' said Borghese, out of nowhere.

'We have,' said Scamarcio calmly.

'You've conducted some searches.'

'We have.'

Borghese flicked some ash from his trousers and let it fall onto the polished parquet. Scamarcio thought of the angry owner.

'The game is pretty much over, then.'

'It is,' said Scamarcio, trying to sound tired rather than excited.

'You got a case?'

'It feels like it to me.'

'You been around my place, looked through my things?'

'Yep.'

Borghese took another long drag, then hung his head. 'Then you'll know how it all happened.'

Scamarcio made a mental note. There had to be something of use on Borghese's laptop that they weren't yet aware of.

'It would be nice to hear it from you.'

'Nice?'

'The wrong word maybe.'

Borghese rubbed the back of his neck, then his shoulders. 'I haven't slept since Andrea died. My brain is mush.'

Scamarcio said nothing.

'It's like I can't find any focus or steady myself. I just keep going around and around in circles.'

Scamarcio still said nothing.

Borghese glanced at him, then at Sartori, standing by the window. Nobody uttered a word.

Borghese sighed and took another long suck on the cigarette. He closed his eyes.

'The way it worked was that I made regular payments to the director-general of the pharmaceutical service, and to the health secretary.' He opened his eyes again and started fidgeting with the fag packet, moving the plastic sleeve up and down, shuffling the cigarettes around.

'The bribes meant that the director-general would favour the entry of some Zenox drugs into the health service. From time to time, my work would take a different form, and I was forced to use the stick rather than the carrot.'

'What do you mean?' Scamarcio held a steady gaze on him and didn't blink.

'Sometimes there were certain drugs, crucial drugs, usually for cancer, that the National Health Service couldn't do without. I had to threaten to withdraw these drugs from the market if the Health Service didn't swallow a 1000 per cent price hike.'

This time Scamarcio did blink.

'Don't looked so shocked, Detective — it's common practice. I'm just a small cog in the wheel. There are plenty of others like me making sure the drug-rationing watchdogs are encouraged to lower the threshold on certain medicines. Their incentives usually arrive in the form of direct payments or renumerations for making speeches or giving advice. Zenox is just one of many who use these tricks.' He paused and smiled tightly. 'We have our own journalists on the outside, we have our own doctors we can rely on to tow a certain line, officials we can call on to chuck inconvenient researchers behind bars.' He paused. 'We pay for our own studies, of course. You see a report confirming the safety of a certain drug? You need to ask yourself who's behind it. Often these papers are ghost-written by the pharmaceutical companies themselves.'

The room grew quiet again. A Vespa roared past on the road below; some cats started a fight. Scamarcio could hear the uniform officer making small talk with the owner down on the patio.

'How did you get involved in all this?' Scamarcio asked eventually. 'Where was your moral judgement?' Sartori turned to look at him, his drawn expression warning, *You're pushing it*.

Borghese brought a palm to his mouth, as if he wanted to stop the words from coming out. 'It all started with a drug my son was given when he was six.'

'I know about it. I spoke to your brother.'

Borghese looked surprised. Sartori looked miffed to have been left out of the loop.

Borghese finished the last of the cigarette, but didn't do anything with the butt, just held it aloft, as if it was the remnant of something lost. 'When I challenged Zenox about my son's reaction, they offered me what they termed a "lucrative side-line", which would require me giving up just one afternoon a month. In a way, I saw it as my chance to give back to Andrea, through material things, so much of what had been denied him.'

'But wouldn't it have been better to have taken Zenox to court, held them to account? You might have helped others.'

Borghese looked at him, his eyes full of regret.

'That is all I can think, now. At the time, I did see a lawyer, but they advised me I'd never win a court case — Zenox was too big, too powerful. Zenox had already said they'd destroy me if I ever tried to go public about Andrea's reaction or their offer — they claimed to have compromising photos of me, and I believed them. I didn't want to lose my family. In hindsight, I think perhaps they offered me the sideline because they were worried. I know other parents had come forward, furious about adverse reactions in their kids and Zenox managed to fob them off. But I was more of a threat because I worked in the pharma sector and might have been able to stir up a bigger fuss than an outsider. I guess their logic was that if they got me involved in their deceit, I'd be too implicated to ever speak out.' Scamarcio watched an old fear come to life in Borghese's eyes. 'They seemed like an all-powerful machine, and I was just one guy trying to go up against all that. I was overwhelmed, intimidated, and I didn't think I stood a chance.' He sighed. 'Besides, Andrea's medical bills were huge, and my salary was modest — we needed the extra money.'

'In your letter to your wife, you said that you believe Andrea was killed as a warning?' Scamarcio tried.

Borghese nodded slowly. 'I've become very disillusioned lately: I saw Andrea's childhood and teenage years wasted, reduced to nothing. I regretted my decision not to pursue Zenox;

I felt guilty that I'd given in so easily. Recently, I'd read about a few cases where families were winning against drug manufacturers, and I started to think I'd been too defeatist … that I should have been braver. We'd been going through a very rough patch with Andrea, and one day, something inside me snapped — I suddenly felt like no money in the world would ever make up for what had happened to our boy. I guess it was a rush-of-blood-to-the-head moment. I told my contacts at Zenox that I'd be able to prove from a sample of Andrea's bowel tissue that the stimulant had harmed him irreparably. To be honest, I wasn't even sure this was true, but I was angry.'

He stopped and studied his fingernails, which Scamarcio noticed were bitten to the quick. 'In that one moment of rage, I may have condemned Andrea to death. Perhaps Zenox decided that they couldn't have this living, breathing potential evidence walking around, so Andrea had to be disposed of. Or maybe, like I say, it was just a warning. I think their plan had been to take his body, but then one of Amato's priests walked in and spotted them, and they were forced to make a quick exit.'

'What? One of the priests was there? How do you know all this?' asked Scamarcio.

'As I was parking outside our block, I saw the priest and these two strangers, both men, running away. The priest looked petrified and kept checking over his shoulder for the men. I wanted to follow them, but obviously my instincts were urging me to get up to our apartment and make sure that Andrea was OK.'

Scamarcio glared at Borghese in frustration and took several moments to let his anger settle. 'Mr Borghese, why didn't you tell me all this before?'

Borghese shook his head tiredly. 'I was still considering my options.'

Scamarcio thought back to Meinero's apparent disquiet during their interview — it now felt discordant with the picture

Borghese was painting. Why hadn't the priest just told Scamarcio what he had seen? Scamarcio couldn't make sense of Meinero's hesitancy if anonymous killers from the drug company were involved. Scamarcio studied his worn shoes. There was an explanation, though: maybe Meinero hadn't understood what he'd seen and had reached his own mistaken conclusion. If he'd suspected that Cardinal Amato had had a hand in Andrea's death, that would explain his silence. But that assumption posed a troubling new question: was there something about the killers that had made Meinero draw a connection? Scamarcio looked out at the velvet hills beyond the window, trying to imagine what Meinero could have seen. He must have doubled back in order to speak to Andrea alone.

He became aware that Borghese was watching him, waiting. 'Did you have any idea about your son? That he might be gay?'

Borghese slumped back against his pillow. 'He was? There were a few things that made me wonder, but it wasn't something we ever discussed.' He hung his head. 'Maybe we should have. Maybe that was my failing — that he felt like he couldn't talk to me.'

Scamarcio rubbed his chin and thought about it. 'Don't beat yourself up. Maybe he just wanted to keep it to himself. Perhaps he wasn't ready.'

'Being a parent is so difficult,' mumbled Borghese. 'You feel like you never get it right, however hard you try.' His voice grew fragile. 'And of course, we didn't get it right, did we? If we had, he'd still be alive.'

'I don't think Andrea's death had anything to do with your parenting. If the murder went down as you suspect, it was your decision all those years back to throw in your lot with Zenox that was the mistake. Things could have been different there.'

'Really? Living in a tiny apartment in a grim suburb — struggling to pay all the medical bills. Sure, they would have been different.'

Scamarcio pushed his hand through the air, trying to wave away the pointless speculation. 'Mr Borghese, my problem with all this is that, while we have some kind of picture forming about Zenox's role in the death of your son, I can't make sense of why Father Meinero was killed.'

'If he saw something he shouldn't have?'

'Then why didn't they deal with it at the time? Faking his suicide a day later just doesn't make sense. It would have given him plenty of time to report the murder, and it's too complicated.'

Borghese just shook his head. He didn't care about the priest, of course. Scamarcio was discussing this with the wrong person. He rose wearily from the corner of the bed and motioned Sartori to follow.

'Thanks for being so open with us, Mr Borghese. You won't be surprised to know that we have been recording your testimony.'

Borghese just shrugged again.

'This will all come to trial, you know.'

'Will it? I think you're underestimating the power of Zenox. They'll come up with some other way to threaten me or my wife. They'll think of something.'

'Have faith. If they killed your son, the courts will find them accountable.'

'And no doubt they'll also find me accountable for bribing public officials.'

'Yes. But a judge may take into account the mitigating circumstances surrounding your initial decision to cooperate with Zenox.'

Borghese glanced up tiredly. 'You know what, it doesn't really matter. My son is dead. Whether I'm in prison or out, my world no longer has any meaning. I'll be living behind bars for the rest of my life, whichever way it goes.'

'Time does make a difference.'

'Do you have children?'

'Not yet.'

'Then you can't imagine my suffering.'

Scamarcio slumped back down on the corner of the bed. 'From what people tell me, and I've encountered many grieving souls in my work, you will get used to carrying the pain around, but it doesn't ever really go away.' He couldn't think of what else to say, so just extended a hand. Mr Borghese shook it weakly, as if he had nothing left to give. 'My colleague Sartori will accompany you to the station — there are formalities we'll need to complete there.' He rose and placed a hand on Borghese's shoulder. 'I'm truly sorry for your loss, Mr Borghese.'

Back in his car, Scamarcio cursed the decrepit heating system that took an age to warm up. He bashed it a few times, but it made no difference.

He fished out his phone and scrolled through the contacts, looking for Meinero's sister up in Piedmont. It was late to be calling, but he knew she was the only person left who might provide the missing pieces. There had to be something about Meinero, or Meinero and Andrea, that she hadn't told him — something that might explain this second death.

She sounded weary when she eventually picked up.

'I'm sorry to be disturbing you at this hour.'

'I was trying to get my daughter to settle.' She paused. 'Has something else happened?'

'No — I'm just worried there are a few things I may have forgotten to ask you last time. I feel like I'm missing something important.'

'You still haven't found him, have you? Alberto's killer?'

'I may have done, but I need to be sure I'm right.'

She drew a sharp breath. 'Oh.'

'Can we just go through the conversation you had with your brother about the cardinal's obsession with Andrea Borghese?'

'… I've already told you everything.'

'I know it's frustrating, but I need to hear it again — please.'

She sighed, then began the story of the phone call once more. Scamarcio sat back and closed his eyes, ticking it all off in his head, detail by detail, trying to match it to the films of the exorcism sessions he'd seen.

He opened his eyes. 'Could you repeat that?'

'He said something needed to be done about Amato, that someone needed to be made *aware*, but he didn't know how to bring attention to it all without getting into trouble himself. Oh yeah, and then I think he said, "At least this new fixation of the cardinal's is healthier than his usual ones."'

Scamarcio had been stuck on the first point, but now his interest was seized by the second. '*Healthier*? That was the word he used?'

'Yes — I remember it because it seemed odd.'

'Did you ask him what he meant?'

'No, I don't think so. He was kind of on a roll, a bit of a rant, and then he went on to say something else, and I didn't interrupt. Albie was like that sometimes — if he got onto a pet subject, he would talk and talk. My role was always the listener.' He heard the beginnings of a tremble in her voice. 'I didn't mind, though,' she added quietly.

'So, he never explained it further?'

'No. That was our last conversation. Is it important?'

'It might be.'

Scamarcio dialled Cafaro's mobile.

'It's past eleven,' growled the chief inspector. Scamarcio heard liquid splashing in a glass and then Cafaro wetting his lips.

'Is something finally happening?'

'What's that supposed to mean?'

'Seems to me that you're taking a hell of a long time to wind this up. I thought you were supposed to be some kind of hot shot.'

'Reputations can be strange.'

'What do you want, Scamarcio?'

'Can I come and see you?'

'What, *now*?'

'Now.'

'I'm at home. I was about to go to bed.'

'I wouldn't be asking if it wasn't serious.'

Cafaro sighed. It came out as a whistle down the line. 'OK.' He gave Scamarcio the address. 'Be quick. I need to be up by six.'

40

CAFARO LIVED IN A modest apartment on Via Tizzani in Monteverde. Scamarcio realised that he had been expecting something grander. When he entered the hallway, he noticed a load of mobility equipment: crutches, wheelchair, plastic ramps, piled along one wall. He guessed it was for the son.

'Excuse the mess,' said Cafaro, waving a tumbler at him. 'I'm enjoying a Scotch. Will you have one?'

Scamarcio smiled, surprised at the courtesy. 'Thanks, Cafaro. Don't mind if I do.'

Cafaro entered the small living room and motioned Scamarcio to a battered sofa. As he sat down, he saw that the wooden coffee table was flecked with paint, crayon, and bits of plasticine.

'So, what's happened?' said Cafaro as he passed him the drink. 'You have that predatory look a cop gets when he's about to nail it.'

Scamarcio took a swig of the Scotch. It was good.

'I dunno, I still feel like I'm left with a few grey areas. That's why I'm here — I can't move on until I shed these last doubts.'

Cafaro studied him over his tumbler. 'Why do I sense it's all about to come back to bite me?'

Scamarcio sank deeper into the sofa and realised that the springs had gone. A throw came away, revealing a threadbare cushion beneath. He suddenly had the feeling that most of Cafaro's salary went on caring for his son.

'Has the cardinal ever been in any trouble in the past?' Scamarcio asked, wishing that Cafaro had put some ice in the glass. 'You ever had to clean up after him?'

Cafaro rubbed the crown of his head and fell silent. Eventually he said, 'I thought we went through this the other day.'

'We skirted around the edges.'

After a few moments Cafaro said, 'It's a problematic question for me, Scamarcio. You understand my difficulty?'

Scamarcio felt like singing 'Hallelujah!'

'I do, Cafaro, but I also know that, despite our different positions, you are a decent man who appreciates the seriousness of this inquiry and the importance that we exercise the law to the best of our abilities.'

At the words *exercise the law*, Cafaro cocked his head to one side. 'You threatening me?' Then he muttered, 'Again.'

Scamarcio scowled. 'I wouldn't do that, Cafaro. Especially in your own home after you've just poured me an excellent glass of Scotch.'

Cafaro narrowed his eyes.

Scamarcio looked away for a moment. 'Just tell me if there's any smoke — anything I need to know. Like you say, I'm nearly there. I just need to make this last push.'

Cafaro studied him for a few seconds, then slowly set down the glass and rose from his chair. Scamarcio thought he was about to show him the door, but instead he headed for a wide desk to the right of where they'd been sitting and pulled out a drawer. Cafaro placed a small leather book on the desk and leaned over to flick through a few pages. When he'd found what he'd been looking for, he reached for a yellow block note and scribbled something down with a felt-tip pen. He tore off a sheet, then walked back to the sofa and sat down.

Cafaro picked up his glass and took a large mouthful, as if the act of writing had caused considerable stress.

'Many years ago, when I was still relatively junior, Amato came to my boss Battaglia's office. I think Amato wanted me to leave, but Battaglia insisted I stay. He then got called away, and I was left to deal with whatever problem the cardinal was bringing us.'

'What *was* the problem?'

'I'm not going to tell you.'

Scamarcio opened his palms in exasperation.

'But it might interest you to know, Detective, that Cardinal Amato thought I was dirty. After he'd unburdened himself of his problem, he said that if I dared tell anyone about our conversation, he'd make it known that I was involved in the Cherubini disappearance.'

Scamarcio felt the air leave his lungs. 'He said that?'

'Before you get too excited, I *wasn't* involved. I knew nothing about it. But now, all these years later, I suspect that the rumours about my boss Battaglia may have been true. I think that, because I was Battaglia's protégé, Amato kind of lumped the two of us together and presumed I must have had an interest.'

'Did you ever tell anyone that you suspected Battaglia?'

'I haven't, as yet. I saw Cherubini's brother on TV again the other day, and it did make me think. I may take my suspicions to someone soon. Before I die, at least.'

'Are they just suspicions?'

'There are a few elements that are a little bit more concrete, so to speak.'

'Wow,' Scamarcio murmured quietly as he swilled his Scotch and watched the amber splash against the sides of the tumbler.

'Amato brought his problems to Battaglia, and Battaglia helped him sort them. There was a mutual understanding. A pact.'

'But you're not going to tell me what these problems were …'

'No.' He rose tiredly and handed Scamarcio the scrap of paper. 'But this man will. Don't go tonight — he's old and ill. Head over in the morning.' He'd seemed about to say more, when a woman in a blue nightie appeared in the doorway. She gave a start when she noticed Scamarcio.

'I'm sorry, sweetheart, the detective just needed to talk to me about something,' said Cafaro.

The unusual tenderness in his voice threw Scamarcio slightly.

'It's OK, I'm leaving,' Scamarcio said, quickly getting to his feet. 'I'm sorry to have disturbed you so late.' He folded the piece of paper, placing it in his pocket.

'Tread carefully, Scamarcio,' said Cafaro as he escorted him out. 'Amato might seem old and frail, but there's a well-oiled machine behind him — and it can be brutally efficient.'

41

SCAMARCIO CLIMBED INTO BED beside Fiammetta, trying to keep as quiet as possible.

'Do you even remember who I am?'

Scamarcio switched the light on.

'You haven't called all day.'

'I called this morning.'

'That was over twelve hours ago, anything could have happened since then.'

'I'm sorry, Fiammetta. I'm close to the end now. I'm trying to wind up the case as fast as possible in time for the baby.'

'That doesn't stop you from taking five minutes out to make a call.'

'It's not as easy as it sounds,' he said, but he knew she was right. He needed to get better at concentrating on more than one thing at a time.

She pulled out a pillow and punched it against the headboard with what seemed like unnecessary force. When she was finally comfortable, she said, 'I feel like I'm losing you.'

He stroked her hair. 'Don't be ridiculous.'

'It's just something I can sense. Like an instinct.'

'Well, your instincts are wrong.' He thought of Aurelia and felt a warmth spread across his abdomen. He needed to see her.

The next morning the sun was bright and confident and, for the first time in a long time, Scamarcio thought he could actually smell spring. Sure, it was cold, but there was a warmer undercurrent, a floral breeze from different climes that whispered through the pines and made him think of the coast. It stirred hope. Whatever happened, he felt that things would be OK. Everything would work itself out.

A few seconds later, he gave himself a mental kicking — self-delusion was for arseholes.

The old man was in a care home on Via Porcari near Vatican City. Scamarcio imagined it would be a church home, probably one of those run by nuns. As he approached the address, he spotted a couple of matronly sisters in blue habits descending from bicycles. He wasn't that happy to have his guess confirmed — nuns could spell trouble.

The one on reception wasn't too impressed by his police ID. 'Cardinal Acatte is ninety-six years old.'

'That doesn't necessarily mean he can't communicate or remember things. Or are you telling me he has Alzheimer's?'

'No, he's as sharp as a button.' She smoothed out some papers on her desk. 'But, physically, he's very weak. You shouldn't stay more than ten minutes.'

'I'll try to be as quick as I can.'

She called for another nun, who led Scamarcio down a corridor that smelled of broiled beef, then up a steep flight of stairs that smelled of bleach. 'The elevator is always occupied at this time of day,' she panted as she struggled her way to the top. They reached another musty corridor that smelled of lavender detergent, and she knocked on a door to her left.

'Come!' boomed a loud, confident voice. Scamarcio imagined that it couldn't possibly belong to Acatte.

But as he entered the small room, he changed his mind. A tall man was standing by the window, looking out at the street below. He was only very slightly stooped, and his head was full of grey hair. He was repeatedly bashing a fist against the glass. 'These fucking pigeons. They drive me mad,' he said as he turned.

'Cardinal Acatte, please mind your language. You have a visitor.'

'Adele, I'm not blind — yet. I can see I have a fucking visitor.'

Scamarcio brought a fist to his mouth and smiled behind it.

'No need to be so moody, Cardinal.'

'Adele, why don't you fuck off.'

The sister rolled her eyes at Scamarcio, then turned. 'No more than ten minutes,' she whispered as she left.

'He can stay as bloody long as I want,' shouted the cardinal.

Scamarcio hovered in the middle of the room until the cardinal said, 'Sit down. You look exhausted, Detective.'

'How did you know I'm a policeman?'

'I can smell it on you — and then there's that look of quiet desperation in your eyes.'

Scamarcio smiled again and took a seat. 'Aren't you going to sit?'

'No, I'm fucking not. I spend twenty-three hours a bloody day sitting down. For at least an hour of my day, I'd like to see the world.' He punched the glass again. 'Fucker,' he shouted.

'Careful, you might break it.'

'You're fucking joking, aren't you? They have it reinforced, probably three times over, to keep us inmates in.'

'I've never met a man of the cloth who swears so much.'

'I didn't start swearing until retirement. It was one of the perks — the only perks. I did screw a bit, too, but it wasn't much cop. Overrated. Maybe it was the whores I chose — big girls from far flung places — a bit of a shock to the system. Kind of put me off.'

Scamarcio swallowed. When he'd got his breath back, he said, 'I'm here about Cardinal Amato.'

'That old cunt? Don't tell me he's dead. Actually, on second thoughts, do.'

'Er, no. The cardinal's still alive.'

'I saw the old fucker on the news the other day. Some kid died who he was doing his hocus-pocus on.'

'Hocus-pocus?'

'Surely you don't believe all that shit?'

Scamarcio swallowed again. 'I take it that you and the cardinal didn't get along?'

'We hated each other. Still do.'

Scamarcio wondered why Cafaro had sent him here. Was it some kind of joke? 'May I ask why?'

'He was a fucking hypocrite — like so many of our old bastards in the church.' He raised his middle finger at a pigeon. 'I can't abide hypocrisy.'

'Why do you think he was a hypocrite?'

'Didn't practise what he preached, did he?' Acatte smashed a palm against the glass again.

'I don't quite understand.'

'At least it wasn't little kids.'

Scamarcio felt a thumping in his chest. 'What?'

'Women,' said Acatte decisively. 'Amato loved women. He slept with hundreds of them.'

'You're joking. The cardinal?'

'Do I look like I'm joking?' Acatte paused to check the ledge outside was finally clear. 'He didn't have a type: fat, thin, black, white, Chinese — he'd shag them all.'

'How do you know this?'

'I had a room on his corridor for years. If you ask me, he brought back all that skirt, 'cos he liked to rub it in our faces — show us his power. Cunt.'

'Blimey,' muttered Scamarcio quietly.

Acatte walked away from the window and leaned down to pull something from a bedside drawer. 'You want a smoke?'

Scamarcio did a double-take. The cardinal wasn't holding up a packet of cigarettes, but a fat spliff, expertly rolled. Scamarcio swore softly. 'Did you make that yourself?'

'Yes, I'm quite the expert.' Acatte waved the joint in the air. 'Do me a favour, lad, and get up on that chair there — I need you to deactivate the smoke alarm.'

'You do this every day?'

'Only when I have someone who can sort the alarm for me.'

Once Scamarcio had obliged, Acatte took a seat wearily in an ugly armchair by the bed. It was the first sign of tiredness Scamarcio had seen in him. The cardinal took a long tote and closed his eyes. 'Nice,' was his only comment.

Scamarcio coughed. He would dearly have loved to partake, but there was a time and a place. Acatte opened his eyes and seemed to remember that they were in the middle of a conversation.

'Do you suspect the cardinal of being involved in the death of this boy, Detective?'

'No, not really.'

'What does "not really" mean?'

'It's still complicated.'

Acatte shut his eyes again and took another long smoke.

'The skirt's not really the story you should be interested in, though. That's not the half of it.'

'What do you mean?'

'Word is that Amato's got kids everywhere … and I mean everywhere. He's sown those wild oats far and wide.'

'Now you *are* joking.'

'Nope, deadly serious. He used to keep pictures of them in his rooms — he may still do. That's brazen if you ask me.' Something at the window prompted him to scramble hurriedly out the chair and smash the pane with the back of his hand. He quickly grasped his bony fingers and grimaced. 'Fuck off and die!' A pigeon was frantically bashing its wing against the glass as it tried to take flight.

Scamarcio was about to ask whether this was just rumour or whether Acatte had seen the photos for himself when the old man said, 'The problem with Amato is that he's obsessed with his reputation. He seems like this unassuming old codger, dedicated in his mission to rid the world of the devil, but the truth is that he's got an ego the size of St Peter's. The cardinal's abiding concern is what people think of him. Me, I've reached an age where I couldn't give a shit — and there's something very liberating about that — but if you ask me, Amato will never arrive at that point.' He took a hurried toke, as if he'd heard footsteps in the corridor. 'It's sad.'

But Scamarcio wasn't listening. He no longer needed to ask if it was all just rumour, because of course he'd *seen* the photos for himself — Andrea as a toddler, Andrea as a young man.

Amato had to be his father.

42

KATIA BORGHESE WAS WATERING the plants on her terrace when Scamarcio walked in. She looked slightly more rested than the day before, and there was a certain focus and determination in the way she went about her task that led him to think she hadn't been drinking. That may or may not prove to be a plus, he told himself.

'Katia.'

She turned and set down a large green watering can. She was wearing tight jeans and a white shirt. Scamarcio realised how attractive she must have been as a young woman. No doubt Amato had found her hard to resist. *But how did their paths cross?* he wondered.

'You look like you have yet more bad news, Detective.'

'You heard from your husband?'

She nodded sadly. 'He called me from the station, told me that the two of you had spoken ...' Her eyes searched his.

'OK,' said Scamarcio, tentatively. How was he to frame this? 'Mind if I take a seat?'

'Of course.' She walked in from the terrace, closing the sliding door behind her. 'You still look like you have bad news.'

'Katia.'

'Now you're really making me nervous. How much worse can it get?'

'Sit down.'

She did as instructed.

'Listen, there's no easy way to say this, but I need to know: did you have an affair with Cardinal Amato, years ago?'

It was as if someone had pierced a vein and was draining her blood. Scamarcio had never seen anyone pale so quickly. Katia Borghese remained quite still and stared at him hard. The force of her gaze was almost too much to take. It felt as if she was trying to kill him with it.

'Who the hell told you that?'

'Nobody. It's just something I pieced together.'

'Well, you pieced it together wrong.'

'Katia, give it up. It's time to be honest. There's too much at stake.'

She opened her mouth, then closed it again. After a few moments, she murmured, 'I just need to know how you got there.'

'It was the photos of Andrea in Amato's room, coupled with some rumours I heard.'

'Give me a second, I just need to fetch something from the kitchen.'

'Don't get a drink, Katia. We can do this without alcohol.'

'You might be able to, but I sure as hell can't!'

Scamarcio rubbed a palm over his mouth and waited for her to return. He tried to guess what she'd poured and felt no satisfaction when she came back with a vodka, proving him right.

'No, it's not water,' she said, defiantly slamming the tumbler on the table.

Scamarcio said nothing.

She took a long slug, almost draining the glass, then sank back against the sofa. 'I was young, just twenty-five. Amato must have been in his early fifties. It might be hard for you to believe, but he was a very good-looking man. There was a twinkle in his eyes, and he had such strength, such *power*.'

Scamarcio had been about to ask how they'd met, but now he had a feeling he already knew.

'I'm still not sure what happened, but, in my twenties, I started to experience what you might call an existential crisis. I was sick of everyone, everything. I began to hate my parents and the way they stifled me, hate my life, my studies, my friends. I became very angry with the world ... very angry with those around me.'

'Rather like Andrea?'

She nodded slowly. 'That was part of my problem with him — he reminded me so much of myself that I just couldn't stand it.'

Scamarcio wasn't quite sure he understood, but he smiled as if he did. 'So, this crisis — what happened? Did things get worse?'

Katia Borghese laughed and raised her eyebrows to the ceiling. 'They did indeed. I threw things; I wrecked the house. I punched my mother — broke her teeth once.'

'God.'

'No, the devil, according to my parents.'

Ah, there it was. Scamarcio's suspicions crystallised. 'They took you to Amato?'

'Yes.'

Scamarcio remained quite still.

'To start with, they were there for the sessions, but after I'd been four or five times, Amato said it was better if my parents left. What they didn't realise was that he sent everyone else away, even the other priests, so it was just him and me — and the devil of course. Amato and I started sleeping together almost immediately.' She paused and glanced at the floor. 'He was an amazing lover. He seemed to still something in me; he calmed me down.'

Scamarcio wanted to look away, but told himself to grow up.

'Of course, I knew it had to end. He was a cardinal, a high-profile cardinal at that — there was no future in it. But my heart wasn't listening. I was in love with him; I couldn't think about anything else.' She drained the glass, but kept it in her hand. 'I found out I was pregnant after I'd been seeing him for a couple of months. I guess I'd been harbouring this romantic fantasy that he'd just leave the church and we'd run away to a new place and start our family.' She stopped. 'But he soon set me straight on that.' The memory of it seemed to steal her breath for a moment.

'Amato didn't want a scandal: his work was far too important; he couldn't give it up — Italy needed him; the *world* needed him.' She paused. 'I was devastated. A friend had dragged me out to a party one night, trying to cheer me up. That's where I met Gennaro. There were no sparks, but he seemed like a decent guy and a solution to a big problem. We married very quickly — at my insistence of course.'

'And did he ever suspect that Andrea might not be his son?'

She rubbed her nose. Her movements already seemed uncoordinated, and Scamarcio wondered if the vodka had been a double or a triple — maybe there'd been no tonic in the glass.

'You know,' she said, 'I don't think he did. I mean, Gennaro is tall and dark, so they actually did look similar in some ways. They've always got on to a certain extent, so that helped.'

She fell silent again and placed the glass carefully on the table. When she looked up, she said, 'You're not going to tell him, are you?'

Scamarcio leaned forward. 'Katia, how can I *not* tell him. He's going to find out anyway.'

'Let me be the one to break it to him, then,' her voice had almost dropped to a whisper. 'It's the decent thing to do.'

A new thought struck Scamarcio. 'Did Andrea know?'

Katia Borghese swallowed. Scamarcio watched as the tears collected in her eyes. 'Well, there's the strange thing. I told him a week before his death. I'd drunk too much. We had a huge argument about Amato and the sessions — Andrea didn't want to do them anymore — and it had all come out.'

'A week before his death?'

She stared back at him. 'A week, yes.'

Scamarcio thought of the photos in the cardinal's rooms. 'Did Amato know Andrea had been told the truth?'

Katia Borghese nodded wordlessly. 'To be honest, *that* was why I was late coming home the day of Andrea's death. Amato and I had had a row on the phone that morning — he hadn't wanted Andrea to ever find out. He was furious.'

'Why?'

'Scandal, of course. He was just thinking about himself. Again.'

Scamarcio fell silent. Eventually he said, 'Katia, you understand the significance of all this? It gives possible motive to Amato. And, if he learned the truth, it draws your husband into the frame, too.'

She looked stricken. 'Surely not?' She buried her face in her hands. Then, she looked up and said pleadingly, 'No, Detective — don't go there.'

43

BORGHESE SEEMED TO BE dozing in and out of sleep when Scamarcio walked into the interview room.

'Wake up,' he barked.

Gennaro Borghese jolted upright and knocked his spine against the chair. He rubbed his lower back and blinked. 'What's going on?'

'Why were there no documents relating to your son's life in your desk? No school reports, no medical notes, no childhood drawings?'

'What?' Borghese blinked again.

'There's no trace of Andrea in your study — it's like he doesn't exist.'

'What … I don't …'

'Get it together. I'm waiting.'

'Katia holds all his stuff. She keeps all his files in the living-room sideboard.'

'There wasn't even a photo of him on your desk. I find that odd.'

Borghese frowned. 'Why would there be, if he's always home with me? I keep a picture of him in my office at work, though — when I'm away from him.' He stopped and hung his head. 'Why am I talking in the present tense?' He paused. 'Where are you going with these questions?'

Scamarcio scraped a chair across the floor and sat down. 'You *knew*. You found out — I don't know when, but you did, and it felt like the ultimate betrayal. You were going to punish Katia in the worst way you could. Your whole life had been turned upside down, your entire existence wrecked, for a boy who wasn't even …'

Borghese sprung to his feet and stabbed a finger at Scamarcio. 'Now you listen here. Things with Andrea were tough, sure. We were under intense pressure, often exhausted, and often desperate, but I loved him like nobody else. It's not right to say my life was *wrecked*. We had so many good times — walks, games, conversations — moments I will cherish for as long as I live.' His eyes were filming with tears. 'Why are you trying to trash my memories of my boy?' He stared at Scamarcio, uncomprehending. 'What the fuck do you think you're doing? Are you some kind of monster?'

'It was you. And you disabled the fingerprint ID on his phone in case it incriminated you!'

'What the hell are you talking about?' Borghese was screaming the words. The tears were rolling down his pale cheeks and dropping from his chin. He seemed dumbfounded and disorientated.

Scamarcio breathed out slowly and closed his eyes. When he opened them, he said, 'I'm sorry.'

He wouldn't be the one to tell him. He couldn't. He'd leave that to Katia.

Borghese slumped back down in his chair, exhausted. His eyes were red, his hair greasy and moist from sweat. 'What do you mean, "I found out"? *What* did I find out? I don't understand.'

Scamarcio rose slowly. 'I'm going to ask your wife to come in. There's something she needs to tell you.'

He was about to leave, but then he turned slowly. 'If it's any consolation, for both of you, maybe you should focus on the fact that Andrea found love before his life ended. He was happy. That's a good thought to hold on to, I think.'

Amato had been taking an afternoon nap when Scamarcio and five uniformed officers knocked on his door. It had taken quite some time to rouse him and cajole him into opening up.

'Cardinal Amato, you are under arrest for the murder of Father Alberto Meinero.' Scamarcio read him his rights. Amato struggled to tighten the string on his pyjama bottoms while repositioning his wide glasses. When he'd finally managed it, he ran a shaky hand through his hair.

'I didn't do it,' he croaked, his voice still hoarse.

'You may not have done, but I believe you may have paid someone to commit the murder for you.'

The cardinal said nothing.

'Andrea Borghese revealed the truth about you being his father to his boyfriend, Meinero. Meinero confronted you with the information, at which point you knew he had to be silenced. Whether or not you had your own son killed, is a separate question.'

'How could I kill my own boy?' Amato suddenly dropped shakily to his knees, as if in prayer. There was a plaintive, pleading quality to the question, which made Scamarcio wonder whether the cardinal was interrogating himself rather than the policeman standing before him.

'I *will* track down the men you paid to do this. I'm well aware of the Vatican's history of collusion with elements of organised crime. I know what I'm looking for.'

'Please, don't.' It was almost a wail now.

'Cardinal, it's my job.'

'I'm begging you. I made a mistake, that's all.'

'A mistake that cost a young man his life.'

'Please, just leave it — don't look for those men.'

Scamarcio stiffened. 'Why? What difference would it make to you now?'

'Because they'll murder me. You know they will.'

Scamarcio felt his skin grow cold with disgust.

As he was heading for the exit to the gardens, he heard someone roar his name from a few metres behind. He turned. Cafaro was striding towards him, flanked by three officers of the gendarmerie corps, their polished gold buttons glinting under the ceiling lights.

'What the hell is going on?'

'I've just arrested the cardinal for the murder of Alberto Meinero. He's in a cop car outside if you want a quick word before we take him to Via Vitale.'

'Couldn't you at least have given me a heads-up — especially after our chat last night?'

'Time was of the essence — you weren't around.'

'I was only at lunch, for God's sake. Someone could have fetched me.'

'It looks like they did.'

'Christ, Scamarcio, you're a bonehead.'

'I'll take that as a compliment.'

'Cardinal Amato has a lawyer. He'll need to call him.'

'Why don't you do that for him — get things moving. Got to dash, Cafaro. Thanks for the Scotch, by the way. I enjoyed our talk.'

Scamarcio threw him a wave as he hurried down the stairs. He jogged towards the squad cars and was just about to take his seat, when he paused to check his mobile and saw twenty missed calls and voice messages from Fiammetta all left in the past hour. His heart lurched. He'd switched the phone to silent when he was heading out to deal with Amato, but now cursed himself for that short-sighted decision. Had Fiammetta gone into labour and not been able to reach him? She usually never left more than one message. His blood throbbed as he spun through the missed calls history. At the top of the list was one from an unknown number, who had also left a message. Was that the hospital? Had the baby already arrived?? He dialled his voice message service. It seemed to take an age to play. His mouth turned dry as he listened to the first few words:

'I'm just watching your girlfriend come home from her shopping. Some women grow drawn and ugly during pregnancy, others blossom. We can safely say Fiammetta falls into the latter category.' Greco sighed. 'I really wish I didn't have to do this, Scamarcio. You should have listened.'

There was a wistful sadness in the way Greco said the words that turned Scamarcio's stomach liquid.

'Don't you touch her,' he heard himself shout, even though Greco wasn't there to hear it.

The others in the squad car, including the cardinal, dishevelled and cuffed between two uniforms, all turned to stare. Scamarcio felt sick. Greco had been following her — to their home. Fiammetta had tried to reach Scamarcio over and over, but as usual he hadn't been there for her. He was never there for her.

Rage at Greco and terror at what he might do overwhelmed him. He had to get to Fiammetta. 'Take Amato to the station,' he shouted to no one in particular. He sprinted to the second Panther parked next to them. 'Get me to Via Boncompagni ASAP — it's an emergency. I'll direct you from there.'

The driver looked startled as Scamarcio scrambled into the passenger seat, but he fired up the ignition immediately and exited the bay with rapid precision. They sped out of the Vatican entrance and tore down Viale Vaticano. The traffic was building, and Scamarcio leaned over to activate the blue light.

'Base, calling base. This is Detective Scamarcio. Get two units to Via Puglie.' His voice was shaky; he was struggling to get the words out.

'What gives, Scamarcio?' asked the operator calmly.

'I've just had a direct threat to the lives of my girlfriend and unborn child, related to the exorcist inquiry. The guy was watching her at our home. You need to get there, fast.'

'Copy that. Locating units,' replied the operator, still calm.

Scamarcio heard the crackle of back-and-forth as the operator mustered the patrol cars nearest to Scamarcio's apartment. After a few seconds, the controller said, 'Two units dispatched; closest is three minutes away. I need your floor and flat number.'

Scamarcio reeled off the details, his voice shaky.

'Entry buzzer or open doorway downstairs?'

Scamarcio's mind went blank, he couldn't remember whether it was the weekend or a weekday when the concierge would be in. 'Fuck, what day is it?'

'It's Wednesday, Scamarcio.'

'What time is it?'

He felt himself falling apart, his mind was shutting down, growing dark.

'It's 2.00 pm.'

'The concierge may still be at lunch.'

'No worries. They'll get someone to let them in. Try to stay calm, Scamarcio. We have this.'

But he couldn't stay calm. He felt as if he was about to be punished — punished for all his doubts, for his appalling act of betrayal, for his self-indulgent reluctance and hesitation. He should have been grateful for everything he had, instead of dissecting it piece by piece and analysing it all to death.

They arrived on Via Boncompagni, which of course had to be unusually busy for the time of day. He wanted to run over the lost tourists dawdling in the middle of the road. 'Keep going, keep going, swing a left now.' The police driver screeched to a halt outside Scamarcio's flat, and he saw that one of the patrol cars had already arrived — a driver was behind the wheel, but the passenger door was flung open, and there was no one on the steps. The officer must have managed to get inside already. The front door was ajar, pinned back by a standard-issue weight the police often used. Scamarcio rushed to the elevator, but realised it was occupied, so took the stairs, three at a time, up to the fourth floor. Immediately, he saw that the door to his flat was open. His blood was drumming in his ears and he could barely make out the words of the officer inside on his walkie-talkie.

'I need an ambulance to Via Puglie, as soon as possible. Flat four, fourth floor.'

Scamarcio wanted to keel over and vomit, but he pushed himself forward, his legs weak. He thought he could hear screaming. As he neared the door, he closed his eyes; he'd had a first glimpse of the scene inside, and it was too much, his heart couldn't cope. The image had lasted less than a fraction of a second, but it now burned on his retina like acid. Fiammetta was on the floor — there was blood — everywhere.

'Oh shit,' he heard the young officer shout into his walkie-talkie. 'I don't think there's time.'

Scamarcio felt the walls around him fall away. He was in a cave, a tunnel — he was spinning, hurtling through space, water was running. There was a whistling in his ears, a cold wind against his face.

Then he heard a cry — a powerful, raw primordial cry — the cry of a human as it tested its lungs for the first time.

Scamarcio opened his eyes. The frightened young officer was pushing a bloody bundle towards him, imploring Scamarcio to do something, take control.

'Congratulations, Detective, it's a girl.'

44

Scamarcio sat in the uncomfortable armchair at the bottom of Fiammetta's bed, cradling his daughter and drifting in and out of sleep. In his waking moments, he realised that he had never felt so content. It was as if this tiny soul had filled the void, cancelling out all the years of sorrow and loss. Her smell, the touch of her, the softness of her hair was a balm, a tonic that flooded him with joy: for the first time since he could remember, he felt complete.

He looked at Fiammetta, asleep in the bed, and vowed to be the best partner and father he possibly could be. Never again would he make a mistake like the one he'd made with Aurelia; never again would he doubt the immense fortune that had been bestowed upon him.

As if in answer to his thoughts, Fiammetta opened her eyes and looked at him.

'How are you feeling, Leo?'

'That's the question I should be asking you.'

'I'm OK.' She gazed at her baby, asleep in his arms. 'Well, more than OK.'

Scamarcio rose awkwardly from the chair, trying to balance the baby without dropping her, and walked over to the bed. He placed their daughter on the blanket and took Fiammetta's face in his hands. 'I love you both so much. You're the best things that have ever happened to me.'

He saw her eyes fill with tears, but she said nothing and just squeezed his hand. Eventually she whispered, 'I love you, too, Leo. More than you will ever know.' Her eyes were closing again.

'Why didn't you call the ambulance sooner?'

'I wasn't sure I was in labour. I thought it might just have been an upset stomach again — there have been so many false alarms. There was this strange guy following me — I tried to tell you. I wanted to shake him off and head home so I could lie down, but as soon as I reached the apartment, I realised the baby was on its way. I was about to call the ambulance when the doorbell rang.' She sighed, fighting off exhaustion. 'I went to answer it, hoping it was you and you'd forgotten your keys, but when I opened it, there was nobody there. It was then that it suddenly became too much, and I couldn't even get back to the phone. I collapsed on the floor right where I was — it was awful.' She closed her eyes.

'I'm so sorry.'

She said nothing.

'You should rest.'

She nodded and laid her head back on the pillow. He picked up his daughter and returned to the chair. He was exhausted, physically and mentally. He felt as if he'd looked into the abyss, but had been pulled back right at the last moment, and now euphoria and anxiety battled it out for supremacy. As he shut his eyes, his mobile rang, and he reached for it reluctantly. The intrusion felt obscene.

'Congratulations, Scamarcio. I'm made up for you,' said Garramone sounding like he really meant it. 'Now you can get on and enjoy the life you deserve. My wife has bought you something from the two of us. But don't blame me if you don't like it — you know how her taste can sometimes be weird.'

Scamarcio smiled, remembering how Garramone's wife had once turned up at a squad summer party in pink wedge shoes, the soles of which glowed in the dark. It had been particularly striking because the rest of her outfit had been perfectly normal.

'Thank you, sir.'

'I can't wait to see a photo. Will you send me one?'

'Of course.'

'How's she doing? Everything hunky-dory?'

'Seems so, yes. We're very lucky.'

'Kids are such a blessing, Scamarcio. They're your treasures, and nothing will ever change that.' Scamarcio had never heard Garramone speak so sentimentally and felt newly disorientated. He heard the boss stop to take a breath. After a few seconds, he said, 'Look, I don't like bothering you with work, but we need to wind things up, and I need to know whether to ask someone else to bring the ship to shore.'

Through his haze of happiness, Scamarcio's mind flashed on Lovoti, and he heard himself say, 'No, don't do that.'

The baby shuffled and sniffled in his arms, startled by the change in volume.

'You want to come in?' Garramone sounded surprised.

'I want to see it to the end.' Scamarcio thought of Greco. 'For a whole load of reasons.'

Garramone exhaled. 'OK, but I think you should put Fiammetta and the baby first — just until things settle.'

'I *will* put them first. I'll just drop in for a few hours, then I'll be back at the hospital.'

'Right you are, then.'

Scamarcio thought he heard a smile in Garramone's voice.

As Scamarcio made his way to the squad room, he pondered whether a father would really have it in him to kill his own son, illegitimate or otherwise. To Scamarcio, it seemed so abominable as to be incomprehensible, but he knew he couldn't allow his current emotions to cloud his intellect. The question was, could *the cardinal* have commissioned a crime of that magnitude? Scamarcio wondered why the lab was taking so long to provide the DNA comparison between the two bodies. He'd chased Manetti several times in the last few hours, but he'd claimed there'd been some kind of bureaucratic hold-up with the processing: budgetary issues and reassessed priorities, it seemed. Scamarcio's jaw clenched at the thought of it. They were in the middle of a major inquiry that had massive global attention, and they were still forced to deal with this shit.

The bottom line was that he couldn't rule out the possibility, as disgusting as it was, that Cardinal Amato had Andrea killed in order to take his secret to the grave. Just because they'd threatened Gennaro with punishment, it didn't necessarily follow that Zenox had murdered the boy. And there was something else playing at the corners of Scamarcio's mind about the cardinal: why the hell had he seemed so scared about Scamarcio going after the men he'd hired? Why was that more frightening than the prospect of prison?

Scamarcio took the stairs to the squad room, exhaustion a lead weight in his chest. How was he going to find out who Amato had used? That calibre of inside knowledge could only be found in a minefield ringed by high voltage fences. He couldn't consult his old sources now that Piocosta was gone. And had the old man still been around, Scamarcio had a feeling even he wouldn't have been able to produce a name.

He pushed the swing doors to the squad room. He knew from bitter past experience that the Cappadona sometimes took out Vatican rubbish. What were the chances they were involved in this? Their horrific reputation might explain the cardinal's considerable fear. That said, they were hardly alone in their talent for instilling terror in their 'clients'.

Scamarcio was on his way to his desk when a disturbing volley of claps swept through the room. It was probably the most genuine round of applause he had witnessed in the bearpit, and he was alarmed to feel a small lump forming in his throat. He tried to suppress it and offered a weary salute as he drew out his chair, willing them all to get back to work.

'Congratulations, Scamarcio,' said Sartori, slapping him on the back. 'We're chuffed to bits for you. There's been a whip-round — I'll bring the present over later. How are they both doing?'

'Well. Really well.'

'Great.' Sartori slapped him again. 'I'm kind of shocked to see you here, but, then again, I'm not.'

Scamarcio smiled. 'I just wanted to tie things up — you know.'

'Sure.'

Scamarcio folded his arms across his chest. 'Any news?'

'Negruzzo got nothing from the laptop, but there were a few things on the USBs — looks like a kind of ledger of monies paid to our dirty head honcho at the pharmaceutical service. There are drug names in brackets by some entries, but not all. Generally, there's not as much evidence as we might have hoped for, but Garramone doesn't really care, given Borghese's testimony.'

'Right.'

'The cardinal's said nothing more since he arrived. He may be waiting for you.'

'OK.' Scamarcio paused. 'Listen, I'm still waiting on the DNA comp — we need to see if we can pin Amato or whoever he hired to both these murders.'

'I've heard nothing from Manetti.'

'What the fuck is going on down there? Are they all dead or something?'

'Want me to shake his tree?'

Scamarcio thought about the 'welcome to fatherhood' conversation he'd now have to have with the chief CSI if he talked to him himself. 'Yes, do that. It's way too late in the game to be waiting on this kind of info. Obviously we're looking for any kind of match: it doesn't have to be Amato, it just has to be someone.'

'Got you.'

Scamarcio decided to wait before speaking to Cardinal Amato. If there was any new evidence to be had, he wanted to enter the interview room armed.

Probably bowing to pressure from a now irate Garramone, Manetti finally produced the goods two hours later.

'Congratulations, man, I hear you've pulled a blinder,' said the chief CSI as soon as Scamarcio picked up. 'It's such lovely news.'

'… Is that it?' Scamarcio asked warily.

'What do you mean?' Manetti sounded offended.

'I was expecting some wisecrack about Fiammetta's fidelity or my nappy changing skills.'

'God, Scamarcio, there's a time and a place.'

Scamarcio reminded himself that Manetti was actually known for showing real emotion at times.

Manetti paused. 'I have a gift for you — well, two actually. One for the baby and one for you.'

'Oh, thanks, Manetti — I'm touched, really.'

'Good,' said the chief CSI briskly, as if he, too, was now uncomfortable and wanted to return to their default setting. 'You want your present now?'

'You downstairs or something?'

'It's a gift I can deliver by phone.'

Scamarcio finally cottoned on. 'Ah — hit me with it.'

'I got your match.'

Scamarcio wanted to shout 'About fucking time', but instead he said calmly, 'You never disappoint.'

'I do what I can,' said the chief CSI, all faux modesty. 'I had to really sing for my supper on this one, cos the lab guys were breaking my balls — if anyone says the words backlog or budget again today, I swear I will poison them and make it look like suicide. Anyway, I got fuck all off the body — the priest's. The match came from a hair on the shower curtain in his hotel bathroom and a hair on Andrea Borghese's trousers. No stone left unturned — praise be to my team. Make sure you pass that up to the old bastard, won't you? He just roasted me for ten minutes when it wasn't even my fault.'

'Sure,' said Scamarcio.

Manetti was talking so fast that Scamarcio wondered for a moment if he was on something. Then he wondered if he was simply putting on a show to distract from his responsibility for the delay. He should have put a bomb under the staff at the lab; he certainly had the power, and Scamarcio wondered what had held him back. Office politics, probably. In Scamarcio's experience, that particular fungus lay at the root of every inefficiency, crap decision, and festering grudge in the squad.

'Any takers in the system?' Scamarcio asked, knowing this was probably expecting too much.

'One, and you're going to love it.'

'Fuck, Manetti, I hope you're not shitting me.'

'Would I?'

'Yes.'

Scamarcio heard the chief CSI rattle some pens in a pot — he seemed to be aiming for the drum-roll effect.

'Vincenzo Candiolo.'

'Should that mean something to me?'

'Well, it didn't to me until the database told me he was Gianfranco Becchi's boy.'

Scamarcio frowned. 'You've lost me, Manetti …'

'According to the latest intelligence, Becchi took over

from Papa Cappadona's replacement after all that fuss last year you were caught up in. So, I mean, if you were looking for a Cappadona link, you've got one loud and clear, bells and whistles.'

Scamarcio felt an icy stab of paranoia. 'Did Sartori tell you I was looking at them for this?' He didn't think he'd even mentioned it to Sartori.

'No, Sartori didn't say anything along those lines. I just meant …'

Scamarcio came to his senses. 'Oh, don't sweat it. You're right, I *was* wondering about them, given their past work, so all this is topnotch. Invaluable, in fact.'

'So,' said Manetti. 'Who were they working for? Don't tell me the cardinal?'

'I think so.'

'Fuck a duck.'

Scamarcio sighed. 'It's a riot, this one. I don't think even the papers could have made it up.'

'Is it me or is murder getting stranger?'

Scamarcio tore the plastic off a fresh pack of Marlboros he'd bought outside the hospital. He took out a cigarette and admired the way the rest in the pack were perfectly aligned, just waiting to be lit. But he wouldn't smoke around his daughter. He could never do that. 'It's Satan's work,' he said, patting his pocket for his lighter.

'You buy into all that?'

'Maybe just a little. Cardinal Amato was fighting the devil,' Scamarcio paused to take a long toke, '… but in the end, after more than forty years, he lost.'

Scamarcio thought of Greco's advice, and his heart turned cold. 'What that means for the rest of us, God only knows.'

45

CARDINAL AMATO'S EYES WERE closed when Scamarcio stepped into the small interview room. The silence rattled his nerves and made him uneasy. It felt like the moment before something terrible happened: the last charged seconds before a bomb exploded or an earthquake struck.

Scamarcio drew out a chair and took a seat opposite the cardinal, expecting him to open his eyes or move. But he didn't. Scamarcio leaned forward. Was he asleep? He leaned in a little closer. Then, just when his head was mere inches away, Amato's eyes sprung open, and Scamarcio jolted back in shock.

'Christ, you scared me.'

The cardinal looked bemused. 'I thought you were a hardened detective.'

Scamarcio ran a hand across his forehead, and it came away damp. 'What are you playing at?'

The cardinal stared at him — Scamarcio read detachment and irritation, then something dark and primal he found hard to define. All he knew was that he'd seen it before.

He took a long steadying breath and folded his arms across his chest. 'Let's begin.' He went to push the button on the recording unit, but the cardinal's wizened hand sprung out to stop him. The force of his grip took Scamarcio by surprise.

'No, let's wait a minute,' said Amato quietly, his pupils tiny pinpricks in the light.

'Where's your lawyer?' asked Scamarcio.

'I didn't call him.'

Scamarcio blinked.

'What's the point? The money would be better off going to charity. Lawyers can do nothing for me now.'

Scamarcio shifted in his chair. 'Listen, Amato, the more difficult you make things, like not allowing me to record this conversation, the harder it will be later.'

'I'm not convinced.'

'OK, let's try this another way: is there something in particular you wish to tell me off the record?'

The cardinal nodded, looking up to the ceiling, perhaps for cameras. He was right to wonder.

Scamarcio opened his hands. 'Please, go ahead.'

Amato leaned forward in his seat and rested his long arms on his lap. Scamarcio noticed that his robes were dragging on the ground. It seemed undignified and, strangely, he found himself hoping the floor had been cleaned.

The cardinal started to cough and seemed to lose control of it for a few seconds. He brought a pristine white handkerchief to his mouth and dabbed shakily at his raw lips. After a few moments, he said, 'It's a difficult story to tell, but I shall try.'

He said nothing more for a long time, and Scamarcio willed himself to be patient. His own breaths seemed distractingly loud, and he tried to make them quieter.

Amato shifted in his chair, then said softly, 'Twenty years ago, the devil came to my door. He appeared in the form of three men. He said that if I ever spoke out about a certain story, a certain dreadful case, he would visit me in the night and murder me. My death would be silent, but it would be painful.'

321

Scamarcio saw Amato's hand flutter to his heart and then return trembling to his lap. He coughed again, and Scamarcio heard phlegm release.

'He also said that if I ever found myself in difficulty, I should call on him and he would assist me. It was in his interest to make sure I did not have any troubles of my own with the police.'

Scamarcio frowned.

'Many years went by, and I almost forgot about that awful day. But then, just over a week ago, I faced a dreadful dilemma, and, in my weakness, I called on him. I asked him to help. He said it was as important for him as it was for me that I remained inside the church with my reputation intact.'

'Did this devil have a name?'

Amato looked up. 'What's in a name? The devil has many names.'

Scamarcio said nothing.

'Maybe you know the name already,' whispered Amato.

'I need *you* to say the name.'

Amato looked away to the wall. 'You will know them as the Cappadona.'

'And this terrible story they wanted you to keep quiet?'

'You will know it as the Cherubini case.'

Scamarcio's hand brushed over the mobile in his pocket. He glanced up to check Amato was still staring at the wall and switched the phone's voice recorder to 'off.'

He leaned over and activated the recording unit in the room.

'Cardinal Amato, you are charged with two counts of murder … The first charge relates to the murder of your son, Andrea Borghese, the second charge relates to the murder of Alberto Meinero.'

As Scamarcio said the words, a small piece of the puzzle finally fell into place. He recalled how Meinero had used the cardinal's ID when checking into the hotel and realised that the dead priest had been trying to give him a clue. He'd feared he

322

was going to be killed and had gone to great trouble to send Scamarcio a message from beyond the grave. But Scamarcio had been too slow to comprehend.

'Andrea was my boy — my favourite,' said Amato quietly. 'I would never have killed him.'

'Getting other men to kill him is the same thing.'

'I didn't ask them to kill him,' Amato shouted, a thin fist trembling. 'I asked them to kill *Meinero*. They killed Andrea as a warning — to make sure I never spoke about Cherubini again. They're monsters, worse than any demon I have ever known. Theirs is an evil that knows no bounds. They're Satan in his purest form.'

Scamarcio swallowed. It all made sense now: there was a terrible logic to it. Meinero was the principal murder, and Andrea's death had been secondary to that. It was just the timings that had sown confusion.

'How did they know Meinero would be at the hotel?'

The cardinal shrugged, almost disinterested now. 'They had been following him, I suppose.'

'Andrea was my punishment from God,' added the cardinal quietly.

Scamarcio looked up from his thoughts. 'What?'

'I broke my vows for the first time when I slept with Katia. The devil was borne from our union. It all started there — the evil started there.'

'You know,' said Scamarcio, his voice rising as he thought of Andrea and the difficult life he had lived. 'It seems to me that that poor boy was never given a chance. He had a few problems early on and was then overmedicated for years. He suffered adverse reactions to a drug, but unfortunately for him, he was surrounded by people who just wanted to turn it into something else, tell some other story. All that boy really needed was love and attention.'

Amato shook his head. 'You will never understand, Detective. You wouldn't be able to recognise the devil. Your soul is lost — I could sense that right from the beginning. There's a darkness in you.'

'In me?' Scamarcio pushed back his chair. 'I think we're done. If I were you, I'd call your lawyer.'

Scamarcio felt very little sympathy for Amato. Sure, they'd killed his son, but he'd covered up a dreadful crime for far too long for his own selfish ends. Now that would all have to come out. He wondered whether the cardinal's testimony would lead to the Cherubini case being reopened or brought back to life, given that it had never been closed in the first place. He wondered if Chief Inspector Cafaro might finally feel compelled to come forward with his evidence.

As he was taking the steps to the hospital, a bunch of red roses in one hand and a box of Fiammetta's favourite chocolates in the other, a hand grabbed him from behind and pulled him back.

'Congratulations, Scamarcio.' Greco was holding his own bouquet: white chrysanthemums, the flowers traditionally left at funerals.

Scamarcio slammed Greco's hand away, smashed it into the wall. The box of chocolates fell to the ground. 'Leave me the fuck alone.'

'Wish I could.' It actually sounded like Greco meant it. 'Why don't we take a stroll?'

Scamarcio looked deep into Greco's lizard eyes and watched the pupils flare then shrink under the street lamps. 'Dante, you are the head of the 'Ndrangheta. I will not be seen walking with you.'

Greco shrugged, as if Scamarcio was being oversensitive. 'I'm just trying to help you.'

'You've threatened me twice.'

Greco sighed. 'I want you to see sense. You can't win this one.' He made a claw of his hand and weighed the air. 'The machinery turning here, the power behind it — you have no idea of its *scope*.' He un-clawed the hand and brought it to his temple. 'It makes no sense to me that you'd risk everything — and right now you have a lot — to fight a war you can't ever win.'

He paused and glanced behind him quickly, as if to check no one was listening. 'You might not believe me, but it pains me to watch this play out. I've been around the block, Scamarcio. I know how it works. Even *I* know when to call it quits.' He shook his head, seemingly perplexed. 'This crusading thing you have — honestly, it's suicide. And, at the end of the day, it's not just you who's going down. You'll be taking others with you: you're putting them both at risk. Just call it a day. I'm not up here in Rome for the weather. I'm here because I'm worried about you. Deeply worried.'

'Greco, you don't give a shit about me.'

'Actually, that's where you're wrong. You're one of the few people I've met who have truly impressed me. I don't know what it is. I never had kids of my own, so maybe it's that. But, somehow, I want you to be OK, Scamarcio — I don't want to see you fail. Just listen to me on this, please.'

'You tried to kill my girlfriend and unborn child.'

'I didn't. It was a warning.'

'You followed her.'

'A warning.'

Scamarcio stared at him in disbelief. Why *was* he bothering with the song and dance? Direct in-your-face threats followed by execution were the norm as far as men like Greco were concerned.

Scamarcio felt lightheaded. 'Let me go and see my family.' He brought a hand to his temple and closed his eyes. 'Just let me think about it. I'm very tired.'

Greco gripped his shoulder. 'That's good. Think. Think hard.'

With that, he turned and made his way back down the steps. Scamarcio had expected to see the usual Bentley loitering, but Greco just walked all the way down the street and continued walking: the head of the 'Ndrangheta had come by foot, it seemed. It was almost as if he was scared of being spotted.

By whom? Scamarcio wondered.

Fiammetta was sitting up in bed with the baby at her breast when he walked in. Her face was contorted in agony. The baby was screaming at the top of its lungs. Scamarcio put the flowers quietly down on the bedside table, for later.

'I'm trying to get her to feed. It's not going well.' Fiammetta bit her bottom lip, which Scamarcio noticed was red and cracked. 'Fuck it.'

'These things take time, I believe.'

'You believe,' Fiammetta muttered, her forehead wrinkled with pain.

He kissed her, then his daughter. 'I read it somewhere.'

'Good for you.' She looked away to the window, her eyes desperate. To Scamarcio, it almost looked like she wanted to jump out. 'Tell me you've nailed it,' she said, through gritted teeth.

'Case is almost closed. It was the cardinal.'

The baby screamed louder. Scamarcio leaned over. 'Can I take her?'

'I don't hold out much hope.'

But as soon as she nestled in his arms, his daughter stopped crying. He wished there'd been more people around to witness it.

Fiammetta just rolled her eyes. 'How could Amato kill his own son?' she said, sinking her head into the pillow.

'That's slightly more complicated, although it seems he

believed that Andrea was both a punishment from God and a message from the devil.'

'That's fucked up.'

'Indeed.'

Scamarcio brushed his finger against his daughter's soft cheek. He had never in his whole life seen a face so beautiful. He was also extremely proud of the fact that she already had a good head of blonde hair.

'Would you mind if I took a nap?' Fiammetta's eyes were already closed.

'Go ahead, we'll be fine.'

'Thank you for the roses …' she murmured.

He eased back into an armchair and studied his child, carefully taking in every feature, every sound, every smell. Again, he vowed to be the best father he possibly could. He thought of his own dad — in many ways he had also tried his best. But what did it really mean, in the end, to be a good father? Did it mean trying to shield your family from the worst? Trying to swing a corruption inquiry so you could all sleep soundly in your beds?

Or did it mean standing firm in the face of threats from men like Greco? Scamarcio looked out at the rain-swept vista. What kind of future would he be leaving his daughter if he ditched his principles and allowed Greco and his ilk to run the country? What would have been the point of Scamarcio's work in the police? He might as well have stayed put in Calabria and raked in millions. But as his baby slept softly in his arms, Scamarcio felt these churning worries gradually fade to be replaced by something new and unexpected: a kind of fizzing energy, a sudden swell of confidence that, in the end, if he tried hard enough, he *would* be able to protect his child, so that she and her peers might one day make Italy a better place.

His thoughts were broken by the ringing of his phone, but the baby didn't seem to notice. Maybe she'd be a solid sleeper.

'Sorry to bother you when you've only just left,' said Garramone, sounding more chipper than sorry.

'No worries.'

'I just wanted to let you know that District Attorney Ercolani thinks we have the makings of a solid case for corruption against the director-general. Ercolani's optimistic, which, as you know, is not his usual state of mind.'

Scamarcio felt his stomach flip. 'Good,' he said quietly.

'All Zenox drugs are being withdrawn from the market and an urgent review is being ordered into those medicines whose licenses were granted in the last five years — there will be a call-out for possible side-effects, medical claims, etc.'

'OK,' Scamarcio said softly.

'You don't sound pleased.'

'Oh, I am.'

'Sometimes, in my lighter moments, I think the tide's turning, Scamarcio. It's starting to feel like we're making headway. Or maybe that's just me going soft in my old age.'

'No,' said Scamarcio, louder than he'd intended. His daughter let out a small cry. 'I think you could be right.'

'Any thoughts on names?' asked Garramone.

'What do you mean?'

'Names for your daughter, Scamarcio,' said the boss slowly, as if he was worried that Scamarcio might have forgotten that he'd just become a father.

Scamarcio looked at her tiny fist bunched against her flushed cheek, her fine expressive brows, strong forehead, and rosebud pout. He wondered how much of his character she'd inherit — how much of his determination and general bloody-mindedness.

'You know,' he said quietly, as an idea took shape, 'I think we'll call her Hope.'

Acknowledgements

I would like to thank the excellent team at Scribe and my ever-supportive agent, Norah Perkins at Curtis Brown.